REVERIE

BRIDGETTE HOOPER

A-

in every life, every world, every breath,

it's you

ONE

The dream started the same way every time.

A warm breeze greeted her first, ruffling its phantom tendrils through her unbound hair in welcome. It caressed her face like a lover, soft and tender and safe.

Aisling's eyes opened to a view gorgeous enough to make her weep. Rolling emerald hills stretched as far as she could see in every direction. Cerulean blue skies smiled down at her. The sun's rays sank deep into her bones.

Long grasses tickled her fingertips. Fluffy white clouds drifted across the sky as if dancing with the wind in an unheard melody. The song was an invitation, a welcoming. She would spend her waking hours replaying the sound over and over again, haunted by the peace it promised.

She tried not to think about reality while in the dream. Everything here was infinitely better than what she would wake up to. The colors were sharper, the sounds and smells more vivid, more bold, than anything she had experienced before.

It had been years of nightmares. She hated falling asleep every night knowing she would experience the worst parts of her past in a never-ending loop. Aisling refused to allow those memories access to this part of her mind. For months now, she had rested here and known nothing but peaceful respite. She found herself looking forward to sleep, foregoing dinner and relaxation to crawl into bed with a giddiness she could never recreate awake.

At first, she would sit for the entire dream. The grass would crunch and fold under her as she rested her head on the ground. She stared into the sky until she woke, watching the clouds dance and change into amorphous shapes for hours, her mind pleasantly empty of stress and thought.

As time passed, she explored her dreamscape with rapt fascination. Craggy rocks poked through the grasses, littering the steep hillsides with pointed edges and splashes of deep gray. Bright flowers in all colors reached for the sun with their faces upturned and happy in flat fields and scattered on the sharp slopes. Massive tree trunks held her as she leaned back and admired all the different views. Small streams gurgled beneath her feet as she leapt with more grace than she would ever have in real life. Birds squawked intermittently. She loved watching them ride the currents, dipping and diving in a confident freefall she would forever envy.

Every night was a new adventure. Somewhere to explore and walk freely without the weight of reality on her shoulders, and she reveled in it. Reveled in the peace of silence, the peace of finally being able to be herself.

The air during last night's walk turned briny, the tinge of salt heavy in the wind. The grass below her feet switched to black sand.

Tears fell freely down her cheeks as the roar of gentle waves and shimmering water greeted her beyond the low dunes. She had never seen the sea before. Real life had never given her the opportunity, but her dream did.

Frothy waves tickled the shoreline with a rhythmic beat that lulled her into a marrow-deep calm. She watched them for hours, never bored of the reliable kisses the water would plant on the infinite grains of black sand. Gold glittered on the surface of the deep blue water as the sun dipped low in the sky.

She worked to keep the sorrow from her mind as she explored. There was so much she hadn't seen yet of the real world. Was the sea as blue as it was in her mind? Was it as calm and constant? Would the real ocean disappoint her?

Would anything she saw in real life live up to what she had created in her mind?

As if it could hear what she was thinking, the wind picked up every time her thoughts ran wild. It sang its siren song, luring her back into the present where peace and calm lived.

The dream always ended the same way, too. A deep pull would start in her stomach, tugging her very soul like she was on the end of a rope. Her vision would blur at the edges before turning gray. The gray turned black, leaving her temporarily blinded as she fell back into darkness. Her eyes would open again in reality.

She would be lying if she said she didn't feel her heart break every morning when she saw her grimy apartment and the bleak city skyline from her windows.

She would be lying if she said she didn't wish she could leave her waking life forever and live in her dream.

TWO

"I asked for nonfat milk," the woman with flawless cherry red lipstick and a permanent sneer snapped. Her long fingernails clacked against the screen of her phone in a jangled rhythm. Her dark bob shone in the soft light, not a single hair out of place. She didn't look up at Aisling, didn't seem to register that she was speaking to a human being.

"I'm so sorry. I'll remake that for you," Aisling smiled. She took the cup from the counter and dumped the contents in the sink. The container of nonfat milk greeted her, seeing as it had already been used in the first drink, but she lifted it and made a point to show Red Lips before remaking the latte.

She would never argue with a customer. Or anyone, for that matter. She needed this job. Needed to be quiet and meek and obedient, always there in dependable silence.

She handed the new latte to Red Lips with a wan smile and dipped her eyes in subservience. The cup disappeared in well-manicured hands. The woman's tall heels clicked loudly against the floor as she made her way to the exit.

The morning rush continued. Red Lips was no longer relevant. The line was full of swaggering businessmen, early-morning exercisers, and a handful of exhausted parents. Aisling went through the motions with robotic accuracy and a blank smile. Troy fluttered around her as they performed the dance they had done for three long years.

"I hate teenagers," he mumbled in her ear at the espresso machine. She glanced inconspicuously over her shoulder, noting the two teenage girls at the counter, their attitudes tangible.

"Did they bully you?"

He scoffed. "I'm immune to bullying. I'm not immune to spoiled brats with undeserved entitlement." He added an obscene amount of sugar to one of the drinks. "When I was young, I wasn't even allowed to have coffee. They don't know how good they have it."

"Someone's grumpy today." Aisling snapped the lid on her cup and felt his eyes roll.

"You're always grumpy. What's your excuse?"

"Life, baby." She shot him a wink before delivering the Americano to the young mom behind the counter, her eyes desperate for caffeine and a break as the two babies in the stroller drooled in their sleep.

Troy handed over the two coffees with a pained smile. The teens sat at one of the five small tables in the café, heads bent together as they whispered and giggled. Aisling couldn't deny the fierce surge of jealousy in her gut while she watched the girls sit and talk without the dark cloud of life hovering over their heads. She always wondered what it would feel like to relax with a friend like that. It seemed sacred, almost, to have that time together.

Her friendship with Troy was sacred, but their time together was spent at work. Both of their apartments were less than ideal, and by the end of the day, they were too tired and too poor to do anything fun besides hang out at the park.

Troy pulled out a new sleeve of reusable cups. "I'm meant to live life poolside, Ash, with bottomless cocktails and sinfully hot cabana boys on rotation."

"You are terrified of hot men."

He tutted and flicked her pathetic excuse for a ponytail. "Your point?"

"My point," she drawled as the frother growled, "is that you would be mute if you lived that life. And I know not being able to constantly yap would be a horrible way for you to live."

"Do you always have to ruin my fun?"

"Yes."

His deep hazel eyes glanced sidelong at her with obvious disdain. She blew a kiss before returning to the counter, drink in hand. The hours flew by until the rush turned into a steady trickle of more relaxed customers. She eyed the last slice of the pre-made lemon cake in the display case greedily and prayed no one would take it so she could claim it as her lunch.

"Maybe if you lick it people will get the message."

She glared at Troy, his glittering smile infuriating. He lifted his fingers to wipe invisible drool from his mouth. Her hand reflexively lifted to flip him off, but three devastatingly good-looking business men walked through the door. "I spy your cabana boys," she taunted before walking into the virtually unused kitchen. She watched him through the tiny window in the door, giggling to herself as he stuttered at the register.

"I'd say that was mean, but..." her boss said with an easy smile. Ryan leaned against the stainless steel counter and angled his strong chin to the front. "I've never seen someone so flustered around attractive people before."

"He's cursed it seems," Aisling slumped onto the stool beside the door. Her feet ached from the long hours of standing. Her four-year-old shoes weren't helping.

"Any issues?"

She shook her head and glanced at Ryan. He was barely older than her, already the owner of a successful café, and adding another to his roster. "Nothing."

"Great. The other site is starting construction tomorrow. I have another meeting in half an hour, but I wanted to check up on you two."

Troy burst through the door. "I am so mad at you." He paused at the sight of his boss. "Oh. Hi, Ryan."

Ryan nodded his greeting. "I have another meeting to go to, I was just telling Aisling. I know I haven't been present as much, but this new location is a lot more work than I imagined." He ran his hands through his sandy blonde hair. "Are you two okay to close?"

"Of course," Aisling responded automatically.

Relief washed over Ryan's shoulders. "Great. Thank you guys. I hope the new people I hired will be as good as you two."

"Highly doubt it," Troy admitted with a shrug of his shoulder.

"I'll take the trash out," Ryan said. "I can't have you two doing everything." He turned to walk out the back door but paused and looked over his shoulder. "Maybe if you picture them naked it'll help, Troy." The door shut behind him.

Aisling couldn't stop her smile as Troy's jaw dropped in shock. A bright blush tinted his light brown cheeks pink. He whirled on her. "You –"

"I didn't say anything," she lifted her hands. "He watched you and brought it up."

He eyed her warily and brushed back a loose strand of short dark hair from his forehead. "Fine. You're cleaning the toilet though."

She groaned and followed him to the front, working diligently for the last hour before closing the café with efficient precision like she did every day. As Ryan's only employees, Aisling and Troy knew the shop better than they knew themselves. Maybe even better than Ryan.

She locked the back door and shut down the register. Troy pulled out a small plate from under the counter, revealing the last slice of lemon loaf. "I hate when you drool," he sighed. "Take it."

Her throat tightened. "Ring it up for me."

"It's taken care of, babe. Just eat."

A blush crept over her neck. She shook her head. "I can't."

"I swear to God, Ash. If you don't take this, I'm going to riot." He nudged the loaf closer, his voice softening. "Take it, please."

She nodded and placed it in her bag. Later. She'd save it for later and enjoy it over time.

Troy grabbed his bag from under the counter. "Let's go." He locked the front door and shoved the keys into his pocket before looping their arms together and merging into the sidewalk traffic of mid-afternoon. The din of city life echoed in the streets. Winter was hanging on as long as she could, but the warm touch of spring thickened the air.

"You know," Aisling started, unable to conceal her smile, "Ryan is a pretty good-looking guy. Why don't you have a problem talking to him?"

Troy jerked his chin and blinked, his jaw going slack. "Oh, no. He is hot, isn't he? Why hadn't I noticed it before?"

"Willing ignorance, maybe?"

He nudged her with his shoulder. "Ash! You shouldn't have said anything. Now I won't be able to talk to him, either." He groaned. "Life just got so much harder."

"Cheer up. It's not like you have to see him every day."

He squeezed her hand. "Devil woman."

They stopped at their intersection and kissed each other's cheeks before parting ways. A few minutes later she stood in front of her derelict apartment building and wondered how much longer it would remain standing before the bricks holding it up crumbled. The entry stairs were sloped. Huge chunks of concrete were missing. It was a safety hazard, but it had a roof and four walls, so she wouldn't complain.

She walked through the poor excuse of a lobby, ignoring the mold on the ceiling and the musty smell in the air. Dingy gray-blue paint peeled on the stairs in frequent patches. Questionable stains littered the walls. Thumping bass vibrated the rickety floor beneath her feet. A dog barked incessantly. Somewhere outside an alarm sounded.

All that and she still could barely afford rent.

Her apartment was not a sanctuary. It was a dilapidated studio with a sleazy landlord and neighbors insisting on anonymity. But it had in-unit laundry, and that was all she cared about. The ability to be clean overrode any and all of the other problems the apartment had.

She unpacked the lemon loaf and placed it on the counter. Did Troy know how much this simple act meant to her? To have someone looking out for her? Someone who cared whether or not she ate that day?

Of course he did. He knew everything about her, even what she couldn't articulate.

Delicately, she broke the loaf into tiny pieces, savoring each bite as it melted on her tongue. It was her lunch and dinner and dessert.

She'd gotten used to the gnawing ache of hunger years ago. If being on her own since seventeen had taught her anything, it was how to survive. She could make food last twice as long as a regular person. She knew how to ration everything and make every cent last. She knew to take every opportunity that came her way and to simultaneously keep her head down and blend in.

She discovered long ago the only way for her to stay out of the streets and shelters was to mute herself. She became quiet, timid, withdrawn. She did not cause any scenes or ask for more than she was given. She quietly took on responsibility until she became indispensable at work.

The loaf soured on her tongue at the flood of memories of her past rushing back. She banished them until the sweetness returned. One day she would be able to pay Troy back for his friendship over the last three years. For his unending kindness and love.

Aisling pouted when the lemon loaf disappeared. She showered in lukewarm water, washing herself as quickly as she could before the chill set in. She glanced at her reflection, marking the deep purple under her bleak brown eyes and the almost translucent sheen to her skin, and sighed. She pulled the band from her tiny ponytail and grimaced at the dryness of her mousy brown hair.

The hem of her only pajama shirt grazed her knees as she lowered herself to the thrifted mattress on the floor and closed the blinds against the late afternoon sun. Her alarm would be blaring before she knew it, so she threw the covers over her shoulders and settled against her thin pillow, closing her eyes as the sounds of the city leaked in through her window.

It wasn't all bad, she admitted to herself with a heavy sigh. At least she had somewhere to escape to.

THREE

The salt air greeted Aisling like an old friend as she opened her eyes.

Black sand stretched in both directions as far as she could see. Chilled water lapped at her bare toes. She knelt and extended her fingers into the damp grains, marveling at their softness and the faint glittery twinkle they gave off in the weak sunlight. A thick layer of gray clouds meshed in the sky above, only allowing peeks of the sun through.

A chill slid down her spine, but she brushed it off and extended her feet into the cold water and her chin higher to the sky. The hem of her brown linen pants was soaked, but she didn't mind. She was free of the exhaustion and soreness that constantly plagued her in reality.

In this place she wasn't poor and uneducated. She wasn't abandoned and thrown in the street. She wasn't hopeless or worthless or useless. She just *was*.

A content sigh left her lips as she shut her eyes and rested back onto the sand. It molded to her body like a cushion. The sand would stain her thin white shirt, but she didn't care. Her dream clothes didn't have to be perfect. When she woke up, there would be no cleanup. She had nothing to stress about for once.

A colony of seagulls squawked with shrill panic. She cracked her eyes open, brows pinching at the sight of them racing across the sky and toward land, screaming as they went.

A thundering boom from above vibrated the sand below her. She sat up and watched in horror as the waves at her toes grew into angry frothy slams. She stumbled to her feet and stepped back from the waves with a sickening tightness in her chest.

It sounded again.

And again.

The wind turned vicious. Her hair whipped in every direction. Sand pelted her ankles like tiny pinpricks.

Another boom, this time just above her.

The clouds parted. She flinched against the glittering reflection of the sun on the water and shielded her eyes.

Her breath caught in her throat. Everything inside of her went numb in disbelief.

A flash of scaled light fell from the sky.

She watched in awestruck horror as it fluttered against the wind, its shimmering brightness a beacon of beauty against the raging sea and black sand below.

It crashed fifty yards beside her, its brilliant white wings a stark contrast to the black grains beneath it. Her bones jolted at the silent impact that reverberated under her feet, the sand shifting with the shock.

Her legs moved before her brain could register what had happened. Sand squished between her toes as she sprinted from the water to the lush green hills just yards away. The grass tickled her ankles as she met the safety of a boulder sticking up from the ground and hid behind it. Chest heaving, she peered around the rock.

It wasn't moving.

The sun shone directly on it like a spotlight, illuminating a broken body against the black sand.

She couldn't explain why her heart clenched as she stared at it. Didn't know why she felt the sudden urge to cry or the fierce jolt of protectiveness entering her bloodstream. She couldn't explain why every instinct screamed at her to walk out from behind the rock and back to the sand.

It happened again, her body moving before she could stop it. Every stride toward the creature was long and confident, the exact opposite of how she felt.

It dwarfed her. The closer she got, the smaller she felt.

Her stomach hollowed as the wings fell limp to the ground.

It was a thing of nightmares made flesh—a promise of fire and pain and death.

A dragon.

Its head was the size of a car. Massive spikes stood as a wall along the back of its head in a permanent crown. Two nostrils puffed steaming hot air against the sand. Razor-sharp teeth the size of her leg glistened under scaled lips.

A hulking body rested behind it. She stared in shocked wonder at the bone-white scales covering every inch like armor. The sunlight peeked again through the clouds, and she let out an audible gasp as each scale turned opalescent, gleaming and glistening like a pearl emerging from a shell.

The sound of her gasp carried in the wind. Two eyes shot open.

Aisling thought she knew fear before when her stepmother bashed her head on a curb. When her mother attempted to sell her for drugs. When she was chased down countless dark alleys in the middle of the night or felt the icy twinge of death as she slept in a box one winter.

None of it compared to this. Her bones had turned liquid, her veins frozen with shards of ice lodged inside.

Bright orbs of amethyst stared back at her. Vertical black pupils pulsed and narrowed.

She couldn't move, couldn't think, as the eyes roamed over her body. Didn't know what to do as it inched its nose closer, sniffing hard enough for her clothes to pull toward its nostrils. She stopped breathing as a low rumble vibrated the sand beneath her feet and a flash of something danced in its eyes. It slowly blinked once before shutting its eyes and letting out a weak wheeze.

Her brain shouted at her to run. To hide and not look back.

But the pull in her chest refused.

This was her dream. She could not get hurt. She would not hide here. She would not be afraid or meek like she was awake.

Aisling stepped around it, marveling at the sheer size of its body, the muscles under the thick scales, the long tail extended into the sea. She walked to its other side as a burst of wind blew its wings up and off its body.

A river of crimson leaked down its shimmering scales.

Everything in her went silent. There was no more lapping of the waves. No more song of the wind or cautious chirping of birds.

An entire chunk under its right wing was gone.

She glanced toward its head, swallowing her fear and stepping closer. "I'm going to check your wound," she said with as much strength as she could muster, her tongue long since turned to ash. The dragon didn't react save for the rhythmic rise and fall of its chest. She took it as an answer and stepped just inches from it, lifting onto her toes.

The border of the wound was jagged like the edges of ripped paper. Blood poured down the white scales, tainting the beautiful sheen with an angry red. Sinew and muscle sat in ribbons inside the massive crater with more blood pooled inside.

She bit down on the bile crawling up her throat. It was more than a single bite. Something had treated this beautiful monster like a buffet. The thought sent a surge of rage through her soul.

An instinctual need to help overwhelmed her. She had no medical training. Had no supplies. She knew this wasn't real. But she had to help.

"Don't kill me," she whispered before throwing off her shirt, thankful that even in a dream she had thought to wear a simple band around her chest. She shoved the shirt into the wound. It was drenched with blood in just seconds. The thick red blood ran down her arms and onto her torso before dripping to the sand in wet puddles. She dipped the shirt into the sea, rinsed it in the surf, and squeezed the water from it before returning to the wound.

It didn't matter that this was a dream. She didn't care that it wouldn't be there again the next night. Her breathing turned ragged against her fear for the creature's life. Her shoulders screamed as she reached for the wound again and again. Her legs begged for a break as she sprinted to and from the sea. Sweat poured down her face despite the chill in the air.

She kept on.

She kept cleaning, kept moving until the blood loss slowed. Until the fascia inside the wound wasn't drowning in blood. She kept going until her shirt was no longer soaked with gore. Until the red in the sea dissipated and once again turned blue.

With shaky arms, she packed the wound with the shirt as best she could, and prayed the salt water would help staunch the bleeding. The dragon let out a small sigh, the only sign of life she had seen besides the unsteady rise and fall of its breaths.

Aisling took a step back and collapsed on the ground. The sun hovered just over the horizon with a crown of orange and red.

Hours, then. She had been doing this for hours. She let herself fall back onto the sand. Thousands of grains stuck to her sweaty body. Water lapped at her toes. Her body ached.

But the wind danced and swirled around her. The sun warmed her bones. Fresh air filled her lungs.

And this creature... this beautiful, horrifying beast was still alive.

A weak smile lifted her lips.

None of it made any sense, but she was happy.

Her vision blurred, blackening at the edges. The familiar tug pulled her stomach.

A bolt of fear paralyzed her. What would happen to it now? What if it got attacked again? It was helpless and out in the open. She couldn't leave it alone, not like this.

She didn't want to go back to reality. But it pulled her back even as she turned to her side, arms and fingers outstretched toward the beast as if it could keep her anchored in the dream.

FOUR

"Does salt heal wounds?"

Troy glanced sidelong at her, brows knitted together. "It's five in the morning, Ash."

"I know that," she snapped, still on edge after waking up. "But does it?"

"I'm a barista, babe. Not a doctor." He placed a tray of pre-made muffins in the display case. "But I think it cleans wounds. I saw it used in a show once."

She pursed her lips in thought. She had woken from the dream with a start, a thin sheen of sweat coating her body. Every minute since she had gone over the events of the previous night, wondering if the salt water had helped slow the blood loss or if the dragon just didn't have any more to give.

"Why do you want to know? Did you hurt yourself?"

"No!" She shook her head. "Forget it. I had a weird dream is all. Maybe I'm still half asleep."

He watched her for a minute before starting a pot of drip coffee. Aisling leaned back against the counter and rolled her shoulders, shaking the emotions from last night off. She watched Troy work, noting the flex of lean muscle in his narrow shoulders beneath his shirt and the cut of his high cheekbones on his warm golden skin.

She thought he was beautiful the first time she laid eyes on him three years ago. He was tall and gangly. A thin layer of muscle peeked from under his impossibly tight shirt. His hazel eyes were warm and bright, and his genuine smile brought her an immediate sense of safety. In a heartbeat, she had imagined them falling in love. Her heart shattered seconds later as it became evident he only preferred men. But the connection she felt was real. They fell into an immediate friendship, one lost soul to another, that saved her on her bleakest, loneliest days when darkness threatened to swallow her whole.

"What? Is there something on my face?"

"No," she pushed off the counter. "Just admiring how pretty you are."

He smirked. "Are you flirting with me?"

"Depends." She turned on the register. "Is it working?"

"Not in a million years, my love. But I appreciate the effort." He planted a quick kiss on the top of her head. "You're more than welcome to continue showering me with compliments while you wait for me to fall in love with you."

She rolled her eyes and started the espresso machine. "You're already in love with me."

Ryan appeared through the kitchen door. It took everything in her to keep from smiling at the bright blush creeping over Troy's face as he took in Ryan's normal uniform of form-fitting jeans and a simple black tee that hugged his slim figure.

"Morning," she pointed to the display case. "We've gotten a few complaints about some of the baked stuff." Ryan's eyebrows rose. "They say it tastes like plastic, especially the muffins."

Ryan leaned against the display case, the stress of opening another location heavy on his young face. "I've been debating whether or not to hire a baker," he admitted. "It would be nice not to rely on an outside source for our food items. Something fresh would eliminate the taste of reheated food. Of plastic, too, I think." He ran a hand through his hair and the muscles in his arms flexed. She bit the inside of her cheek to keep from laughing at Troy's eyes widened. "Hiring someone will take a while, though. And we'd have to figure out how they'd fit in here with you two, plus the other location..." he mumbled.

"I could do it," she answered, surprising herself. Both men turned to her in shock. She cleared her throat. "Someone would have to teach me specifics, but I can follow a recipe. This way you don't have to train someone else. It would save a lot of time and money."

With each second that passed, the plan made more sense to her. She was making herself indispensable. Necessary. Vital. Securing the roof over her head and making herself important.

"That's not a bad idea," Ryan whispered. He pushed off the display case. "But we'd need someone to be in the front with Troy, too."

"No, you wouldn't." She allowed herself a tentative smile. "I can come in earlier. That way everything is done or almost done by the time customers come in."

"You wouldn't have to worry about new employee issues, either," Troy said, his hazel eyes bright and locked on Aisling in silent approval.

Ryan glanced between them. "Would you be okay coming in that early? I would still need you to stay the whole day."

"Pay me overtime," she responded with a flutter of confidence. "That way it's legal." Ryan angled his head as if seeing her in a whole new light. She shrugged. "I'm already here early. What's one more hour?"

After a minute of silence, Ryan smirked. "I'll find some recipes, then." He disappeared behind the door a second later.

A new emotion fluttered in her chest, foreign but welcome. She couldn't name it, but it warmed her veins all the same. The morning rush came and went. Ryan had ventured to a slew of meetings for the new location at some point in the morning. She and Troy closed and grabbed cups of tea for their walk home.

"Clever minx," Troy smiled.

"I wouldn't say clever," she responded. "It was just…"

"Don't make it less than what it was, babe. It was clever. We don't have to add someone else to this codependent relationship. We can keep it just us." He wiggled his brows. "Plus one more if – "

She lifted her hands to stop him. "That's enough. Do not finish that sentence."

"You're telling me you wouldn't if offered the chance?"

She rolled her eyes. Ryan was handsome and successful, but she'd never given a thought to a relationship. She'd been on her own for ten years now barely scraping by. There was no room in her life for someone else. She didn't know what a healthy relationship looked like, either. It was better that she stayed alone for everyone's sake. "You could hardly even look at him today without blushing. How would you expect to go further than that?"

He snorted. "Part of that is your fault, you know. But you're right. I can dream, though."

"Do me a favor and keep me out of that dream."

He slung his arm over her shoulder. "I can't make any promises." His arm tightened around her. "Take the compliment, Ash. You deserve it."

They parted ways at the intersection. She barely remembered the walk home.

Barista. Baker. Small titles, but they were something solid. Something tangible. It was more than she'd ever had before. What she could do with them, she wasn't sure, but maybe all those years of struggling would be worth it in the end.

She found a bag of stale tortilla chips and topped them with the last remnants of shredded cheese in her fridge before shoving them into the microwave while she rinsed off in the shower and donned her sleep shirt. The chips were chewy between her teeth. Someone screamed from another door down the hall. The fuzzy black mold in her bathroom had grown.

She didn't care. She was happy for once.

FIVE

The early morning sun and sea breeze welcomed her back, jolting her exposed torso with a brisk chill. Aisling opened her eyes, shocked to find the enormous white body still on the beach. Its chest moved up and down steadily. She sighed in relief before moving to its side.

The wound glared at her, still angry, still red. It gaped under the beast's massive wing like the opening of a chasm. Her shirt remained inside, still dry save for a spot or two of damp redness. Dread sank into her bones. The shirt had to come out. The wound needed fresh air or infection would set in. She walked up the length of its body and stopped a few feet to the side of its snout.

"Hello," she called out weakly, "I'm back. I have to take my shirt out now." There was no reaction. Its eyes remained shut. Her heart stuttered when the morning sunlight reached its hands toward the scales. They were no longer shining and shimmering. Instead, they were almost matte, dull and lackluster and seemingly drained of life.

Aisling swallowed thickly before reaching into the wound and grabbing the shirt by the hem. She lifted it slowly, cringing as bits and pieces of tissue came with it. A dull rumble started beneath the scales, and she paused, her hands prickling with sweat. It quieted down after a heartbeat. She pulled again and the sound of skin tearing carried in the breeze.

The dragon woke up. Its long neck lifted and twisted toward its side, bringing her face to face with its burning amethyst eyes. She froze. Her stomach pitched forward with fear as its lips pulled back, revealing too-large teeth sharper than blades.

"I'm just removing my shirt," she said with as much bravado as she could muster. "It will help you heal. I told you this already, but I think you were sleeping. Or just ignoring me."

Its lips lowered halfway over its teeth. Aisling's shoulders relaxed the tiniest bit. Its snout inched closer. Hot air swirled around her as it sniffed once, twice, three times. With a snort, it moved its head and glanced at the wound as if in invitation.

She didn't let herself think. Her arms yanked on the shirt with as much power as possible. The force knocked her off her feet and onto the black sand below. The dragon let out a rippling snarl, its teeth bared in response. Terror slid down her spine.

But she refused to fear or bow to anything in this dream. This was the one place she didn't have to be scared or worried, and this dragon would not change that.

"I told you it would hurt!" Aisling yelled. She jumped onto her feet with the crusted shirt clenched in her hand. It didn't retract its teeth or lower its lips as it narrowed its stare at her. She lifted her chin. "I'm going to make sure it all came out. I won't touch anything if I don't have to. Don't bite my head off. I'm helping you for some stupid reason."

She lifted onto her toes and hovered her hand over its hide for balance. There was no more blood, but there was a layer of clots in every shade of green and yellow where red tissue should have been. And the smell... she'd spent a lot of time in filthy places full of unknown smells, but this topped them all.

Her lip curled reflexively. Infection. She could recognize the sickly sweet scent from a mile away. The smell imprinted on her brain, a warning sign she had memorized for survival during those dark, terrible years. Without proper treatment, even the smallest cut could be a death sentence.

She knew it was a dream, knew it wasn't real. But it didn't stop the raw fear slithering down her spine as she met the dragon's eyes.

This creature had to live. She didn't know why. She didn't care how insane it made her sound. Real or not, it mattered to her.

The dragon searched her face, its eyes softening as they flashed with an almost human expression of pain. Aisling's heart snapped in two. Her hand lifted to the snout but stopped just inches from the dulling scales. "I'm going to get you fixed. I promise." She took one step back, then another. "Stay here. I'm going to find help."

It blinked once as if in response.

She dipped her pink-stained shirt into the ocean to soften it before wringing it out and throwing it on to air dry. Her feet carried her to the grass, and she flew across the fields with a lightness and agility she never knew before. The flowers passed in a kaleidoscope of blurred colors around her. She leapt over rocks and streams in gentle arcs. She wasn't sure what she needed, but she knew she couldn't help the dragon herself. She needed help.

Foot after foot, mile after mile, she saw no other signs of life bigger than a fox. With every step, her pace became more frenzied, more panicked.

Every sharp breath felt like it was on borrowed time. Every step was a breath that the dragon was losing. She couldn't let it happen. Couldn't let the beast go.

The wind propelled her forward. She cursed as the sea met her again and again. No matter which direction she went, the ocean met her with a taunting, glittering smile.

She skidded to a stop at the edge of a cliff standing hundreds of feet over the sea. The sun hung low in the sky, flirting with the horizon. Angry water hurled onto the garden of sharp rocks in the shallows below, their sharp tips pointing up at her like daggers. Frothy waves sizzled with every crash and overpowered the sound of her gasping breaths.

There was no one else here. No one and nothing to help the dragon.

She had made an island of torture for herself. Her mind could never let her have something peaceful, even in a dream. Not without a cost.

The sun dipped lower in the changing sky like a taunt. Her vision frayed at the edges, turning black as the pull in her stomach strengthened.

Aisling screamed against it. Screamed her defiance and rage, into the sea, the sky. Her throat burned raw, and she liked it. Liked the self-imposed pain she somehow craved even in her sleep. She screamed at the wind circling her, suddenly furious with its touch.

She screamed as the darkness pulled her under to the sound of the sea and the scent of her despair.

SIX

Aisling woke with a cry trapped in her throat. Sweat lined her brow as she sat upright, her hands at her neck. She peeled thin strands of her hair from her face and coaxed her erratic breathing to a normal rhythm.

Her alarm hadn't gone off. Stars twinkled outside her window, blanketed by the deep blue hue of night.

Sleep never came for her. She twisted and turned in panicked exhaustion for half an hour before grunting her annoyance and rolling out of bed. She showered and dressed for work while her mind whirred with unnatural, unexplainable concern.

The dragon was infected. If she didn't find a way to help it, the infection would spread, weakening the beast until it died alone on the beach. Painfully. Hopelessly. Alone.

It deserved more than that. Something so beautiful, so fierce, had to be saved, and she was going to do it.

She knew she wouldn't find a doctor or medicine in her dream. Even in sleep, her mind was unable to allow her to have anything easily. She would have to find answers in reality. The internet would be her best bet, but her apartment didn't have it, and she had a turn-of-the-millennia flip phone. She filled a glass with water and decided to visit the library after work. There would be answers there.

A building full of books was a portal to knowledge and enlightenment, both of which she desperately needed.

Questions swirled in her mind that she tried to ignore. What if tonight's dream was somewhere different? What if the dragon was gone? What if she met a dead dragon, its wound black and festered against the beauty of its scales as scavengers ate their fill of its beautiful corpse?

It's only a dream, she told herself through gritted teeth over and over until it became her mantra. It did nothing to calm the nausea curling in her gut or the panicked thoughts haunting her every breath.

It felt too real – the scent of the beach, the sand, the sea. The wind against her skin. The warmth and thickness of the blood on her hands. The pain in its eyes.

The clock glared at her. There was still an hour before she had to be at work. She left anyway, unable to tolerate a moment more in the shoebox of an apartment with only her thoughts as company. She walked through the sleeping city, not paying any mind to the shadows lurking in the darkness, and entered the café.

An hour later, Troy waltzed in with sleep still heavy in his eyes. He squinted, brows furrowed, as he looked at the café. Aisling sat quietly at the only booth in the back with a cup of coffee in her hands and a tight smile on her face.

"Why does it look like everything is done?" he croaked.

"Because it is."

He shut one eye and glanced at the clock. "Am I late?"

"No."

"So you're here early because..."

She shrugged. "I couldn't sleep."

He threw his bag on the back of a chair and poured a cup of coffee, adding in an exorbitant amount of sugar and flavored syrup before sitting beside her. She leaned into his warmth and breathed him in. The panic ebbed, allowing her thoughts to drift from her dream to real life. He sipped his coffee. "Nightmares?"

She grimaced. "Kind of. Figured I'd be productive since I was up."

"Making me look like a slacker, Ash." He took a sip of coffee and grinned. "First the baking, now this. How are Ryan and I ever going to fall in love when you're outshining me?"

She snorted. "First, you have to talk to Ryan about something besides work. But until you can work up the courage, I'll dim myself for you any time."

"Ugh, stop," he whined, hanging his head between his shoulders. "Talking to him would mean opening up to him. Meaning I'd have to be vulnerable. Meaning," he emphasized with a flip of his hand, "I'd simply be preparing myself for rejection. I'd rather save myself from the hideous embarrassment, thank you."

"So I can still shine?"

He angled his head toward her. "You shine as much as you want, babe. I'll be here to reflect your brightness."

Something in her cracked with his words. He was the only person in her life who valued her. The only one who had kept her from sinking into hopelessness. He had saved her time and time again and still thought she was brighter than the sun. Still thought she was worth something when the world was determined to show her she wasn't.

Her throat tightened but she forced the words out anyway. "I love you."

Troy's eyes flashed with concern. His arm found its way to her shoulders, and he pulled her tighter into his side. He didn't say anything, but he didn't need to. She knew he loved her, too. They were soulmates in the most platonic sense of the word. "Tell me about your nightmare," he murmured after a few beats of silence.

Aisling pulled back slowly. "You're going to think I'm insane."

He rolled his eyes. "As if I don't already?"

She leveled a stare before taking a quick breath and giving him every detail from the first dream to the one last night. When she finished, he was staring at his cup with wide eyes, blinking slowly. "Say something," she whispered.

He shook his head. "I don't know what to say. I've never heard of someone having the same dream for months."

"Do you think I'm going insane?"

"No. Truly, I don't." He shrugged both shoulders. "Maybe it's your brain's way to escape."

"Why would it send me somewhere nice and then bring in all this mess, though?"

"Because you got bored."

Aisling grimaced. "I did not get bored. I loved that stupid dream."

"Do you not love it now?"

"I still love it," she muttered. "But it's not as relaxing as it used to be."

Troy gulped the last bit of his coffee and licked his lips. "I don't see you as a person who can relax, Ash. No matter what you tell yourself. You need something to do. You're like a dog." Her jaw dropped and he laughed, soft and warm. "I'm not taking it back. You'd make an adorable dog. I'd even let you sleep in my bed."

She groaned. The kitchen door opened, and Ryan's eyebrows lifted as he took in the sight of them lounging in the booth. "I came in early," Aisling said before he could speak. "Just practicing."

Ryan poured a cup of black coffee for himself before sitting opposite them on the bench. He rubbed the sleepiness from his eyes. "Grandma was thrilled when I asked her for recipes. You'd think I was telling her I'd gotten married." He took a sip. "I've ordered the equipment and ingredients in bulk. They should be here in the next two days. We can start then?" Aisling nodded in agreement.

"And Troy, I'll need your help, if you're willing, to create the menu board. You have nice handwriting. Better than Aisling's, anyway." He pointed to a spot on the wall above the espresso machine. "It will hang there." Troy nodded his acceptance, his tongue apparently not working anymore. Ryan's shoulders loosened and he gave a weak smile. "I couldn't run this place without you two. I can only hope the new kids I hired will be as good as you."

Aisling cleared her throat. "Are you training them here? Or at the new place?"

"Here. I know it'll be tight for a while, but I want them to learn from you guys. I think it'll be the best way. If there are too many of them, let me know and I can work on staggering them."

Aisling stood and took Troy's cup, glancing at the clock on the wall. "How many are there?"

"Four," Ryan called out as he twisted to face her. "Just enough to get the other location started. Would you guys like one of them here? They could take some of the load off for you."

"No!" Both Troy and Aisling said at the same time. Ryan smirked and disappeared with his coffee through the kitchen door into his tiny office. Troy unlocked the front door, and the day began in a flurry of caffeine and sugar, a welcome distraction from the haunting memories of her dream.

They closed with brutal efficiency. Troy handed her a mug of tea. She transferred it to a travel cup and glanced up at him. "Do you have plans?"

He cocked his head. "Are you asking me on a date?"

"Do you consider the library a date?"

"Yes."

"Then yes. Would you like to go with me?"

He pursed his lips. "What are we looking for?"

"Books."

"Then no."

She nudged him with her elbow. "I need to find something that could be used to heal it."

"The dream?" She nodded. He sighed. "It's not like I have anything better to do. Of course, I'll help you find a cure for a dragon in your dream like a sane person."

They entered the library and were greeted by the nostalgic smell of books and warm light of the old chandeliers above. It brought back a slideshow of memories from her earlier days when she had no home, no friends. The library was her school, her social life, her sanctuary. She would spend an entire day devouring new worlds and drinking in as many words as she could before returning to an alley or shelter at closing. It was a safe place for her. One she never took for granted. She had stopped reading recently, preferring her dream to anything else.

They walked up a grand wooden staircase to the nonfiction section. Wordlessly, they split. Troy went to the medical section. Aisling stared at the books on botany and homeopathic remedies. She didn't know what she needed, but she knew the answer would most likely be in the plants that decorated the dream. She grabbed an armful and met Troy at a table, his nose already stuck in a book.

"Would you call it a minor wound?" he whispered. She shook her head violently. He turned the page. "Never mind, then."

She pictured the wound. What would it look like now? What would her mind conjure when she went back? Had the tissue already gone black? Had the infection seeped into the blood?

A warm hand covered hers. "Relax, Ash. We'll find you something to work with." He jerked his chin to the pile of books on their table. "There has to be something here that your brain can transfer to your dream."

They spent the next half hour in silence. "There's no sutures?" Troy asked.

"It's a beach. Not a hospital."

He tutted. "You should work on making it a hospital, then. Because all the answers are here."

She sighed and tossed her book to the side to grab another. Her heart rate jumped at the first page. It was exactly what she needed. Pictures and diagrams of multiple flower varieties littered the pages. Paragraphs on their medicinal properties yielded recipes for tinctures and salves and oils.

"I've seen these there," she whispered, pointing to a page of bright orange flowers.

A piece of paper appeared in front of her. Troy took a pen from his bag and handed it over. "You haven't stopped gasping. Write it down before we get a noise complaint."

She grabbed the pen and let it fly over the paper. Troy added notes of his own until both sides were devoured by ink. Happy with their work, they returned the books and yawned as they walked back into the street.

"It's almost bedtime," Troy said as he stretched. He squeezed her hand. "Good luck tonight. Heal your new fake friend, and make sure you give me credit, too."

She ignored her rumbling stomach as she threw herself into the shower and onto her pilled sheets. She read and reread the notes clenched in her hands until her vision went hazy and her eyelids drooped, letting numerous possible cures be the last thing she saw before the dream transported her away.

SEVEN

The beach was empty.

Aisling ran to the water, scanning the coastline for a hint of a body, a wing, something. There were no puddles of blood on the sand or dark stained patches. She saw nothing. Nothing but the spray of the sea and the seagulls flying above.

She shut her eyes against the rising tide of anger in her chest, her fury with herself almost too much to bear.

Maybe Troy was right. Maybe she was never meant to have peace. Maybe her mind had conjured up this entire scenario because it got tired of the lack of pain, the lack of struggle. It had spent almost thirty years battling life. It was all it knew.

She forced her eyes open. Forced herself to take a deep breath and banish her anger, her frustration. She drank in the sight of the sun glittering on the water's surface and the sound of her steady breathing. But even the beauty around her wasn't enough to quell her thoughts.

She would not accept it. She would not accept her need for pain and despair even in sleep. She created this creature for a reason, and she was going to find out why.

Her eyes scoured the beach and stilled when she saw car-sized footprints embedded in the sand and the distinct line of a tail dragging toward the green hills. The long grasses parted, revealing a path over a hill and through a small valley. A bubbling river bordered by thick bushes and purple flowers followed the dragon's trail. The path disappeared at the mouth of a cave embedded into the hillside. A pair of massive vertical boulders stood at each side of the entrance like pillars. Darkness hung heavy inside where dirt had been disturbed.

She knew it was inside. Felt it in her chest like a pull on an invisible thread.

There was no fear in her heart save for the state of the wound. She did not need to fear a creature of her mind's own making. She did not need to fear anything in this dream.

The sound of her footsteps was swallowed by the inky darkness. Her ears throbbed with the hollow silence inside. "I know you're in here," she called out. Her voice bounced against the rocks. The scent of the infection wafted toward her. She clamped down on a gag. "Come out. I need to see the wound."

Dark silence responded.

"I can smell you. You're hurt. Let me try to help."

Silence.

She rolled her eyes. "Fine. Die in here. You'll have no one to blame but your own stubborn ass." She turned on her heel and walked toward the light.

A moment later, a rustling came from inside the cave. She smirked as the ground rumbled under her feet. The birds stopped singing. Aisling turned. The dragon stood beside her, its scales duller than the last time she saw it. The bright violet hue of its eyes had turned milky.

"Are you going to let me look at it?" she asked. The dragon leveled a stare at her. She cocked her head. "I might be able to help you. Which is good, because you smell like death, and you know it." She walked to its right side and looked at it expectantly. Her jaw dropped as the dragon answered with an eye roll. It lifted its wing enough for her to see the damage. She sucked in a deep inhale as the smell permeated everything around them.

The green and yellow clots inside were chunky and thick. Purulent drainage oozed from the edges of the wound and down its hide. Her eyes scanned for anything black but found nothing. It didn't mean it wasn't lurking beneath the surface.

"I think I know something that can help," she said as she took a step back and turned to the dragon's face. "I've seen it here before. I just have to find it again. Don't leave this place, okay?" The dragon blinked as if in answer. Its legs folded beneath it, bringing it to the ground with more agility than she thought possible of a creature that big. It rested its head on the ground and lifted a scaled brow in question. She couldn't stop the grin that spread on her face. "Yeah. Just like that."

The dragon huffed once before wrapping its tail around its body and covering its face. Aisling sprinted from the cave, praying her memory served her right. Her legs conquered the hills with a strength she'd never had in reality. Every pump of her arms was in tandem with her steps like she was a natural-born runner.

Craggy rocks stuck out of the ground like ledges, allowing her feet to find purchase on her way up another steep incline. She cleared the top and scanned her surroundings. Lush green grass spread out in every direction around her. Shadows filled the valleys where ribbons of blue snaked across the land. Sprinkles of every color but orange dotted the ground.

Frustration boiled. She swallowed a cry and tilted her head to the sky. They were here. She had seen them before. She'd seen fields of flowers. Seen the bright orange like a beacon against the timid pastels for months.

Why would she do this to herself? Why couldn't she let herself have a single break? Did she hate herself so much that even in her sleep she had to make sure she was having a shitty time?

She swayed as a strong gust of wind blew her to the left. Her hair pulled like a leash as it followed the current. She twisted it and tucked it into the back of her shirt. Another burst of wind hit her, sending her stumbling to the left. Again and again and again.

"I get it!" She shouted to the open sky. The breeze swirled before gently pushing her down the hill to the left. It guided her over three hills, a stream, and a thicket of thorns before dying down as she stepped onto a flat stone. Her throat tightened as she looked at the meadow before her and the thousands of flowers blowing in the wind. Pastels in every shade lifted their faces to the sun. Green leaves danced in the breeze.

And in the center was a splattering of bright orange.

She charged from the rock and slammed onto her knees before the bright orange petals. With a shaky hand, she plucked a flower. Sticky to the touch. Tall green stem. She popped a petal in her mouth and didn't cringe at the bitter taste. This was it. This was what she had been looking for.

The flowers came out of the soil with a pop, flinging dirt everywhere. She clutched as many of them as she could before hurtling through the field and over the hills. She raced along the bank of the river against the current. The power of the bubbling water increased as she followed it to the valley. The dragon remained outside the cave, its scales painfully dull in the sunlight.

It removed its tail from its eyes at the sound of her hurried steps. Aisling threw the flowers at its feet and pointed to the river. "I found them," she panted, "but we need to wash it out first. Get up."

It didn't move.

"Do you want to die? Is that it?" She spit, her anger boiling. "You get hurt and give up? We don't get to do that. We push forward. We ignore the pain and keep going." The dragon didn't move. Its vertical slit of a pupil narrowed. She scoffed. "I don't care. I don't care what you want. You have to live, damn it." Her throat tightened. "You have to. So get your sorry ass up and into the river."

Emotion clogged her chest. She didn't know why it was so important to her that this creature, this thing her subconscious had made up, lived, but it had taken over all her thoughts awake and asleep. Selfishly, she needed it alive for her own sake.

The dragon blinked once before lifting itself from the ground with a low moan. She contained her sigh of relief. It entered the river gingerly and rolled on its good side. The wound glared at her, begging for help.

"Just going to rinse it out quickly," Aisling said, ignoring the dragon's unending glare. She stepped onto a large rock and cupped her hands into the frigid water, dumping it directly into the wound with a splash.

A sharp hiss left the dragon's lips. It bared its teeth. Aisling didn't care. She dumped a few more handfuls of water in and watched the byproducts of infection slosh and rinse from the wound. Bright red tissue stared back at her after a few minutes of work.

"That wasn't so bad, was it?" she asked as she stepped off the rock and picked up the flowers. "Come on."

The ground reverberated under its gigantic feet. Aisling stepped aside at the mouth of the cave and allowed the beast to enter first. It lay on the dirt in the only chunk of light available and rolled on its left side, allowing her access to the wound.

She picked up a flower and held it out in front of her. "This is what I'm going to use. According to a book I read, it has antiseptic properties that can help stop the infection and maybe allow your wound to heal faster." She extended the flower and held her breath in wonder as it sniffed the orange petals. "I don't know if it will work. But I don't know what else we can do. This is the best option right now."

In answer, the dragon rested its head on its front legs and let its eyelids droop shut. She took it as consent and tore a handful of flowers from their stem. The book instructed her to rest the flowers in a jar and let the oil seep naturally from the petals, but she didn't have the luxury of time. She clenched her fingers around the flower until her hands shook, then she repositioned the thick mess of petals and squeezed again. And again. And again.

Her forearms begged her to stop. Her fingernails sliced into her palms. She kept squeezing.

The petals turned into a pulp, staining her skin bright orange like a sloppy sunset. A choked sob left her lips as she opened her hands to find a sweet, thick liquid coating her palms.

Delicately, reverently, she hovered her hands over the cavernous wound. Each drip of oil was a miracle she couldn't look away from. The pulp succumbed to gravity, landing with a small wet thump on the ravaged tissue. She didn't remove it. She left it, hoping it contained more oil she hadn't been able to expel.

She looked at the dragon in excitement but found it sleeping soundly, hot air puffing from its nose.

Why hadn't it tried to hurt her? Why did it allow her to work on it? Did it actually understand what she was saying?

She shook her head. A dream. This whole thing was a dream. Nothing had to make sense.

A sheen of sweat lined her brow as she continued and the minutes stacked into hours. Her forearms screamed. Her hands quivered as she crushed the flowers, the bright petals of hope, in her grasp and let the oil cover the wound inch by inch.

Gray and black tinted the edges of her vision.

No.

No.

Not now. Not when she had finally done something right. When she had made good on her promise to help.

She would not allow herself to wake up.

Darkness swarmed in her eyes. She clenched her teeth together, willing herself to stay grounded in the moment.

A sweet floral scent in the air. Sticky oil covering her palms in an iridescent sheen. The dryness of her mouth. The warm body beneath her hands. A small pebble digging into her leg.

She was here. She was not leaving.

Her eyes remained open, forced to see through the darkness that threatened to overpower and take her under. The dragon snored soundly beside her. She locked her stare on its face, willing herself to stay at its side.

She would not leave it like this, vulnerable and alone. Not again.

The tightness in her stomach tore at her very soul, pushing it toward a dark current she wouldn't be able to fight.

She fought anyway – her hands planted on the ground, dirt shoved beneath her fingertips as if an anchor. A guttural scream left her lips as she pushed away from the current, from the pull, and felt her soul shudder at the resistance.

A heartbeat later, darkness devoured her.

EIGHT

A thin sheen of sweat covered her with a damp chill. Aisling's chest ached. Every muscle burned with a sharp acidity even in stillness.

She didn't want to open her eyes. Didn't want to see her depressing apartment or the light of the moon from her window. Didn't want to hear her alarm going off with its shrill screams.

Hot air tickled her cheek.

The smell of dirt coated her nostrils.

Her heart heavied as she opened her eyes to find a dark ceiling of rock and a pair of bright violet eyes staring at her in concern from above.

She'd done it. She fought reality and won.

"Go back to sleep. Everything is okay," she murmured to the dragon as she forced herself up and wiped the sweat from her brow. It stared at her for a few heartbeats longer before resting its head again on the ground.

Aisling knew time was not on her side. Eventually, she would have to answer to the darkness and return to reality.

Oil pooled in her palms with each handful of flowers she pressed. Every drop was sacred. She coated the entire wound with it. When the last flower had been crushed, she took a step back and admired the shimmering tint of yellow that covered the angry tissue inside.

Briefly, she wondered if she should get more flowers but decided against it. Wait and see how it works – if it works – and go from there.

She tiptoed from the cave and washed her hands in the crisp water of the river, watching as the yellow film of the oil drifted in the current. Cotton candy pink clouds reflected on the surface of the water. Her eyes drifted upward to where the sun peeked from behind a hill, tinting the pale blue sky with ribbons of oranges and pinks.

Gratitude flooded her soul. How lucky was she to have fallen into a dream like this when her reality threatened to crush her spirit every day?

Her entire life had been about surviving. Surviving her mother's erratic moods. Her father's anger and subsequent departure from their lives. Her mother's insane ramblings. Her father's laugh as she bled at his new wife's hand.

She spent ten years floating between homeless shelters and the streets, barely making it through some winters. She went days without food. Years without medical care. For a decade, all she dreamed of was a safe place to rest her head at night and a steady influx of food and water to keep her nourished.

It was as if her mind knew she would never attain it in reality. Instead, it sent her to a state of tranquility in her sleep as an apology for what she had to endure during her waking hours.

She was grateful. Grateful to have a job that allowed her to have a roof over her head. Grateful to have made a friend who shared her struggles. Grateful to be alive after the injuries and terror she had been through.

But she wondered if it was all she would ever have. How could she have more? She was uneducated. Barely scraping enough money to pay rent, let alone buy food or have fun. She had no time, no energy for any relationship. There was nothing she had to offer anyone. She was, for all intents and purposes, useless. Worthless. A wraith in the world, a shadow of a soul, whose only purpose was to suffer and survive, not live.

She cupped her hands in the cool water, letting the chill freeze her thoughts and bring her back to the present. The water slid down her dry throat and she let out a sigh of relief. The last rays of the sun warmed her back as she turned back to the cave. The wound glittered in the dimming light. The dragon slept soundly.

Something in her chest tugged at the sight of it.

A creature of nightmares, born to instill fear and terror, sleeping like a baby just feet from her. It listened to her and let her attempt to help it when it could have easily just eaten her or burned her to ash.

Maybe it would when it healed. She wouldn't put it past her mind to create some nightmare tragedy like that.

She sat against the cave's rocky mouth and crossed her arms over her chest as she watched the sun disappear behind the hills and the shiny film of the oil seep into the tissue. All she could do was wait. Wait until the next night to see if her mind would let this be enough to help.

Her eyes shut against the first twinkles of night. She welcomed the darkness she had fought and allowed herself to be pulled back into reality.

NINE

She was late. Very, very, late.

Toothpaste clung to her finger as she rushed out the door. Her greasy hair begged to be put up and hidden away. Her bag slammed against her hips with every step she sprinted across the city. It was not like running in her dream. She was no longer agile and lithe. Gravity held her with a tight fist, barely allowing her to leap over a puddle that smelled strongly of urine.

Gone were the flowery fields and hills of emerald green grass. Gone was the salty mist of the sea and the song of the wind. Instead, her burning lungs filled with smog and bitterness.

Aisling yanked the door to the café open, looked over her shoulder to spit out the last of her toothpaste from her mouth on the sidewalk, and ran inside. Troy stood at the counter. His eyes and jaw were wide in shock as he took her in. Strands of unwashed hair clung to her forehead. Sweat covered her skin in a layer like the oil she spent the whole night harvesting. A glob of toothpaste had turned to cement on her upper lip.

Troy glanced over his shoulder at the kitchen door. He turned back with his finger over his lips to hush her. Her brow furrowed just as Ryan walked in, his eyes immediately widening at the sight of her.

Aisling held her breath. In three years she had never been late. Never called out sick. Never did anything to jeopardize her job. Now she risked it all for a dream.

"Did you get that emergency plumber?" Troy asked, his eyes begging her to play along. "I know it's almost impossible to find one this early. Judging by your hair, it looks like they didn't fix the shower in time."

Aisling nodded quickly, ignoring his jab. "Yeah. Yeah, thanks. He said it would be an easy job, but he's still there now." She turned her sheepish gaze to Ryan. "I didn't want to leave him alone in my apartment, so I waited as long as I could, but..."

Ryan's posture loosened. He shook his head. "No, please. Don't worry about it. I'm sure it's been a rough morning already. But text me if it happens again, not just Troy."

She nodded, the perfect picture of submissive embarrassment. He tucked his hands into the pockets of his black jeans. "Baking will start in two days. There are two new mixers and supplies in the kitchen. I have copies of the recipes here for you to familiarize yourself with if you'd like." He pulled out a small stack of index cards and placed them beside the register. "I'm meeting with the construction team again today. If you need me, please keep calling until I pick up. I could use a break from them."

He flashed a quick smile before disappearing through the kitchen door. She let out a sigh of relief and threw her bag under the register, ignoring Troy's pointed stare and pursed lips. A gasp of horror left her lips at the sight of her reflection on the register screen. Dark purple pooled under her eyes. Her cheeks were hollow. There was a dullness to her already pallid skin that made her nauseous. She pulled out a rubber band from a drawer and yanked her short hair into a slick bun before splashing a handful of cold water on her face.

"The words you're looking for are *thank you*," Troy said over the mouth of his mug.

"Thank you," she mumbled, patting her face dry with a paper towel. She met his eyes. "I mean it. Thank you. You're a lifesaver."

"Now we're even."

"Even?"

"Yeah. You showed me up yesterday coming in so early. I covered for your sleepy ass. Now we're even."

She took the mug from his hands and gulped his coffee, grimacing at the amount of sugar inside. "You're going to get diabetes from this cup alone."

He snatched it back. "Did our hard work help or did your brain sabotage it?"

Memories of the night came flooding back. Her voice came out quieter than she intended, full of unspoken fear and concern. "I'm not sure yet."

A pause. "Well, there's nothing you can do right now. So let's focus your attention on something else." He looked around the café and frowned. "Nothing here worth your time except me, it seems."

"You want me to focus all of my attention on you?"

"How could you not?"

She rolled her eyes but let a smile creep onto her face. "You're delusional, you know that?"

"Says the one trying to save a dragon in a dream."

"Touché," she sighed, throwing her apron on and tying the thin strands around her waist. They cinched tighter than she remembered.

Troy's face tightened but he said nothing as he unlocked the doors, allowing the three customers already lined up outside to come in.

Aisling didn't give herself a single second to think about her dream. Troy was right. Her attention needed to be focused elsewhere. She made drinks. She cleaned. She reheated the baked items as needed. She organized and restocked when it was slow. There was a moment when she even debated cleaning the bathroom.

"You haven't taken a breath all day, you nut job," Troy mumbled beside her at the espresso machine. She ignored him and reached to the top shelf for a large mug, but his hand covered hers. "Let me."

He reached for it slowly, deliberately forcing her to take a single second to do nothing. She hated it. She hated him for knowing her so well. Hated herself for –

No. She didn't hate herself.

She had done the best she could with the cards she had been dealt.

She hated life. Reality. She hated leaving her dream to return to the nonstop grind of work and settling.

She didn't hate herself. She was proud of herself. Proud that she didn't return to an abusive household. Proud that even in her darkest moments, she hadn't turned to the same vices that plagued her mother. Proud that she wanted *more* even when the world made it obvious she would never have it.

And she was proud that even though it was in a dream, she had been deemed valuable. Someone like her, with no skills, no anything, wasn't useless like she was in reality.

"Better?"

She blinked the burning in her eyes away and took the mug from his hand, nudging his shoulder with her forehead. "Much."

"Good. Get back to it." He lifted a brow. "You're slacking."

Hours later, they found themselves at the lone booth with mugs of tea in front of them. Troy stuffed a pale pastry in his mouth and looked pointedly at her. "Spill." Aisling dunked her tea bag in the water absentmindedly, watching as the water turned from clear to a weird shade of yellow-green. Sparing no detail, she told him everything from the night before. He smirked when she was finished. "Bossy little thing, aren't you?"

Her brows pinched. "What?"

"Little miss meek and mild bossing around a fully grown dragon. Who would have thought?"

"I am not meek and mild," she countered.

"You absolutely are. You're like a quiet little mouse unless you're with me. And it's fine. I love you for it," he patted her hand. "But I like this dream version of you, too. I think it's the person you are deep down. It's like your subconscious is forcing you to be yourself."

Aisling pursed her lips and leaned against the puffy plastic behind her. "Are you a therapist now?"

"Should I be?" He angled his head. "Tell me how you feel."

"Annoyed," she responded dryly.

He smiled, his bright teeth a beam of light against his warm skin. "Then it's settled. That's my destiny."

"You don't want to sling coffee forever?" She knew it was the wrong thing to ask when the brightness in his eyes and the smile she adored dimmed.

"No. This is not what I want to do forever." He glanced around the café. "I'll do this until I'm able to do something worthwhile. Something I can be proud of." She nodded in understanding. He glanced back at her. "What about you?"

"I've never been able to think about my future much," she admitted. Her future was nothing but a black void when she imagined it. Never had she allowed herself to dream or hope that her life could be something worth living. She knew from a painfully young age that she was not someone of importance. She was placed on this earth only to work, only to survive, and she forced herself to be okay with it because what was her other option?

"Maybe you should," Troy said gently. He lifted from his chair and extended his arm to her. "Shall we?"

They walked arm in arm through the streets, two souls lost in the world together. He wrapped her in a bear hug before they parted ways. Her apartment building seemed to sag in on itself as if it felt the weight of the world on its beams and couldn't hold it any longer. She knew the feeling.

She skittered up the stairs, ignoring the trio of mice hiding in the corner of the entryway and the questionable new red stain on the stairwell. A TV blared from under a door. A dog howled incessantly. Her fridge was barren. So were the cabinets. She found a single bag of popcorn and threw it into the microwave. While it cooked, she jumped into the shower and let the lukewarm water soothe her entirely too busy mind.

Making coffee was not what she wanted to do for the rest of her life. She wanted to make a difference, even if it was just for a single person. Where to start and how to find the time with her awkward schedule was the hard part.

The microwave beeped. She dressed and ate the popcorn in silence while looking over the notes from the night before. If last night's work hadn't been fruitful, she needed to be prepared.

Her eyes crossed. She pulled the blanket up over her shoulders, not bothering to close the blinds. Her hands rested under her cheek, and she took a deep breath before allowing the pull in her soul and the call of her dragon to bring her under the darkness.

TEN

Ice cold water lapped at her ankles. She jumped up and let out a curse before sprinting from the riverbank onto the grass.

The morning sun had barely made itself known over the hilltops around the valley. The deep blue sky of night paled as a yellow haze lifted from the horizon. Birdsong tickled her ears. A rabbit jumped between a bed of long grass beside the river. Small flowers tilted their faces toward the incoming sun, ready for another day.

The dragon wasn't seen, but she wasn't worried. Something inside her chest pulled her toward the cavity where darkness lurked. The grass under her feet switched to dry dirt littered with flat rocks as she stepped into the mouth of the cave. "Good morning!" she called out.

Immediately, the darkness shifted. A pair of bright violet eyes shone through. Aisling grinned, her heart soaring with hope as it moved forward on silent feet, bringing its entire body into the light. "Hello, sunshine," she cooed. "How was your night?"

A puff of hot air was its answer. Its long serpentine neck stretched in the light. A yawn escaped its gigantic mouth, allowing the first rays of sunlight to illuminate teeth sharpened to points she knew could destroy her. But no fear pulsed in her veins.

Admiration did. Respect did.

"Can I take a look?" The dragon didn't hesitate to turn to its side and lower to her level. The wing drew back slightly, allowing her unrestricted access. "Thank you," she whispered and stood on her toes, holding her breath.

The wound greeted her like an old unwanted friend. The oily sheen was gone. Small chunks of orange pulp remained scattered over the tissue. The smell was gone. There were no more clots.

It wasn't magically healed, but it wasn't worse.

Hope sunk its claws into her chest, leaving her breathless. She hadn't self-destructed this. She'd allowed herself this singular victory.

She lowered to the ground and walked toward its head. "Much better. Still have a lot to do, but better." She allowed a smile to lift her lips. "Does it feel better?"

It blinked once. She sighed. "I know you can't talk. I don't know why I asked." Her eyes traveled to the wound again. "If I do all of that again, it could help more. Are you okay with that?"

Another single blink. She nodded just as a deep rumble echoed from its torso. They both stared at its stomach.

"Are you hungry?" How many days had it been since it last ate? It blinked once. She took it as a yes. Aisling gestured to the wound. "I don't think you can hunt like this."

It blinked twice in answer. She pursed her lips and looked beyond the mouth of the cave. She hadn't seen anything bigger than a rabbit or fox in all her time here. How much did it eat? And how often?

"Do you like fish?" A strong puff of hot air was its answer. She swiped her hair from her face and cocked her head. "Well, you're going to. I can't hunt, so it's the only thing I could even have a chance of feeding you."

It lifted its top lip in a grimace, and she smirked. "Would you rather starve? Because that's always a possibility, too." The lip lowered as its eyes narrowed. She flashed a quick smile. "I'll be back soon. Well...

hopefully soon. I've never fished before, but it doesn't seem that hard. Don't fly away."

It lowered to the ground and tucked its membranous wings tight to its side with a hint of annoyance. An overwhelming urge to run her fingers over them took her by surprise. Clenching her hands at her sides, she turned and ran into the light.

Three hours later, the sun was well on its way to midday. In one arm were a few bouquets worth of bright orange flowers. In her other were four fish that cost her dry clothes and her dignity.

The dragon's brows lifted as she walked in, eyes narrowed on the fish. She shot it a look. "Don't even." The fish landed with a sickening thud on the stone ground. Both Aisling and the dragon grimaced. "Bon appétit," she murmured and walked to the wound with the dozens of flowers still in her arms. She sank into a squat and peeled the petals from the stems, watching the dragon stare at the fish like they were garbage.

It scooped all four into its mouth at once, swallowing loudly and shaking its head in distaste. Aisling knew the fish wouldn't sustain it, but they didn't have any other options.

The next few hours were spent over the wound. They sat in companionable silence as she worked. After a while, she stopped noticing the burning ache in her arms or the near-permanent tone of orange on her palms.

The dragon's eyes never left her. It sat with its neck curved toward her, purple eyes always watching. Aisling felt the tickle of its gaze on her back, her arms, her neck, like a constant shadow. Barely there, but enough to notice. It was oddly comforting.

The sun made its way over the valley, spreading shadows in its wake. A pile of green stems littered the floor when she finished. She stretched her stiff back and rolled her shoulders. "Let's get you some water."

The dragon followed soundlessly, its heavy footsteps the only indication it had obeyed. Aisling stopped at the edge of the bank and watched it walk in completely unbothered by the chilled water. Its long neck lowered in a graceful arc as it drank gallon after gallon.

She noted the lack of stiffness in its walk. The brightness in its eyes. There was frustration written in them, frustration and exhaustion, but no pain. A glimmer of pride ran down her spine. She did that.

Aisling stepped into the river until it covered her knees and cupped her hands, bringing the water to her lips and shutting her eyes at the crisp relief it brought. She lowered her hands again but stopped at what she saw reflected on the surface.

It was her, but it wasn't her, either.

Her hair was no longer short and choppy. It was still brown, but it had a warm depth to it. Every strand was thicker and healthier, ending just at her waistband with the slightest hint of waves.

Her brown eyes were still dark, but there was a brightness there she never noticed in reality. The heavy purple bags beneath were gone. Her cheeks were no longer sunken but full of life. A golden radiance glowed beneath the surface of her skin.

She tore her eyes from her reflection to her body. How had she not noticed it before? She was taller here. Her legs and arms were longer and stronger than they ever were in her waking hours.

A lean finger lifted to trace her face. She looked at her reflection in wonder as it slid across her cheeks, the narrow bridge of her nose.

Every plane, every angle, her but not.

Aisling, but better.

Purple eyes reflected behind her. She didn't know what to think of the comfort they brought, the safety she felt, as she met its gaze. "This isn't me," she whispered, turning her stare back to her reflection. "This isn't what I look like. I don't know who this is."

She wanted to be this person. Wanted to be beautiful like this. Strong like this.

Maybe Troy was right. Maybe her dream was just her subconscious showing her what she would be without the heavy weight of surviving on her shoulders.

Which version of her was the real one?

If she wanted to disappear into this world where she felt the most like herself, could she? Could she shed her skin, her life, like a snake and become the woman she wanted to be?

If she couldn't go back to reality, would that really be the worst thing?

Would she ever have a say in her reality? Or would she be thrown into whatever fate chose to give her, teasing her with snippets of a life worth living?

Her heart pounded in answer. She had known from the first night of the dream months ago that she didn't want to leave this world. It felt like peace. It felt like what a home was supposed to feel like – safe. A luxury she'd never truly felt before.

Something moved under her left hand, throwing her from her head. She glanced down and inhaled sharply.

White scales as large as dinner plates rested beneath the pads of her fingers. They were warm, not cold like she'd imagined.

Every thought eddied from her head. She didn't dare move, didn't breathe.

The beast pressed its snout into her hand. She spread her shaking fingers, letting each scale glide under her palm, and marveled at the smooth texture between the divots and ridges.

A soft vibration rumbled from its throat and shook her hand. It traveled up her arm and landed in her chest with a soft glow. A thought barreled through her, taking her soul with it.

This dragon was hers.

ELEVEN

She barely remembered the last week.

Of reality, at least.

She remembered everything about her dreams. Her day off was spent in bed, healing a dragon and feeling free.

"Ash, did you hear me?"

She snapped her head up. Troy peered into the kitchen; his hazel eyes sharp as they assessed her blank stare. A flicker of concern washed over his face, disappearing as quickly as it came. "I said, they've been devouring the cranberry orange muffins. You might want to make an extra batch."

She blinked. Muffins. Yes.

She was at the café. Baking.

This was real life.

She nodded once and returned her attention to the unknown dough underneath her palms. What was she making again?

Warm hands covered her narrow shoulders. She flinched against the touch. They disappeared instantly. "Ash…" Troy whispered, "What is going on with you?"

Her voice felt foreign. "Nothing. Why?"

"You haven't been here this whole week." His gaze danced between her eyes. "Well, okay. You've been here, but not mentally. Not emotionally."

She didn't know what to say. So she lied. "I know. I'm sorry. I've just been thinking about what we talked about last week."

He cocked his head to the side. "What did we talk about?"

"You asked me what I want to do with my life. Remember?"

"Yeah. Now I do."

She nodded. "I haven't stopped thinking about it. There are so many options, you know? I'm sorting through each one." In truth, she hadn't thought once about their conversation. She'd only thought about her dream life and her friend waiting for her, now beautifully healing and back to life. "I'm just trying to figure out who I am, I guess."

He smiled softly. "Aren't we all?"

Her gut contracted with the acid of the lie. He was the one person in this world she actually cared about. Actually trusted. But to tell him the truth would make her look...

She returned the smile. "They've been enjoying the bakes?"

His shoulders relaxed and he leaned his hip against the counter. "They're like animals. Are you almost done?"

She had no idea. She glanced around the room. He followed her stare, noting the various tools and ingredients spread haphazardly on the steel island in the middle of the kitchen. He pushed off the counter. "Okay. Well, I have to open. Come out soon, okay? I miss you."

She swallowed thickly as he walked out front, leaving her alone with the unknown dough as her only companion. She tossed it in the trash. Whatever it was, she had kneaded it to oblivion. The oven would only turn it to brick.

Ryan's recipes were easy to follow and perfect for a first-time baker. He had given her a whole page of notes about baking bread from his grandmother, and Aisling caught on quicker than she could have imagined. The café constantly smelled of coffee and warm bread, and the customers raved. Ryan couldn't have been happier.

After mixing muffins and throwing them in the oven, she shoddily cleaned the kitchen before meandering to the bustling front. Troy shot her a look of thanks, his beautiful face frazzled by the length of the line and the handsome man ordering in front of him.

She didn't see any of the customers. Didn't register them or what they said. It was like she was a robot, interacting with only half of her brain while the other half was left in her dream.

The wound had started to shut. There was no sign of infection. Grainy pink tissue sewed it together bit by bit, encouraged by the orange flower oil she processed. The dragon had started stretching and exercising its wings as best it could, stopping when the pain became too much.

She marveled at the sight of them. The pearly white leather went translucent in the sunlight, filtering whatever was under them in a haze of dreamy pastels. The scales brightened with each day, making the dragon even more of a sight to see in the sun.

She didn't know how much a dragon was supposed to weigh, but she knew it was too thin. Her fishing had improved, but it snarled each time she threw one in front of it. Luckily, it had started hunting foxes and rabbits during the night when she wasn't around. The remnants of fluff between its teeth were the only sign.

"Excuse me? Excuse me! I asked for nonfat milk," a voice called out from the pickup counter. Aisling turned toward the familiar voice, noting the woman waving her down.

Her bob remained immaculate. The red on her lips was perfectly painted. She had the same air of impatience as before. The same condescending tone.

Aisling glanced down at the counter where the nonfat milk was still out. With a blank smile, she took the drink back and dumped it before starting over. She lifted the nonfat milk to make sure Red Lips saw it before she poured it in. She placed the new drink on the counter. "So sorry about that." Red Lips gave a tight closed-lip grin before turning on her heel and flouncing out the door.

Aisling wanted to throw the milk at her head.

"Sometimes I think she does that because she wants everyone to think she's skinny," Troy mumbled beside her. She let out a breathy laugh. He glanced at her with a hint of surprise before continuing with his order. "I like to picture her super fat just for that reason."

She laughed out loud. "Maybe I should try that. It would make it easier not to throw the drink in her face."

"I would pay to see that, Ash." He turned but glanced over his shoulder at her. "Big bucks."

She couldn't picture herself doing it. Dream Aisling would throw the drink and then set the dragon on Red Lips. But real Aisling needed this job.

With a resigned sigh, she continued working until her mind was pleasantly blank and her only thoughts were of what awaited her that night.

"So."

She tilted her head. Troy leaned on the kitchen counter beside her, watching as she finished cleaning her mess of flour and egg. "Tell me about the dreams."

She paused for a second before continuing her cleaning. "What about them?"

"Tell me what's got you so distracted."

"I'm not distracted."

"I may be gorgeous, but I am not a bimbo, babe." He angled his shoulder closer to her. "Tell me."

She shrugged. "The books we read worked." His mouth parted slightly in a half smile. She nodded, attempting to hide her satisfaction and pride. "The wound isn't infected anymore. Every night it looks more healed. I think it'll close by the end of this week."

"So... we're doctors now?"

A smile lifted her cheeks. "I don't know why we don't go to school for it. We've obviously got a knack for medicine."

"It hasn't eaten you yet, then?"

She laughed again. "No. It's eaten other things. I had to catch fish for it once." She glanced at him with wide eyes. "You should have seen it. I was soaking wet. It was awful."

He dropped his head between his shoulders and laughed. "I wish I could have. I'm sure whatever I'm picturing now doesn't do it justice."

"I'm glad no one was there to see it."

"Have you named it?"

"No." She had no desire to name it. There was no point in naming something if it wasn't going to be permanent.

"So what now? You're friends with it? Or has it left?"

Her stomach sank at the thought of it leaving. She swallowed thickly. "We're just friends now, I guess. Until it feels good enough to fly. Then..." She trailed off, unable to finish the sentence

She didn't want to go back to the dream if it wasn't there.

Troy picked up on her silence and rested his head on her shoulder. "I'll be your dragon when the time comes, Ash. You can take care of me."

She pressed a quick kiss to the top of his head. "If you come to me with a giant gaping wound, I'm taking you to the hospital. Okay?"

"Fine. But you pay all the medical bills. Deal?"

She leaned her head against his. "Deal."

TWELVE

The dragon wasn't in the cave. Or the river. Or in any of the fields they'd frequented. It wasn't at the beach or swimming in the sea.

Aisling's pulse thundered in her ears. Every inhale turned acidic.

It left.

An oily roll of nausea sank into her gut before a tidal wave of despair rocked her entire body. Her knees collapsed beneath her, connecting with the loam cushion carpeting the hard ground.

The only thing she looked forward to, gone. The little sliver of happiness she craved, vanished. Her purpose, gone.

Despair dried as raging fury roared to life in its place.

How dare it leave without saying goodbye? After everything she did for it? She thought they'd formed a real connection, that it felt the same pull she did. The same comfort in her presence that she found in it.

She was a fool, tried and true. Even in her dreams, she did not value herself enough to even warrant a goodbye. She'd allowed herself to get close to a creature of her own imagination just to rip it from her heart like it was nothing.

A rich bellow echoed in the wind.

Everything in her body stopped working as she snapped her gaze to the sky. A thick cover of clouds the color of dried ash hung low, moving slowly on a weak breeze.

Again, the call.

Again, her heart stuttered.

A shadow flew behind the clouds, disappearing as quickly as it appeared through a puff of dark gray. Ahead, the clouds parted, leaving a single ray of morning sunlight touching the grass.

And through it came her dragon.

Her sob was drowned by a tremoring roar as the dragon fell from the sky in a graceful twist. Like an angel falling from grace, it sliced through the air toward the ground at a dizzying speed.

She opened her mouth to scream, only to be silenced as it opened its wings to their full length, banking on the wind back into a lazy ascension.

There were no words for the beauty above her. No words for how the light hit the pearlescent scales. For the shimmering radiance that emanated from it as it soared through the air, its wings covering the land in sweeping shadows.

A tear fell down her cheek as she watched it ride the current of wind, dipping and bobbing like it was born to do. Hours could go by, days even, and she would never tire of the ethereal beauty made of both nightmares and dreams making the sky its own.

It landed just feet in front of her. The ground shook on impact, but Aisling did not. She met its eyes, the amethyst inside nearly glowing. Its magnificent wings splayed across its back and hovered just over the ground.

"I thought you ditched me," she said through a wide smile, hiding how broken she had been at the thought. It dipped its head in answer, a silent apology.

She extended her hand and stepped forward confidently. The beast met her halfway, nuzzling its nose against her skin. The crack in her heart instantly healed at the touch.

With a step closer, she placed her other hand on it's neck and stroked the cool bony plates. Hot air danced around her as it sniffed her in greeting. She angled her chin toward its wound. "How's it looking?"

It lifted its wing for her to inspect. The wound had finally healed completely. Pale pink skin stretched and melded together, awaiting a new layer of scales to cover it. Her hand traced the scar with awe. She had done this. "Did it hurt? Any of it?"

It blinked twice, their only way to speak to each other. *No.*

"Did you eat?" It blinked twice again, much faster than before. She pursed her lips. "Fish?"

It leveled a disgusted look at her before slowly blinking twice. *NO.*

Aisling glanced around their little island, painfully aware they were the only two things besides a few bunnies and foxes. And if it didn't want fish...

"Are you going to leave, then?"

No.

Her shoulders loosened but confusion tightened her face. "Then how?"

It lowered its shoulder, angling its front leg toward her in a silent request. Her mouth dropped open. A nervous laugh bubbled from her lips. "There's no..." She waved her hands in the air, words difficult to come by. "There's no saddle! I'm just supposed to sit on you without any safety harness? And what if you fall? Did you think about that?"

It rolled its eyes. Aisling gawked. "Did you just roll your eyes at me?"

One blink. *Yes.*

Her mouth snapped shut. She stared at the dragon.

What else was she going to do? Sit on the island and wait for it to come back? Pace until she made a trail in the grass and worry that it got hurt again? Twiddle her thumbs?

No. She'd had enough of watching life fly by. Besides, it was all a dream. A painfully realistic dream, but a dream, nonetheless. If she fell, she'd still be fine in reality.

"Fine." Her voice cracked. "Okay. So I just climb up here, then?" Without giving herself a chance to back out, she gingerly placed her foot on its leg. "Am I hurting you?"

Bright amethyst eyes rolled again. She gritted her teeth and gripped the scales, using them to both guide and haul herself onto its broad back. It leveled its shoulders as she stood. She swayed, splaying her arms out for balance before crawling on her hands and knees. "Watch it! I have no idea what I'm doing up here!"

The bony plates were far thicker on its back than on its stomach. She put herself just behind its wings, a foot or so past the end of its neck. A few scales stuck up like a short wall of spikes in front of her. She latched onto them. "Is this okay?"

It blinked once. *Yes.*

She nodded, more to herself than anything else. Her voice came out breathless. "All right. Okay. So if you could just –"

Aisling didn't get to finish her plea to take it slow. Its legs sprung up as its massive wings splayed to their full length and pumped against gravity with impressive ease.

Her scream rattled her bones. Every muscle tensed as she shrunk herself against its body, holding onto the spikes with a white-knuckle grip while a brutal downforce of wind pushed against her.

She didn't understand how she could feel a terror so visceral in her sleep. For one moment, she forgot it wasn't real and panicked for her life.

The wings beat steadily beside her as its body leveled out. Her face pressed into the scales; her hot breath pushed back at her face as she attempted to keep from hyperventilating.

Ignoring the dread and terror and nausea coursing through her, Aisling lifted her head cautiously from its back. Blinking forcefully against the incessant wind, she inched herself into a seated position by lengthening her spine and tightening her thighs against its strong back.

Clouds hung just over their heads. Gray mist tickled her hair, leaving some strands damp in their wake. The dragon angled itself up, its head disappearing in the clouds for only a second before Aisling followed. Her mouth opened against the cloud, and a heavy thickness immediately soaked into her tongue like cotton candy.

With two flaps of its wings, the clouds disappeared, replaced by the clearest cerulean sky Aisling had ever seen. It stretched eternally around her in every direction, an invitation and a welcoming.

The creature soared along the current, keeping her steady on its back despite the random gusts of wind that threatened to turn them around. The wings tilted and angled against each burst with innate accuracy. She watched the thin membranous skin ripple and send shimmers of color in their wake.

Time became a loose construct as they sailed above the clouds. There was nothing but them and the sky. They conquered it, taking up as much space as they could against the infinite air around them. The wind, cold and overbearing, hugged her and sang sweet nothings in her ear like a lover.

Tears slid down Aisling's cheeks.

She'd never known happiness like this, this deep, peaceful content-ment. Never felt as serene as she did on the back of the magnificent dragon below her with the wind dancing in her hair and wrapping her in its brisk caress.

Her hands slowly loosened from the spikes. She rested one hand against the dragon's back and gently rubbed small circles on its hide. It turned its head enough for her to see one eye before it let out a gentle rumble that reverberated in her bones.

It slowly angled its body downward in warning and she replaced her hands on the spikes. Her body instinctively hinged at the waist until her torso was flush against its back. Small pops of pressure burst in her ears as they steadily descended from the blue sky.

The clouds here, wherever they were, were a deep gray. The mois-ture in them slapped her with a surprising burst of cold. She let out a sigh of relief when they passed through them and into clear skies again.

Shock rolled through her, coated with a layer of gut-wrenching unease.

They were over land. But it wasn't their island.

THIRTEEN

It was land tainted by humans.

She could see it even from the clouds.

Fences divided the green and brown land into different shapes. The wide open spaces were littered with small barn-style houses. Black smoke danced upward from chimneys, polluting the sweet fresh air in her lungs.

They drifted in and out of the clouds, never staying under for more than a few seconds. Every peek she got of the land beneath them made her shiver.

They weren't alone. They never had been. How much had her mind created?

And the wound, she had assumed another one of its kind was the cause. But now...

If a human had done it, she would make them pay and collect her pound of flesh.

They flew silently. Even the flap of its wings was mute. She felt it tense, felt its eyes narrow and scan the landscape and sky every time they drifted below the cloud cover. The land opened up below them. There wasn't a fence to be seen. No house, no sign of humankind, but there were cows. Hundreds lingered about in vast fields without a single brain cell between them.

The beast turned its head, locking eyes with her in a silent conversation she understood too clearly. She nodded and squeezed onto the spikes in front of her, lowering herself tighter against its flesh. It gave a quick chirp that took her by surprise. She'd never heard that sound before.

It dove. Its wings tucked in tightly against her, shielding her from the relentless rush of wind screaming past. She kept her mouth shut and willed her scream to disappear. Her dragon needed to eat. She would not get in the way.

In seconds they were on top of the herd. The cows bellowed and kicked but were no match for the monster as its giant maw opened and devoured them like grapes. The scent of warm iron and fear wafted in the air with dust and dirt as it feasted.

She didn't know how many it ate. All she saw was a pool of blood beneath them and a river of angry red spilling down its throat when it turned to check on her.

Aisling smiled, broad and unrestrained. "Eat," she commanded, rubbing one of the scales by her thigh. Its eyes flickered before it tore into a cow too stunned to move. There were no more livestock to be seen as her dragon chewed. The lucky ones that escaped had run off far into the distance.

The dragon stretched its wings wide and it took a few steps backward. Flecks of blood fell as it shook its head and neck. She glanced at the ground where it had landed. It didn't leave anything to waste. There was nothing left, not even an ear or tail. The only sign that something had happened was the pool of crimson left in its wake.

Its head snapped to the right. Aisling heard it a few seconds later. Screaming.

Human screaming.

In the distance, three horses raced toward her and kicked up clouds of dust in their wake. Riders sat atop their backs with a slew of weapons strapped to their chests and torches of flame in their hands.

Her dragon turned toward the party, a deep rumble building in its stomach that sent a rush of pressure through Aisling's veins. The men didn't falter. Their horses didn't stop.

The promise of violence glowed in her beast's eyes.

"Go!" she screamed at it, unable to think of any other word. It lifted its head and widened its wings until they stretched taut. It opened its mouth. A thunderous roar filled the air and sank into her very soul, making its home inside her heart.

The horses stopped without warning. Two riders fell off them instantly, their torches snuffed out by the dirt below. Aisling swallowed as they looked up, their faces morphing quickly from anger to terror as her dragon stepped closer, snapping its maw while the blood of its meal ran over its teeth.

None of them reached for their weapons. What could a bow and arrow do against it? What could fire to do a monster who carried it inside its chest?

Their bravado disappeared. Nausea churned in Aisling's gut. They were farmers. They were simply protecting their investments. She couldn't blame them for their fury.

But this was not a creature to exact revenge on. It *was* revenge, cold and icy and unyielding.

"Stop," she whispered. "Stop, please." Her hand rested on its scales. The dragon paused, shaking its head from side to side and flapping its wings in argument. She gritted her teeth. "Don't hurt them."

It turned its head, rage glittering in its eyes.

"Don't look at me like that," she snarled. "They don't stand a chance. Leave. Now."

It blinked once. She waited for the second.

It never came.

The vitriol in its eyes dissipated. Its lip lowered over teeth. It rolled its head again, slowly this time, before turning its gaze skyward.

The horses pawed at the ground, stirring up puffs of dirt in their panic.

The dragon's legs lowered into a spring. Aisling instinctively curled into herself and gripped the spikes with all the strength she could muster. Aisling took a final glance at the men. The oldest, his hair white and bold against the brown dirt covering him, looked straight at her with his jaw wide open as her dragon launched skyward.

"Don't huff and puff at me," Aisling called over her shoulder. They landed minutes prior and took to the river for water and to clean up. "They were angry at you for eating their cows. You can't blame them."

A low grumble was its response. She watched as it waded and sank its body as deep as possible in the crystal clear river. The dragon drank and drank without coming up for a breath while Aisling wiped her face with the chilled water. Some of the lingering blood on its jaw pooled in the water at its feet and disappeared with the current. Dried streaks of it remained on its neck.

"If you turn this way, I can wash it off for you," she offered. It lifted its nose into the air. Aisling contained her laugh and lifted a brow. "You're acting like a child." It lifted its nose higher, stretching as far as it could in the opposite direction of her. She rolled her eyes and sat on the river bank. Sand and dirt latched onto her wet pants, but she didn't care. She had ridden a dragon and survived.

Her joy was tainted by their encounter with those men. The entire ride back she barely looked at her surroundings, barely marveled at the clouds in her hair or the sparkling of the sea beneath her. All she could think about was what had happened.

They were not alone in this dream. It was not as serene as she had thought.

Her body ached with the thought. Her mind raged against it. This was her peace. It had to be. She deserved to have a place to rest her soul. How dare she construct a dream so complicated where she couldn't get a break from other people.

"Do you have to eat like that every day?" she asked. The dragon blinked once before adjusting its gigantic body to rest beside hers on the bank, its attitude lessened. *Yes.*

A dozen cows every day. And for how long had she been forcing it to eat a few fish or rabbits? It had to be starving. She spoke around her tight throat and blinked quickly against the pressure building behind her eyes. "You're hungry, aren't you?"

One slow blink. *Yes.*

Aisling nodded, her heart straining against the inevitable. She leaned into the beast and rested her head against the shimmering scales she knew as well as her own skin.

The sun slowly descended behind a thin veil of clouds. The gurgle of the river was the only noise as they sat in companionable silence, letting what little time they had left together wrap them in an embrace.

"You have to go home, don't you?" she asked after a while. It turned its neck to her and blinked once. *Yes.* The purple eyes flashed with something she couldn't translate. It rested its head at her feet. She palmed its snout, committing every inch of the scales to her memory as her heart tore itself apart.

"I'm going to miss you," she whispered as a traitorous tear fell down her cheek. What would she do now? What was the point of returning to this dream? To walk an island she already knew? Part of her heart would be flying somewhere far away, and she had no desire to interact with humans even in a dream.

She didn't want to sleep again.

Her subconscious heard her desire. Black tinted the edges of her vision.

Her chest seized. She locked eyes with the dragon, letting the tears fall down her face freely. "Thank you," she whispered, her voice frantic and fast. "I know this is only a dream and you aren't real, but meeting you, helping you..." She sucked in a sharp inhale. "You've changed me. And I will never, ever forget you. Wherever you go, I hope you know how much you mean to me."

The darkness pressed in. Her vision became nothing but a small tunnel. She forced herself to meet its eyes. "Be safe when you fly home, wherever that is. And be nice to people." The pull of reality yanked. She pushed back for only a moment, memorizing every facet of the beautiful dragon's face. "I have to go now. I'll miss you."

The last sound she heard before reality devoured her was a desperate growl.

FOURTEEN

Her alarm went off. Again and again and again.

Aisling couldn't move.

Her eyes were open. She saw nothing. Heard nothing. Was nothing.

There was nothing in her chest, nothing in her head, except a palpable void.

Eventually, the alarm stopped blaring. Clothes appeared on her body. Her teeth were clean. She was at work. Her hands were in a ball of dough.

"Ash?"

She knew that voice. Knew it, and still didn't react. Her head turned slowly, her eyes following like a doll, and met a piercing hazel gaze.

"Babe..." Troy whispered, his eyes darting over her crumpled face and landing on the deep despair in her eyes. "What happened?"

Aisling knew she would look insane now. Knew she had allowed this dream to take her too far, too deep. She cleared her throat and turned her attention back to the unknown dough under her palms. "It won't be there tonight."

Maybe she was stupid. She was a true idiot for allowing herself to believe she was able to do something wonderful and amazing. That she could be strong for once.

An idiot for believing she could be happy in any life.

Warm arms wrapped around her. Troy's hand rested at the nape of her neck. Aisling breathed him in, breathed in reality. "I'm so sorry," he whispered against her lank hair.

She knew he meant it. Knew he wouldn't be making fun of her for the heartbreak she had brought upon herself.

Somehow it made her feel worse.

She nodded, her throat in danger of collapsing with pain, and gently pulled away. She attempted a smile, unable to meet his eyes. "Pretty pathetic to let a dream mess you up this much, right?"

Troy didn't return the smile. "It meant something to you, Ash. And that's important." His hands pulled hers onto his chest, his warmth seeping into her. "Don't ever downplay something that makes you feel something in this shitty world." There wasn't time to stop the tear from falling down her cheek. He wiped it away with the pad of his thumb. "We'll get through this together. After work, we're going to the park."

She started to protest but stopped. She had nothing to do and no desire to go back to sleep. There was nothing for her to look forward to after she left work anymore.

Troy nodded at her silent acceptance. "Good." He glanced at the clock before examining the mess of flour and egg on the steel table. "We have to be presentable in twenty minutes. And whatever that is needs to look remotely appetizing by then." She nodded and moved to clean, but his hands gently clenched around her upper arm. "Live now, Ash. Dream later."

With that, he disappeared behind the door. A second later she heard the whir of the espresso machine awakening and the sound of cups clinking. The smell of coffee found her moments later, warm and comforting, and lulled her into a temporary state of unfeeling calm as she attempted to save her bakes.

"So you steal things now?"

They sat beneath a large maple tree in the sprawling park. He pulled two muffins from his bag. "I like to think I am allowed a sweet treat a day since I work there. Ryan never explicitly told us otherwise." He peeled back the paper and took a bite. "And I can see your cheekbones in far too much detail now. Be grateful I'm allowing you to eat like this and not forcing more food down your throat."

She swiped the muffin from his hand, ignoring the truth in his words. Too much had happened in the last few weeks. She didn't even know how long it had been. Days and nights and dreams and reality became one complicated mix. All she wanted to do was dream, and she forgot to take care of herself in reality.

She couldn't find it in herself to care about it just yet.

"Do you want to talk about it? Or would you rather mope in silence like a lonely little mouse?" A crumb tickled the top of his lip. She didn't tell him. But she told him everything about the dream. "Why do you think your mind brought the dragon in in the first place?" he asked after a few moments of silence.

"To make sure I'm never happy," she answered instantly. Troy narrowed his eyes. She shrugged and wiped the crumb from his lip with her thumb. "Truly? I don't know. Maybe to make my life seem more exciting. Or to make me feel like I had a purpose."

"You don't think you have a purpose?"

She let out a distressed laugh. "Look at me, Troy. Really look at me and tell me you see someone of importance. Someone who will do something with her life." The heel of her hands pressed against her eyes for a breath. "I have nothing to offer. I think my dreams, my subconscious, recognized that and tried to fill a void for me."

Troy stared at her, his anger tangible in the silence. Her eyes fell to the ground with shame. He leaned back against the tree after a minute. "You still have to sleep."

"I know," she replied quietly. He'd seen her gulping cup after cup of coffee all day. Watched her hands shake as she forced more caffeine into her body in a desperate attempt to ward off sleep. "I just don't want to dream."

"Would you take sleeping pills?"

She shook her head violently. After dealing with her mother's addictions and insane ramblings, she refused to take anything more than the occasional over-the-counter painkiller. Troy's eyes registered her reasoning. "Shit. Sorry. I knew better. Delilah ruined that one."

Aisling flinched at the sound of her mother's name. "Stop. It's fine. Frankly, it's not a bad idea."

"There's always a natural route."

"But how effective are they, really?"

"There's only one way to find out."

Aisling took a bite of the muffin, inwardly groaning at the perfect sweetness she had somehow achieved in her sorrow. "Remember that research we did?" Troy nodded. "I think there was something in there for sleep."

"Great." He leaned forward. "What was it?"

"It started with a V."

He shot her a withering glare. "Helpful."

"Can't you look it up?" He sighed, pulled out his phone, and began typing. She watched in rapt fascination as the screen followed his every movement. "How can you afford that?"

"What? This?" He held up the phone. She nodded. "Before everything happened, I squirreled away money for myself. I had a feeling I'd need it." He kept typing. "And there's too many of us. They never thought to check if my phone number was still under their account. So I only had to pay for the physical phone. If they figure it out, which they won't, I'm fucked."

A low hum of rage heated her bones like it did every time she thought about his family. "Has anyone reached out?"

"Nope," he responded, emphasizing the word with a pop of his lips. "Same number and everything. No one is blocked. But it didn't matter if they were. I haven't heard a peep."

"In five years?"

"In five years," he replied quietly.

"I'd text you."

Troy laughed, the darkness around his eyes lightening. Her heart jumped with relief. "You've texted me three times in three years, Ash. I'm not holding my breath. What with that brick of a phone you have."

She pouted. "Don't be rude. He's been good to me."

"Valerian root!" he shouted, showing her the screen of his phone. "That's it."

He stood. Crumbs fell from his pants. He held out his hand and she grabbed it. "Let's get you some drugs, dream hater."

They walked to three different pharmacies before spotting what they needed. Troy grabbed two bottles and paid for them, pushing Aisling and her wrinkled cash away like she was an unruly child.

"Here." He held out a bottle. "Take one tonight. If it works and you like it, I'll give you this other bottle when you're done with the first."

She scowled. "What? You think I'll take too many?"

"I think," he said softly, the warm flakes of brown in his eyes glistening, "you're going through a lot. And I cannot handle the thought of something happening to you. So in..." he glanced at the bottle, "one month, I will give you this one if you're so inclined."

"I'm not going to –"

"It's not a risk I'm willing to take, Aisling." He pocketed the other bottle. An unmistakable tone of command laced his voice.

"You should be a nurse," she said as they walked to their intersection.

"Stop giving me ideas, Ash! First a therapist, now a nurse. I'm not meant to work. I've told you this a thousand times."

"Look into it," she responded, lifting on her toes to kiss his cheek. "Thank you for this."

"Anything for you, my girl."

Aisling was barely in the doorway of her apartment before she ripped off the label packaging and took two pills with water. Troy had said one, but she wasn't going to risk it.

She showered and made a bowl of pasta with butter, adding salt and pepper and pretending like it wasn't one of the more pathetic meals she'd ever made. By the end of it, she was painfully full and exhausted. Heaviness plagued her, both emotionally and physically.

Her limp bed welcomed her with open arms. The lights remained on, the blinds open, as sleep took her into its depths.

FIFTEEN

Three weeks passed without a single dream.

It felt like she was missing a limb. There wasn't a single hour where her thoughts didn't drift to her dragon, her island. Every flower she passed reminded her of the fields. Every burst of wind reminded her of the sky that sang its sweet song in her ears.

Aisling cringed every time and forced herself to focus on the present moment. Forced herself to keep her head out of the clouds and her feet planted firmly on the ground.

Forced herself to become numb to it. To accept her reality.

She started putting on weight. Her hollowed cheekbones and sunken eyes had filled in. She started baking a few extra treats a day for them to take to the park after work. Ryan never wanted anything to go to waste, and she varied the bakes enough that he didn't catch on.

The bakes became her personal experiments. Ryan encouraged her to play with the spices and fillings, and she dove into it, relishing in the sense of purpose she had missed in her sleep. If Aisling had a single talent in life, it was baking. Every recipe was a success. Her favorite was an orange and ginger morning bun. She adored kneading and twisting the dough and watching it rise before baking. And the smell...

"Do you think he knows I think he's hot?" Troy asked, leaning his head against the trunk of their tree.

"Who, Ryan? Yes. I think Helen Keller would be able to see it."

"Yikes." He sighed. "I'd already pictured our wedding."

"I'll marry you if worse comes to worst." She leaned her head against his shoulder.

"That's a very nice sentiment, Ash. But no. We deserve more than that."

"There is no one who can top you, my dear. I'd be a lucky, lucky girl to have you forever."

"You already have me forever."

She nuzzled into his side. The park glittered with life around them. Dappled sunlight tickled the rolling hills and small pond in the distance. There was no way to stop the low rumble of jealousy in her blood as she watched parents playing with their kids, gigantic smiles on all of their faces. Every peal of laughter, both adult and child, was like a razor slice to her chest. "Do you ever miss your family?" she asked quietly.

Troy stiffened beside her. "Do you?"

"I never had a family," she responded baldly. "Not a real one."

Troy had a real family five years ago. Then he came out and was promptly dropped on the street like trash. He only talked about it over cheap wine and popcorn on dilapidated park benches, but she tried anyway.

"Why do you ask?"

"I'm curious. We don't talk about our pasts much. Sometimes it helps me feel better if I do."

He considered her words before shrugging. "I do miss them. Not all the time. But there are moments…" His throat bobbed. "There are times I feel like I'm drowning. And I know they're the only ones who can save me. But instead of helping me, they stand at the shore and wave as the water fills my lungs. So yes, I miss them, but I know it's not worth my time or energy. I'd rather drown than have their hands on me." He looked up at the green leaves above them. "They aren't my family though. Not anymore." He lowered his gaze to hers. "You are."

She squeezed his bicep. "You're mine, too."

He grinned weakly. "Why do you really ask?"

"I told you."

"No. I know what you said, and I know you're full of shit."

She lifted her head from his shoulder and crossed her arms. "I hate how well you know me."

"Noted."

She tightened her jaw. "I never had a family. I had people who shared blood with me, but that's it. I have you, and I can't imagine a single day without you. But..." she paused, steeling her shoulders. "When I met the dragon, I swear something in my soul snapped, like it was part of me. Like family." Her hands clenched in her lap. "I don't know what a real family feels like. But I know that feeling was it. And I know it was just in my head... a creature of my imagination, but it was so real. I miss that feeling."

The past three weeks had been the longest of her life. She'd never had heartbreak before, but she wondered if it was like this feeling. Troy had kept her together, kept her from falling apart, but he could only do so much. He couldn't stop the torrent of memories or the gut-wrenching pain every morning when she woke up from a night of nothing but blackness.

They were quiet for a long time. Children laughed on the playground. Dogs barked at squirrels. A dull breeze slid through the air. It didn't talk to her here.

"Family can be something you choose," Troy said gently, breaking the silence. "And I think in some cases, it's better that way. Better to choose the people you love unconditionally. And maybe it includes animals or fictional people, but does that make the love any less real?" Troy's eyes were lined with silver, his voice thick. "I think if you find a connection with something it should be cherished no matter what anyone says or believes. Too much time is spent fighting feelings. Sometimes, it's worth it to give in."

Aisling wasn't sure when she started crying. She watched a lone drop fall down Troy's cheek and felt her chest burst with love for her friend. Her soulmate. Her confidant. The one person in this entire world she cared about.

Time passed. They remained side by side with golden rays of sun peeking through the leaves above them, dousing them in a bath of warmth.

How could his family drop him like that? How could they look at him, a man they loved, a man worth more than any diamond or ruby, and remove him from their lives so easily?

She didn't wonder the same about her family. Her mother never forgave her for ruining her life. She blamed Aisling for keeping her tied and anchored when all she wanted was adventure, which she later found in drugs. And her father never wanted her. Her stepmother made sure she knew it.

She had been blamed, been punished for something out of her control her entire life, then forced to fend for herself for years. Forced to live with a target on her back: *Lone young female. Hopeless and struggling to survive. Easy shot with no consequences.*

She was sick of it. Tired of feeling like she had zero worth. Tired of being looked over and ignored and spoken down to. Sick of being weak and docile and invisible.

"I'm done," she whispered, resolve sparking in her veins. "I'm done living like this. With all this..." she waved her hands in front of her. "This emotion and exhaustion and fear. I'm so tired. And I think you are, too."

Troy turned to her, dried tracks of salty tears on his cheeks. His eyes screamed in agreement.

"So let's be done together. Let's start living. Not just surviving."

His answering smile dazzled her. "I think I'll follow you anywhere, Aisling."

An hour later, she washed and dried her face before crawling into bed, exhaustion heavy in her bones. Too much was fluttering through her mind. She could plan her future, her plans for living, tomorrow. Sleep was calling, and she would answer.

Her eyelids shut. Her breathing evened out.

The bottle of valerian root sat on her floor, forgotten.

SIXTEEN

Aisling's first thought was a string of vile curses.

She knew this grass. The flowers and hills and clouds. She knew the beach would be three hills behind her as she stared at the familiar river just ahead.

It hadn't changed in these last three weeks. The long grass and squishy moss were still perfectly soft under her feet. Every color bloomed across the fields in pockets of different flowers. The river water was still immaculately clear.

She refused to look at the gray sky. Refused to sit at the riverbank or venture into the cave. Every muscle tensed as the memories came swirling back in a kaleidoscope of technicolored pain.

She begged herself to wake up. She tried to force the pull and blackness in her vision. Her face stung as she slapped it. The skin on the back of her arms yelped with every pinch. She didn't wake.

Anger boiled. She pictured the unopened bottle of valerian root on her bedroom floor, somehow taunting her even in her sleep, and remembered crawling into bed without it.

She did not want to be here. She didn't ever want to walk the undulating hills, smell the sweet scent of flowers, or hear the gurgling of the water she'd spent so much time in again.

So she walked and walked. Away from the beach she knew too well. Away from the cave and the river and the meadow. She climbed and scaled every gigantic slope, sweat lining her brow, until she felt like she could breathe again.

Her calves burned with the steep incline. This hill was the biggest, one she would almost categorize as a mountain if she knew what the difference was. Her balance faltered but the wind wrapped around her in a cool embrace to steady her. Her lungs drew in each gust, relishing in the crisp coolness she had missed so much.

The slope crested. The wind slowed to a constant steady current, gently nudging her forward. The ground flattened. She stopped along the edge and stared down into the raging sea beneath. Foamy caps of white threw themselves against the rock wall. Seagulls cawed as they dove toward it, narrowly missing the jagged rocks peeking up from the waves.

How was it possible, she wondered, to feel like both the wave and the rock wall? To feel raging anger and also nothing at all?

A slit of light opened through the clouds, and she reflexively lifted her chin to it, letting the warmth seep into her skin. A small part of her calmed, the resentment and anger inside dulling enough for her to lie down in the grass while the roaring waves beneath her pummeled the stone.

Time passed with the arc of the sun. It warmed her body and soul like nourishment. She shut her eyes and let her other senses take the brunt of her return. The wind blew intermittently, keeping her from getting too hot, and she wondered if she could start easing herself back into this world if only for this intense feeling of rightness in her heart.

The pain would eventually diminish. With time she would come to enjoy the solitude of it again. The memories would stop hurting.

She wondered what her mind had conjured for the dragon. Had it simply disappeared, erased from time and memory like so many dreams were? Or did she give it a happy life full of love and food and freedom? There would be no way to know.

Maybe years from now it might come back to visit. If things in her reality got too bad, it would sense her pain and come to bring her comfort again.

Her hands folded beneath her head. The sun moved in the sky. The clouds followed.

She sighed in annoyance and furrowed her brow as a cloud covered the sun and stayed there. A shiver sent goosebumps down her arms and legs. With a groan, she ran her hands over her arms but found no heat. She was freezing. Movement would warm her. She opened her eyes, and promptly stopped breathing.

A pair of amethyst eyes bright as stars stared at her from above.

Aisling blinked. Rubbed her eyes. Pinched her arm.

The eyes were still there.

"You came back?" she whispered, her voice barely audible against the wind and water.

The dragon blinked twice. *No.*

No.

Her heart began working again, picking up at a rapid, unsteady pace as she worked through the single word that said more than an entire novel could. She sat up slowly, turning to face it. "What do you mean, no?"

It sat back, its tail flicking over the edge of the cliff. Two more blinks.

"You... you never left?"

One blink.

Yes.

"Why?" she asked as emotion threatened to undo her completely. It was too much, all this *feeling* after weeks of bleak nothingness.

It leaned forward in answer, nuzzling its snout against her chest and surrounding her with puffs of hot air. Her body absorbed the touch like a person starved. The shimmering scales were warm under her hands as she pulled herself closer and leaned her forehead against it. "I missed you," she admitted against the warmth she didn't know her soul craved so desperately. A deep purr rumbled through the dragon, and Aisling smiled, bright and uninhibited as she pulled away.

"Have you eaten?" *Yes.* "Fish?" *NO.*

She smirked. "You really didn't go home? Not even for a day?" *No.*

Guilt washed over her. Three weeks spent alone, waiting for her to come back. Three weeks she had wasted in reality forcing herself to stay away from this dream world when she could have been happy. "This place isn't meant for you. You need more. You have to go home."

It let out a sigh before turning sideways and extending its front leg out at a slant in invitation.

Aisling stared at the leg. She shouldn't. Life had just started to become halfway manageable again. The café needed her. And Troy...

But this feeling in her chest, this glimmering pulse of something against her heart wasn't possible to ignore. Nothing in reality gave her this feeling.

The sun drenched them in light. Aisling stared in awe at the dragon before her. Every scale glimmered. A hazy border of light surrounded it like a halo, a beacon, as if the dragon was her own guardian angel. And her decision was made.

The scales gave her purchase as she climbed up and onto its back, settling in the seat she claimed all that time ago between its wings and grasping the spikes in front of her. The dragon stood to its full height without jostling her. It extended its wings to their full length. Leathery skin rippled with the wind as it stepped to the edge of the cliffs.

As the wind danced around them, Aisling knew she was on the precipice of something wonderful and devastating. Something other-worldly and insane. This flight would be the one she wouldn't come back from. Her soul would be lost to this world, this dream, the second the dragon leapt from the cliff, and she would have to claw her way out of it if she ever wanted to leave.

As if it sensed it too, the dragon turned back to look at her, its purple eyes glinting in the sun.

"Go," she smiled.

Aisling could have sworn the dragon smiled back.

SEVENTEEN

There were no theatrics or acrobatic feats as they took to the sky. They were grace and power bolstered by the wind at their backs guiding them forward and up.

Aisling glanced down and watched the island turn into an amorphous blend of green and blue and brown with every powerful push of her dragon's wings. She looked away, not an ounce of anxiety in her bones as the place she loved shrank to a dot on the horizon and she hurdled toward whatever her mind created.

The dragon lifted them higher and higher until the fizzy dampness of the clouds flirted with her hair. Light filtered just above them, dotting the deep blue sea below with glittering waves.

They were infinite. The sun and wind, the clouds and sea were their only companions, and she'd never felt so surrounded by happiness in all her life.

Her dragon must have felt it, too. It glanced back at her with a gleam in its eyes, a brightness in the face full of harsh lines and angles. It gently rocked them from side to side, playing with the current as it took them forward. To where, she wasn't sure. She didn't particularly care anymore.

A coastline appeared to their left a few minutes later. She recognized it from their last flight and wondered if the farmer would ever recover from the dragon's feast, then shook her head. It was her dream. She could create a whole story for him if she needed to where his livestock multiplied rapidly, leaving him bathed in money.

The coastline followed them like a shadow. The brown livestock fields turned to green squares of crops. The crops changed to meadows and hills littered with small houses and tiny villages. A ribbon of blue cut through the land at various points. Small puffs of smoke ascended from chimneys.

Aisling couldn't understand how she had created this entire world with just her mind. Maybe it was from the books she'd spent hours reading or from the pictures she'd seen from old history books in the library. Where was this creativity in her reality? It had been tamped down, forced to recede in her mind. There was no time for creativity or imagination in her life, so her mind hoarded it and created something spectacular for her to experience only in sleep when the constant pounding of reality took a break.

The dragon tensed beneath her. Its head whipped to the left and scanned the sky. A breath later, they were darting up through the clouds.

"What's wrong?" she shouted against the wind. Unease tainted her blood. The dragon responded with a single short chirp. She didn't know what that meant, but something inside told her not to press.

A plume of black smoke rose through the sky on their left. They lowered just enough to see the land through the thin layer of clouds beneath them.

Scorched earth glared back. Black clouds reeking of smoke danced in the sky, their tendrils twisting and writhing in the wind. She saw no humans. No movement save for the remains of the fires. Her beast saw it all. It shook its neck, tension and aggravation in every muscle as it flexed and grumbled beneath her.

A shrill screech rang through the air, shattering the illusion of solitude she had fallen into. Something in the sound made Aisling's blood curdle, but her beast didn't flinch. Soundlessly, it soared deeper into the clouds, its massive wings pumping faster, harder, than before until they were nothing but a blur.

The screech sounded again, this time from just beneath them. Aisling didn't breathe, didn't dare move, as they continued flying in tense silence. A guttural rumble vibrated from her dragon and pressure thudded against Aisling's ribs.

She braced for flames, but they never came. The pair flew silently for miles, never leaving the dense cover of clouds. Her heart sank as the clouds thinned out, but her beast flew higher until it reached another thick patch and disappeared inside.

With every foot of elevation, a deepening cold sank into her bones. She forced herself closer to the beast as the thin air seeped through her thin linen shirt and pants and caressed her skin with its icy fingers. The sky around them darkened. Static pulled at her hair as they passed through the thick clouds. The darkness turned violent seconds later and her dragon dove when thunder cracked just above them. Fat drops of rain fell in a slant, pelting against her face with incessant sharp stings. Two wings pulled back to shield her as they careened toward the sea.

The dragon banked. Aisling squinted through the rain and sighed in relief as they moved toward a steep cliffside of black stone. A large opening gaped high above the sea. They flew past it twice before her dragon stopped in the middle of the sky, making Aisling's stomach lurch. It flapped slowly and lowered them to the ledge.

It reminded her of the cave on the island. A small sliver of light peeked in at the opening, but darkness devoured it further inside. The dragon shook its neck and stared into the darkness, its scales almost bristled against some invisible threat. Seconds passed in strained silence, the only sound the pelting of rain just feet away.

The dragon finally lowered its head and extended its front leg. Aisling begged her frozen body to comply. A deep ache had settled in her bones, from the wind or the rain or fear, she wasn't sure. Her feet landed against the hard stone, and she stretched, her eyes darting around the cave. "Are we alone?"

Yes.

"Is this your home?"

No.

"Thank god," she whispered. She rolled her shoulders and leaned against the rock wall. "So... we'll stay here tonight and continue tomorrow?"

Yes.

"Are you going to be okay not eating?" She glanced over the edge of the opening to the fuming sea beneath and saw nothing but fog and rain. Fishing here would be nearly impossible, and she had no desire to go hunting in the rain. The dragon blinked once. "Great. I'm going to get out of these clothes then, or I might freeze to death."

Her simple linen set had drunk all the rain, leaving her a sopping mess. She peeled them off and wrung them out, surprised to see the inky stain of the dragon's blood still on her shirt from so long ago, before hanging them on a rock jutting out from the wall. Her body, left in just a simple bra and underwear set, shook uncontrollably with cold. "Can you make a fire?" she asked through shivering teeth.

No.

She groaned. "Please?"

No.

"What do you mean, *no*? You're a dragon. That's what you do." The chattering of her teeth echoed against the stone walls. The dragon lowered to the ground, blinking twice again in refusal. She stared into the violet eyes that haunted her waking hours and frowned. "You're really not going to do it?" It swiped its tail on the ground in response. "Is it not safe or something?" she asked, unable to hide the desperation in her voice. She was so violently cold. It blinked once. She paused. "The screech we heard…"

Yes.

Something had spooked it. The risk of lighting a fire and being seen was too much. It was still healing. And based on the wound from the beach, she wasn't sure if it would be able to fight again.

"We traveled north, right?" *Yes.* "And we still have further to go?" *Yes.* Her body shivered in response. Going further north would only be colder.

As if it could hear her thoughts, the beast opened a wing and looked expectantly from her to its side. Aisling didn't hesitate. The ground was cold and hard beneath her as she curled into the dragon's warmth. It lowered its wing against her like a blanket. "Thank you," she breathed.

Her teeth stopped hitting each other after a few minutes. The muscles in her back and shoulders relaxed as the dragon's warmth soaked into her. "I'm glad you didn't leave," she whispered. Her eyes fluttered shut.

EIGHTEEN

Her alarm blared. Shrill. Exhausting. Unrelenting.

Aisling opened her eyes to find her ragged apartment staring back. The moon hung heavy in the sky. The bottle of valerian root glared at her from the floor.

The alarm turned off. Silence bathed the apartment. She wasn't going to be late for work.

But relief didn't come from that thought. It came from her dream. From reuniting with her dragon. From the wind in her hair and the fresh air of the heavens in her lungs as she flew on its back into the unknown. Relief came from the dream she denied herself for too long, the escape she craved from her reality.

Lukewarm water brought her back to the present. Chipped tile peeked up at her from under her feet in the shower. Fuzzy black mold taunted her from the ceiling, its shape growing daily.

Her soul quivered with the unfamiliar heat of rage. What was the point of going to work? Of slinging coffee for people who didn't see her, didn't acknowledge her when she could be somewhere she wanted to be? Why did she let herself come back to this shitty life every morning?

It was torture, exquisite and self-imposed, to dream as vividly and passionately as she did. To create a world so wonderful and right that she would rather live in it than in reality.

A numb emptiness filled her chest as she dressed for work. She couldn't tell Troy. Not after everything they'd discussed. Not after dumping a heap of raw hope in his lap that they would trudge through this life together.

He was the only person in this world she loved. Hurting him was not an option.

The soft lights of the café greeted her as she began working. Batter mixed and filled pans. Dough spread and twisted beneath her hands. A weak tick echoed as the oven warmed. She lost herself in it, forcing her memories of the dream into the recesses of her mind. There would be boundaries this time. Her sanity depended on it.

The kitchen door opened and Troy's bright face peeked in. "Morning, my love. Ryan texted me that he wants two of these little babies in with you today. Are you ready and willing?"

She rolled her eyes. Ryan's new hires for his second location had come by yesterday to see the café. She had been too busy to do anything but say a quick hello as she filled orders. Today was their first day. "Did he request anything specific for me to do with them?"

"Nada. Just show them the kitchen, I guess." He glanced over his shoulder before sneaking in and letting the door shut quietly behind him. "Don't hate me." Her hands stopped kneading. She looked up at him expectantly. He cringed. "One of the girls I'm sending back is great. You'll love her. But the other..." he sighed. "Let's just say Ryan has his work cut out for him."

Her head tipped back. She closed her eyes with a groan. "I hate you."

"Sending them in now!" he called brightly before disappearing through the door. Seconds later her small kitchen had two extra bodies in it. A young girl with dark hair and dead eyes stared at Aisling.

Another girl looked around the kitchen and twirled a long blonde hair around her finger.

Aisling cleared her throat. "Uh, hi. I'm Aisling. Ryan wants me to show you how we do our bakes I think." She gestured a flour-covered hand over the steel table. "So –"

"Do you really get here at four-thirty?" the blonde asked with a voice too soft, too high. It sent a burst of annoyance down Aisling's spine.

"I do."

The girl groaned. "I thought he was joking."

"Why would he joke about something like that?"

The girl blinked. "I don't know. To be funny?"

Aisling glowered at her, patience dwindling. She latched her eyes on the other girl. "Your name?"

"Eva."

"Eva. Have you baked before?"

"No." She lifted her chin. "But I'm willing to try."

Aisling grinned. "Good. Do you have an issue with the hours?"

"No. I need this job," she admitted without shame.

Aisling liked her already. "Me too." She turned her eyes to the panicking blonde. "Your name?"

"Vivienne," she responded, her wide green eyes darting between Aisling and Eva.

"You'll get here at the ass-crack of dawn every day. Ryan has graciously shared his family's recipes with us. We make them in time for opening, then help out front. It's not bad. The baking is the best part. It's quiet and peaceful. You get to work with your hands." She shrugged. "I think it's one of the best ways to start a day, honestly."

Something glimmered in Eva's dark eyes. Aisling studied her for only a blink, unsure of why she looked so familiar. Vivienne didn't look convinced, but Aisling couldn't care any less about her already. "Wash your hands." She jerked her chin to the sink. "Put on the cap. And then we'll get started."

Aisling was glad for the distraction of the two girls in her kitchen. It kept her reveries at bay. Hours later, Ryan refused to let Troy and Aisling clean, instead making the four new employees try their hand at it before going over a slew of new hire paperwork.

"How much do you hate me?" Troy asked as they walked to the park.

"Vivienne complained that her extensions would get caught in the cap all morning." She glared at him. "Then out front, she told me she didn't know there was a difference between regular and decaf."

Troy snorted. "Stop it."

"I swear. She told me she adds water to regular coffee and it makes it decaf because there's less caffeine." She shook her head. "You should have seen her face when she realized it was a completely different roast."

Troy's eyes widened. "God. She's been serving caffeinated coffee all day? Ryan would kill her if he knew."

"Are you going to tell him?"

"No. Are you?"

Aisling scrunched her nose. "I don't know. Not yet. If she's still insufferable in a few weeks..."

"Agreed." He leaned against their tree and slid down to the ground. Two twisted buns appeared in his hands. She groaned with happiness. "I know they're your favorite. I figured after a morning with Vivienne, you'd need it."

"I need a lobotomy," she griped, swiping the snack from his hands. The bread melted in her mouth. Her tongue danced with the orange and ginger mix, spicy and warm and bright. "God, who made this? She's so talented."

"Please," Troy rolled his eyes. "So I've been thinking about what we discussed yesterday." She lifted a brow. "And I was too tired to come to any conclusions at all about what we should do."

She laughed, barely able to remember what conversation he was talking about. "Same." Her eyes lifted to the sky where pale white clouds hung low and no dragons flew. "We can think of options later. Maybe living just means choosing to be happy."

Troy gave her a heartbreaking smile. Her chest cracked. There was no way to tell him she didn't care about this life anymore. That he was the only thing keeping her tethered to reality. That she had found happiness somewhere else.

NINETEEN

Aisling had fallen asleep with dread in her chest for the cold she knew she would fall into. But a leathery wing was wrapped around her, swaddling her to the beast's side. Inside was nothing but warmth.

The hazy light of morning shone through the wing, casting the rocks below them in a pastel glow. She smiled and nuzzled closer, savoring the stability of the dream and the safety of her mind. Minutes later, the wing drew back and a pair of bright violet eyes peered in.

"Morning, sunshine," Aisling croaked.

Hot air wafted from her as it retracted the wing fully, leaving her exposed to the chill. She yelped against it and ran to the rock where her clothes sat, exhaling sharply in relief at their acceptable level of dryness and ignoring the damp spots. Dressing quickly, she peered over the edge of the opening and instantly regretted it as her stomach pitched forward. Any fog from yesterday had dissipated and left a perfect view of the drop hundreds of feet down where relentless waves pummeled the stone.

She turned to the dragon. "Time to go?" It let out a groan and stretched its long neck and wings, taking up the entire width of the cave. "Wherever home is, it has to be better than this, right?"

One blink. She smiled with relief as its stomach rumbled, the sound bouncing off the rock walls around them. "You're hungry?" *Yes.*

"Do you need to hunt before we go?" *No.*

She cocked her head. "So home is close, then?" *Yes.*

"Thank god," she whispered. The beast yawned, its giant maw opening to expose brutally sharp teeth that would have sent her running a few weeks ago, but she was a different person now. At least in her dreams.

The dragon glanced outside before extending its leg to her. She climbed up, thrilled to be leaving the damp cold of the cave. It lumbered to the edge with sunlight dancing over its scales, coiled its legs, and became one with the sky.

It was not as graceful as their last leap from a cliff.

A squeal left Aisling's lips as gravity took hold. The wind was vicious, pulling and pushing as if it wanted a taste of them. Her dragon soared through it with an agility she'd never be able to recreate, dodging three tall rock arches and pointed shards with ease.

The dragon chirped as they soared out to sea where the force of the wind lessened. It lowered until its stomach scraped the surface of the water and dunked its head for a heartbeat. It came up and shook its head, turning back to her with a happy chirp.

The black-tipped mountains disappeared behind them as they followed the coastline of thin beaches. Green hills, lush and rolling against the morning blue horizon, urged them forward toward some unknown destination.

She turned her head constantly, waiting to hear another shrill screech, but the only sound was the wind in her ears. Slowly, with every mile they covered, she began to relax. There was no point in panicking. She was in a dream. In a world she had created. If things got bad, she could wake up.

The land to their left changed again. Rolling hills flattened into little bumps. Forests spread in every direction, littered with meadows full of flowers with bright pops of color. Craggy gray rock peeked from the ground sporadically.

The dragon pumped its wings faster as the landscape grew rockier. A heavy breeze seemed to recognize its want and nudged them past small villages and towns in a flash of blinding color. The beast extended its neck to the sky in happiness. She could feel it rolling off its scales, feel the joy in every tiny chirp that came from its mouth.

The coastline elevated until it became a steep cliffside of dark gray rock. Thundering waves crashed into it from below, leaving frothy sheets of white in their wake. At the top of the cliff, two turrets stood on either side of a long walkway with a giant stone bell tower standing proudly in the middle.

Aisling's breath stuttered as the dragon lowered and flew over the stone with just inches to spare. Men and women shouted. The dragon huffed a chip like a laugh as it sailed over.

They ascended higher over a massive stone building shaped like a horseshoe. It blended in with the rocks surrounding it, lying low to the ground as if it wanted to remain hidden and unseen. A small meadow sat behind it with pops of purple and pastel pink to brighten the hardened landscape.

At the edge of the meadow was a gigantic square building of windows and dark stone. A hundred yards behind it was a gigantic ravine that opened to the sea. Aisling held her breath as they flew over it. The black slice of open earth stared up at her in a taunt of sharp rock and darkness. The dragon circled back to the square building.

The top of it was open, revealing a sandy pit that could rival the size of any major stadium. A deep rumble left the beast's chest as it lowered them in and landed on the sand with practiced grace. Flames from hundreds of small candles fluttered along inside small alcoves in the stone, adding a comforting warmth to the sunlight that peered inside from above.

There were no doors, just gigantic openings carved into the stone walls inside the sandy pit. There was an opening to their left, just as large as the two other ones straight ahead and to their right. Human-sized torches hung on the walls, illuminating her dragon's scales in ripples of bright orange and red.

The darkness shifted in the doorway directly in front of them. Her dragon lifted its head.

Aisling sucked in a sharp breath as another dragon made itself known.

It was twice the size of hers. Viridian green scales covered its massive body like armor from the land itself. It opened its wings, revealing leathery green skin that faded to black at the edges. Neon yellow eyes narrowed on them.

Her dragon snapped its jaw, the sound jarring against the stone surrounding them. It tucked in its wings as it widened its stance and lowered into a pouncing coil.

Aisling forgot how to breathe as the green dragon opened its mouth and lunged toward them.

Their massive bodies collided with enough force to rattle the building. Aisling gripped onto the scaled spikes and swallowed a scream as a string of chirps bounded through the air. Her eyes widened.

They weren't fighting. They were... talking.

Their foreheads bumped together like two friends spilling secrets after a night out. Chirps rang out. Wings fluttered. Huffs and puffs and growls punctuated the air.

After a particularly long string of chirps from her dragon, the giant green one looked at Aisling with the brightest, most unsettling yellow eyes she'd ever seen. It stared at her unblinking and sniffed the air before returning its gaze to her dragon with long low rumbles.

"Damnit, Neera!" boomed a male voice from the doorway. Her dragon lifted its wings, shielding Aisling from sight. The green dragon, Neera, rolled her eyes as a man burst through the darkness, annoyance written clearly over his devastatingly handsome face. Aisling's heart stuttered as she peeked through the tiny opening behind her dragon's neck and took in his broad frame and lean muscle, his cut jawline and dark eyes that matched his chestnut brown hair. He was tall, dressed in a simple black tee and black leather pants.

"I told you I'd be out in five minutes, but -" he stopped, his jaw dropping at the sight of her dragon in the sand. Neera stepped back and let the man inch closer. "How?" he whispered after a long minute, his deep voice quiet as if in awe.

Neera's eyes glittered, her excitement palpable. Aisling's dragon growled low in its throat before its wings lowered, exposing her to the man.

Aisling didn't know what to think as she took in his shock. His chest stopped moving. His eyes widened. His face flashed with a mixture of pain and shock before he composed himself. "Who are you?" he demanded. The beast beneath her rumbled at his tone, but the man didn't blanche. He didn't take his eyes off her.

Aisling smirked. She'd been talked to like that her entire life. But this was her dream. And she would not be intimidated by anyone, man or beast, anymore.

"You first," she cooed.

His eyebrows lifted for a fraction of a second. "Koen."

She paused for a full minute, long enough to make him squirm. "Aisling."

Koen whispered her name. A dull roar of flame burst in her gut. She ignored it. He pointed to her dragon. "What are you doing on Morana?"

Morana. The name of her beast, the one she'd refused to name for fear of getting too close, but she'd been too close from the moment they locked eyes.

Morana turned her neck and met Aisling's stare, something akin to a smile in her violet eyes. Aisling patted the scales on her neck and smiled. "Nice to meet you, too." Her attention drifted back to Koen. "I'm teaching her to fly."

"You're teaching her to..." he shook his head, anger flashing in his dark eyes. "Answer the question."

"I did. She needed a refresher."

"Did she give you permission to ride?"

Aisling blinked slowly, her patience dwindling. "No. I'm just very, very convincing."

He took a step forward. The flicker of torchlight illuminated strands of gold laced in his dark hair. Morana let out a ripping snarl. A dull huff left Neera's snout. Koen glared at her but rescinded his step. "How did you find her?"

Her blood froze. She found Morana because she needed to feel like she had a purpose. Because her mind knew she was struggling needed something to bring her back to life.

"She fell out of the sky. I helped her heal."

Koen's hands clenched at his sides, flexing the corded muscles in his forearms. "Do you ever give a straight answer?"

"That is a straight answer. You can ask her yourself." She angled her chin to Morana. "One blink is yes. Two is no."

His dark gaze traveled between her and Morana. "Where are you from?"

"Not here."

"Where?" he pressed.

"I just told you."

He turned his harassment to Morana. "Have you bonded?"

The air evaporated from the room. Every inch of Morana went tense. Aisling felt her beast's shoulders tighten, her scaled body prepped for a fight. She gripped the spikes in front of her in case.

Morana didn't blink. She lowered her massive head, eyes like purple flames, and bared her teeth.

Koen smirked, the movement too confident.

Morana's wings opened to their full length. Neera let out a cautious chirp. A flicker of fear passed over Koen's eyes.

"Stop it," Aisling commanded, her eyes trained on Morana. The dragon shook her head and took a single step back as her wings folded in. Koen's throat bobbed.

Movement came from the darkened doorway on their left. Aisling steeled herself as three women crossed through the opening.

Was everyone here gorgeous? Did she need therapy for creating people so beautiful it hurt to look at them?

Each of the women reeked of strength. They were athletic and lithe, and all dressed in skin tight leather pants and corsets that accentuated muscular curves. Two of them, both brunette, had their hair in intricate braided updos. A tall blonde stood behind them, her hair short and wispy. Silver flickered in the light from their pockets as multiple daggers swayed with their movement. Aisling tensed.

All three of them stopped at the sight of Morana. Their jaws dropped as they met Aisling's eyes.

The blonde looked to Koen. "What..." she whispered.

"Morana has taken a rider," he responded, his glare burning Aisling's skin.

TWENTY

The silence was overwhelming.

"Fucking finally," one of the girls cried, breaking into a smile bright enough to blind. Her dark skin was like silk, smooth and radiant and warm. Her thick black hair was braided into a crown at the top of her head, held up by a slim neck. There was a brightness to her hazel eyes that made Aisling think of Troy.

Koen rolled his eyes before running his hand through his hair. Aisling didn't miss the flex of his swollen biceps or the glimpse of his lean waist under the tight black tee. "Can you come down? It'll be easier," he called.

Aisling hesitated, but Morana turned to her with painful gentleness. "Is it safe?" she whispered.

Yes.

"Swear it."

Yes.

Aisling nodded and gritted her teeth. If this was Morana's home, it was safe. If not, she could always wake up.

Morana extended her front leg and Aisling slid down, landing in the sand with as much grace as she could muster with her tight back and sore thighs.

Sick of the show, Neera strode to the large doors, forcing everyone in her wake to stand aside. With a low chirp, Morana nuzzled her snout into Aisling's side before following her friend and disappearing into the darkness.

She'd never felt so laid bare in her life as she watched her dragon walk away.

The woman stepped forward. Aisling took a step back. The woman lifted her hands in placation, dimming her smile just slightly. Her voice was calm and even. "I will never hurt you." She lowered her hands slowly, never taking her eyes off Aisling's. "My name is Amerie."

"And I'm Elaila," the other brunette chimed in, taking a hesitant step forward. Her piercing blue eyes warmed as a slight blush tinted her pale cheeks. "We are so happy to meet you."

Something inside of Aisling relaxed instinctually. Amerie came closer. She pointed at the blonde with a layered pixie cut. "And that is Cielle. Don't let her little scowl fool you. She's perfectly docile."

Cielle stuck out her tongue and smiled at Aisling. "It's an honor to meet you. What's your name?"

She took a deep breath. "Aisling."

"Aisling," Amerie repeated. "Well, welcome to your new home." She came beside Aisling and looped their arms together, clasping her hand on Aisling's bicep. "Come on. You have a lot to tell us, and you look absolutely frozen." She glanced to her right. "Koen, be a doll and grab her something warm?"

Without waiting for a response, Amerie guided her through the doorway. Cielle and Elaila walked ahead, frequently turning with tentative smiles over their shoulders.

Amerie's bright aura could blind. "This is the Pit. You probably passed over the Keep. It looks like a horseshoe." Aisling nodded. They turned a corner, arm in arm. The hallway was the same dark stone as the exterior, lit with orange flames from numerous torches guiding the way, and enormous. "This is where we live. Someone should have come up with a better name besides *Pit*, but it's too late now."

"We live and train here," Cielle offered. "The dragons live here, too. They have a wing called the Lair. Each one of them has their own stall and staff."

Aisling tensed at the thought of someone else taking care of her beast. Amerie noted it. "Do not worry about her here. Trust me. Right now she's gossiping with the rest of them, telling them the whole story of how she found you. And Declan has missed her far too much to let her want or need for anything."

"Will she have enough to eat?"

"Always," Elaila reassured. "Every human here is vegetarian. It keeps the dragons fed and the farmers from stressing about their livestock supply."

"Unless your cycle comes. Then you get red meat for the first three days." Amerie smirked. "They want to make sure all their beasts are fed and happy. That includes the women."

They turned another corner. Two massive iron doors intricately designed to look like they were covered in dragon scales were left open. Aisling swallowed a gasp as they entered the room.

The ceiling and far wall had been replaced with windows. The light of late afternoon poured in, illuminating the dark walls and specks of glitter in the smooth stone floors. The wall on the left had a countertop with a small, recessed fireplace in the middle. A French press and kettle sat on one end with various jars scattered about. Empty buffet trays lined the other end of the counter.

Elaila and Cielle walked to the back of the small room where a scattering of mismatched couches and chairs sat in front of a grand roaring fire. A family-sized table with ten chairs rested closer to the right wall. The two girls plopped side by side on a large red couch. Amerie guided Aisling to a velvet purple armchair.

"I hope you enjoy mediocre tea," Amerie said as she placed full mugs on the low coffee table in the middle of the couches and chairs. The girls scooped their mugs and Aisling followed, cradling it between her hands and letting the warmth seep into her aching body.

"This is perfect," she murmured. "Thank you."

"None for me?" Koen asked from the doorway, a blanket bundled under his thick arm.

"Oops," Amerie whispered with a wink.

Aisling worked to keep her eyes from widening at the sight of him. He was tall. Taller than Ryan or Troy, and cut from stone. He frowned and stomped to Aisling before extending his arm. She reached up for the blanket in his hand only for him to drop it in her lap and walk to the kettle. Aisling murmured her weak thanks and wrapped the blanket around her, nearly groaning with the comforting scent and relief of warmth.

"Okay, Aisling. Tell us everything." Amerie tucked her legs under her, bright hazel eyes glittering with anticipation.

"Wait," Elaila interjected. "Shouldn't we wait for Kaida and Oryn?"

"They're with Aedan then out on patrol until tomorrow. I am not patient enough to wait that long."

Aisling smiled tentatively, already feeling questionably comfortable in the company of these women. "What do you want to know?"

"Everything!" Amerie shouted at the same time Koen said, "Who you are."

Aisling shot him a glare before speaking. "I was on a beach, and —"

"Where?" he asked, sitting on the green recliner on her left.

"I have no idea. It was an island."

"An island?" Elaila's small voice asked, her brows pinching. "The one down south? Do you know how you got there?"

Aisling swallowed. "I don't know. But I woke up one day and was there." A lie, but a decent one on such short notice. Elaila nodded and silently urged her on.

Koen frowned. "You don't remember anything before that?"

"It's not an interrogation. Get a fucking grip, Koen," Cielle grumbled, kicking his shin from her chair. "Go ahead, Aisling."

"Were you hurt?" Elaila asked.

"No, not at all," Aisling shook her head. "But Morana was. She fell from the sky. Gigantic chunks were taken out of her right side just under her wing. She was bleeding so much." Flashbacks harassed her. She took a steadying breath. "I washed the wound out and –"

"Wait," Amerie said. "She let you clean the wound? And you'd just met?"

"I wouldn't even say we met," Aisling admitted. "She fell, and she didn't try to get up. I knew she was hurt, and I couldn't leave her. So I told her I was going to help as best I could. She didn't fight it." She shrugged. "It's not like she had a choice, really. It was either accepting my help or bleeding to death." She lowered the blanket from her shoulders and pointed to her dirt and blood-stained shirt. "All I had was this shirt. I used it to soak up the blood then squeezed salt water into the wound to staunch the bleeding. An infection started the next day. I stopped it with the oil of some orange flowers. And the wound started knitting back together." The four of them had gone quiet. Aisling continued. "She got better. And now we're here."

"Do you know where here is?" Cielle asked softly. Aisling shook her head.

"It's okay. Don't stress. We're just happy you're here," Elaila smiled. "We were terrified Morana wouldn't return at all."

"Why?"

"She was gone for so long," Cielle said. "We figured..."

Aisling glanced at the somber faces around the room. "Well, she's back. And healthy." She took a sip of her tea, grateful for the warmth sliding down her throat. "Anything else you want to know?"

"Uh, yeah. I have a thousand questions," Amerie said, beating Koen to the punch. "How long were you two together before you came back?"

"I think a month or so? I'm not sure." She didn't want to admit how confusing it was to live a full life in your sleep. The days and nights molded together with her reality.

"How's her wound now?"

"Perfect. Everything is healed and closed."

"Are you hurt at all?" Elaila asked again, her blue eyes assessing for an invisible wound.

Aisling shook her head. "No."

"Did you encounter anyone else on this island?" Koen asked, his eyebrows lifting at the last word.

"Yes. Well, not on the island. We saw three farmers when Morana got hungry. She ate some of their cows." She pursed her lips. "We heard something on our way up here, but I didn't see it. Whatever it was, it was enough to spook Morana. We spent the night in a cave." She shivered at the memory of the cold darkness and tightened the blanket around her waist.

The girls all looked at Koen. He sat up with tense interest. "Where was this?"

"Up the coast from the island. We passed a town on fire. There was a screech. Morana didn't like it. Then it started raining and she tucked us away inside some cliffs beneath a mountain range."

"What color were the mountains?"

"Black."

"The attack," whispered Elaila. Aisling's brow pinched.

"We were too late," Amerie said. "We can't do anything about it now."

"One lived?"

"I thought we got all of them?"

"Did you see anything else at all?" Koen pressed, silencing the women.

She racked her brain but found nothing. "We were alone." Koen watched her for a moment, his dark eyes piercing against the soft golden light of the sinking sun. Aisling noted the flecks of gold in his irises that matched the tiny wisps of gold in his dark hair. She tore her eyes from his face. "What is this place?"

"The home of the Ferox," Elaila responded.

"What's a Ferox?"

"It's you. Me." Elaila looked around the room. "All of us."

Cielle put her mug down. "There are six of us. Well, seven now, including you."

"Seven dragons. Seven riders," Amerie said with pride as she brushed a dark stray hair from her face. "Finally a full set. Took Morana long enough to find you."

Aisling didn't understand. Why did her dream become so complicated? Why had her mind deemed all of this necessary? Was she really in such bad shape that she needed to create an entirely new world for the sake of her mental health? She couldn't possibly be this starved for friendship. Adventure, yes, but friendship? She had Troy. She shook her head, utterly overwhelmed, and whispered, "I don't..."

"You will," Elaila murmured, her soft voice like a hug. "In time you will. Just like the rest of us."

There was a promise in those words. A threat of a future. It terrified and enthralled her.

Gray haze wrapped around her field of vision. A tug formed in her stomach.

No. *No.*

Aisling lurched to her feet. The chair underneath her slid with the force.

She swayed, pushing the now black tint to her vision back as much as she could. "Morana," she rasped, forcing herself to remain standing. "I need Morana."

She needed the one soul that made her feel safe. The one who waited weeks for her. Who fell from the sky for her like an answered, unsaid prayer.

Without waiting for help, she stumbled out the door and into the hallway. A hand grasped her elbow and pulled her forward. She gritted her teeth. Forced herself to stay present, to fight until she felt the safety of the scales near her.

Voices muffled in her ears. Something warm and spicy sank inside her nose. A hazy light appeared through an opening. She stumbled through it, the hand on her elbow steady and strong, an opponent to the pull in her gut.

A glimmer of bright white took over her tunnel vision. A low rumble vibrated her feet. She reached out, relieved to feel familiar scales under her fingers.

"Morana," she breathed, just in time for the blackness to take over.

TWENTY-ONE

She barely heard Vivienne's complaints. Barely registered Troy's smiling face or Ryan's nod of approval as he tried her bakes.

Aisling moved robotically. She kneaded dough. Mixed batter. Made coffee. Put it on the counter. Smiled as needed. She made sure to drink water once an hour and put food in her mouth at least once a shift to have energy. She focused on looking alive and human with both feet in one world.

But her thoughts drifted and anchored in her dreams.

Morana. Her dragon had a name. She had friends of her own kind, a warm home, and people terrified of her. She had a life. Aisling didn't know what to make of it, a creature of her imagination having a better life than she did.

And the people... she liked them. A lot. The women had taken to her without hesitation. Had welcomed her with open arms like a long-lost family member. Did she ache that badly for the female friendships she saw? Was her jealousy that potent?

But Koen... she didn't know what to make of him. He was rude and commanding and brisk. Everything about him was painfully intense. She'd never felt a gaze as searing as his. But she refused to let anyone made from her imagination put a damper on her dream. She would not allow herself to be bullied and made smaller by someone not even real.

What would they think now after seeing her fall victim to their setting sun? She looked so vulnerable, so weak – the exact opposite way the dream always made her feel. She wanted to pretend to be fierce and strong. She ached to be taken seriously. To be seen as someone of value, of importance. But her reality had snuffed that possibility, deeming her unworthy of those feelings even in her sleep.

"You have to get it together," Troy whispered in her ear.

Aisling jumped out of her mind and into her body with a gasp. She hissed as the cup of hot coffee in her hand spilled onto her skin with a scalding burn. Troy wiped it up immediately, his lips pursed tightly in disapproval before taking it from her and refilling it. Eva stood on Aisling's other side, her dark eyes somehow seeing everything. Aisling gave her a strained grin. "Oops."

"Alright, minions," Troy shouted an hour later as he locked the front door. "Time to close up shop. Vivienne and Eva, kitchen. Annabelle and Levi, everything else." The four bustled to their spots like obedient soldiers. Troy met Aisling's eyes. "And you're with me."

She blinked and glanced at the clock. Was the day done already?

He made two cups of herbal tea and led her to a back table. He sat across from her, mouth tight. "You stopped taking the valerian root." It wasn't a question. Her throat bobbed in answer. His jaw feathered. "When?"

How long had it been? So much had happened. She was getting everything mixed up. Reality morphed with dreams. Sunsets became sunrises.

"I think two days ago," she whispered.

"You think?" he hissed. She nodded with her eyes planted on the table, shame blooming on her cheeks. He leaned forward. "It's only been two days and you're this far gone?"

She didn't know what to say...

"Why?"

"I didn't mean to," she whispered, her voice cracking. "I was so tired that night after the park. I crawled into bed and forgot to take them." She ran her hand through her greasy hair, hesitantly lifting her eyes to meet his. "I swear to you it was an accident."

"But you won't take them now." Again, not a question.

No. She wouldn't. She would never take them again.

She wanted to dream. Wanted to fall into her new world and stay there. She wanted to dive into an escape where she was more than what she was here. She wanted to feel something more than oppression and despair.

But she couldn't tell him that. He'd already heard too much of her moping.

So she shook her head, the words dying in her mouth.

Troy's disappointment was palpable. Heat pricked at her palms. He looked toward the kitchen for a few painful heartbeats. "If you're going to divide your time between two worlds, you need to make sure you're present in each one." His gaze bore into hers. "I don't care if you dream. I want you to. Fuck, I wish I could find an escape, too." He shook his head. "But I need you here when you're awake. I'll listen to everything that happens while you sleep as long as you're here with me when you're *here*." His throat bobbed as emotion clouded his eyes, overpowering his anger. "I cannot do this without you. Don't make me live alone again, Ash. I can't do it."

Guilt devoured her. He deserved so much more than her. They could live a thousand years together and she still would never find a way to be worthy of his friendship. Aisling swallowed a sob, remorse and relief combining in her blood with an acidic rush. Her cold hand closed around his. "You're my heart, Troy."

His palm twisted upward and squeezed hers, accepting what she could give him. She knew he recognized her not-apology. Knew he refused to acknowledge it. He cleared his throat. "You left me alone with Vivienne's nonstop bitching. I may never forgive you for that."

A raw laugh escaped her lips, loosening the tension in her back. "I wouldn't forgive me either." A clatter rang out from the kitchen, and she groaned. "She couldn't tell the difference between salt and sugar yesterday. I had to remake everything."

"The jars are labeled."

Aisling laughed. "Yes. Which makes the whole thing that much funnier. Or scarier, depending on how you look at it."

Troy looked at the ceiling and let out a puff of air. "We might have to talk to Ryan about that one. I know we said to give her time, but she might be beyond help."

They sat in silence, hands still clasped together over the table as the new employees familiarized themselves with closing. A steady warmth filled her in his presence. It always had. But it wasn't as strong as when she was with Morana. She found herself addicted to that feeling, that contentedness she hadn't found anywhere else in life.

She could do this. She could be here with him to give him the attention and devotion he deserved. She could live in two worlds and give her all to both.

There wasn't another option. She didn't want to give up either of them.

Eva appeared silently beside them like an apparition. They both jerked back in surprise. "Vivienne clogged the sink. She put an entire thing of flour in it, like, bag and all," she emphasized, "and tried to let it dissolve instead of just throwing it out. She wants me to say I did it, but I have more than two brain cells."

Aisling's eyes widened. Troy covered his mouth with his hand to keep from laughing. Aisling cleared her throat, barely able to keep the smile off her face. "Thank you for telling us. For what it's worth, we would never have believed you if you said you did that." She winked at Eva as they walked into the kitchen. A faint smile hinted on Eva's face.

An hour later, they had closed without any more issues. Vivienne received a full education on where trash goes after learning how to unclog a sink. Aisling and Troy leaned against their tree, sharing an ice cream cone she had splurged on in the shade.

"The dragon is a she."

Troy snapped his head to her. "No way."

"Her name is Morana." The ice cream trailed down her hand and she lapped it up.

"Oh, that's beautiful. I wonder what it means." He took the cone from her.

"What does your name mean?"

He scoffed. "Foot soldier. My parents got bored with naming kids once they reached me, I guess." He licked the ice cream. "And it sucks because I love name meanings. I think they're prophetic in a way."

"Maybe they thought you'd be in the military?"

He leveled a look at her. "Do I look like I could do anything those people can do?"

She took the cone from him. "They didn't know that when you were a baby. At least give them that." She handed him the last of their melting treat, but he shook his head and pulled out his phone, tapping on the screen too quickly for her to follow. His brows pinched as his fingers hovered over the screen. "What?" she asked, lifting her back from the tree.

"It means death," he murmured, turning the screen to show her. She felt her breath catch as she read:

Morana: Derived from the Latin words mors and mortis, meaning death.

She shook her head. Her voice came out weaker than she intended. "No. They just named her that because it sounds pretty."

"They didn't name her, Ash," he said evenly. "You did. She's from *your* dream."

"Okay, well what does my name mean then?" she asked, forcing him to talk about something else. Troy's fingers tapped on the screen. His jaw went slack. "Tell me it also means death," she drawled.

Troy shook his head. "Dream."

Time stopped. The din of the busy park faded.

"Your name means dream, Ash." He tilted the screen to her, but she didn't look at it. Didn't need to.

Had her mother known when she named her? Or did she just like the way it sounded? Delilah had started drugs shortly after Aisling was born, apparently unable to handle the baby she had brought into the world, the one she had labeled as a dream. She barely knew who Aisling was half of the time. Naming her *dream* was ironic in the most painful sense of the word.

Troy's hand covered hers and squeezed softly. "Tell me everything about the dream since we last talked. Leave nothing out."

Aisling swallowed and followed his command, telling him everything and ignoring the questions swirling in her head.

"It – Morana waited for you? For three weeks?" He whistled. "Dedicated little beast. And these people, what do you make of them?

Aisling shrugged. "From the little bit I saw, I like them. The girls made me feel comfortable. Like we'd been friends for a while."

"But the guy?"

She sighed. "Koen. I don't know. He doesn't like me. It's like he thinks I'm hiding something."

"You are. You haven't told him he's a figment of your imagination."

"Won't that ruin it?" she asked. "It's like a sleepwalker. You don't wake them. Why would I ruin the only good thing that I have?" She regretted the words as soon as they left her tongue.

Hurt flashed across Troy's eyes, but he nodded. "Best not to tell them then." He let out a heavy sigh. "What a complicated little weave you've made, Ash."

"I didn't want it."

"Don't lie. It's okay to want more than what you have. Why shouldn't you have fun in your dreams? Isn't that what they're for?"

"Do you dream?"

"Daydream or in my sleep?"

"Sleep."

He shook his head. "No. I fall asleep quickly. If I do dream, I don't remember it in the morning. It's a blessing and a curse. I think having a little nook totally my own would help sometimes."

She rested her head against his shoulder. "I wish I could take you with me."

His chin pressed into the top of her head. "If you took me with you I don't think we'd ever come back to this nonsense."

"Would that be the worst thing?"

He was quiet for a moment. "No. It wouldn't be."

She suffocated in the reek of the sadness in his voice, wishing she could wash it from him. Wishing she could bring him with her, to show him why she preferred the dream, preferred to be asleep and away from everything else.

Time passed in silence. A heaviness sank between them that she couldn't shake.

He stood to leave as the sun crept lower in the sky. "You have to keep eating. Last time you looked horrible."

She took his extended hand and stood. "I didn't look *horrible*. I just didn't look great." He rolled his eyes. She sighed. "Fine. Yes. I will eat."

They walked to their intersection side by side. With a weak smile as her goodbye, she stepped off the curb. His hand wrapped around her bicep. "Be careful, Ash. Come back to me, okay?"

They were off the next day. She had forgotten. She ignored the rush of glee that ran through her at the ability to sleep as much as possible for an entire day.

He disappeared in the mob of movement in the other direction. She followed the current of bodies to her apartment, not sparing a single glance at the new deterioration she saw accumulating daily.

She didn't look for food. The ice cream would be enough.

Her hair begged to be washed. Her stomach growled. She promised Troy she would take care of herself, but she could do that tomorrow.

Aisling ignored it all, an addict to her unconscious mind, and fell into bed with a smile.

TWENTY-TWO

The air smelled of brine and smoke. Aisling smiled to herself.

She was bathed in warmth. She nestled further into the softness and stretched her arms above her head. Morana's wing lifted. Bright purple eyes peered in.

"Hi," Aisling whispered. "I'm back."

She glanced around the room at least three times the size of her apartment. The soft orange glow of multiple torches flickered across the tall stone walls. A trough of fresh water sat in one corner. Under her was a pile of large blankets lusher than anything Aisling had ever owned or seen. Instead of a door, there was a gigantic opening in the stone wall leading to a dark hallway.

"Is this your room?" *Yes.* "It's very nice." *Yes.*

Aisling sat up and rolled her neck. How was she going to explain this to them without causing suspicion? Koen already had it in for her. She wasn't smart or clever enough to keep him off her scent for long.

"Am I usually out all night?" she whispered. Morana blinked once. *Yes.* "And I arrive in early morning, right?" Another yes. Aisling cataloged the information. She needed to keep track of her days and nights.

She stumbled as she fought for her footing amongst the sea of blankets. Morana let out a huff of a laugh as Aisling's foot sank into a soft spot. Aisling sent her a glare and grunted as she lifted her foot. The movement sent her flying forward. She threw her hands out and grabbed the doorway before flying into the hallway.

She turned to her dragon. "I don't know what to do. Where do I go?" Morana stared blankly. Aisling groaned. "Come on. A nod of your nose. A flick of your tail in the right direction. Anything. Please." Morana blinked twice and rested her head on the blankets, curling her wings tightly to her side. Aisling gawked at her. "You're joking."

Two dramatic blinks. *No.*

Aisling swallowed a string of curses at her ungrateful beast and turned out the door on her heel. She made it two steps before she stopped.

Koen sat against the open doorway beside Morana's. His head tilted back against the stone, revealing the gentle slope of his throat and a sliver of broad chest from beneath his shirt. The angle of his jaw was sharp enough to be a weapon. His lips were parted slightly in sleep, the lower the tiniest bit bigger than the upper. His dark hair was ruffled in a way that made her stomach flip involuntarily. What would it feel like between her fingers?

She cringed at herself. Morana poked her head out of her door and let out a low grumble. Aisling glanced over her shoulder and flicked her away with her hand.

Koen's dark eyes met hers when she turned back around.

They regarded each other in tense silence.

Her skin burned where he looked, and she hated herself for liking it. He stood and leaned against the wall, arms crossed over his chest. "What was that?"

"What was what?" she asked sweetly, her mind fumbling for a halfway plausible reason for her disappearance. His eyebrow lifted. "I fell asleep," she replied with a shrug. "Long day."

"Hmm," he responded, a low purr to his voice that made her blood sing. "And that's normally how you fall asleep?"

"Yes." Her throat bobbed with the lie. He saw it, narrowing his eyes enough to make her squirm.

"So we shouldn't worry that your eyes turn milky and you lose your vision? Or that you collapse? Because I've never seen someone fall asleep like that."

She gave him a saccharine smile. "Do you watch many people go to sleep, Koen?"

The corner of his mouth twitched. "I've seen enough." His eyes glittered like a cat who had cornered its prey, playing before devouring it. "Tell me, Aisling. Do you always crumble in front of Morana with a gasp?"

She didn't respond. Didn't know how to.

He pushed off the wall and stalked toward her with leonine grace. "I don't think you do. Do you know why?" He took a step closer. "If you did, Morana wouldn't have looked as panicked as she did." He stood before her, just inches away. She lifted her chin to meet his eyes. "Morana took you in her mouth and disappeared into her room. She wouldn't even allow us to peek in and check on you without baring her teeth."

Aisling barely controlled her breathing.

"What happens to you?" he asked, a deceptive softness in his voice. "Where do you go when the light disappears from your eyes?" She swallowed and lowered her gaze to his chest. Koen scoffed. "Do you know how terrified the girls were? They got the medical team, but

Morana scared them away. We saw the light leave your eyes. We didn't know if you were alive or dead and we were left in the dark for hours. I had to force the girls to go to bed. Then you pop up just before sunrise attempting to sell me a lie like we made the whole thing up."

He leaned down, leveling his searing gaze with hers. She held her breath as the candlelight flickered and illuminated the streaks of gold against the russet brown in his eyes. "I think you're a liability, Aisling. Not just to us, but to Morana. I'm glad you haven't bonded yet. I hope she doesn't do it because I know you're hiding something."

His warm breath caressed her face. His eyes flashed again with predatory confidence.

Aisling saw red.

This was her dream. Her attempt at peace.

She was not prey. Not anymore.

Her hand lifted. She extended a single finger, placed it on his forehead between his eyes, and pushed him back. He blinked in shock and receded a step. She stood to her full height, rolling her shoulders back and steeling her spine despite barely coming to his shoulder.

"Would it be easier for you if I was dead, Koen?" she asked softly, her voice full of gentle fury. "Would it be easier for you to accept no one as Morana's rider instead of me?"

He didn't speak.

"Your approval of me means nothing. Morana's is all I need. It is all I will ever need here. And as far as her protecting me, why is that a surprise? She saw how you've reacted to me. It makes sense that she would want to keep me safe from you." She took a step closer and marveled at the way his eyes widened. "I don't know a lot. I will admit that. But I do know that you should never question Morana about her choices. Especially about me. And you should never," she snarled, "question my devotion to her."

He opened his mouth in retort but slammed it shut, his eyes following movement behind her. With a final furious glance, he walked down the stone hallway and disappeared through the giant doors she knew led to the Pit.

Aisling let out a heaving breath of adrenaline. Her hands shook as she ran them through her hair. She turned to find Morana's head peeking out of the doorway, her eyes full of a brutal violet glow. She walked back to her dragon and placed her hands on either side of her snout.

Koen's words hit their mark. "I am a liability," she whispered against the white scales. "I don't know why you chose me. Was it because I helped you? Because that shouldn't be your litmus test. You should find someone else." Her heart cracked with the admission. "I think you were wrong about me."

Morana pulled away. She blinked twice. *No.*

"Yes," Aisling breathed. "I'm the worst person you could have chosen. Trust me."

No.

Frustration bloomed. Frustration and anger. Anger at herself for creating a scenario like this. For allowing someone to make her feel small in her own head.

"You chose the weakest, most inept person you could have found, Morana! I don't know where I am. I don't know who I am anymore." Her throat burned and she shook her head. "I can't be here for you like you need. This isn't –"

"In my experience," drawled a low feminine voice from the darkness, "telling a dragon that it's wrong is the best way to end up as a pile of ash."

Aisling jumped and whirled on her heel. A petite woman dressed in black leather leaned against the far wall across the hall. Bright white-blonde hair cascaded to her waist in loose waves. A pair of luminescent silver eyes met hers. "Morana does not make mistakes. None of them do."

"Who are you?" Aisling asked, unashamed of the fear in her voice. The woman pushed off the wall and strode forward. Silver daggers hung from her pants and twinkled in the light of the torches. She barely stood to Aisling's shoulder and looked up at her with unsettling, all-knowing eyes.

"I'm Kaida. Leader of the Ferox. Soren's rider." She jerked her chin to a room further down the hallways shrouded in darkness. "He's in no mood to meet anyone right now or I'd introduce you."

Aisling glanced down the hallway. "I don't –"

"Koen wasn't wrong."

She paused. "Sorry?"

"Koen wasn't wrong. But he wasn't right, either."

Aisling's brows pinched. Who was this woman? And how much had she heard?

"Morana chose you for a reason, Aisling. A dragon does not choose their bond lightly. It is the single most important decision they make in their lives."

"How..." Aisling took a step back toward Morana, "How do you know my name?" Kaida only smiled; her delicate face bright and beautiful with a hint of something terrifying just under the surface.

Aisling shook her head. "Morana made a mistake this time. I'm no one. I have nothing to offer."

"Everyone has something to offer. We just have to figure out what your gift is."

She snorted. "I have no gifts."

Kaida cocked her head to the side, silver eyes roaming over Aisling's face with measured slowness. "Tell me. When you collapse here every night, how early do you wake up in your other world?"

Aisling blanched.

Her fingers tingled. Her stomach hollowed.

Kaida's eyes glittered in the warm torchlight. "We haven't seen someone like you for almost three decades now. The others wouldn't know the signs, but I knew one of your kind all those years ago. The second Koen told me about your episode I knew what you were. That's why I stayed in Soren's room after patrol until you came back. I needed to see it for myself to make sure."

Her heartbeat thundered in her ears.

Her lungs filled with sand.

"You're a *plane stepper*," Kaida explained. "One foot in each world. How long have you been floating between?"

Aisling blinked slowly, digesting each word. "I-I don't…" she croaked. "Months."

"The same dream every night? A feeling of a broken soul every morning when you wake?"

It was the perfect description of how she felt the last few months – the pain and the pull of every breath in her waking life, the discomfort of reality and raw happiness in her dream. Aisling nodded slowly.

"Koen wasn't wrong. You are hiding something. But you didn't know what you were hiding. Not really." Kaida took another step closer. "Your soul sensed what you needed and brought you here. And now with every switch, it begins to shred. Tiny cracks have already started forming, right?"

Her tongue turned to ash.

This couldn't be true. It had to be another mind game created by her sick brain. What Kaida was telling her –

"Take a deep breath," Kaida instructed, her voice taking on a maternal command Aisling instinctively followed. The sand disappeared as air filled her lungs, and she gasped at the relief. "Good. Keep breathing. I know this is a lot, but you have to keep a clear head." She waited until Aisling's breath evened and slowed. "You will only be able to divide your soul between two planes for so long before it starts to shatter. When Morana bonds with you, you'll feel it in your other world. At some point, you will have to choose which world your soul remains in or it will hang between the two worlds for eternity."

Aisling's bones softened. She swayed on her feet. Morana's snout at her back held her up.

Kaida continued, unbothered by the distress on Aisling's face. "I will not tell anyone. It can be your secret for now. But I will not cover for you. You need to figure out a way to make it work until you decide on the path your soul will take." She turned and walked through the hallway in the next breath, disappearing with an agility and quietness Aisling had only ever seen before in snakes.

Morana lowered her to the ground. A chill ran through Aisling's body despite the warmth in the air.

Plane stepper.

She wasn't just dreaming.

Some small part of her knew it all along. It was all too real from the beginning.

Her head spun. She cradled it in her hands, willing her breaths to slow, her heart to calm.

Morana laid her head at Aisling's side and nuzzled against her. Aisling lowered her hand to the scales, running her hand atop them absentmindedly.

It wasn't a fair choice. Not really.

"Did you know?" she whispered, her voice a broken rasp. Her dragon met her eyes, a sadness tainting the purple, and blinked once. *Yes.*

She couldn't stop the lance of pain in her chest. "So it's true? What she said?"

Another single blink.

The ground vibrated beneath them. Neera's head appeared from the doorway Koen had rested in front of. Her long neck extended through her door and rested on the hall floor just feet from Aisling. Aisling stared into her bright yellow eyes. "Did you know too?"

Neera glanced at Morana for a breath before blinking once.

Aisling nodded to herself as numbness took over.

This wasn't a dream. It never had been.

This was her other life—the other half of her soul.

The soul that was going to fracture either way.

TWENTY-THREE

"Morning, sunshine!" Amerie called as Aisling walked into the common room. Buffet trays of breakfast food adorned the countertops. "How do you feel? Morana wouldn't even let us near her."

Aisling hid her cringe and forced a grin, ignoring all the new information she was forced to digest earlier and the vomit she left in some random corner of the building. "I'm fine. Thank you for asking."

Cielle came up beside her. "Very glad you're better. Eat up. There's a full day waiting for you."

There was too much: eggs and oats and fruit, fresh bread, muffins, and multiple juices in beautiful glass carafes. She'd never seen so much food in her life. Never had options like this.

"You okay?" Cielle whispered. Aisling swallowed and gave her a tight smile before spooning a random mix of food onto her plate. She turned and found Elaila, Koen, and Kaida at the family-sized table, only one of them glaring at her from under his lashes.

"This is Kaida," Elaila said as Aisling sat beside her.

"We met already," Kaida said with a simple nod of welcome from across the table.

"Oh! Then never mind."

Kaida smiled at Elaila. "No. Keep going. I want to know what you were going to say about me."

"I was going to say," Elaila said after a sip of juice, "that you're the leader of the Ferox. And your dragon is Soren."

"And she's old as dirt," Amerie joined in, plopping down beside Koen on the opposite side of the table.

"So you want a full week of patrols, then?" Kaida asked blandly over her mug of tea.

Amerie paused. "Being old isn't a bad thing. It means you know a lot."

"I'm not old as dirt, by the way," Kaida said as she turned her attention to Aisling. Amerie grimaced. Aisling couldn't tell if they were joking or not. This tiny woman looked no older than her mid-twenties. She was heartbreakingly beautiful and innately dangerous. "Just the oldest one here."

"Only by a minute," Cielle piped in.

"Oryn couldn't stand to be without me longer than that. But who can blame him?" Her eyes shifted to the open doorway. "Speaking of."

His white-blonde hair was the first thing Aisling noticed. It was just like his twin's, but instead of waves, it hung pin-straight just below his shoulders and was pulled back into a sleek half-up ponytail. There was an ethereal grace to him Aisling had only ever read about. He was stunning and severe with his pale skin and high cheekbones. His piercing green eyes nearly glowed in the morning sunlight.

Unlike his twin, he was tall and willowy, towering over them as he stood beside the table. His eyes traveled over each person as if assessing for injuries. They landed on Aisling and flickered with a single second of surprise. "You must be Aisling," he said, his low voice lyrical and soothing. She nodded, somehow incapable of speaking. He smiled softly, his lips parting to reveal a set of perfect teeth. "Welcome. I'm Oryn."

"Hungry?" Amerie asked him, her mouth full of food. He took his eyes off Aisling and shook his head, depositing himself in the seat beside his twin. Kaida nudged her plate over, half of it bare, half of it piled high with food. "Ugh, twins," Amerie groaned.

"Is the food okay?" Elaila whispered, her eyes on Aisling's untouched plate.

"Yeah. It's wonderful. I just…" she cleared her throat, "I haven't had this much food to eat for a while. It's an adjustment." A heavy silence hung over the table, one she instantly regretted. She ate a forkful of scrambled eggs, refusing to look at anything but her plate.

"When I got here, I felt the same way. It's a lot to get used to." Elaila offered a warm smile.

"You need to eat," Oryn said. "You're going to be flying the rest of the morning."

Aisling's brows pinched. "Are we going somewhere?"

"The sky," he replied.

Koen didn't glance up from his plate. "She doesn't have a saddle."

Oryn cocked his head at Aisling. "You've been riding Morana bareback?"

"Yes."

He looked at her appreciatively. "We won't do anything crazy today, then. Just some basics."

"You don't ride bareback?" she asked the table.

They shook their heads. "The dragons prefer to be saddleless," Oryn explained. "But for what we do, it's safer for us to have an anchor to them."

Aisling took a sip of tea. "What do you do?"

"*We,*" Kaida responded, "are weapons."

No one elaborated. Oryn nudged her plate closer. "Eat."

Aisling panted against Morana's back.

Her inner thighs ached from gripping her dragon. Every finger screamed to let go of the spikes as Morana took another sharp turn, angling her body to fit through a narrow rock archway above the roiling sea. Her loose clothes billowed in the wind. A brisk chill ran down her spine.

They'd been flying for hours now.

She wondered what Oryn considered advanced if this was just basics. She and Morana had fallen from the sky. They twisted and turned at steep angles. They had stopped mid-air, and her head slammed against Morana's back every time.

Morana turned back to the cliffside where Oryn stood at the edge, assessing their every move. She landed and shook her long neck. Aisling grunted as she peeled her chest off Morana's back and sat up.

"Not bad," Oryn called over the brisk wind. The sunlight turned his hair nearly white, a stark contrast to the black leathers he wore. "Need a break?"

She whimpered a yes and slid down Morana's extended leg, almost collapsing with soreness. Oryn's hand found her elbow and coaxed her to standing. He handed her a flask of water. "We haven't flown like that," she explained after a long gulp. "It was just straight, boring flying."

Morana huffed.

Oryn nodded. "Going on a flat ride can be challenging enough, especially without a saddle. I'm impressed by your instincts. Not everyone knows how to move their body to compliment a dragon."

She warmed at the compliment. He looked over the sheer cliff into the sea and she marveled at his profile, his beauty. "You have a dragon, too?"

"I do," he grinned. "Her name is Nyssa."

"Do you ride her bareback?"

"No. It's dangerous for us to do that, Aisling. We need to have control of both the dragons and our bodies. In battle, the saddles keep us safe, which is reassuring for both our dragons and our family."

Family.

That's how it felt at the table that morning. There was a deep level of comfort, of safety and protection between each of them. She was unfamiliar with the concept, but it felt like they had the same bond she had with Troy, and he was the only person she considered family.

"Wait," she shook her head. "Battle?"

He turned to her, a gleam in his green eyes. "My dear, you didn't think we simply rode dragons for fun all day?" He laughed. "Kaida was not lying. We are weapons. Which is why you need to start training."

Her eyes fluttered shut and she took a steadying breath. It was all too much. "Weapons for what?"

"Justice," he replied, the word definitive and final. "Now, back onto Morana. The best time to train is when your body feels like giving up." He pushed her toward her dragon. She climbed up, numb to her overwhelmed mind and the pain in her body. Oryn lifted his hand to Morana's snout and gently stroked her scales. "As fast as you can without losing her, Shadow Bringer."

Morana chirped in response and lifted her wings to catch the current. They hovered above the sea, lazily following it outward until the water turned so blue it was almost black.

"Why did he call you that?" Aisling asked over the wind. Morana let out a low rumble of a reply and launched forward. Aisling barely got her grip on the spikes in front of her. Barely tightened her legs or lowered herself in time.

Morana was a flash of white light over the sea. She was a lightning bolt, a shooting star. She was light and beauty and terror in one scaled package.

Aisling gritted her teeth against the pull of the wind. It blew her hair back against her head and her shirt against her skin. It pushed against her ears with a keening wail. Her eyes begged to shut against it, but she refused. She needed to see this. Needed to feel everything, to know that it was real. To understand it wasn't just a dream.

Her skin chilled. Her jaw ached as her teeth clenched tighter. Every muscle in her body screamed for relief. The cliffs got closer. The sea grew angrier.

The wind sang its song and her heart beat in time with its melody.

Aisling smiled as they blew past Oryn, tilting up, up, up into the clouds, and leveling out with a sigh. She patted Morana's side, unable to quell the ferocious happiness in her bones. Morana kept them in the clouds, just the two of them with the wind and the sun as their companions. They lowered after a minute. Oryn watched Aisling dismount with an upward tilt on the corners of his mouth.

"Tell me we're done for the day," she begged.

"You're done with me. But the rest of the day is booked, I'm afraid."

She groaned. "I don't like the way you said that."

"We have to see where you are physically." He pulled out an apple from a small satchel and handed it to her. "Eat this while we head back. Walking will help your muscles relax just in time for some sparring." He started toward the Pit.

She tilted her head to the sky in a silent whine and followed. The apple was crisp on her tongue. They passed the ravine on their left, keeping a wide berth from the opening drop. Morana soared high above them before dipping into the Pit.

"Your saddle should be ready tomorrow," Oryn said.

"Will Morana wear it?"

"If she wants to keep you alive."

Aisling lifted her brows. "And if she doesn't?"

He smiled. "Then you need to learn to hold on tight."

"Reassuring."

"I wouldn't worry if I was you."

"You mentioned battle." His smile faded. She pressed. "For what?"

"The girls will tell you everything. I'm simply the flight instructor. I don't want to take their job."

"I won't tell them."

He smirked. "It's better coming from them. Nice try, though." He opened two massive wooden doors at the entrance. He gestured for her to follow and guided her to the giant sandy Pit where the rest of the team had divided into sparring pairs.

She watched in wonder as Elaila, so narrow and thin, wielded a sword almost as tall as her. A single dark braid lounged against her shoulder and moved seamlessly with her. Cielle narrowly dodged the strikes. She lifted her own sword, much smaller than Elaila's, but easier to maneuver. The two of them danced in a tight circle with the shrill scraping of metal as their song.

"Boring!" Amerie cried from the sidelines as she unsheathed two daggers from her belt. Aisling watched in wonder as the playful woman she knew changed in the blink of an eye.

Amerie was a predator. Every move was too easy, too natural. Cielle and Elaila attacked her as a unit, their longer swords no match for the two daggers that seemed to be extensions of Amerie's hands.

Aisling blinked again. Both Elaila and Cielle were breathless and weaponless, their swords glistening in defeat against the sand. Amerie shot her a wink over her shoulder. "Size doesn't always matter."

Oryn chuckled. The girls picked up their weapons with smiles and wiped the sweat from their brows. "This is the matchup you always want to see," Cielle whispered, jerking her chin to the far corner of the Pit.

Kaida stood with her back to Koen, her face a picture of beautiful boredom. Koen prowled in a circle around her, his brown leathers contrasting her black. He was almost twice her size and at least that much heavier than her, but Kaida didn't balk, didn't flinch, as he stepped behind her with his blade clenched in his hand.

Koen brought his arm up and Aisling gasped as the sword dropped over Kaida's head.

But Kaida was a viper. She moved faster. The blade came down onto the sand. She winked at Koen from his right side. Two sharp daggers twinkled in her hands.

He lunged for her. She parried. Sand flew under their feet. They attacked again and again, their weapons scraping and clashing with a bone-jarring sound.

Kaida increased her cadence. Koen surrendered his steps. His blows became sloppier, wilder. Her blades became her fangs as her tiny body twisted and whirled with preternatural serpentine grace.

Koen swung with his right arm. Kaida blocked it and stepped into his body, angling the point of her other dagger against the flesh of his neck. They panted against each other for a beat, his eyes wide.

"Maybe next time," Kaida said before lifting to her toes and planting a chaste kiss on his cheek. Koen wiped it off with a scoff but smiled and stepped back, giving her a mock bow. He didn't stop smiling as he wiped the sand off his blade while he and Kaida talked. Aisling couldn't look away from the brightness that transformed his face of harsh planes and angles into a thing of beauty.

"Catalog that," Cielle whispered. "Doesn't happen much."

Heat bloomed on Aisling's cheeks. "Oh, no. I wasn't -"

Cielle shot her a wink. Koen noticed her then, his eyes flashing before the smile dropped like it had never been. Kaida turned, looking from Aisling to Oryn. "And?"

"A natural," Oryn responded. "A saddle could almost be a detriment."

"She can't ride without one," Koen chimed in.

Aisling bristled at his commanding tone. "I thought Kaida was in charge."

One of the girls inhaled sharply. Oryn smirked. Kaida sheathed her two blades somewhere in her leathers. "Koen, assess and teach. Aisling, don't kill him. The girls will be back in an hour or so to take you."

Silently, the rest of the Ferox disappeared through the darkened doorway.

Amerie's head popped back in. "Good luck!"

TWENTY-FOUR

Venom laced Koen's stare, burning her skin.

Aisling held it, refusing to back down.

Maybe this wasn't a dream and Kaida was right. Maybe all of this was real. If it was, she would not allow herself to become weak here, too.

"Do you like what you see?" she cooed, her voice sinking into the sand.

A hollow laugh was his only response. He stepped forward, the predatory gleam from before back in his eyes. "Do you know how to fight, Aisling?"

"With my tongue or my fists?"

Koen scoffed. "So no. Not surprising."

"Do tell me what you've already assumed about me, Koen. I'm dying to hear."

"I haven't given a single thought to you."

She rolled her eyes. "Liar. You -"

She hadn't even seen him move. He came at her with more speed and strength than she'd ever felt before. Her next breath was with her face to the sky. Sand tickled her scalp. She lifted to her knees with a crimson rage burning in her chest. "What the fuck is your problem?"

He squatted beside her with an infuriating gleam of pleasure in his eyes. "Share your truth and I'll share mine."

"I told you the truth," she seethed.

"No. You told a story that frees you of any suspicion."

"I don't know what you're talking about."

He smirked. "Of course you don't."

Burning hot rage overflowed her throat, and she liked the way it felt.

Koen lifted to stand. Aisling shot forward, wrapped her arms around his knees, and twisted him to the ground. He grunted in shock as he met the sand.

She had never fought before. The years she lived in squalor were spent actively avoiding them, but she'd seen enough to know the basics.

She pummeled him with her fists. Slapped him with an open hand. Pushed and shoved. Shouted obscenities and threw her rage for the last twenty-six years of her miserable life at him. She threw every ounce of confusion and pain for her future at his solid body, somehow knowing he would be able to take it.

The wind left her lungs as her back slammed against the sand. She gasped, eyes wide. He hovered over her with one of his massive hands pinning both her wrists over her head. "Is that all you have?" he murmured, his breath hot and oppressive against her face. She kicked feebly as her lungs attempted to fill with air again. He laughed again, this time bitter and without humor. "Of all the people in this world, Morana had to pick you."

As if he summoned her, the ground beneath them rattled. His eyes flashed with recognition at the same time Aisling's did. She smiled, big and bold and bright as Morana's furious snarl ripped through the air.

His weight disappeared. Morana consumed Aisling's field of vision. Bright purple eyes roamed her face, her body, before she turned to Koen with her teeth bared.

A second rumble shook the floor. Aisling sat up with her hair full of sand. Neera landed beside Koen, her neon yellow gaze darting between him and Morana before settling on Aisling. She let out a series of low chirps.

Morana didn't answer. Her attention was locked on Koen, and for once, he had the sense to look unnerved.

Sharp trills echoed from the sky. Three more dragons in an array of colors and sizes fell into the Pit, their eyes wild and wired as they took in the scene. A fourth hovered above, shimmering gold in the sunlight.

Aisling's stomach lurched when the floor trembled and the sand jumped. When she looked up and saw a creature of nightmares enter the Pit – a dragon with eyes of crimson red and scales blacker than the darkest night. It towered over every other dragon and splayed its wings to their full length, blocking the sun indefinitely. She cringed at the bone-shattering roar it released.

"It's been five fucking minutes!" Kaida shouted as she reentered the Pit, her silver eyes fuming. Oryn followed at her heels with his lips tight and tense. The girls came in behind him. Elaila covered her mouth with her hand at the scene.

"Pay up," Amerie nudged Cielle. Oryn shot them a look that had them blushing.

"What happened," Kaida demanded, her voice terrifyingly calm.

Aisling looked at Koen. He shrugged, unbothered by the chaos. "We were sparring."

"And the entirety of our force is here because?"

Koen ran a hand through his hair and Aisling hated herself for not looking away from the flex of muscles beneath his shirt. "They're nosy."

A laugh bubbled in her throat. She smiled and caught herself, but not before Koen noticed. "Ask Morana," she called to him, forcing her face back into steely anger. Every eye landed on her. She stood and wiped the sand from her body. "Ask Morana any question since you don't believe a word of it."

"Don't believe what?" Oryn asked.

"Me," she answered, refusing to take her eyes off Koen. "One blink means yes. Two means no." She turned to her beautiful beast glimmering in the sunlight. "Are you okay with that?"

An instant blink. *Yes.*

Aisling crossed her arms, leaned against Morana's chest, and smiled at him in invitation. Koen's shoulders tightened, but he took a few steps before stopping ten feet from her and her beast. The rest of the Ferox, human and dragon, stood around them in silence. His deep voice sank into her bones.

"Did you land on the island? *Yes.*

"Was she alone?" *Yes.*

"Were you injured?" *Yes.*

"She healed you with flowers?" *Yes.*

"Did she leave at any point after you met?"

Aisling's blood froze. She had left to live her other miserable life for three weeks.

Morana blinked twice. *No.*

Koen's jaw feathered. Aisling could have collapsed with relief.

"Your injury, was it from the Cruento?" *Yes.*

The air charged in the Pit. Something shifted that Aisling couldn't understand. Fury lit the eyes of every human. The dragons stomped, their tails swiping and slapping the sand. Morana stood still behind Aisling.

Koen took a deep, heavy breath and glanced at Aisling. There was something in his eyes she couldn't decipher – defeat or acceptance, a desperate kind of hope, something mixed and convoluted. He looked back at Morana.

"You trust her?" *Yes.*

The air thickened with a static force. The thin hairs on the back of Aisling's neck tingled.

"You choose her?"

Morana lifted her neck to its full height. Her wings splayed at her sides, reflecting and refracting the sun's light. Her attention swiveled to Aisling.

She blinked once.

Yes.

Aisling's heart stilled. The pull she had felt from their first meeting on the beach, the pull that defied all logic, awakened with vicious intensity.

A glowing golden cord flickered alive in her chest. It wrapped around her bones, twisted and twined up her spine and around her ribs like vines, and tied around her heart with a vise grip.

Her blood turned to fire in her veins. Pain as she'd never known before flooded her body as her heart began beating again, furious and strong as if stoking the flame inside.

She gasped and covered her chest with a hand, leaning against Morana's side in excruciating pain. A white wing covered her, shielding her from every pair of eyes except the bright purple ones she had come to know better than her own.

She writhed in silence against the fire inside. Gritted her teeth and clenched her fists as the flames devoured her very soul.

Time slowed and stopped completely as the cord around her heart and bones turned molten and solidified.

Aisling was dying. Dying, but furiously alive at the same time.

Dark mist came from nowhere, snuffing out the flame like a soothing balm. It traveled through her veins like wildfire. Everywhere it traveled, it doused the pain, the searing burn. It came to rest in her heart, finally allowing it to beat at a regular, unhurried rhythm.

The dark mist dissipated after a few beats. Her body became hers again. She panted as she lifted her eyes to Morana. "You choose me?"

Yes.

"Even though?" she left the question unsaid.

Morana blinked once. *Yes.* Even though Aisling was teetering between two worlds. Even though she was weak and useless.

She lifted shaky hands to either side of Morana's snout and rested her head against the comforting scales. The words came to her on instinct. "I choose you, Morana," she breathed.

The golden cord through her soul snapped in place with the words, the knot at the end melding together to form a single unending string. A bond so strong, so permanent, she knew losing it would kill her.

A purr rumbled Morana's throat. Aisling took a few steadying breaths before bursting into a smile. Morana lifted her wings, exposing them again to the sunlight and sky above. Aisling didn't know what to think of the sight before her.

Six dragons stood in a line before them. Neera lowered her head first, her yellow eyes never leaving Aisling's. The rest of the dragons followed, resting their heads in the sand at both her feet and Morana's.

Morana trilled sweetly, stretching her neck and flapping her wings with the attention. Aisling could feel something through the golden cord in her chest, something warm and bounding that made her feel a deep sense of pride.

The dragons lifted their heads and opened their wings in unison to create a wall of power, of fury and dominance. Together, they bellowed to the sky, long necks and teeth exposed. The foundation of the Pit shook with the strength of their call. Pressure built behind Aisling's eyes, and she furiously blinked it away while the dragons' song swam in her bones.

Morana took to the sky first. Then Neera. Then the rest. They circled high above the Pit in a flock of wings and teeth in a dizzying dance against gravity.

"What was -" she stopped. Each of the riders stood in a line before her, their right arms bent, their palms splayed over their hearts. Amerie and Cielle beamed. Elaila's eyes were glassy as her lips tilted upward. Kaida and Oryn stood together, their twin faces stoic save for the glimmering tint in their eyes. Koen stood beside them with his hand over his heart. His jaw feathered and he lifted his chin, staring down at her with forced respect.

Morana let out a roar of claiming into the sky. It slithered through the bond, eliciting a rush of goosebumps down Aisling's arm. The dragons echoed it. Morana dropped from the sky to land silently beside Aisling without shaking the ground. Her snout nudged Aisling and another jolt of warmth ran through the cord between them.

Kaida stepped forward as the rest of the dragons landed behind the humans. Her chin bowed. "Welcome to the Ferox, Aisling."

Aisling's soul sang.

Amerie let out a squeal while Cielle and Elaila clapped. Oryn stepped up. "Now we can show you why we're weapons." The rest of the Ferox obeyed the silent command. Each of them stood beside a dragon.

Elaila spoke first, her soft voice carrying through the Pit with musical grace. She rested her palm against a dragon almost the size of Morana. "Aisling, this is Osiris." Lavender-blue scales shifted under her touch. His near-white eyes shimmered as he lifted his head and shot a plume of pure orange fire into the sky. A blast of heat warmed the electric air around them.

The rest of the dragons shifted with excitement. Cielle winked at Aisling. "This is Aylim." Her dragon was the smallest, barely half Morana's size, but lithe. She was the color of the moon with a blend of silver and matte gray scales that matched her eyes. After a quick kiss on the snout from Cielle, Aylim threw her flames into the air, twice the size of Osiris's.

A dragon the color of dried blood stomped its feet impatiently. Its scales looked almost like velvet. Aisling's fingertips ached to touch them. "Ugh, Calen!" Amerie pouted. "Stop it. I wanted us to look cool." She rolled her eyes. "Anyway, this is Calen." The dragon let out a low rumble, his strong body twisting as if Amerie prevented it from releasing its flames. He was the most athletic of all the dragons. Thick muscles that reminded her of a thoroughbred flexed under his scales. Amerie clicked her tongue, and he burst, throwing flames just inches over her head. When the fire cleared, Amerie was tickling his chin. "Good beastie," she murmured.

Oryn smirked and rested his hand against the dragon beside him. Its body was beige sandstone, but its leathery wings were dipped in pure gold. "Aisling, this is Nyssa. Nyssa, this is Aisling. Welcome her, my love."

Aisling knew there was such a thing as fate as she stared at Oryn and Nyssa. There had to be some entity that forced them together, two things of otherworldly beauty and grace. Nyssa's flame danced in the sky with a shimmering metallic quality the other dragons didn't possess.

Koen crossed his arms and angled his chin up. "This is Neera." Neera narrowed her eyes at his weak introduction. Aisling bit back a smile. The giant green beast extended her neck and exhaled long and slow and controlled. The fire extended outward above them, reaching for more sky, more space, until it created a thick wall of red-orange flame. Neera pulled back. The flame barrier stayed.

Aisling didn't want to give Koen any satisfaction, but she couldn't help it. Her jaw dropped as the flame spread and molded to the outer edges of the Pit, covering the opening above with a dome of orange and red. Adoration flashed in Koen's eyes as he leaned against Neera's chest and looked up at her.

A boom sounded. Aisling jumped. Bright blue flames from the black dragon's mouth cut through the wall of flame like a knife through butter.

The blue flames stopped. The last embers of the wall of fire disappeared. The black beast looked down its nose at Kaida. It was almost comical how much the beast dwarfed her. The brightness of her hair was a stark contrast to the scales as bleak and dark as a void behind her. Kaida didn't look up at it. Her arms remained crossed in front of her, daggers and swords at her back gleaming against the black of his scales. "This is Soren." She gestured to the rest of the dragons. "They are all bonded. This means the dragons cannot hurt you, nor can they hurt each other. You are now one of us. You are Morana's bond, a title both coveted and feared." She jerked her head to the riders and dragons. "They are a family. We are a family."

Family.

Morana let out a low rumble of impatience. Kaida laughed, low and breathy, and took a step backward into Soren's chest. "Yes. Now it's your turn, Morana."

The rest of the riders tucked in close to their dragons as Morana inhaled deeply and pushed Aisling against her side with her wing.

Morana exhaled.

Aisling stopped breathing as the Pit descended into darkness.

TWENTY-FIVE

There was no more sunlight.

Aisling couldn't see her hand in front of her face. The scales at her side shifted slightly, anchoring her in the void.

The blanket of shadow brushed against her skin with a misty chill like the clouds above. Her blood recognized it immediately. Her body responded with a song of triumph, the bond between them the only source of light.

Aisling shuddered. Morana was a weapon. She could blind entire battlefields. Obliterate the sun. She could disappear in the darkness and reappear wherever she pleased.

She was a harbinger of death and destruction disguised as the pearl of the sky.

Aisling twisted and rested her hands against the scales she knew and loved. Morana's hot breath tickled the top of her head. She took a steadying breath and whispered into the darkness, "I've been a shadow my whole life. Never seen. Never noticed. And I thought I was okay with it." Her hands stroked the bony plates. "Until I met you, my future was nothing but a terrifying, endless void I couldn't escape."

She didn't have the words to explain what was happening in her heart, her head. Wasn't able to articulate what it meant to be chosen as the bringer of shadow, not the shadowed. There were no words to describe what it meant to be not only seen but seen even in darkness.

So she said nothing. She let the warmth of her love spread down the golden cord against her heart, the bond, and allowed her emotions speak for her.

The shadow slowly evaporated above, allowing her to meet Morana's bright amethyst stare. Her breath caught in her throat as she took in the wild gaze of her beast, the glimmering radiance of the entire universe dancing in her eyes. The bond shimmered bright and overpowering between them.

"Morana's gift is also a curse," Kaida said as she stepped forward, breaking Aisling from Morana's trance. "She is a weapon – one many would seek to destroy or keep for themselves. You've seen for yourself what the Cruento can do."

The memory of the wound flashed through her mind.

"As Morana's bond, you are going to be hunted with as much vigor as her. Potentially more so." She came to a stop before Aisling. "We are in a war, Aisling. A war with an enemy a step ahead, hidden in plain sight. We need Morana. And we need you."

Aisling knew what Kaida was telling her. Knew what the piercing stare was really saying.

"Oryn will help you fly. The girls will handle diplomacy and history. Koen will teach you to fight. I will oversee it all." Kaida nodded to the girls. "Lessons start now."

"So this," Cielle pointed to a large land mass on the map hanging on the wall, "is Kairossen. And this," she pointed at a small bulge in the northeastern corner, "is us."

"Anguid. Home of the Ferox and bleak weather," Amerie groaned and leaned against the back of her chair. They were in a large room full of maps and books and comfortable chairs down the hall from the common room. Floor-to-ceiling windows covered the far wall, allowing Aisling an unimpeded view of the gorgeous cliffside.

"Irrelevant," Cielle muttered. "It's our home. Where the first dragons came hundreds of years ago and decided to stay. Where they came from, we have no idea, but that's also irrelevant." She pointed to a star in the middle of the map. "This is Impellor, our capital city. It's where King Aedan lives."

"And where Kaida visits often," Amerie said, wiggling her eyebrows.

"Can you just -" Cielle hissed and threw a book at Amerie's head.

Elaila leaned forward. "The King visits us often. We're his only true force against the Cruento. During battle, Koen handles the ground. We handle the sky. If Aedan's men arrive and need us when we're done with the beasts, we dismount, but that has only happened a few times. By the time they get there, we're usually done. When Aedan needs us, a falcon will come, and the bells at the front of the Keep will ring. Kaida, Oryn, or Koen will tell us where we're going." Elaila gestured to the map. "We go anywhere on the continent they need us. It's relatively small, so it only takes about an hour or so for us to fly from top to bottom."

"And you get there in time?" An hour was a long time if your city was on fire.

Elaila cringed. "Usually. There's only been a handful of times when we don't."

"Who are the Cruento?" Aisling asked, tired of not having an explanation for Morana's gaping wound.

Cielle sat between Elaila and Amerie. "Before Aedan became King, a string of rulers believed women weren't worth as much as men. I think you can picture what that was like." She rolled her shoulders. "Aedan became King after his father died, and he changed everything radically and quickly. He was relatively young and most viewed his age as a hindrance, but it proved to be his biggest asset."

"Not his biggest if you know –"

"Shut up, Amerie. I swear, I will –"

"Aedan declared your gender did not determine your importance," Elaila picked up, glaring at Cielle and Amerie. "And that's when things began to change. The dragons were isolated up here for all those years. There was a healthy respect between them and humans and we didn't socialize for centuries. But the dragons started appearing day and night over our cities as if hunting for something. They sensed the unrest growing in the kingdom and their bodies adapted to it, seeking a bond for protection and strength against the conflict they felt growing. They somehow knew what was coming and knew what side they were on. That's when Soren and Nyssa found the twins."

"There was a steep learning curve," Cielle chimed in. "Kaida and Oryn were mercenaries before. They knew how to fight but they had to learn to ride. And the dragons had to learn to listen and follow commands. The twins will tell you it was an exercise of trust and patience for a few long years."

Elaila nodded. "Meanwhile, the kingdom was a mess. Women began working, began living, and small groups of men hated it. They worked endlessly to stifle the women's growth and keep them for breeding or whatever else they desired. Aedan refused to let it continue. He wants a world of equality. A world where women have just as many options and possibilities as men. He made sure the men who fought against the progress were killed. But there were too many of them hidden amongst everyone else."

"They formed the Cruento," Amerie said with a sneer. "Their fight is to place women under the fist of a man again."

Elaila's blue eyes burned. "They take women during their attacks and force them through an underground network of horror that spreads throughout the entire Kingdom. We have yet to infiltrate it. Their leader is an unnamed, unassuming man hidden amongst the rest."

Disgust curdled in Aisling's gut.

"The progress of Aedan's work is mind-blowing. Women are in every facet of life now. But the Cruento have tainted the progress."

"That sound you heard when you were coming to us? The screech? That was one of their beasts." Amerie pursed her lips. "They're black as night and smaller than our dragons. They have a single brain cell between the lot of them. They live to fight and only stop when they're dead. They follow no commands. But they are fast and agile, and that's where the danger is for our dragons."

"They're not dragons?"

The girls shared a glance. Amerie sat up. "We have seven dragons now, but there were eight. Almost ten years ago, the Cruento captured Favilla. She looked like Soren, but her eyes were bright blue. About a year after her capture, the beasts started appearing. They can spit small, rapid bursts of fire and fly. They decimate entire towns. And we still have no idea where they're coming from or how they get around."

Aisling balked. "How did they capture a dragon?"

"We don't know the details. Kaida and Oryn don't like to talk about it. Koen was still young when it happened. We weren't even here yet." She sighed. "The bond between dragon and rider is stronger than what the dragons feel between each other. If she had bonded, we would likely have been able to find her using her human bond. It's what the dragons had feared when all of this started."

"They need us for protection from the Cruento," Elaila clarified. "By anchoring to us, we can hopefully keep the rest of them from Favilla's fate."

Aisling rested her elbows on the long table. "How do they make the beasts then? If there are only eight dragons and seven of them are here…"

"Their beasts are stupid because the Cruento are stupid," Cielle replied baldly. "They took Favilla and mated her with some unknown creature. Against her will."

Elaila's jaw feathered. "They do not know how special dragon mating is. They don't know that it needs to be not only consensual but *wanted* by both parties. Our dragons are only made when power respects power. When the Cruento took Favilla's choice from her, they unwittingly created monsters instead of creatures equal to ours."

"Our fight," Amerie said with reverence, a gleam of fire in her warm eyes, "is for equality. Justice. We fight to ensure no woman feels used or useless. We destroy the men who come for them. We fight to keep the past from becoming the future."

Aisling could think of no better cause.

"The dragons have bonded with mostly women. This infuriates the Cruento. But what they don't understand is that a dragon sees soul, not gender. They do not look for brute strength or power in a bond.

They aren't looking for someone to give them what they already have. They look for the strength of will. The ability to stand up for what's right. They're looking for a soul that matches theirs."

Aisling's throat bobbed. Morana...

Elaila offered a small smile. "I know it's a lot. But being seen for your soul instead of your gender is a privilege. Many go their entire lives without being known as intimately as our dragons know us."

Aisling glanced at each of them. "How long have you guys been here?"

"Eight years," Amerie replied. "I came about two months before the beasts started appearing."

"Seven. And Elaila six," Cielle answered.

"And Koen?"

Amerie pinched her face in thought. "About twelve years. The twins have been here almost thirty, I think. They had a long, long time of just them and their dragons before things went sideways."

"How old are they?" Aisling asked in a shocked whisper.

"I have no idea," Cielle admitted. "They look as young as us. It's terrifying."

"You couldn't pay me enough to ask Kaida how old she is," Amerie laughed. "Did you see her with Koen today? He's the one that taught all of us to fight. If he didn't stand a chance against her, neither do we."

"He taught all three of you?"

They shared a smile. "He's called the Blade of the Ferox for a reason," Cielle shrugged.

"His methods can be..." Amerie laughed again. "Well, in the end, you'll be a fighter. Keep that in mind."

Aisling sighed as she leaned back against the chair, her body and mind exhausted in the best way. Her eyes closed.

A familiar tug in her gut made itself known.

She slammed her eyes open. The sun hovered above the horizon through the floor-to-ceiling windows. The other world was beckoning.

"Can I go see Morana?" She fought to ignore the gray creeping into her vision.

"Is it happening again?" Cielle asked. Aisling could only nod. They stood at once. Elaila wrapped her deceptively strong arm through Aisling's and walked her toward the Lair. Cielle and Amerie followed close behind.

Aisling worked to keep her feet from scraping along the floor. Every step was an effort to keep her body awake. She gritted her teeth against the growing pull.

"Almost there," Elaila whispered as the massive doors came into view.

"What's happening?" Koen's deep voice boomed from down the hall.

"None of your business!" Amerie shouted back, pushing Elaila and Aisling through the doors. "Nosy ass," she murmured under her breath.

Aisling whined in relief when Morana appeared from her room, her eyes narrowed on the three women around her. "They're helping me," she managed to breathe. "Be nice."

Her vision blackened. Her feet gave out. Morana was there a heartbeat later, catching her in a clawed foot before she hit the ground.

"Do you need –"

"I'm fine," Aisling whispered. "Please don't worry. It's a waste of time."

Her vision disappeared. The pull in her stomach intensified. Morana rumbled as another set of footsteps raced in and echoed against the stone ground. The bond tightened in her chest before darkness took her under.

TWENTY-SIX

There was no reason for her to be here. She was off today.

Aisling groaned as she woke to the first rays of dawn and her musty apartment. The air hung heavy against her skin. She threw open a window, immediately regretting it as the sounds of the city raced inside.

A fierce ache sat in her chest.

She showered and washed the heavy layer of grease from her hair.

She forced herself to dress in clean clothes. To eat something. To drink water.

Time passed. Sunlight poured in. She closed the blinds.

She thought about what Kaida told her. What the girls explained.

The bond around her bones pulsed. She stroked it.

The sun grew hotter.

She sat and waited.

The sun lowered, casting a bright glow around her blinds.

She crawled into bed and let the golden bond against her chest bring her back.

TWENTY-SEVEN

Kaida leaned against the doorframe of Morana's stall. She lifted her eyebrow as Aisling sat up. "Good sleep?"

"How did you know?" Aisling asked, keeping her voice low. "How did you know I was a plane stepper?"

"No one passes out for over eight hours unless their brain is frying."

Aisling stared at her. "I can't... I don't understand any of this."

"It's not for us to understand," Kaida shrugged. "The journey of a soul is too complex to be able to fit it into one single ideal. We have to roll with what we're given."

"What am I supposed to do?"

Kaida pursed her lips. "That is not for me to say, Aisling."

"Help me," she whispered desperately, her voice breaking. "Please. I'm so lost."

"In what life?"

"Both."

Morana trilled lightly behind her, a comforting vibration against Aisling's back. She blinked quickly against the rush of warmth floating through the bond. Kaida came to her dragon's head and patted it softly. "I can't tell you what to do. But I can tell you what I know." She leaned against the wall. "Your soul already knows where it belongs. It's instinctual. The soul is selfish. It knows what it wants and it takes it. Our minds, our egos, keep us from following what the soul wants.

What would you choose if you had to pick with your heart? If you stopped thinking, stopped worrying?"

She would live here.

Aisling's eyes widened.

One corner of Kaida's lip lifted. "The other plane stepper I knew never asked questions. So ask. And what I can answer to ease your mind, I will."

"How many of us are there?"

"I have no idea. I've only known one other."

"Why does it happen?"

Kaida shrugged noncommittally. "Part of me thinks it happens when the other world feels the need for the new soul, or your soul feels a need for more. But another part of me, a very large part, has no idea. After the one I knew left, I tried to read about it. There was only one book I could find that mentioned it, but all I could find was a single page with almost no details. Before I could explore the book more, the Cruento sacked the library in the middle of the night and the book was destroyed."

Aisling sat up against Morana's stomach and frowned at the lack of actual answers. "How long do I have before..."

"You shatter?" Aisling nodded. "I don't know. You've been here for a long time."

"Do you think that matters?"

"Your other life... physically, how are you faring?"

Aisling shrugged. "Fine, I guess?"

"Weaker? More tired?"

"Yeah," Aisling murmured. "I'm not eating. I can't focus on anything."

"You're not eating at all?" Kaida's eyes widened.

"No, I'm eating, just not a lot," Aisling lied. "I... there isn't much. So I make do with what I have."

"You cannot allow your body to deteriorate too far in either life," Kaida warned. "The stronger you get in one life, the weaker you get in another. If you are not conscious or strong enough to make the switch, you will keep both of your bodies in a constant state of flux. It will destroy you, Aisling. Not just shatter you. It will be something you cannot recover from. Your soul will float between two lives, unable to rest or plant in either."

Aisling shuddered. "So I really do have to choose."

"Yes."

"How do I make the switch?" She grimaced. "If I wanted to, I mean. How would I do it?"

"You simply choose," Kaida said. "It isn't a momentous ceremony or procedure. The thought, the intention, has to be there before you fall asleep. And once you fall asleep, your soul will do the rest."

Could it really be that easy?

"But my other body – it would, what? Die?"

"Yes."

"So either way," Aisling gritted her teeth, "either way, my body will be a burden for someone I care about to take care of."

Kaida's eyes flared. "Do you care more about your body or your soul, Aisling?"

"My soul, obviously," she snapped, running her hands through her knotted hair. She couldn't leave her body for Troy to find. But she couldn't leave her body here for Morana, either.

"It's a terrible choice," Kaida offered. "I would not be strong enough to make the decision, I can promise you that. I don't know many that could. But this gift has been given to you for a reason. It's up to you to figure out what that reason is."

"What if I don't want the gift," Aisling whispered, her throat constricting. "I... my other life sucks, and this has been a peaceful little break from it. But now it's not peaceful. It's real. And violent. And terrifying." She shook her head against the tears in her eyes. "I'm not cut out for this. I'm not strong enough."

Morana's piercing violet stare latched onto hers. *No,* she blinked.

Kaida cocked her head. "Do you think Morana would have chosen a weak soul to bond with?"

"No," Aisling whispered.

"Do you think we would allow someone weak in our ranks?"

Aisling shook her head, unable to stop the tear from falling down her cheek.

"The decision is yours to make, Aisling. What I can tell you is that time is running out. With every day here, and you haven't been here long at all, you're more vibrant. You're stronger. Which means your other life is deteriorating. You're letting it happen, which should tell you something." She walked to the open doorway. "And as far as pain – physically, there is none. You just fall asleep like you have been doing. The true pain will be mental and emotional. But should you choose us, you will have people here to guide you through it. You will never have to face anything alone again." Kaida smiled, soft and heartfelt. "Isn't that the beauty of all of this? That you have the opportunity to be loved in two separate worlds? To be surrounded by nothing but adoration and support? Yes, it makes the decision harder. But how often do you get to be adored on two planes?"

Wordlessly, she walked out the door, leaving Aisling to rest her head against Morana in exhausted defeat.

She hadn't told Kaida that this was the only place she would ever be surrounded by love and support. That her other life was only for one single person. She had no true family, no network of happiness or guidance or hope.

She couldn't leave Troy alone.

But she couldn't leave Morana. She couldn't leave the Ferox.

Tears fell silently down her cheeks as she stared into the billowing torches, willing the flames to tell her what to do.

TWENTY-EIGHT

"So this," Elaila said as she pushed open a gigantic set of wooden double doors, "is the Keep." She had shown up shortly after Kaida left and pulled Aisling from Morana's room, her eyes lingering on the dried salty tracks of tears down Aisling's cheeks. She said nothing but led Aisling through the Pit and meadow separating it from the Keep.

The hallway, like everything else, was made of dark gray stone. Iron chandeliers hung from the ceiling with hundreds of candles aflame. The outside walls were mostly windows, allowing unbroken streams of light to blanket the stone. Long velvet rugs lined the halls and brought a warmth to the Keep that the Pit lacked.

It was busier, too. People bustled about with smiles and quick bouts of chatter. Laughter rang out. A man with a small child in his arms waved at Elaila. She waved back with a smile.

They stopped at an unmarked door and knocked. A short woman answered. Her curly gray hair was pinned back from her face in a loose updo. Her warm eyes crinkled on the edges as she smiled and gestured Elaila inside. Aisling followed and glanced around the enormous room full of fabric and clothes in every state of disrepair. In the middle of a clearing of clothes was a stool topped with a basket of measuring tapes inside.

Elaila gestured to the woman with a warm smile. "Aisling, this is Maura, seamstress extraordinaire." A sweet blush crept up Maura's cheeks. "And Maura, this is Aisling. Morana's rider."

Maura's eyes widened. "I heard the rumor, but didn't believe it." She looked Aisling over. "What can I do for you, Shadow Bringer?"

Aisling lifted her hands in a shrug. "I have no idea why we're here, so I couldn't tell you."

"An entire new wardrobe, please," Elaila chimed in, crinkling her nose at Aisling's dirty clothes from the island. "Full rider ensemble." She nudged Aisling to the stool in front of the mirror. "Let her measure you."

Maura made quick work of her measuring tapes before disappearing into the wall of fabrics, coming back with a basket full of clothes in Aisling's size. Maura took Aisling's old clothes, her face tight at the state of them, and Aisling dressed in a pair of black leather pants and a simple black tee. "These will do for now," Elaila said as they left with the basket minutes later. "Maura might be done by tomorrow with your stuff."

"What clothes am I getting?"

"A few sets of leathers like those," she pointed to Aisling's pants. It's what we all wear, just in case we have to fly on a moment's notice. You'll get a few corsets like this one," she pointed at the leather tightly wrapped around her narrow waist. "It makes flying easier and acts as extra armor around our stomachs if needed. Maura makes a few pairs of linen pants for lounging if we have time and a few sleep sets, underwear, and bras." She pinched her tight gray tee. "And an abundance of these in a bunch of colors. They get so dirty between flying and battle and the Pit. Our launderers do a great job of keeping us clean and dressed."

"Someone... does your laundry for you?"

Elaila lifted her brows with a smile. "I know. It's amazing. One of the best things about living here."

"Maura looked busy," Aisling replied, thinking of the clothes scattered about. "Being done by tomorrow seems like a stretch."

"She is. But she's brilliant. You'll have them by tomorrow." She led Aisling down a spiral staircase. The air warmed with each step. A sharp clatter rang out down the hall, accompanied by a chorus of shouts. Elaila grinned. "You're going to love this guy."

They walked through another set of doors into a kitchen infinitely better than the tiny one in the café. Five long wooden islands stood opposite a room-long countertop of pale butcher block. Pots and pans hung from the ceiling. An entire wall of wood-fueled ovens stood against the far left wall. In the back left corner was a locked door Aisling assumed was the refrigerator.

A burly older man with white hair and wire-rimmed glasses bustled between the islands. A pristine white apron hung across his stomach. He checked the food the younger staff were working on with a permanent frown.

Elaila cleared her throat. "Leonard?"

He looked up. The frown disappeared. A sweet smile took its place. "Elaila," he beamed, "my sunrise and sunset! Finally, she comes to see me again!" He swallowed her in a hug.

Elaila's face was bright pink as he released her. She breathed a laugh and lifted her hand to fix the ruined knot of dark hair at the nape of her neck. "Leonard, I brought you someone to meet. This is Aisling. Morana's rider."

Leonard's eyes widened. He took a tentative step toward Aisling, his eyes devouring her face as if he, like Morana, knew what was in her soul. "Aisling," he murmured, taking her hand in both of his. "My most sincere welcome. Tell me, is Morana as lovely as she looks?"

"Even more so." A genuine smile lifted her lips. "And thank you. You have a lovely kitchen."

"Leonard's kitchen is the best, my love. Only the best for my Ferox."

The smell of warm bread wafted through the air, and she stifled a groan. "The breads smell amazing. Mine never smell this good."

A flicker of light burst in his eyes. "You like to bake?"

She shrugged. "I like to, yes. Doesn't mean I'm good at it."

"You don't have to be good at something to like it. Here." He ripped open an oven and took out a steaming loaf of bread with his bare hands. He wrapped it in a clean cloth and handed it over. "You can come bake with me anytime, Aisling. I'll make you a good baker, you'll see." He winked and bowed his chin before kissing Elaila's cheek.

They left to the sound of Leonard yelling and the smell of fresh food lingering in the hall. "He's…"

"Oh, he's insane," Elaila agreed. "But he's wonderful. He's been here forever. And his food is phenomenal. Wait until he makes his chocolate cake. The place goes wild." They continued through the Keep on a short tour. The third floor was strictly for staff, each bedroom with its own private bathroom. "Refugees come here when their homes are destroyed by the Cruento," Elaila explained. "They become staff wherever they feel most comfortable. Unless they're children or too old, of course. After a few months, Aedan gives them the option to take what money they've earned and go, or stay under the employ of the Crown. Most tend to stay here."

Aisling glanced around at the friendly faces as they walked through each level of the Keep. She didn't see a single frown. The air was full of laughter and gentle chatter. The walls were full of warmth, of comfort.

Elaila showed her the dusty ballroom and the door to the throne room. "Aedan is very different than his father. You'll see."

"How often does he visit?"

"Pretty frequently."

"And what Amerie said?"

Elaila laughed. "About him and Kaida? Yeah. It's true. He's like a lovesick puppy around her. It's really cute. Kaida pretends she doesn't see it but..." She sighed. "He should be here soon. Kaida's told him about you, and he'll want to meet you."

Aisling tensed. A King. She had no idea how even to approach meeting royalty.

They walked through the meadow separating the Keep and Pit. Clouds streaked the air in stripes of gray and white. Flowers of every different color danced with the wind, their faces tilted to the sun. She swallowed the fresh air, addicted to its brightness in her veins.

"Lunch?"

"I thought Oryn wanted to do lessons?"

"He's out. Kaida sent him to Impellor for the day."

"Oh, why?"

Elaila opened the door to the Pit. "Either Kaida or Oryn holds a weekly council with Aedan at the castle. The people come and tell them what they know, if they've seen Cruento movement, that sort of thing. Some offer their livestock for the dragons in gratitude." They entered the common room where Cielle and Amerie were bickering. "So no lessons today. Your saddle isn't ready yet, either."

"Is that Leo's fresh bread?" Amerie asked with her nose in the air. Her bright eyes landed on the wrapped loaf in Aisling's arms. She threw her braid over her shoulder and lunged for it. Aisling twisted away.

"Ask nicely."

Amerie's jaw dropped. A playful smile parted her lips a second later. "Can you please share the fresh bread with me, Aisling? I'll make sure to pay you back in full."

Aisling pursed her lips, a smile dancing in her own eyes. She put the loaf on the table. "I collect interest."

Amerie planted a quick kiss on her cheek and tore off a piece, moaning as she chewed. Cielle rolled her eyes and pulled a knife from her leathers. "Pretend for a single second you're civilized." She cut a piece for Aisling and Elaila before cutting one for herself.

The simple white bread melted on Aisling's tongue. She'd never had anything like it. What she made at the café was trash compared to this.

"I know," Cielle said after swallowing. "It's rare that we get it this fresh. By the time it gets here, it's usually cooled off. This is a treat."

"I've never made bread this well," Aisling said. "He's amazing."

Amerie angled her head. "You bake?"

"Not like this," Aisling admitted. She took another piece and let a groan leave her lips.

"Oh, look," Amerie cooed, her eyes on the door behind Aisling. "It's time for you to learn from the big strong man."

Aisling glanced over her shoulder to where Koen leaned against the open doorway with a hint of a smile on his lips. Black leather pants perfectly accentuated his strong legs. His hair, weakly curled at the ends, was pushed back from his forehead. The skin on his face was smooth, perfectly highlighting the angles of his strong cheekbones.

Her blood boiled. She popped the rest of the bread in her mouth. "I don't think that's how Kaida would have described him yesterday."

Cielle and Elaila's jaws dropped open. Amerie let out a howl.

Aisling turned and walked out the door, brushing past Koen like he wasn't there. His footsteps clipped behind her as she made her way to the Pit. The sun illuminated tiny grains of sparkling sand, each one warm under her feet.

There was no one else inside. No humans. No dragons. No buffer.

She turned on her heel. "So about yest–"

His fist came from nowhere and landed in the middle of her stomach. The air leeched from her lungs. She collapsed backward with sucking breaths. "You *ass*," she seethed through her teeth. "I was going to apologize."

"Then apologize." He prowled around her hunched body, an ember of light in his dark eyes.

Was he enjoying this?

The fire in her blood came roaring back.

"No." She stood up. Her stomach screamed with the movement. "You aren't worth the breath."

His eyebrows lifted. "I already took your breath, Aisling. It was too easy." His fist came at her again. She barely dodged it before his leg swept out and clashed with her ankle, sending her face-first into the sand.

She didn't give herself time to recover or think. She pushed herself up, sand caked to her skin, and lunged. He was bigger and more skilled, but she was angrier. Her hand clenched and she threw it at his chest. He clasped his hand around her wrist, his fingers overlapping, before she could make contact. His scent and warmth seeped into her skin.

"You're sloppy," he said. "I can see your plan from a mile away. Even if I couldn't, you're weak. You don't stand a chance."

She sneered. His hand only tightened against her wrist as she fought to pull out of his grip. "Let me go."

"Why? So you can flail around?"

"Yes."

"Do you even want to learn?"

"I want to learn from someone competent," she spat, staring up at him with nothing but disgust in her eyes. "Not some power-hungry dick."

He smiled and dropped her, shoving her chest back just enough for her to stumble. His hands rested at his sides. "Fine. Show me how much you want to be taught."

She panted and rubbed her wrist. "I don't know anything. That's why you're here. I need you to help me." She rolled her shoulders back, refusing to feel as pathetic as she sounded. "But if you're not up to the task, I'll ask someone else. You aren't the only good fighter. You're just the worst teacher."

Koen cocked his head. "Say it again."

"What?"

"Say you need my help."

Her lip curled. "Fuck you."

He was on her a breath later. She dodged a punch, a kick. But he was too fast, too strong. She was on her back seconds later, breathless and furious as he pinned her hands beside her head, the muscles in his shoulders rippling. "Do you expect everything to fall at your feet? Everyone to bow to you, coddle you until you get better?"

"I don't expect anything but common decency," she spat. Her body writhed unsuccessfully under him. He was everywhere. "Nothing has ever fallen at my feet except a dragon."

He scoffed. "What luck you have."

"I have no luck. You know nothing about me. Nothing of where I came from or what I've had to go through."

"And you do?" he challenged. "You remember your past now? Or did you ever forget it?" She blinked quickly. Bitter amusement lit his eyes. One of his hands disappeared. He knelt beside her with the other hand still wrapped around her wrist. "Get out of this."

"What?"

He lifted her arm. "Fight your way out of this. All I'm doing is holding your wrist. You have three limbs and a whole body to fight with. Show me you want to fight. Prove you aren't useless to us."

Useless.

The word hit home, latching onto her heart.

The one word she used to describe herself.

Because she was, wasn't she? She was worth nothing. A useless sack of skin with no skills, no prospects, no future.

And here the word was again, in the one place she'd been able to escape it. It tainted the very air, suffocating her with its unbearable weight.

What was the point of her fighting? Of learning anything here? If she was going to be as useless in this life as her other one, why would she waste her time even trying?

Her body stopped fighting. She went limp.

The fire in her eyes died. The fury in her heart snuffed out.

There wasn't a point anymore. Fighting fate wasn't worth it.

Her eyes looked to the sky above. The sky she had come to love, to crave. The sky she needed like she needed air to breathe.

Koen's grip loosened. "Aisling?"

She didn't respond.

She saw him out of the corner of her eye. A deep crease sat between his brows. His eyes were on her face, on her body, with a warmth that seeped into her bones.

"I didn't – I didn't mean –"

She felt the pull in her gut despite the sun high above. Saw the gray hue at the edges of her vision and welcomed it. It would just prove his point, anyway. She was a liability. Useless. Let him see her like this, weak and helpless to the pull of something she could never control and would never understand.

Her name on his lips was the last thing she heard as reality took her in its grasp.

TWENTY-NINE

Useless.

Useless.

Useless.

The word played on repeat in Aisling's head. It wormed its way into her every thought, every breath, and made itself at home in her soul. She had woken hours before her alarm and stared numbly at the ceiling until it went off, letting the vile word be the only thing to keep her company.

Flour and egg swirled in the mixer, slapping against the steel bowl like flesh. She had no idea what she was making. No idea how she'd gotten here or why the clock still said she had over an hour before Troy would walk in. She added the miscellaneous ingredients with robotic efficiency. On instinct she chose a dash of ginger and orange zest, picking whatever made her feel comforted and warm as her mind echoed the word.

The despair she always kept bottled up began leaking out.

She had thought, had hoped, that she had finally found her home. But now...

The kitchen door opened. Aisling glanced at the clock. Almost two hours had passed.

"Add these," a small voice said beside her. She jumped and found Eva at her side with a bowl of blueberries. Eva reached over and slowed the mixer before tilting the bowl and dropping the berries into the unknown batter with a wet slop. "Blueberry muffins," she whispered with a tight smile.

Aisling nodded, her throat painfully tight. "Thank you."

"I need this job, too," Eva responded, a knowing sadness in her eyes. "I can't afford to be bad at it."

Aisling finally realized why Eva felt so familiar. Finally figured out what had bugged her since she first laid eyes on her.

Eva was her mirror. A quiet desperation and furious tenacity to survive was written clearly on Eva's young face as it had been on her own for her entire life. She was looking at her younger self and hated what she saw. Hated the thought of Eva struggling like she did. Hated the thought of what the future would bring to this kind, quiet, strong girl.

The tears came without warning. She barely lifted her hand to her mouth in time to muffle the sob that echoed in the kitchen. Eva's eyes widened. She took Aisling's elbows and yelled. Seconds later, Troy's hands hooked under her knees and lifted her in one fluid motion before walking somewhere and placing her on his lap.

Aisling sobbed into Troy's shoulder, her body shaking as she released every ounce of pain she'd kept hidden for a decade.

It was never going to end. Her struggle, her barely scraping by, was never going to end. She would spend her whole life in a daze of survival, never once to feel the obliterating happiness she felt in her dream life. The dream life that was another reality where her uselessness was again on display.

Troy said nothing, but his hand never stopped running up and down her back with a heartbreaking softness.

Part of her wanted to die. She'd never said it out loud. Never even admitted it to herself. But now, after everything...

Her life was not getting any easier and the other world was now tainted by that ugly word. Her dream had morphed into a nightmare. A nightmare turned reality.

The golden bond against her heart tightened, pulsing and twisting with a painful rub, and forced her out of her head.

Even a world away, Morana was there. Kaida hadn't been lying. Her soul had been split.

She felt it more than ever as Morana stroked the bond with her love, her loyalty. Aisling's heart was split between her dragon and Troy as their care and comfort surrounded her.

She slowly stopped crying and wiped her nose with her sleeve as she looked around the room. They were in Ryan's office, on his chair in the dark. "Is it this place? This job?" Troy asked against her hair after a few minutes of calm.

Yes. But she shook her head, her voice a croak. "I just feel useless."

He gently pushed her off his shoulder and cocked his head. "Are you out of your mind?" He laughed, a booming cheerful thing. "You're the most important person to me. Probably to Ryan, too, if we're being honest. I cannot imagine my life without you in it, Ash. The highlight of every day is seeing you, being around you. Our days off are both the best and the worst. All I want to do is hang out with you."

His hazel eyes warmed. "Your job does not determine your worth. What other people think of you does not determine your worth. Yes, things are shitty. But our lives are not worth less than anyone else's because of how we're handling what we've been given. We just have a different path than most, and our paths mean just as much as anyone else's." He brushed a lingering tear off her cheek. "The sooner you realize your worth, the better your life will become."

She spoke through a tight throat, needing to voice it out loud, just once. "Sometimes I think it would be better if I –"

"I swear to God," he gritted through his teeth, "if you say what I think you're going to say, I'll lose my ever-loving mind." He closed his eyes. When he opened them again, she went breathless at the silver tears on his waterline. "You are worth everything, Aisling. And you will fight those feelings because that is who you are. Your whole life has been a fight, and still, you remain quiet and steadfast and kind when it would have been easier for you to fall into the same pits of uselessness as Delilah and your father."

The string at her heart pulled tighter. A faint glow lit in her soul.

"This is just the beginning of your story. You can write the rest however you want. Don't stop the story because you don't like the direction it's going. Change the plot until you're happy."

The bond around her heart sang. Shadow danced in her blood as warmth sank into her bones, replacing the cold numbness from before.

The two most important people in both her lives agreed with each other and would never know. They would never know how much she adored them. How much she would do for them. How well they would get along.

But she had to choose. Every day that passed was another jagged crack in her soul. It was held together by a thin golden cord. If she tore that cord...

She smiled at Troy, knowing she would break his heart with her choice. But she didn't have to leave him just yet.

THIRTY

The warm blankets of Morana's room molded to her body. A leathery wing surrounded her. Morana had to have gotten her from the Pit. Maybe she killed Koen in the process.

Aisling watched Morana's chest rise and fall in a soothing rhythm and decided she could wait to wake her beast for a little bit. She rested for a while longer, her heart a steady beat in her chest.

Troy was right. She could rewrite her story. She could eliminate that awful word from her vocabulary, never to think it again.

Her life would be worth something in the end. She would make it so or die trying.

Quietly, she crawled from underneath the giant wing through the sea of blankets onto the stone floor. Morana continued to lightly snore, unbothered by her wiggling. Aisling relaxed her shoulders and stepped into the giant hallway.

Her outfit smelled of sky and dragon and sand. She ached for a hot shower and shampoo. Where she would find that, she wasn't sure, but she was going to find out. The stone floor echoed her footsteps as she made her way to the giant doors leading to the hall.

"Going somewhere?"

She stopped. Her chin dropped to her chest. She took a deep breath and turned. "I'm going to clean up."

Koen appeared from the darkness in the same outfit from earlier. His dark hair was tousled in the annoying way she liked. Every step was slow and deliberate. "Where do you imagine you'll do that?"

"The sea."

"The sea..." he repeated slowly as if she had spoken another language.

She nodded. "Yes. So if you'll excuse me." Turning her back to him, she took a step and cursed herself for her stupidity. Of all the types of water, she chose the ocean at sunrise.

"You have a room here." Her feet stopped. "I can show you if you'd like. There's warm water, unlike the sea, which is about freezing right now. It's up to you."

"I'd find it eventually," she responded after brief consideration.

"Before your next episode?" he asked as he brushed past her and into the hall. She gritted her teeth and followed. Her pride could wait until after she bathed. She came to his side and followed him down the hallway.

"The riders used to stay at the Keep, but it was too far from the dragons. Kaida and Oryn oversaw construction." His voice was quiet and conversational, not a hint of the normal disdain in the deepness. "The dragons stay on the top floor. It gives them easy access to the Pit when they need to fly. Our weapons store is in the Pit, just before the entrance to the Lair so we can grab them quickly before battle. The riders get a wing of the lower floor."

He led her down a spiral staircase. Torches sat high on the wall, casting the dark stone in flickering orange and red. He turned left into a dark hallway once they hit the bottom.

"Where do the soldiers stay? Here?"

He nodded. "Yes. Some stay in town, but most prefer to be here."

"Why? If the dragons are here, why do they need to be?"

"They keep watch over the sea and offer aid in other ways when they aren't being used to fight Cruento."

"Have they ever come here?"

He glanced at her. "The Cruento? No. They're stupid but not that stupid." They passed unmarked doors on the right wall and stone on the left. Koen pointed to the second door. "Some of the medical team keep supplies here. There's always at least one of them on staff at all times in case. Don't knock on the door unless it's an emergency, though. They can be cranky." He jerked his chin to another door. "Cleaning supplies are in this closet. There's anything you could want in there. Toiletries, too."

"And laundry?"

"Maura's apprentices do it. There's a basket in your room. They come daily."

Aisling balked. "Daily?"

"Yes," his forehead pinched as he glanced sidelong at her. "Is that an issue?" She shook her head. They turn left again at a hard corner. "The common room is upstairs. The Keep brings food three times a day. The chef –"

"Leonard," she chimed in.

Koen's brows furrowed. "How do you know him?"

"I met him today with Elaila. He was wonderful."

"You liked him?"

She smiled despite herself. "How could you not?"

Something flickered in his eyes. He turned his attention back to the hallway. "If there's something you need dietary-wise, the kitchen will sort it out for you. You just have to let them know."

They walked in silence for a few steps. "Kaida mentioned patrols."

He nodded as they turned another corner. "Every night two of us go. It's on a rotating schedule. We patrol the whole kingdom from the sky and come back in the morning. Morana was doing it alone the night she disappeared."

Aisling couldn't keep the acid from her voice. "Why was she alone?"

His jaw feathered. "We were on patrol together. Neera scented something up north. Morana scented something to the south. They decided to split. Neera didn't find anything. Morana didn't come back." He stopped walking, his eyes almost pained. "You have to understand. No one could control Morana. She did what she wanted when she wanted. For her to go off on her own wasn't unusual. But when she didn't come back…" He shook his head. "She and Neera have been together since they were hatchlings. They haven't known a single day without each other. Neera was distraught when Morana never came back. I was sick over it. So every night we did patrol. There was no chatter about her. No one knew anything."

Aisling soaked in every word. Weeks, maybe months he had spent doing night patrols because of his guilt.

"When she showed up, Neera and I had just gotten back from patrol that morning and had barely slept. We were exhausted. Seeing her was a shock. And to see her with you…"

She couldn't stop herself. "So being surprised makes you an ass? Or is that just your default mode?" She crossed her arms over her chest. "Or have you just transferred your guilt for losing her onto me? Is blaming me easier?"

He blinked. "I was looking out for Morana's best interest. For the safety of the Ferox."

"I was the one who saved Morana. I was the one who nursed her back to health. I'm the one who saw her bleeding to death, Koen."

Her throat tightened with the memory. "So is looking out for her best interest really what you were doing? Questioning our bond – which was obvious to anyone with eyes – is that how you support her?"

His throat bobbed. "You wouldn't understand."

"No, I wouldn't," she admitted. "But I know never to treat someone like that unless it's warranted. And I did nothing to you to earn the disrespect I've been shown. I have shown up day after day for Morana, for the Ferox, even though I have no idea what's happening. I show up willing to do whatever I have to for her." Her voice shook. She reigned in the emotion as best she could. "I love Morana. And I care deeply about every single person here. Including you." She forced herself to stare at him, to make him see the honesty in her words. "I don't expect you to like me or care for me, but I do expect you to show me respect, if only for Morana."

On weak legs, she turned her gaze back down the hallway. "Just tell me how to get to my room and I'll let you be."

Her heart raced. Her palms prickled with sweat. She had never stood up for herself before. It was terrifying. And exhilarating. She wasn't sure if she liked it or not.

Koen came beside her, silent as a lion, and turned a sharp corner. There were more torches in the hallway illuminating a wall of doors evenly spaced apart. He stopped at the second door on the right. "This is your room." He pointed to the staircase at the far end of the hallway. "That will take you up to the main level. Mine is the last one, right here." He pointed to the last door beside hers and ran a hand through his hair. "Morana's saddle is ready. Oryn will take you early for a few hours, then you'll come to the Pit for training."

Her fingers traced the lines of the wood on the door. "Do I have a key?"

"None of us do." He stilled. "Do you need one?"

"No. I don't have a single thing of value." She looked up at him. "Thank you for helping me."

Aisling didn't allow him time to answer. A heavy exhale left her lips as she shut the door and stepped inside her new room.

It was bigger than anything she'd ever had before. Dark stone covered every wall except the far one where large floor-to-ceiling windows allowed the first rays of the morning sun to come pouring in. She gazed in wonder at the horizon and cliffs leading to the sea and the great expanse of sky she would never tire of.

A fireplace sat embedded in the wall on the right. A red velvet couch and coffee table were in front of it. A gigantic wooden bed stood against the left wall. Her fingertips traced the simple beige bedding with reverence as she stared into the open windows and devoured the beauty around her.

A chest of drawers and a closet rested on the left of the fireplace. A single door in the back right corner was closed. She opened it and let her gasp echo against the sanctuary she would never have dreamed of.

It was nothing like her apartment's bathroom. There was no fuzzy black mold or broken tiles. The windows from her room continued inside. An enormous tub rested in front of them. A table of oils and soaps and shampoos were lined up on a small table. A toilet hid behind a tiny door in the back. And under a large oval mirror was a beautifully ornate vanity.

She threw off her clothes after turning the tap of the bath on and watched in wonder as tendrils of steam licked her face while water poured in. For too long she had settled for lukewarm showers and poor water pressure. The heat melted into her bones as she stepped in. She released an audible groan of relief. Her head rested against the edge. She closed her eyes, allowing herself a moment of peace.

Her mind was blissfully blank as she sat submerged. She washed absentmindedly and watched the sun creep up over the horizon and paint the ground in her colors. She donned a fluffy white towel as she stepped out and looked in the mirror above the sink for the first time.

It was *her*. The real her. Not the mousy, meek girl she crawled inside of in her other life.

This woman was capable and strong. She glowed from inside with a soul deep radiance beneath her skin. This woman was unstoppable. Uncompromising. Aisling loved her.

She opened a drawer under the sink to find numerous toiletries she never had the chance to own before. She brushed her long hair and toweled it dry while exploring her dressers. An entire new wardrobe sat inside courtesy of Maura. She chose a simple white tee and black leather corset like the ones the girls always wore, paired with black leather pants covered in tiny loops at the waist and a new pair of insulated boots.

Her hair dried quickly. She attempted to braid it but ended up using a few pins she found in the back of the vanity drawer to make up for her lack of expertise. With a final glance at the woman in the mirror, she grabbed a fur-lined jacket and stepped out of her room into the hallway. Two doors down on her right, Cielle appeared. She eyed Aisling's outfit and broke into a grin. "Breakfast?"

Aisling's heart fluttered. Home. That's where she was.

THIRTY-ONE

"This is Declan," Oryn announced, gesturing to the tall blonde man outside of Morana's room. "He's been Morana's keeper for..."

"Eight years," Declan answered with a glittering smile. He was tall, not as tall as Oryn, with pale white skin and bright blue eyes. Lean muscle hid beneath his tight white shirt.

"Eight years," Oryn repeated. "He was just a boy when he started. But Morana took to him instantly."

Declan nodded sheepishly. "I've grown up with her, ma'am."

Aisling grinned at him. "It's nice to meet you, Declan. But please do not call me ma'am. Aisling will do just fine."

"Yes ma -" He stopped. "Aisling."

"The saddle is ready," Oryn said as he pointed to the massive leather object in Morana's room. "It's the smallest one we have. Morana wouldn't allow anyone near her wings to size her, so we may have to change things depending on your preferences."

Aisling trailed her fingertips on the cool brown leather. "I think this will be fine. I'm used to riding bareback, so anything would be an improvement." Morana huffed a response from the hallway.

Declan smiled at Aisling. "Shall we?"

Together they placed the saddle on Morana's back, carefully avoiding her wings and the shimmering flesh from the wound. The dragon gave little resistance but made her displeasure known with a chorus of grunts and huffs. Aisling ignored her and climbed on, surprised at the comfort of having her feet in stirrups and not hanging heavy at her sides.

Oryn sat atop Nyssa and Aisling blinked against their beauty. "The clips you see everywhere? Attach them to the loops in your leathers. Never," he emphasized, "unhook the clips unless you're getting off your dragon." She nodded in understanding and attached them to the numerous loops on her waistband.

Nyssa walked into the Pit. Morana followed close behind. Aisling gripped the pommel as Morana took to the sky and sighed her relief as the fresh air infiltrated every breath. A minute later they hovered over the dark ravine. She glanced over Morana's side and grimaced. "It's half a mile through to the sea," Oryn called out.

"How deep is it?" she asked over the wind, refusing to look down.

Oryn shrugged. "A mile maybe? We've never measured it. It doesn't matter. All you have to do is trust her instincts. Don't fight her. The two of you are one soul, so become one."

Nyssa dove, disappearing into the darkness.

Morana didn't give Aisling time to think as she followed. The dragon's wings tucked in tightly against her as they dropped inside the crevice. The air cooled drastically. Aisling was nauseatingly grateful to finally have warm clothes to fly in and a tether to keep her on Morana.

The darkness ate the light. They kept dropping. Rock surrounded them.

A sudden jerk had Aisling gripping the pommel and swallowing a gasp against the total blindness. Morana banked, leveling out for only a beat of her wings before angling so sharply to the right that Aisling let out a squeal. Morana leveled out again, and Aisling dropped her chest to Morana's back just in time for them to slant sharply again. She fought the urge to steer and heeded Oryn's instructions, forcing herself to trust Morana's skill.

Her shoulders relaxed first. Then her thighs. Her jaw loosened, taking the pressure off her teeth. She breathed in slowly and forced her lungs to inhale in a steady rhythm as air rushed past her.

They were doused in darkness, in cold, and Aisling came alive in it. With each sharp turn and dive, her heart grew stronger, more purposeful, with every beat. The bond between them glittered, the only bright thing she could see.

A slit of light opened in the distance and a flash of gold glittered just ahead. Morana's wings pounded against the air, sending them faster through the rock. Nyssa's metallic wings came closer with every breath.

Oryn turned his head, his green eyes widening in surprise at the short distance between them. Nyssa burst forward like a golden missile in the darkness. Morana followed, careening through the ravine as if she did it daily.

Nyssa blew through the opening with Morana on her tail. Aisling smiled as her beast continued to ascend into the clouds, riding the current of wind above the sea like a kite. Aisling sat up and extended her arms to her sides, inviting the wind to twirl against her fingers and in her hair. Her chest felt as though it would break from the joy coursing inside. Morana echoed the sentiment and chirped happily into the ether.

They lowered from the clouds and hovered above the sea beside Nyssa and Oryn. "Seems she's been holding out on us," he murmured. Nyssa chirped in response. Oryn smirked, his hair still somehow perfect despite the ride. "Let's see if it was a fluke."

They were in the ravine a second later. Aisling barely had time to fold herself against Morana's back before they launched back into the darkness.

Again, they ended up on Nyssa's tail.

For hours they flew, testing the boundaries and weaknesses of their bond, and found none. They landed on solid ground as the sun shone high above. Oryn shook his head with a hesitant smile. "This is the first show of pure trust I've ever seen between a human and a dragon. Even Kaida and I didn't achieve this level for at least a year."

Aisling didn't try to control the pride that flooded her at his words. Neither did Morana. Their bond glowed bright and beaming. Aisling stroked it, eliciting a low purr from her dragon.

"She's faster than she ever let on. I don't quite know what to make of that yet." He lifted his brow at Morana. Aisling reached for her clips, but he tutted. "Don't unhook. Koen's waiting for you in the Pit. If he gives you trouble about being late, blame me."

She steeled her shoulders, the happiness from earlier dimming. Oryn noticed. "Keep fighting him."

"Oh, no. I don't –"

His emerald green eyes sparkled. "You're meant to be here, Aisling. You're our missing piece. Make him see it." He nodded at Morana, and she followed the silent command, launching into the air without giving Aisling a chance to respond.

"Again."

Sand tickled her scalp. Her breath seared her chest. Every muscle begged for reprieve as she lay panting and unmoving on the soft ground.

They'd been at it for hours. Possibly for days. She couldn't be sure. Koen hadn't eased her into training. He threw her into the fire without a rope and watched as she struggled to keep from burning.

They started with a mile-long sprint that ended with her vomiting in a bush of purple flowers. He'd grimaced at her attempts at pushups and various other exercises she knew were made by Satan himself. Sparring wasn't proving any better.

Her other body was weaker than this one. Even at this point, covered in sand and struggling to breathe, she was stronger than she'd ever been in her other life. She didn't want to tell him that. She gritted her teeth and stood, wiping the caked sand from her leathers. Her hair somehow remained in the messy braid despite his best attempts to ruin her.

Koen stood two feet from her and watched her grimace with a hint of a smile on his face. A thin sheen of sweat covered his face and thick arms. "Relax your shoulders."

"I can't."

"Why?"

"Because I'm going to end up on the ground any second now. I'm bracing myself."

He breathed a laugh. "Then don't let it happen."

"I don't stand a chance, and you know it."

"You can try to fight," he stalked in a small circle around her. "There's always a chance you can win."

His breath was warm against the back of her neck. She inhaled deeply, preparing to meet the ground, and froze.

That smell, the one from the café – ginger and citrus and warmth and spice. It was him.

She'd made bread that reminded her of him. On instinct and paralyzed by her own despair, she had brought Koen into her other life.

He stopped in front of her, a deep crease between his brows. "What?"

She locked eyes with him. Her tongue didn't work. Her brain short wired. The crease between his eyebrows deepened. He took a step back; she fought the urge to follow.

"Nothing," she whispered. "Nothing. Sorry. Continue."

Koen paused. "Why don't you think you stand a chance?"

"Look at me," she said, exasperated and glad for the change of subject. "I can't even do a single pushup. How am I supposed to fight for anyone?"

"No one came here knowing to fight."

"Kaida and Oryn did."

"I didn't. None of the girls did."

"Amerie?"

"She couldn't lift a sword. Still isn't great at it, if I'm being honest. Which is why she uses the daggers." He rubbed his smooth jaw. "The point of this is to figure out where your strength lies. Not to be the best or the strongest. Amerie isn't brutally strong, but she is fast. Elaila is graceful like a dancer and Cielle is relentless. Kaida and Oryn are just…"

"Perfect."

He smiled. "Yeah. They are."

"And you?"

He angled his head. "What about me?"

"What's your strength?"

A devilish gleam flashed through his eyes. "Are you trying to figure me out, Aisling?"

She shrugged. "I think it's only fair. You've seen my strength, which is nothing. What's yours?"

"I don't know anymore," he admitted after a silent pause. A rawness hung in the words, tainting the air between them with heaviness.

"What's your weakness, then?"

"Tell me your truth and I'll tell you mine."

She rolled her eyes as the fire in her blood billowed. She wasn't ready to tell anyone her secret. Wasn't even ready to handle it herself despite knowing what her soul wanted. "Just throw me down and get it over with," she muttered.

"Horrible attitude from the Pearl of the Ferox." He began his slow walk again, hands clasped behind his back.

"Don't call me that."

"Why not? Would you rather be the diamond?"

"I am not anything."

She felt him this time. Anticipated his movement, felt the air move around them. His hand found her wrist, but she twisted away from his grip. Delight danced in his eyes. "You're selling yourself short."

She dodged a barrage of punches and blocked one with her arm. Her bones screamed at the contact, but she didn't balk. "You can't sell yourself short when there's nothing to sell."

His leg slammed into her waist, and she crumbled onto the sand. He stood over her. "Morana chose you. Do you think she would have chosen someone hopeless?"

Aisling snarled as she stood. "I am not hopeless."

"I know," he replied, stepping close enough for his scent to wrap around her. "So prove it. Prove you can fight. Prove you aren't weak. Make Morana happy with her choice. Make –"

Her body moved before her mind could register what was happening. Her fist slammed into his gut. A satisfying grunt left his lips as he staggered back. Aisling followed and shoved him onto the ground, reveling in the shock in his eyes.

"I am not weak," she whispered as she stared down at him. "And I am not useless."

A shackle around her mind broke. She'd spent her whole life chained by those words, believing she was exactly what she thought.

There would not be a single second that she would believe them now.

An impossibly heavy weight fell off her shoulders. She lengthened her spine and smiled as her hand extended toward him. "Get up and teach me."

He stared wide-eyed at her for a breath before breaking into a matching smile that threatened to buckle her knees.

THIRTY-TWO

"The Cruento hide in plain sight. It's their biggest strength – their ability to blend in." Amerie rested her clasped hands on the table. Her hair was in one thick braid over her shoulder, her eyes tired from last night's patrol. "We have no idea who the leaders are or what their structure looks like. They're quite literally a faceless, nameless enemy."

Aisling leaned back against her chair, her stomach pleasantly full after lunch with Koen. It had been mostly silent, but it wasn't uncomfortable. She took it as progress.

"They have no markings or sigils. Aedan has soldiers stationed in almost every major city and numerous undercover agents scattered about. No one has been able to break into their network in all these years."

"Then how do you fight them?" Aisling asked.

"*We*," Cielle corrected, "fight what we can see. They never work in silence. Their calling card is fire and chaos."

"The fire you saw on your way here? That was them. We missed the attack by seconds. The smoke you saw was the remnants after two days. Our network is fast, but sometimes it isn't fast enough."

Aisling balked. Two days and the smoke had shown no signs of clearing.

"We haven't figured out where they keep their beasts. They appear out of thin air it seems. We've checked as many caves around the Latebros mountains as we could and all the little unknown places." Cielle shook her head. "Somehow they keep appearing and wreaking havoc and destruction."

"So…" Aisling thought out loud, "If you figure out where their nest is, you can root them out. Right?" All three women nodded in agreement. "If the beasts are killed, what chances do they have of succeeding? And when will they consider themselves victors?"

"They'll never consider themselves the winner until every woman is back under their thumb." Elaila's jaw feathered. "And yes, if the beasts are gone, they don't have anything else to make chaos. And no chaos means no chance of them being able to take anyone without being noticed."

"The chaos they make breeds fear," Cielle said with a glance at Elaila. "The fear keeps the women contained and pliant."

"So we kill the beasts."

Amerie nodded. "Kill the beasts. Stop their ability to strike fear without exposing themselves."

Aisling glanced out the large window and stared at the sky above, stretching for eternity in a mix of blue and gray. Her voice wavered. "But they keep making them, right?"

The women's mouths tightened. They nodded.

"Favilla," she whispered, the ugly truth dawning. "You have to find Favilla."

Kill Favilla and destroy their ability to breed. Kill Favilla and end the war.

But to lose a dragon, to kill a member of the Ferox…

"The King has ordered it," Cielle said with unfeeling quietness. "If we see her, we kill her. Either us or our dragons."

"Why not try to free her?"

Amerie swallowed, a rare flash of despair in her eyes. "If we know them as well as we think we do, she's either dead or in no shape to be able to function at all. Killing her would be a blessing at this point."

Her stomach pitched at the thought. She could never ask Morana to do that.

"None of us want to do it," Elaila grimaced. "But if it means ending the war…"

Aisling nodded. If she was given the ability to stop it, she would take it.

They sat in contemplative silence for a few minutes, each one lost in their own little world as the truth of what they would be forced to do seeped into their skin. The crack of the roaring fire was the only noise inside the stone walls. Finally, Amerie cleared her throat and pointed at the map. "So we've searched –"

A shrill cacophony of bells pealed. The stone walls shook.

The girls stood without hesitation and shouted at her to follow them as they sprinted into the Lair.

A feverish energy zapped her skin. The dragons were snapping their maws, stomping their feet, and shaking their necks as a flurry of bodies ran around in controlled chaos. A large man herded the beasts into the Pit, his warm eyes vaguely familiar. Men and women, other dragon handlers, wrangled and readied their assigned dragons with brutal efficiency.

Declan took her hand, guiding her to a small table littered with sparkling white metal. "Your armor, Aisling."

She balked. "I have no idea how to –"

Kaida appeared beside her. Her tiny body was covered in intricate black armor shaped like dragon scales. Each metal scale hung against the other to allow for natural movement and protection. Her bright hair was braided back, and her eyes glittered with caged fury. She lifted a section of bright armor and placed it on Aisling piece by piece. Aisling glanced down as Kaida wrapped the metal around her stomach, her thighs, and marveled at the gorgeous white scales now adorning her body.

"To match your dragon," Kaida explained. Aisling glanced around, noting each rider's armor matched their dragon perfectly. "You will come with us, but you will not," she emphasized with a glare, "engage. You will watch us from above. No matter what happens, no matter what you see, you will stay in the clouds with Morana. She will know when to leave." Declan handed her two small daggers. Kaida tucked them into the loops on Aisling's side. "The pointy end first," she winked.

Oryn and Koen appeared, both devastatingly beautiful and dangerous in their armor. Oryn's golden scales made him look even more ethereal, more regal than she thought possible. His long hair was twisted in a knot at the back of his head. Koen's armor was viridian green, the color bringing out the gold in his hair and eyes. He glanced at Aisling and looked over her armor, his jaw clenched. "Amicitia." He called out. "Started minutes ago. Twenty beasts."

"They counted twenty, but attacks later in the day can conceal the number of beasts with the fading sun," Cielle whispered beside Aisling. "We have to consider that since it's almost dusk." A ripple of panic ran down Aisling's spine. Dusk. She had to stay awake as long as she could before her other life pulled her back.

"Are they ready?" Oryn asked the burly man who took the dragons.

"Fed, rested, and ready to fight," he growled in a deep voice. The riders moved at once at a sprint into the Pit. Aisling found Morana immediately. The bond zapped with an electricity matching the bright purple in her eyes.

"She knows to stay above," Kaida called from Soren after Aisling mounted and clipped into the saddle. The rest of the riders nodded curtly. They were in the weakening golden rays of the sun a heartbeat later.

Aisling had never moved so quickly in any life. Morana was a bolt of lightning against the clouds. They soared high above the rest of the Ferox.

Soren flew in the front with Nyssa at his right wing. Aylim tucked in between Calen and Osiris. Neera flew at the back, her green scales almost blending in with the green grass far below them.

They made no sound. Every flap of their wings was silent.

She smelled the smoke before she saw it. It filled her nostrils with the nauseating tinge of seared human flesh and scorched earth. She forced herself to breathe deeper, to inhale every scent particle of the hatred plaguing the air around her.

Morana lowered just below the clouds. Aisling's mouth ran dry.

Chaos reigned below.

Screams curdled her blood. Houses burned in pools of orange and red. A black haze tinted the air. Entire herds of livestock sat in piles of ash and bone.

Small shadows flew through the air, there and gone in a blink. Fires appeared where they flew. A shiver ran down her spine as they screeched into the sky. It was the same sound from their ride to Anguid, but Morana didn't tense this time. Her body hummed with the need to fight.

Soren appeared in a blink and snapped his massive maw just feet from Morana's face. "He won't tell her again," Kaida yelled over the din of battle. "Get up and stay up."

The pair disappeared a second later. Morana begrudgingly lifted them into the sky, just low enough in the clouds for Aisling to see the frenzy below.

Soren struck first with a cloud of bright blue flame.

Nyssa and Osiris took the right flank. Calen and Aylim went left.

A battle cry left Nyssa's mouth, lyrical and heart-wrenching. The rest of the dragons followed with their own calls before dousing the heavens in explosions of flame and death.

Unholy screeches filled the air as the Cruento beasts met them in the sky. Aisling's breath caught in her throat at the clashing of wings and teeth.

The beasts didn't stand a chance. Soren's jaw snapped, sending two monsters tumbling from the sky in pieces. Osiris danced with Elaila swirling her blade on his back, both in time with each other. Aylim and Cielle shot across the sky like a silver star, sending sprays of blood and bodies in her wake. Calen and Amerie squealed in delight as they took on three beasts at once, daggers and teeth sparkling in the light of the fire. Nyssa and Oryn were silent agents of death as they attacked relentlessly, twisting and weaving as one flash of gold.

Neera hovered just above the ground like a guardian angel of pain and fire. She lifted her neck and exhaled a barrier of flame. It stretched and morphed to cover the town in its entirety. As the Cruento beasts fell through the flame, the sound of their sizzling flesh crackled through the air.

Morana chirped as she watched her family fight. Her muscles tensed against Soren's order. Aisling felt her frustration through the bond and let it mix with hers. She knew she had no skills, no ability to fight, but it didn't stop her from shaking with need.

The beasts went down one by one, some in pieces as they crashed through Neera's shield. The barrier began to weaken as Neera turned her focus on the monsters that had fallen, making sure none of them survived.

Aisling saw them through a weakened corner of the shield – two beasts stuck under Neera's flames and hovering behind a smoking barn, nearly camouflaged against the dusky sky. They watched Soren soar higher to meet a clump of their kind. The rest of the Ferox continued to fight, oblivious to the threat.

Neera landed and ripped into a writhing beast somehow still alive. Koen's eyes were trained on the sky above, monitoring the shield's weaknesses and the status of the fight.

Neera's back was an open target. Koen was an easy meal.

The beasts saw it.

So did Morana.

Her giant head turned, violet eyes pleading.

Aisling didn't think, didn't hesitate. "Go, Morana!" she growled, lowering herself against the saddle.

Morana dove from the sky at the same time the beasts angled toward Neera. The wind tore Aisling's hair from its braid. She heard nothing as they plummeted. No din of battle, no screech or scream, only the promising song of violence in the wind.

They became a spear of iridescent light against the darkness and flame around them, falling as one body, one soul.

Neera looked up first. Her neon yellow eyes narrowed.

Koen looked up next. His face twisted in horror. His mouth opened in a scream as he gestured wildly for her to return to the sky.

Aisling didn't waste her time arguing.

The beasts edged closer to Neera's open back, claws outstretched and mouths open.

Morana sailed over Neera's neck, narrowly missing Koen, and collided with the two beasts just inches from the brilliant green scales.

Aisling didn't clench her teeth as Morana fought. Didn't shrink against the brutality she somehow now craved.

One beast was stuck between Morana's maw, its black eyes wide and wild as it fought, writhing and screaming against the teeth sinking deep into its flesh. Crimson crawled down Morana's neck, tainting her beautiful scales with violence.

Aisling smiled, her hatred and desire for blood overpowering. Morana's throat rumbled in response. Her jaw snapped against the black scales in her grasp. The beast's black eyes flashed before going blank. Morana spat it out like bad meat and turned her attention to the beast in between her claws, its tail flailing like a whip.

Morana lifted them higher into the air through the hole in Neera's shield. The monster screamed against the sizzling heat. Morana dug her claws deeper as if encouraging the sound. In one swift motion, she tore the beast in half and dropped it through the sky, watching as it fell through the flames for a second time and onto the ground.

Morana's head tipped to the dark sky. She let out a roar of defiance and power. A promise. A threat.

She swore her revenge to the ether, and the bond nearly exploded with justified wrath.

Aisling's heart was a living, thrashing thing in her chest. She was alive. Her blood sang with the carnage, the fight. Morana launched them into the clouds, making them disappear like the shadows they were.

A familiar tug pulled at Aisling's stomach. The sky tinted every shade of dark blue.

The sun had set.

She screamed against the pull and focused on the glowing bond.

Darkness claimed her as Morana let out a panicked roar and careened to the ground.

THIRTY-THREE

Her alarm blared.

She slammed it off and threw her phone across the room.

She would not leave them, not now.

There was nothing in this life that could keep her from the fight.

She shut her eyes and anchored herself in the bond.

THIRTY-FOUR

"Is she okay?"

"I don't see any blood."

"Check her for injuries."

Hard ground poked into her back. A warm hand pushed her hair from her face. Smoke filled her nostrils. A cool breeze tickled her skin. Aisling opened her eyes to find six pairs locked on her.

Koen knelt beside her, his face contorted in calm panic. She could have sworn his eyes fluttered in relief as she pushed onto her elbows. "Sorry," she mumbled. She glanced up. There were no more beasts in the sky or acidic screeches in the air.

"The first battle is a lot," Amerie responded, her silky dark skin splattered with blood. "I peed myself the first time. You're fine."

"You were badass," Cielle smirked. Elaila and Amerie nodded in agreement. Kaida's eyes flickered as her eyebrow lifted. She disappeared a second later. Koen dragged his hand against his face before following her.

"What now?" Aisling asked, shaking off the shock of her return to the dream.

"There's work to do," Oryn answered, extending his hand. She took it and stood beside him while the rest of the team scattered through the town.

The ground was charred. Smoke lifted to the sky in stacks. Amicitia was decimated. There were no standing houses. Ashes danced in the wind. A crowd of people stood huddled by what was once a barn. "We never leave them until the cavalry arrives," Oryn explained. "They should be here any minute."

A child wailed. An elderly couple sobbed silently in each other's arms. Utter despair and disbelief tainted the thick air.

"These people are hurt. They're terrified. They may spend the rest of their lives in a constant state of fear because of what happened tonight. All we do now is give them peace of mind." He looked over the crowd. "Sometimes knowing you have someone fighting for you can make all the difference. It can keep the soul alive. Keep hope alive."

He walked to the edge of the crowd where a young woman cradled a wriggling infant against her chest. Tracks of tears cut through the dirt and ash on her cheeks. There was nothing in her eyes – no pain, no sadness. Just bleak nothingness. He wrapped his arm around the woman's shoulder and gently urged her to a broken tree stump. Oryn kneeled beside her, his face a mask of beautiful calm. His mouth moved. The baby stopped squirming. The woman broke her trance and met his eyes, her shoulders sagging with relief as she stared at him. Oryn smiled.

Elaila came beside her. "It's a lot, the first battle. I threw up six times after mine. You handled it beautifully, even if you disobeyed a direct order." She jerked her chin toward the perimeter of the town. "Come on. You need to see the different work we do."

Aisling followed, her eyes absorbing everything she passed. There was nothing left. No homes, no food for these people now. Their town had fallen prey to chaos, their lives the victims.

A muffled scream came from inside a leaning husk of a building. Aisling's chest tightened. "Nothing to worry about," Elaila murmured, a flicker of something in her eyes as she opened the rickety door. A single candle was the only light in the dingy room inside.

Koen's eyes met Aisling's from across the darkness. She swallowed a gasp at the sheer fury and bloodlust in them. Blood splattered his armor. He blinked once in acknowledgment before turning his hardened stare back to the floor.

Three men lay sprawled on the ground, their arms and legs bound. They reeked of smoke and urine, acidic and burning. Her stomach threatened to retch, but she clamped her teeth in refusal. Blood dripped from their bodies onto the floor in small puddles. Kaida stood almost camouflaged in the corner, her silver eyes the only thing visible in the darkness.

Elaila stepped forward, an air of quiet power in her posture. She walked to one of the men and nudged his head with her foot. "This is a Cruento," she said quietly over her shoulder without taking her eyes off the man's battered face. The man began to protest. He stopped when Elaila's boot rested atop his throat. "Koen found these three in the chaos. It's easy to tell who they are. Despite their size, they're very small."

Rage glittered in the man's eyes. Sweat dotted his bald head despite the chill. "Whore," he spat, blood flying from his mouth, "you're worth nothing more than what's between your pretty little legs. You'll get what's coming for you."

Koen stepped forward, his knuckles white as they gripped his dagger. Elaila simply held her arm out and stopped him in his tracks. She cocked her head at the man, a tantalizing shimmer in her eyes. "The universe is between my legs, darling. You have nothing."

As if on cue, Kaida and Koen knelt beside the man and held his writhing body down. His screams filled the air as Elaila gently, sweetly, unbuttoned his pants and slid them down to his thighs. She tutted and shot him a pout. "All that talk for what little you have to offer."

She laughed, severe and blunt. It sent a chill down Aisling's spine. "Wait, sorry. That's not right. I meant what you *had* to offer."

With a swipe of her delicate wrist, her small blade hit flesh, cutting off his most prized possession. Blood splattered Elaila's smiling face.

Kaida and Koen stood, faces blank. The man screamed and attempted to reach for himself through his bindings but found only blood. Panic and hatred lined his face as unintelligible screams leaked from his mouth. The other men lay with wide eyes, their fear a potent, tangible thing.

Elaila wiped her blade on the sleeve of her shirt and walked past Aisling. "Come on," she whispered, the bravado dissipating from her paling face. Aisling followed, ignoring the screams that echoed inside as they shut the door. They walked to the edge of the town in silence. Elaila tilted her face to the sky, her dark braid hanging low on her back, and shut her eyes. "I was sold to the Cruento as a girl."

Blood rushed from Aisling's face.

"My parents died when I was a child. The orphanage placed me with a young couple. I thought I had found a family again, but the man beat his wife to a pulp and had his fun with me." She cleared her throat, keeping her gaze on the sky. "When he got bored, he shared me with his friends. I was shuttled around the kingdom like a piece of meat for a long time. Luckily, I was barely fed, so I had no cycle. No chance of getting pregnant. After my seventh year of it, I decided I would rather die than be used like an animal any longer. The driver of the caravan got drunk and forgot to lock the door of the wagon one night.

I escaped from beneath the crops and ran for miles. I was weak. Barely alive. But I knew if I allowed myself to get captured again, I would be dead anyway. I wanted to go on my own terms, so I ran to the cliffs. I thought it would be a pretty place for me to leave this life. The sea was as angry as I was. It could wash me and make me clean and pure again in death." She turned to Aisling. "That's where Osiris found me. I didn't even notice him at first, he was so quiet. He stood between me and the sea.

"I wasn't scared of him. It was like my heart knew I was finally safe. So I followed him. I was too weak to fly, but I was able to lay on his back while he walked to the Keep. Kaida and Oryn took me in right away. They didn't ask questions. Amerie and Cielle talked to me like I was a normal person, not a dirty waste. And Koen taught me to fight for myself. I built up my strength and learned to tolerate human touch again."

Tears threatened to fall from Aisling's eyes.

"I know how much of an adjustment it is to come here. I know how hard it is to relearn who you are. Some days I'm still stuck in that caravan, or I can feel the hands on my skin, but Osiris tugs on the bond, and none of it matters because I know I'm home. I'm with my family." She took Aisling's hand in hers. "Whatever happened in your past doesn't define you. And when you want to face it, we will all be here to help you get through it." Aisling wiped a tear from her cheek and nodded, her throat too tight to speak. Elaila smiled, softly. "Did I scare you?"

"No," Aisling admitted through a thick throat. Elaila had only stuck a sense of awe in her with that quiet graceful rage. "Not once I understood what was going on."

"Good. Kaida insists I get first dibs on the men they catch if I feel like it."

"As you should." She cleared her throat and blinked away the burning behind her eyes. "When does she catch them?" There wasn't any time to find and fight the men when they were in the sky battling the beasts.

"Koen does it during battle. Neera's shield gives him the ability to hunt on land while we hunt in the sky. He finds the men in the chaos and brings them down. When he has them contained, he puts whatever girls they were trying to take into safety, usually somewhere by Neera."

She couldn't help the wave of awe for Koen that coursed through her. To fight multiple men alone... she could never. "Then what? He waits for Kaida?"

"Yes. They... have methods of wringing out information."

Aisling paused. "Do the men ever get to live?"

"Never." Elaila guided her through the town toward a small group of young women close to Neera.

"What if they're wrong? What if the men aren't Cruento?"

"We've never been wrong. In darkness, in fear, secrets come out easily. It helps that the Ferox is mostly women. It infuriates them. They expose themselves."

"What is everyone's job, then?"

"Oryn does general supervision. He monitors injuries and herds the survivors. You saw him, he's a natural healing presence. Koen finds the Cruento while Neera guards wherever we are. Kaida helps him interrogate them. Cielle, Amerie, or I protect the women the men attempted to capture in the chaos of battle. We alternate patrols in the air in case the Cruento try to come back."

Cielle stood in front of the group of girls of varying ages, sword in hand. Aisling swallowed her bile as a girl no older than ten stared up at her. Cielle tracked the salty tracks on Elaila's face. "All good?"

"Amerie's up there?" Elaila asked, ignoring the question.

"Her, Calen, and Soren."

"Kaida's okay with Soren flying alone?" Aisling asked.

Elaila laughed. "Have you seen the beast? He's fine. No one can see him up there until it's too late for them. And if he runs into anything, he can speak down the bond with Kaida."

Aisling's jaw dropped. "You're joking."

"Nope," Cielle answered. "If you're bonded long enough, you sort of become one being. They can have full conversations without speaking even miles away from each other. It's wild."

Elaila glanced at the sky. "It's how Kaida always knows what everyone's doing. The dragons talk."

"Where are the rest of them?"

"They stand at the borders of wherever we are and watch for the cavalry."

"Oryn mentioned that. What is it?"

"Aedan's men. He has soldiers stationed in posts all over the kingdom for this very reason. They come in and take over so we can go back to Anguid. Sometimes if they get here in time they fight with us, but it's very rare."

On cue, a horn blasted through the night. Over a hundred armored soldiers appeared through the darkness. Oryn met with the leader and exchanged handshakes before delving into the details. The longer they spoke, the deeper the groove between the man's eyebrows grew. Kaida appeared a moment later and shook his hand before joining in the conversation.

"Come on," Cielle nudged as the soldiers dispersed. A group of armored female soldiers took control of the young girls, exchanging quick nods of thanks with the Ferox. "Time to saddle up."

Aisling took one final glance at the little girl, her bright eyes hardened and blazing, and swallowed the rage that boiled inside.

They met their dragons on the outskirts of town. Morana lowered her head and nudged Aisling's chest. "Is Soren mad at you?"

Yes.

Aisling grimaced. "You can blame me. Tell him that."

Something pushed her back. She whirled to find Neera's bright eyes in front of her. Her breath snagged at the sheer size of her, but instinct took over and she stroked the green satin scales. Neera purred at the touch before quickly pulling away and walking toward an approaching Koen in the dark field.

Aisling mounted Morana and patted the scales. "Home please, my love."

Morana obliged.

Declan was waiting in the Pit when they landed. He took Aisling's armor and weapons with a smile. "Glad you're back," he whispered, glancing adoringly at Morana. "I'll make sure she gets what she needs."

Aisling said goodnight to her dragon before he led her to the Lair. She followed the rest of the riders down the stairs. Kaida's room was the first one on the left, and she walked in without uttering a sound. Amerie was almost asleep before her door shut.

Aisling rested her hand on the doorknob and turned to face Koen on her right. "Who's on patrol tonight?"

"No one. The Cruento never attack more than once a day."

"Why?"

He shrugged. "Not enough manpower. Plus, they can't control the beasts. To let too many out at once would be catastrophic."

"Are we still training tomorrow?"

"Yes."

She nodded. "Great. I'll see you then." The handle turned under her palm.

"Wait." He rested his forehead against his door, his face twisted as if in pain. His voice came out tight. "Why did you do that?"

Her answer was automatic. "It was the right thing to do."

She didn't want to admit that she had been terrified for him. That she couldn't imagine him getting hurt for some reason. That she didn't hate him.

He turned to face her, the darkness in his eyes from earlier replaced with a warm golden brown. "You disobeyed a direct order."

"Yes."

The corner of his mouth flirted with a smile. "You saved Neera."

"And you."

"And me."

"Yes. Is there a question?"

He shook his head and opened his door, his voice a whisper. "Goodnight, Aisling."

She let the tug of her other life take her as soon as her door shut.

THIRTY-FIVE

Aisling dressed quickly, grabbed her phone from across the room, and sprinted out her door.

Panic sliced through her when she looked at the screen.

14 Missed Calls from **Troy**

No voicemail. No text.

She burst through the back doors of the café and past Ryan's office. "You're two hours late," he called out.

"I'm sorry," she lied as she passed his door. "My phone died so I didn't have an alarm." Aisling rushed through the kitchen door to the front. Troy stood at the register. The other two new employees, she couldn't remember their names, fluttered around him with orders. She tugged Troy's elbow. He recoiled at her touch.

"Troy, my phone," she explained breathlessly, "I didn't hear it. I was sleep—"

A gasp left her lips as Troy turned around. She clasped her hands over her mouth.

"Your dream needed you, right?" he seethed. His lower lip was cut open and scabbed. Deep purple and black covered his swollen right eye. "A dragon needed you?"

"What happened?" she whispered, ignoring the acid in his voice.

"If you had answered your phone, you would know."

"I didn't hear it," she cringed. "Tell me what happened to you."

His answering glare involuntarily made her cower. She had never seen his eyes so icy before. Gone was the warmth she knew and adored. In its place was a seething, bubbling rage that sent a flicker of terror down her spine.

"We have it covered here, Ash," Troy whispered with a brittle smile, his low voice laced with something so acidic her stomach clenched, "go back to sleep."

He turned back to the register and greeted the next customer. The two employees jostled around her. Aisling stared at his back, dumbfounded.

Troy didn't speak a word to her the rest of the day. At closing, he disappeared while Ryan reprimanded Aisling for the first time over her tardiness. She ripped out her phone on her walk home, constantly hitting his name, but Troy never answered. She showered, ignoring the gaunt wisp of a human in the mirror, and ate a few stale crackers while continuously calling his phone.

She fell asleep with her phone against her ear. He never answered.

THIRTY-SIX

Something tugged at her—an incessant pull against the fibers of her soul.

She fought against it.

Aisling woke up on her bedroom floor in the Pit with a twinge of exhaustion in her bones.

THIRTY-SEVEN

"You have got to work on your core," Koen mumbled as he pulled her up for the thousandth time that hour.

Aisling had spent the entire morning on Morana's back with Oryn and the girls. They worked on formations and protecting blind spots. The girls helped desensitize her to attacks by flying at her from all angles, and she had been terrified. The dragons were so much bigger than the Cruento beasts, but Morana deftly avoided every claw and tooth with idle boredom.

Koen threw her into training immediately after she landed. She was thrilled when she didn't throw up after the mile-long run, but the excitement disappeared quickly when Koen forced her into the numerous exercises she had hoped were a one-time thing.

They'd sparred for half an hour with no end in sight. She was sweaty and hungry and tired. And, she decided, eternally covered in sand.

"What if we all acknowledged I was the weakest and made it work somehow?" she panted.

Koen scoffed. "We're only as strong as our weakest member. So that means," he threw out his arm in a swipe she dodged, "we're only as strong as you. Which means," he ran his hand through his hair as he regrouped, his chest and arms flexing, "we're a group of worms with legs." His strong leg jutted out, catching her at the ankles. Her knees crumbled with the impact, and she collapsed onto the sand.

A worm with legs. She rolled onto her back and laughed. That was the perfect way to describe her. Her brows pinched at the gray clouds rolling in the sky above, darkening the Pit with a chill.

"I don't think working on my core will help," she admitted as a shiver ran through her.

"Why not?"

She leveled a look at him. "There isn't enough training in the world for me to be even remotely prepared for any of this." She lifted to sitting. "I feel bad for you. You're wasting your time."

After a beat of silence, Koen sat down beside her and wrapped his arms around his bent knees. She couldn't tear her eyes away from the strong column of his neck or the broad thickness of his chest. Even his eyelashes were something to look at, long and curled over his dark eyes.

"No one comes here because they're ready. That includes Kaida and Oryn. We come here because whatever is in us is enough for the dragons. We learn how to fight when our souls demand it. For Elaila, it took a long time. Amerie and Cielle caught on quickly. And I'm pretty sure the twins used each other as practice in the womb."

Aisling grinned. "And you?"

His lips hinted at a smile. "Neera chose me pretty young. I was barely fourteen when she found me. My family life was…" he pursed his lips in thought. "It was tumultuous. She found me and that was it. Kaida and Oryn became my parents and friends."

"And they taught you?"

He nodded. "Them and Gareth, yeah."

"Who's Gareth?"

"The head Dragon Master. You haven't met him yet? Big burly guy. He used to be in the King's guard."

"I've seen him, just never been introduced."

"He's great. You've met Declan?"

"Yeah," She smiled. "He's wonderful."

"They all are. Everyone here."

A splattering of small circles pelted the sand around them. Cold drops fell on her head, but she didn't want to move. "Do you -" she shook her head. "Never mind."

He faced her. "Ask."

"Do you ever see them at all? Your family?"

His answer was instant. "No. Not since Neera found me."

"I'm sorry."

"Don't be." He cleared his throat. "And you?"

She shrugged. "I've never had a family."

His voice softened. "Do you remember now? Even a little bit?"

"I remember pain. And fear." Dark alleys where she hid behind dumpsters for a few hours rest. The trio of men who followed her around the city for days with hungry looks in their eyes. She remembered the bladder infection that almost killed her, and her stepmother's boot pushing her neck into the curb. "I remember enough to know I don't want to remember more."

That life wasn't real anymore. It hadn't been for a very long time, longer than she cared to admit. Her memories could be something she dumped into the back of her mind. She could replace them with whatever she wanted now like dragons and friends and happiness.

Troy's swollen, bitter face crossed her mind. She swallowed thickly and shut her eyes against the image.

"Who were you before you came here?" Koen asked, his voice almost a whisper.

"No one." She met his eyes and let him see the person she was, the honesty she was willing to give. "I was no one."

Silence hung between them as they stared at each other. Something intangible built in her chest with a pressure that bordered pain and pleasure simultaneously.

He opened his mouth. His eyes darted over her shoulder to the door behind them.

"Aedan!" Amerie panted, her eyes widening at the two of them sitting together without killing each other. "He's here." She was gone in the next second.

Koen sighed and stood before extending his arm. "Come on. The King wants to meet you."

"What do I do?" Aisling asked frantically. "Do I bow? Or curtsy? How do I address him?"

Her heart was a thundering gallop in her chest. Royalty. She was going to meet actual royalty. She had read so many books like this, but her memory was failing her on protocol. She glanced at her sand-covered outfit and lifted her hand to her hair, cursing at the grains she felt on her scalp.

Koen glanced sidelong at her. "You do not bow to anyone, Aisling. You are Ferox. Dragons bow to you."

She tilted her head back and groaned. "Unhelpful."

He guided her through the Keep, nodding at the people they passed with warm familiarity. She tried to smile but knew it looked like a grimace. Koen stopped in front of the throne room doors. "Take a breath. You're overthinking this."

"I'm not."

He leaned down until they were eye to eye. She stilled, every thought emptying from her head at his closeness. His voice dipped to a low timbre. "You are." He opened the doors, and she followed him in with her heart in her throat.

There was no need to worry. The throne room was nothing more than a more ornate common room. A massive wooden table sat in the middle of the space with numerous chairs scattered around it. A fire roared in the back.

The man at the head of the table stared at her. She stared back. Freckles dusted his tanned skin. Sandy blonde hair hung in a shag to his shoulders. He was well-built and athletic in a simple tunic and leather pants. His bright eyes ran up and down the length of her body before landing pointedly on hers.

"Aisling," Koen purred in a voice she wanted to hear more of, "this is King Aedan."

She opened her mouth, but Aedan stood and opened his arms. "Our newest rider. Morana has finally chosen her equal." He stepped around the table with confident grace and stood in front of her. She was surprised to see he was barely taller than her. "Kaida tells me you healed Morana on the island, is that correct?"

She nodded curtly, still unsure of how to speak.

He whistled. "Amazing. And Kaida tells me your memory of how you got there is poor."

She swallowed, sparing a glance at Kaida's blank face. "That's correct, unfortunately."

"Well, you'll get it back eventually. And if you don't, we will just fill your head with wonderful memories instead." He gestured for her to sit in an open chair. Koen sat beside her. She stole a glance at Amerie and Elaila across the table. They sat with their backs against the chairs, as relaxed as they would be any other time.

Aedan sat at the head of the table with Kaida and Oryn flanking him on either side. He smiled warmly and brushed his hair from his face. "I am thrilled to have you, Aisling. Honored to have the missing piece to our little family at last." He rested against his chair and glanced at the rest of the Ferox. His voice rang with quiet authority. "Business first, though. What did we learn from Amicitia?"

Koen spoke first. "They didn't have anything to say that we didn't already know. We searched for an entrance to any sort of tunnel but found nothing."

"The girls they rounded up were able to fight back long enough for us to get there," Cielle offered. "They were never shown a door or entrance to anything." Aisling swallowed her nausea. That young girl had fought for her innocence, fought for her life, against grown men. A low ember of rage tickled her gut. Morana sent a plume of mist down the bond to douse it.

Aedan nodded. "Refugees?"

"In house."

He nodded. "Keep looking for an opening. I know we've searched everywhere, but the only reasonable explanation is an underground network of sorts. We just have to find the gate." He turned his attention to Amerie, Elaila, and Cielle. "I'll have Anwir bring updated maps. Pretend you're one of them. Show me where would make the most sense for them to be." The girls nodded. "Anything on patrols?"

Oryn shook his head. "Nothing. It's been quiet for weeks. We believe they've been recuperating their losses. They can't have many beasts left."

Aedan's brow creased. "You think they're making more?"

"If I was them, I would," Oryn admitted. "It would make sense for them to build an arsenal. They only brought a handful to Amicitia."

Aedan blinked slowly in thought before turning his attention to the rest of the table. "Are any of the dragons willing to mate?" Silence encompassed the room, tense and electrifying. After a heartbeat, he swallowed and rested his hands on the table with a sheepish grimace.

"The only ones that seem to be… willing, would be Soren and Neera." Kaida offered, her voice flat and stoic.

Koen's spine went rigid. He cleared his throat. "Neera has shown no interest in mating. But," he clenched his jaw, "I can ask her if she'd be willing to try."

Aedan shook his head. "Absolutely not. Do not even bring it up. If she's unwilling that is all I needed to know. We will find different avenues of success." Koen visibly deflated with relief. "I'll increase the number of troops at all the major cities and send out a few more covert operations."

"Let us focus on the fighting. Tell them to focus on the people's safety," Kaida said.

"Of course." Aedan tapped his fingers absentmindedly against the table. "There is one more thing." He cringed. "We have a new weapon against their monsters. It's an automatic device that can shoot spears into the air faster and with more accuracy than a human could."

Oryn met Kaida's glance from across the table and gave a subtle nod. Kaida started, her voice laced with venom, "If those spears come anywhere near my dragons on land or in the air, I will raze your soldiers to the ground without a second thought or apology."

Aedan clenched his jaw. "I do not take orders from you, Kaida."

Her answering smile was bitter and terrifying. "No, you do not, *Your Majesty.*" The smile faded. The temperature in the room plummeted. "But the dragons take orders from Soren. And he is bonded to no one but me."

Aisling held her breath as the two held each other's stares, daggers flashing in both their eyes. After a minute of tense silence, Aedan sighed. "The spears will not be in use when the Ferox arrives at any battle. You have my word."

"Soren will be pleased."

Aedan rolled his eyes. "Anyway." His bright green stare locked on Aisling. "How is training going?"

The door opened. A tall wraith of a man walked in, averting his eyes to the ground as he came around the table and whispered in the King's ear. Aedan nodded and gestured to Aisling. "Anwir. This is Aisling, the newest member of the Ferox. Morana's rider. Aisling, this is Anwir, my right-hand man. If you ever need me and I'm not available, he's your next best option." She nodded a hello. Anwir returned it, his small dark eyes locking on hers for only a second before shuffling from the room and shutting the door. "He's a bit shy," Aedan murmured with a shrug. "Training?"

She cleared her throat. "It's... going."

He smirked. Amerie leaned forward. "She's doing wonderfully. She absorbs the information we give her like a little sponge." She shot Aisling a wink. "My favorite student so far."

"Her flying comes naturally," Oryn said, giving her a nod of recognition. "It's as if she and Morana have known each other for years."

The King pursed his lips. "And how do you feel your flying is?"

"I have nothing to compare it to. But it feels... good. Like it's what I'm supposed to do." She stole a glance at Oryn and blushed at his encouraging smile.

"She rode bareback from the island," Cielle offered.

Aedan's eyebrows rose. "Impressive." He turned to Koen. "Her training?"

She swallowed tightly, prepared for the onslaught of embarrassment.

"It's going well. She shows promise," Koen said swiftly. "With time, I think she will be able to bring down any enemy if needed."

The King grinned. "Wonderful. But don't let the praise get to your head, Aisling! Stay on Morana's back in battle until Koen gives you the all-clear."

Aisling nodded, words lost on her tongue.

"Girls," he flashed a devious smile that would have anyone with eyes crawling for him, "you must show me your dragons. I feel I haven't seen them in ages. I know they miss me terribly." He stood, sparing a secret glance at an unbothered Kaida before looking at Aisling. "An honor, Aisling. I look forward to many more years of our friendship."

She swallowed a gasp as the King bowed at the waist before lifting his head with a wink. He stood and clapped his hand against Oryn's back as they walked from the room. The girls followed.

The King bowed to her.

The *King*.

THIRTY-EIGHT

Kaida looked at Koen. "Soren is open to mating. We both know they've been in love with each other for years."

"I will never ask that of her," Koen responded evenly despite the anger in his eyes. "She has to be willing on her own without pushing or prodding."

Kaida stared at him blankly for a minute before standing and walking to the door. She glanced over her shoulder. "Unlike Aedan, I've seen Aisling spar. She eats more sand than food. Get back to training."

Aisling sank low in her seat as embarrassment washed over her. Koen smirked and walked to the door, motioning for her to follow. She inhaled deeply as they left the Keep, letting the fresh air coat her lungs. "You lied."

His eyebrow lifted. "Did I?"

"To the King."

"And?" he challenged.

She huffed. "I'm trash at training. Kaida is right. I wash sand out of my mouth every night."

"You are awful," he admitted. He lifted his hand in placation before she could argue. "Do you know how many times Kaida threw me on my ass? Or how long it took Cielle and Elaila to spar because they didn't want to hurt each other?" He breathed a laugh at the memory.

"Being awful now doesn't mean you can't get better. Give yourself a little grace."

"Not my strong suit," she mumbled. She glanced up to the darkening sky and smiled at the sight of Soren and Neera riding the current. "Do they really like each other?"

He followed the path of his dragon above. "Yeah. It's distracting. Sometimes she floods the bond with her feelings. I have to tell her to share that with Morana."

"That's not very comforting for her. What if you did the same thing? Would you want her to yell at you?"

He glanced sidelong at her. "I have better control of my emotions than she does."

Aisling laughed. "I'm sure you do. Should I ask Morana to get the truth from Neera?"

He chewed on the inside of his cheek, a hint of a smile on his lips.

"Is the bond really stronger the longer you're with them?" she asked, pocketing the image of him relaxed and relatively happy.

He nodded. "It becomes second nature, too. You don't notice it as much because it's just part of you."

"What does it feel like for you, then?"

"It's like I can taste her feelings. They used to be bursts down the bond. Anger was always hot."

"Yeah. But then the mist calms it down."

He stopped. "The mist?"

"Yeah," she kept walking. "It kept me from feeling like I would explode during the bonding." He said nothing as he came up beside her, his brows pinched. She glanced again at Neera's beautiful body in the sky, her dark green scales a stark contrast to the ever-deepening gray of the clouds. "You wouldn't ask her to mate?"

"Never. That's not my decision to make. It's up to her what she wants to do. I support her either way." He opened the door to the Pit and followed Aisling inside. Sand squished under her shoes as she made her way to the middle of the giant arena.

His hand shoved her back and sent her flying into the grains below. She spit as she stood, not bothering to brush the sand from her face. "What the fuck, Koen? Do you always have to be an ass?"

"Fight, Aisling," he responded, a light in his eyes as if begging her to play. "Fight back. Stop being on the defensive. Make moves. Be the one striking, not the one waiting for one."

She lunged like an animal in a flurry of fists and feet. Koen blocked each attempt like she was made of paper. She stopped to catch her breath after a minute. He smiled and lowered his arms to his sides, the perfect picture of cocky boredom, not a single dark hair out of place.

Her blood boiled.

She couldn't fight him. Not yet. But she did have other weapons.

Her face softened. She didn't dare take her eyes off him as she took a tentative step forward, forcing a blush onto her cheeks. "Your smile..." she breathed, "you should smile more." Her voice came out quiet, almost awestruck.

He stilled. She took another small step forward, letting her eyes dance along his face, his body, just inches from hers. Her mouth parted slightly as she increased the cadence of her breathing. "It's hard to look away when you do."

She knew it was dangerous. Knew that her actions, her words, weren't lies. There was a careful line she was teetering on; one she didn't want to fall off of yet.

The electricity between them had nothing to do with the storm overhead. Her skin buzzed with his closeness like it did every time he touched her. And his scent – the ginger and citrus, warmth and brightness – she could bathe in it, and it still wouldn't be enough.

His gaze darted between her eyes and mouth. His posture softened, his hands falling slack at his sides. With every inch she moved closer, his chest rose quicker.

Aisling gave him a small sheepish smile.

Then shoved her knee into his groin.

He staggered backward with a gasp, his eyes flashing with shock. She kicked his legs out from under him and watched him fall to the ground with a grunt. Satisfaction bloomed in her gut as she straddled his chest and pinned his biceps to his side with her knees.

"Is this enough of a fight for you?" she seethed. Her heart pounded in her ears as every emotion he ignited came flooding back. Her voice cracked. "Or am I still too weak? Am I still useless?"

He froze under her. His eyes swam with a range of emotions too complex for her to understand.

Aisling knew she wasn't useless. She wasn't weak. Not anymore.

But she wanted him to see it. For some stupid reason, she needed him to see it, see her. She wanted him to know she was worth more than what she'd been given. There was a fight in her, a fight she had doused for years. Koen brought it back. Morana brought it back. And she wanted more of it.

She stood on shaky legs and stepped away from him, her hands trembling at her sides. Her breathing came too shallow, too quick. The clouds opened and pelted them with cold, fat drops.

Koen remained on the ground for another moment longer, staring into the sky before standing much slower than normal. He didn't bother to remove the sand from his clothes or fix his unruly hair. He lifted his head, and her lungs seized at the pain in his eyes. "I regret ever saying those things to you. You didn't deserve it. I never thought you were either."

"Then why did you say them?" she asked, her voice softer than she intended.

He stared at her, a war in his eyes. "I don't have a good reason."

Her breath came out in a heavy exhale. She shook her head and glanced upward, letting the cold drops land on her face. "Is it something I said? Something I did?"

"No," he breathed. "It's not... you didn't do anything wrong."

"So you just treat everyone you meet like shit then?"

He ran his hand through his hair, and she worked to keep her focus off the way his soaked shirt clung to him. "I have no excuse, Aisling. None. And it makes it all the worse because despite everything I said, you went and saved my life." He laughed, sour and heavy. "I haven't even thanked you yet, but it doesn't matter, because you never thought I would. You think so little of me that you didn't expect me to thank you for saving my ass. And I am so sick with shame over it."

She stood unmoving, unblinking, as her heart thundered in her chest and the clouds covered her with their tears.

He took a small step forward, his palms splayed. "I can't say thank you because it would never be enough. Thank you will never make up for how I made you feel. It will never encompass how grateful I am that you were there and defied a direct order to save Neera. But I want you to know I'll make it up to you. I swear it."

She soaked in the violent honesty in his eyes. Felt the urgency of his words and the desperation of his breath. Hers came bubbling involuntarily to the surface.

"I lied to you," she whispered, barely audible against the rain. "You were right. I do have a secret. But I'm not ready... I can't tell it yet. You just have to trust me, okay?" she pleaded. "You have to know that it's something I'm working on. I just..." She shook her head to keep the tears prickling her eyes at bay.

She wanted to tell him, of all people. Wanted to tell him she chose this life. Chose the will to live. Chose to fight, to act.

The answer had been simple. The choice didn't seem like much of a choice at all. Somehow it was so simple and natural, while also being the most horrific, terrifying realization she ever had. But she couldn't tell them. Not yet. She needed time. For what, she wasn't sure, but she needed it all the same.

Her shoulders dropped in exhausted defeat. "I need you to trust me. Please."

Something broke in Koen. She saw it in his eyes, a final snap of his will. The hardened look she had come to know vanished. His rain-soaked face was softer than she'd ever seen it, more vulnerable than she ever could have imagined, and it terrified her how much she liked it, liked being the one he showed it to.

"I trust you," he murmured after a long beat of silence. "When you're ready, we're here."

Relief washed over her, softening her tense body enough for her to want to crash into the ground. "Thank you."

His answering smile blinded her, a dazzling beacon in the storm around them. "Come on, training is done for the day. Kaida will understand." He arched his brow over his shoulder while he walked to the door. "Was it real?"

She followed him out of the rain. "Was what real?"

"What you said."

She looked at him in confusion. "Yes…"

He pursed his lips and walked to the stairs. A devilish gleam flashed in his eyes. "You think I should smile more."

Her response was a laugh deeper and brighter than any she could ever remember.

THIRTY-NINE

"Tell me what happened to you."

Aisling cornered Troy in the kitchen. He leaned against the fridge, unable to move past her without knocking her over, just as she had planned.

"Why do you care?"

"Tell me."

"Why? Think you can heal me with some flowers?"

Aisling clenched her jaw. "Troy."

He rolled his eyes, the right one less swollen than yesterday, and loosened the tightness in his shoulders. "I went to the pharmacy for cough drops, and –"

"You're sick?"

"Not the point, Aisling," he growled. She grimaced. "I was jumped on the walk home by three guys. They didn't even take anything. They just beat me and ran."

Her eyes fluttered shut.

"Luckily someone saw it happen and called the cops. They took me to the hospital." The ice in his voice refroze. "I called you because I was scared."

Guilt flooded through her, oily and rancid in her blood.

Troy laughed. "But I should have known better. I only get you during waking hours, and even then, it's a half-assed relationship." He lifted his lip in a sneer. "They asked me who I wanted as an emergency contact. I told them I had no one."

Her fractured soul quivered at his words. "Troy, I..." she trailed off, unable to verbalize what she so desperately wanted to.

"I needed you, Aisling." His voice shook. "I needed you there with me, but you were so lost in your dream that I couldn't reach you. It's happened so many times these last few weeks. I've needed you, and all I've gotten is an empty husk of the woman I love." He rolled his shoulders back. "You're lost to your dreams and lost to me. I don't know who you are anymore. I'm alone again after you swore you'd be here."

Nausea churned in her gut.

"But it's okay. I know how to be alone. So go be with your dream world, with your dream friends, and have fun. I won't hold you back with reality. But I might not be here to pick up your broken parts when your mind ruins what you've created."

It was the last thing he said to her.

Three days went by. He ignored her very existence. No matter how desperately she tried to talk to him, how many times she called or begged him to forgive her, she received nothing but icy silence.

She wanted to scream and cry and rage. Wanted to tell him every single thing she had learned in her sleep. Wanted to tell him what was happening with her soul and how terrified she was to make the final decision because she couldn't imagine leaving him.

But he wouldn't breathe the same air as her.

So she swallowed her fear and guilt and pain, and continued to live in a world she no longer cared about. There was a numbness that coated every cell of hers in this reality—a feeling of being lost or separated from half of her soul. The bond flickered incessantly when the panic began to set in. She held onto it, letting the warm golden glow anchor her when she felt like she was drifting aimlessly into the sea.

She survived off a single muffin she swiped from the kitchen and a guzzle of water a day. There was no food left in her cabinets or refrigerator. She wouldn't tell Kaida.

Bills piled under her door. She threw them in the trash.

She was off tomorrow. She lived to sleep.

As the darkness came to take her home again, Aisling wondered what she was still doing in both worlds – why she felt the need to split herself when it was obvious she was done with this one.

Troy's furious face popped into her mind. She fell asleep.

FORTY

She was in a black void.

There were no stars, no planets or sun or signs of life.

Just... darkness.

Her body was shadow. A thin golden cord wrapped around her torso in an unending loop.

She floated aimlessly. The space was empty, and she was empty of all thoughts. But she was cold. Cold and... terrified.

To her right was a tunnel of black. An oily sheen covered and rippled the end of it.

To her left was another tunnel ending in a brilliant warm glow. The bond around her chest pulsed as if it recognized it.

Aisling shivered as realization washed over her. This was what Kaida talked about. This was the partition between her lives. The veil between worlds. This was where her soul would float forever if she didn't choose.

She would become nothing. No one. Whatever she thought she was before was nothing compared to what her soul would endure here.

Panic flooded through her. She pushed forward through the heavy, thick darkness. It clung to her with a stickiness like molasses, attempting to keep her in its eternal grasp. Her soul ached as it plunged toward the beaming light on the left.

She knew Troy was behind the dark veil. Knew he deserved to know what was happening and what she had decided to do, but she couldn't force herself in that direction.

The bond hummed with every inch she gained toward the warm brightness. Her exhausted soul twitched in pain against the constant push and pull of the two realities and the unrelenting pressure of the void.

She heaved a broken sob of relief as she tumbled forward into the bright light.

FORTY-ONE

"Reports say they're moving northwest toward Solisse," Kaida called out as they dressed in their armor. The bells tolled with a frenetic beat, shaking every exhausted bone in Aisling's chest. "We might be able to intercept them and avoid any civilian loss if you move your asses now."

"Can't go any faster!" Amerie shouted as she sheathed her blades at her side, all traces of her bubbly personality dampened. Cielle and Elaila mounted their dragons and disappeared from the Lair. Aisling's fingers shook as she worked to clasp the corset armor.

"Stop," Kaida commanded, taking the armor into her hands and clasping it in less than a second. Aisling moved toward Morana, but Kaida grabbed her elbow. "Take this." She shoved something cool and small into Aisling's pocket. "Wear it. Give it back to Declan when we return."

Aisling looked into Kaida's bright eyes. Her mouth opened. She needed to talk to someone about her broken heart in her other world. She wanted to tell Kaida everything that had happened when she stepped through the planes just before. She wanted to speak it out loud to someone, wanted so badly to tell someone that she was close to breaking. She wanted to scream to anyone who would listen that she had seen the void, the endless nothing of her soul's future, and threw up on her bathroom floor minutes ago as soon as she woke from terror.

But this was her burden. Her choice. And she would handle it alone like she always did.

She slammed her mouth shut.

Kaida stared up at her, brows pinched with concern at whatever she saw on Aisling's face. Aisling scurried away from the all-knowing eyes of her leader and jumped onto Morana's back. They entered the Pit. The dragons were electric, fires curling between their teeth as they stomped and chirped impatiently. Soren and Kaida appeared a moment later, a beacon of silver and darkness wrapped in one soul.

"Do not get off Morana," Koen called from Neera's back. "You aren't there yet. But you can fly."

She nodded, the bond between her and Morana effervescent with anticipation. The Ferox shot into the sky, traveling westward at breakneck speed. The ground below them changed quickly from craggy rock and grass to lush rolling hills and bubbling streams. They passed houses and towns, sailing high above the rooftops in a race against time.

Aisling reached into her pocket for whatever Kaida put inside. She opened her hand but curled her fingers against the wind. Kaida had given her a necklace: a long black cord made of leather with a vial on the end. She didn't know what to make of the glow inside, the brightness that seemed to shine like a captured star contained in glass. She fought the wind and threw it around her neck before lowering her stomach against the saddle.

The landscape changed minutes later. The green became sparse, intermixed with bright pockets of red and orange dirt. The trees thinned until they were nothing but islands against the angry tint of the land. Dark gray clouds littered the sky, heavy and oppressive with the threat of a storm.

Her throat tightened at the sight of a city miles ahead. Rooftops of red clay baked in the intermittent sun. People scattered in the streets with palpable tension. Their fear seeped upward, tainting the air as she flew closer.

Morana chirped as specks of black emerged from the endless sky ahead. Aisling's fury was instant, almost blinding. Fire boiled in her blood, and Morana didn't send a wave of her shadows to cool it.

The beasts became clearer with every flap of wings. There couldn't be more than twenty. Their wild dark eyes devoured the morning sunlight. Their black scales glittered like a layer of slime on rock. She bit back the bile of disgust.

"Stay on Morana!" Koen shouted again from beside her before Neera dove toward the city. Morana peeled upward, barely escaping the jaws of a Cruento in time.

The beasts screeched as they collided with the dragons. The air shuddered with every wild flap of wings. Morana dove, eliminating three beasts in the span of a second. Blood danced in the air before falling prey to gravity.

Oryn and Nyssa shone against the morning sun, his silver blade and her golden wings a treasure trove of violence as they sliced through body after body. Soren made quick work of his prey, dropping them unceremoniously into Neera's shield. The sizzling sound of their bodies burning crackled through the air.

It was over before it had started.

There was no more shrieking. No more beasts.

Neera's shield faltered before fizzing out. The rest of the dragons dispersed in every direction, scanning the horizon but finding nothing. Soren rumbled fifteen minutes later, and the dragons answered, landing just outside the town on the warm dirt. Kaida sheathed her blade. "Injuries?"

Aylim had a small gash on her cheek that Cielle inspected while whispering comforting words Aisling couldn't make out. Amerie leapt off Calen and stretched. Elaila and Oryn unclipped and looked over their dragons while Kaida came to reassure Cielle.

Koen jerked his chin toward the center of town where Neera remained, her head tilted to the sky. "No casualties or injuries on the ground."

"Any missing?"

He opened his mouth but snapped his head toward Neera. She bellowed to the sky in a frantic, panicked tone that sent a shiver down Aisling's spine.

A wall of black careened toward them from behind a string of dark clouds. At least fifty beasts flew directly toward the city. Directly for the grounded dragons and riders.

There was no barrier. Neera's shield wouldn't go up in time.

The bond flickered with a question.

Aisling answered.

Morana hit the sky. Aisling gripped the pommel as a concoction of adrenaline and fear and rage bubbled in her veins.

Someone screamed at them. Morana didn't stop. Aisling kept her eyes on the beasts swarming closer with bloodlust and insanity in every flap of their wings.

Their black eyes latched onto Morana, a single beam of light and hope against their darkness.

Morana rumbled deep in her chest. The bond trembled with shadow, a pressure Aisling had grown to crave.

They were feet from the wall of claws and teeth. Morana opened her mouth.

Aisling smiled as the sky turned blacker than night. Her necklace glimmered in the darkness, the only sign she was still alive.

The darkness didn't terrify her like it did in the void. It was part of her in this life.

Screeches echoed. Leather shredded. Teeth snapped. Confusion and disorientation blared around her. Something sharp sliced the back of her neck. Morana answered with a bellowing roar, jostling and twisting until Aisling didn't know up from down.

She unsheathed a dagger and twisted in the saddle, aiming the point up as Kaida instructed. It connected with flesh in the next breath. Thick, hot blood coursed down her arm and splattered her face. Again and again, she shoved the blades up, reveling in the screams they encouraged.

Flesh tore. Teeth snapped. Hot breath puffed on her back, her face.

Blue flame burst through the darkness.

Then red. And orange. And gold.

Burnt flesh hit her nostrils. Beasts screamed. Panic tainted the air.

Aisling felt Morana's unfiltered rage through the bond. Felt her teeth and claws destroying sinew and muscle. Felt the searing heat of fire just inches from her face as the dragons lit the sky with their wrath.

It went on forever or for seconds, she couldn't tell anymore. She was lost in the darkness, a herald of death and flame against the invisible enemy.

The sun eventually broke through the dissipating shadows.

Soren's crimson eyes were the first thing Aisling saw. Fear jolted through her as he opened his maw just inches from Morana's, snapping hard enough for the blood on his teeth to splatter and fall to gravity.

Morana didn't balk or flinch. She snapped her jaw back, a deep growl in her throat.

"So you're just as impulsive as your beast?" Kaida yelled, her silver eyes ablaze as she scanned Aisling's blood-covered body.

Aisling shrugged. Adrenaline coursed through her. "There wasn't time to think."

"I should ground you for that stint."

"Go ahead," she threw back, high on her boldness.

Kaida's eyes raged. "He's livid," she replied, dipping her chin to Soren.

Aisling met his crimson stare. "I'm not sorry, Soren."

His eyes flashed, the narrow slit of his pupils widening.

Amerie whistled just above them. "The pair you have, babe!"

One corner of Kaida's lip curled up. She said nothing as she and Soren angled downward. Neera's shield was a wall of flame feet thick, each inch of it licking and looking for flesh to burn. Black piles of ash and smoke sat beneath it, the beasts demolished into nothing more than dirty powder. Soren's blue flame created a hole for the rest of the Ferox to fall through.

Oryn and Amerie remained in the sky on patrol as Aisling, Cielle, and Elaila landed. Soren huffed dramatically as Aisling dismounted. She rolled her eyes and angled her head at the nightmare made flesh. "Be mad at me, not her, Soren. But we did the right thing."

Morana chirped in response. Aisling assessed her for injuries, releasing a breath of relief that none of the blood was Morana's. She planted a kiss on the shimmering scales. The bond pulsed in answer. Morana moved with the rest of the grounded dragons to form a perimeter around the town as Aisling followed Elaila and Cielle into the maze of buildings. No one was in the streets. No eyes peeked through the windows. An eerie quiet filled her ears.

Neera stood guard in the center of town. Her eyes locked on Aisling's. Cielle cringed and let out a low whistle. "Elaila. Come on, we'll canvas."

Aisling's brow pinched. "What about –"

"AISLING!" Koen's furious rumble echoed through the empty street, bouncing off the stone walls and tiled rooftops.

"Good luck," Elaila whispered with a grimace before disappearing with Cielle.

"Do *not* follow them," he roared from somewhere close. Aisling turned on her heel, the familiar bubble of anger he incited back inside her chest.

Her retort got lost on her tongue as he appeared around a corner and stopped just feet in front of her. Bright red blood drenched his armor. It seeped between his hair and sat in splotches on his tight face. His chest lifted and fell rapidly as his eyes devoured her, assessing her in the same way. "Are you hurt?"

She shook her head despite the slicing pain at the back of her neck. "Are you?"

He glanced down at himself as if just noticing the blood. "It's not mine."

A sharp hum of relief ran through her. "Who's is it?"

"No one's now." His eyes traced her face with a fierce heat. "What were you thinking?"

She shrugged. "I wasn't."

"You could have died! It was two of you against fifty."

"And?"

He recoiled. "And? Do you really have so little concern for your own well-being?"

"We did what needed to be done, Koen. I never got off Morana like you said." She lifted her chin in defiance. "And we never had a direct order not to go."

His hands clenched at his sides. "You can't just..."

"I can," she said, her voice steady and strong. "I can. And I did. And I would do it again." She gestured to the houses and buildings around them. "They wouldn't have had a chance if we didn't stop the attack in the sky. Blinding them was the fastest way to stun them and slow them down."

"She's right," Kaida said from a darkened corner, surprising them both. "I hate the way she went about it, but it was the right move. A smart one." She stepped forward, her boots clinking on the ground. Blood splattered her bright hair. "Instinctual."

"But –" Koen started.

Kaida turned her razor-sharp gaze at him. "But what, Koen?" He snapped his mouth shut. Kaida smirked. "Thought so."

Aisling forced herself not to shrink under the bright silver eyes boring into her.

"Morana needs to relay her plan before she brings out the shadows. We were a step behind, and that's unacceptable. We're a team. A family. It only works if we communicate. Tell Morana to do her part or Soren will make sure she stays grounded for the next week."

Aisling nodded, refusing to feel ashamed. "How were we not hit by the fire?"

"The necklace," Kaida said, angling her chin to the string still around Aisling's neck. "It's like a tracking device for us to find you in the shadows. The dragons know to avoid your light."

"Smart," she murmured, her finger absentmindedly finding the cord. "What is it?"

"I have no idea. Aedan had it made a long time ago. Whatever it is, it's the only thing that can penetrate Morana's shadows." She turned on her heel, pausing as she looked over her shoulder. "Good work, Koen. Did they talk?"

"Nothing of importance."

She snickered as she turned a corner. "The girls are canvassing now. If they find anything, they'll bring it to Neera. And Aisling, when we get back, go straight to medical for the back of your neck."

Koen's eyes cut into her. She grimaced internally. "How many?"

"Show me your neck."

"How many?" she repeated.

"Four."

Nausea bubbled in her gut. "How many women?"

"None. The three they tried to take are tucked under Neera's wings."

Her eyes fluttered with relief. No one taken. No one forced into a life of horrors.

"Show me your neck," he demanded. She gave in and turned from him, tugging her braid over her shoulder. He pulled down the back of her armor and she inhaled sharply against the air against the wound. His finger rested on the back of her neck, barely touching her skin, but her blood still fizzled. "When?"

She turned back around, desperately trying to ignore his warm body just inches from hers. "Recently."

The thin shred of patience Koen had left guttered from his eyes. She bit her lip to keep from smiling at his obvious fury.

"In the shadows?"

"Yes."

He took a single step back, all traces of anger gone. Defeat sagged in his shoulders. A heaviness hung in every measured breath he took. She found herself filling the spot he left. "I helped, Koen. I fought. Isn't that what you want me to do? What you keep telling me to do?"

His voice was flat. "Not at the expense of yourself."

"Every time we fly to battle, we risk that. Each one of us knows the possibilities." She clenched her jaw. "Why am I the only one getting a lecture on it?"

He opened his mouth. And shut it.

Aisling fumed. "My whole life has been a fight in a very different way than what we're doing now. I ached for something like this. To be able to make a difference. To do more than just survive." Her throat tightened. She swallowed against it. "I'm not going to apologize for what I did. It was the right thing to do. And I'll do it again and again until we don't have to do this anymore. Don't encourage me to fight and then yell when I do. It can't be both ways. I can't... I can't be broken down to nothing again," she whispered, her voice catching.

Koen's forehead creased. She didn't wait for him to question her. She followed the path Kaida took, leaving him alone on the empty street.

FORTY-TWO

The water forced a groan from her lips as she sank into its warmth. The mid-afternoon sun sparkled on the surface of the bath as she scrubbed the blood and dirt from her skin. She refilled it twice before finally relaxing, her body now clean and sparkling without a memory of battle beside the slice on her neck.

The medical team had treated it in less than five minutes. They were perfectly pleasant as they flushed the blood and slapped on a poultice before sending her on her way, instructing her on basic upkeep to keep it from infection. She wanted to tell them she healed a dragon using only flowers so this wouldn't be an issue, but she couldn't find the energy.

The water ran cold. She dried and dressed, throwing on a pair of simple linen pants with a white tunic and letting her hair fall to her waist to dry. The whole team had missed breakfast. The bells had started ringing just after sunrise, just after she woke up vomiting on her bedroom floor, and her stomach was furious.

"Hungry, too?" Oryn called from down the hall, shutting his door at the same time as her.

"Starving!"

"Come on. Let's eat."

"Your room isn't next to Kaida's?" Aisling asked, noticing he was two doors down from his sister. He made a face.

"Absolutely not. There are some things better left unknown, even to a twin."

She bit back a smile. "So her and Aedan..."

"Enjoy each other's company far more frequently than we realize." He shuddered as they took the stairs. "How did you like him?"

"Oh, he was not what I was expecting at all."

"Don't let his laid-back façade fool you. He's brilliant and devious and an absolute animal on the battlefield."

"He fights?"

"As well as any of us."

She wondered why his chest was so broad and why he filled out his shirt so well. "It makes it easier to fight for a leader who would do the same for his people."

"Perfectly put," Oryn said, slowly hesitating before stopping a few feet from the common room door. "What you did today, Aisling... was very brave. And I'm sure Kaida already talked to you, but you have to know how terrifying it was to see you and Morana attempt to take on the Cruento alone."

She nodded once and ducked her chin. Shame flooded her at his paternal tone. His hand rested on her shoulder. "Don't shy away from this. Look at me." She stared into his bright green eyes. He leaned forward. "You are not alone anymore. Whatever happened before, wherever you've been waking up, it's not here. The rules are different. Do not think that you are replaceable."

The air knocked from her lungs. "You know?" she whispered.

The corners of his mouth tipped up. "Kaida isn't the only one who knew a plane stepper all those years ago. You've been hiding it well."

She swallowed and tore her gaze to the floor. Her voice shook. "How long?"

"The moment the girls explained what happened. The eyes are the tell. They go milky and glassy, very different from someone who simply faints."

She glanced at the common room where voices trilled behind the door. "I'm not ready... I don't know how to tell them yet."

His hand dropped from her shoulder, and she ached for his comforting warmth. "You are ready. You're letting fear hold you back. They will think no less of you. In fact, I wouldn't be surprised if the girls ask you a thousand questions a day for the rest of your life." He breathed a laugh. "I know you haven't chosen yet. But you are getting stronger here, which indicates you're getting weaker there. Soon, you will have to decide. You know that, right? We cannot divide our souls and expect to live full lives."

"I have chosen," she started, shocking herself by speaking it out loud. "But –"

"I thought I heard voices out here," Amerie said from the common room doorway. She glanced between Oryn and Aisling and lifted her brows. "Is there something wrong?"

"Not at all," Oryn replied smoothly. "Aisling had a question about flying."

Amerie rolled her eyes and smiled. "He's like the dragon whisperer. Somehow he knows everything *and* he's gorgeous. Totally unfair." She disappeared behind the door. Oryn winked at Aisling before walking into the common room. Kaida rested on a loveseat with her legs dangling off the armrest, her back angled against Aedan's side. Cielle and Elaila laughed at something Aedan said, his handsome face animated and exuberant. They waved as Aisling walked inside.

"The Shadow Bringer!" Aedan called out with a smile. "I heard you had quite the morning."

Aisling shrugged noncommittally. "We all did."

"Oh, humility. That's rare in your type." A bread roll slammed into his face. He glared down at Kaida. She responded with a saccharine grin.

"Come eat," Amerie called from the counter where numerous trays and pots were lined up. Aisling chose a vegetable soup and an assortment of cheese and bread. She sat at the table beside Oryn and listened to the gentle chatter of relaxed conversation while she ate.

She felt full. Her heart, her mind, her soul. Is this what having a family was supposed to feel like? A bone-deep comfort surrounded by relief you could never replicate? She had been deprived of such basic human connection in her other life for so long that she wasn't sure anymore.

"How's the soup?" Oryn asked, nudging her from her thoughts.

She wiped the corner of her mouth and glanced at her almost empty bowl. "Uh, good. Looks like I've enjoyed it."

"Soup is the best lunch," Amerie declared, ripping off a piece of bread from her plate. "I'll stand by that until I die."

The rest of them made their way to the table. Aisling ate side by side with her friends as stories and jabs flew through the air. She found herself laughing more than she could ever remember. Cielle threw a grape at Amerie at one point and got it stuck in her hair. Amerie retaliated by putting small slices of cheese in Cielle's tea when she wasn't looking, creating a melted congealed mess that made Cielle gag.

Aisling got up twice for more food, filling not just her soul but her ravenous body as well. "Where are you putting it all?" Kaida asked with a laugh as Aisling sat down with another full plate. "You eat almost as much as Koen."

"Leave her be," Koen called from the door, heading straight to the counter. He filled his plate and made his way to the table. "She's put in some work training recently. Her body is probably begging for food."

Aisling swallowed her bite with a gulp. "Put in *some* work?" she mocked. "If I recall correctly, I've put you on your ass at least twice so far."

Kaida's eyes widened with delight. Aedan roared with laughter. Koen looked over his plate at her, a wicked gleam in his eyes that sent jolts of electricity down her spine. "Eat more. You'll need the energy for patrol tonight."

She balked and glanced at Kaida whose face remained neutral despite the challenge in her eyes. It had to be punishment for what she and Morana pulled today. Aisling's heart flared with panic. How was she going to manage to fight against the pull and stay in this world all night? What if she couldn't?

"Relax," Cielle murmured. "You won't be alone. Koen's going, too."

"Neera insisted," Koen said, sliding his eyes to Aisling's from across the table. "After their last patrol, she refuses to let Morana go out without her."

"It wasn't her fault what happened," Elaila said.

Koen brushed it off. "She'll never see it that way. I want to ease her mind. If Morana left with someone else, Neera would be beside herself all night, and I do not feel like dealing with that."

"Sweet beast," Aedan said. "And a wonderful friend. How lucky we are that the dragons adore each other!"

Kaida rolled her eyes and glanced to the corner of the room. Aisling reigned in her gasp at Anwir's lanky frame hidden in a corner of the stone walls. "Is he always this sentimental?" she asked. Anwir blinked before allowing himself a quick grin and nod. Kaida sighed. "You poor thing, Anwir. I hope he pays you spectacularly well for it."

Aedan scoffed. "I am not sentimental. Forgive me for having human feelings, Miss Lack-of-Emotion."

"Bicker downstairs," Oryn drawled over his cup of tea.

Amerie stood behind Aisling and ran her fingers through her hair. "I've been dying to braid your beautiful hair," she cooed. "Can I? I'll put it in my favorite style for patrols."

"You wear it down for patrols," Elaila responded.

"Because my hair doesn't look like this," Amerie snapped. "Hers is so much longer."

Aisling gave permission and Amerie dove in, her fingers expertly dividing and plaiting the hair. No one had ever touched her hair before unless you counted her mother yanking it or her stepmother hacking it off with a rusty pair of scissors. Aisling's eyes fluttered shut at the addicting touch.

It was like flying or being around these people. She was addicted but wasn't scared. It wasn't like her mother's addictions. They wouldn't destroy her. They would build her up bit by bit until she was the best, happiest version of herself.

A content breath left her lips. Every second she spent here was hardening the cement on her decision to leave. She and Troy's friendship had become... she had no words for it. He wanted nothing to do with her anymore. She couldn't blame him.

She had no family. No friends. No true future. There was nothing left for her there.

Maybe that was what terrified her the most – that she could leave another world completely and no one would even notice her absence.

The conversation drifted from the table to the couches. She sank into the cushy fabric beside Cielle and rested her head against the soft back. They grazed, devouring one snack plate after the other. Anwir had disappeared from his corner at some point, obviously bored with the casual conversation.

The afternoon sun began to dip, casting all it touched in a soft golden glow. Exhaustion still hung in her bones from her battle against the void. She glanced at the counter and spied the French press. "Is there coffee?" she whispered to Cielle.

"Behind the tea. I don't know if it's good anymore, no one has used it in so long."

Aisling put the kettle above the fire and placed the dark coffee grounds in the bottom of the press. Just before the kettle screamed, she took it off the flame and poured it on top of the grounds, pressing the handle down slowly. While it sat, she whipped milk by hand until it came to a beautiful froth. Moments later, she had a semi-decent latte cupped between her hands.

Cielle's brows pinched as she peeked into the mug. "What is that?"

"A latte."

"Latte," she repeated, the word foreign on her tongue. "Is it good?" Aisling handed the mug over and watched with delight as Cielle's eyes lit up.

"Would you like this one?" Aisling laughed. "I can make more."

"Wait, I want to try!" Amerie shouted. One by one, each person took a tentative sip from the mug. And one by one, every person begged for more. So Aisling got to work doing the one thing she could do with confidence. Her arm ached by the end. She placed the mugs on the coffee table and watched as they nabbed them like animals.

"Where did you learn this?" Aedan asked, his upper lip foamy.

"Who cares," Kaida wiped his lip and saved Aisling from lying. "Just keep making them."

Oryn shot her a knowing look and leaned back, resting an arm against the back of the couch. "This should perk you up for tonight."

"What exactly am I going to be doing?" she asked.

"Flying the length of the kingdom and monitoring for any suspicious activity."

"How will I know if it's suspicious?"

"Oh, you'll know," Kaida responded. "Morana will, too. Her eyesight is better than yours in the dark, so if she says something is wrong, believe her."

She took another sip. "And if something is wrong?"

"It's up to you and Koen to figure out what to do. If you can make it back in time to wake us, that's fine. If it's something the two of you can handle, even better. I personally don't like being woken up unless there's blood everywhere."

"They're never subtle," Amerie said. "If they're up to something they're stupid enough to make it known."

Dinner came and they ate on the couches, filling their already full stomachs to the point of bursting. She'd never felt so sated in her life. A quiet hum hung in the air, everyone perfectly content as the fire roared.

"You know what sounds good?" Koen said, his voice lower and more relaxed than she'd heard before. He leaned back against the couch with his eyes shut and smiled, his strong neck exposed. "Another latte."

Aisling cocked her head. "Say please."

His head lifted from the couch, the golden flecks in his eyes glowing against the light of the fire. He smiled again, brighter this time, causing her stomach to give a sickening lurch. "Please, Aisling, can you make me a latte?"

Elaila's eyes were wide as saucers. Aedan chuckled. "I like you, Aisling."

"Thank you, Your Highness," she said sweetly, making Aedan laugh more. She refilled everyone's lattes and smiled as they murmured their thanks with lips covered in frothy goodness.

She glanced at the sky above, the bright blue darkening with every blink of her eyes. "We'll leave in an hour," Koen told her, noticing her stare.

"Will this keep me up all night?" Amerie asked, pointing to the mug.

Aisling shrugged. "How well do you handle caffeine?"

Cielle snorted. Amerie glared at her and started speaking, but Aisling didn't hear it. The corners of her vision tinted gray and turned black within two blinks. The pull in her stomach tightened unbearably.

"Fuck," she whispered, placing her mug on the table as softly as she could with trembling hands. Every head snapped in her direction. The conversation stopped.

She forced herself to find Koen through the darkness. "Don't leave without me, okay? I'll be right back."

She slumped sideways against Cielle.

FORTY-THREE

The apartment was bathed in the weakening light of the moon.

Heavy bass pounded through the thin walls.

A siren blared from the street.

The bond fluttered.

Reality sunk into her body. Her exhausted, weak body.

Her bladder screamed even though she couldn't remember the last time she had anything to drink. She walked to the bathroom without opening her eyes, refusing to let herself anchor to this world.

Aisling had to get back. This world was now her nightmare — one she didn't want to return to.

It didn't matter that she was off work today, Aisling realized. She wouldn't have gone in anyway.

She met her bed again, ignoring the sharp springs against her now bony frame, and shut her eyes, praying the strength of her will and the subtle pull of her bond would be enough to push her through the void she knew was coming.

FORTY-FOUR

Aisling was floating.

Not in Anguid. Not at her apartment.

Just... floating in the abyss.

A bright glow twinkled at the end of the tunnel in the distance. The bond pulsed.

Morana.

Her soul was so, so tired.

She reached forward, forcing her arms to swim against the thick blackness around her.

Every inch gained was agony. But she pushed, gritted her teeth, and kept moving. Kept crawling through the thickness of her panic and despair toward the light. To her home. Her dragon. Her family.

It was so close, and yet, so far.

It would be so easy for her to give up, she realized. So easy to finally stop fighting. To give into the fear coursing through her soul and let the darkness devour her.

But Aisling refused to stop. Refused to allow her soul to be stuck in this terrifying abyss forever. She was going to be worth something even if she had to force it from fate.

A cry left her lips as she stretched her shadowed hand forward, her fingertips barely grazing the bright, pulsing glow she knew was the other half of her soul.

FORTY-FIVE

"Again?"

"Does she have a fainting disorder?"

"This happens often?" Aedan asked, his voice concerned and demanding.

Aisling's eyes opened. Cielle's thigh rested under her head. Her hand stroked Aisling's hair with soothing gentleness. Aisling sat up, panting, and refused to meet anyone's eyes. "It happens every day," she answered, attempting to calm the ragged breaths of fear in her lungs.

She had to choose. The void was going to take her.

"Why?" Elaila asked in an almost whisper.

Aisling's heart pounded. She couldn't hold it in any longer. Couldn't pretend or lie. She would not be a liability to these people. She looked at Oryn, his eyes warm as he gave the slightest nod of his chin. Kaida arched her brow expectantly.

"How long until we leave?" she asked Koen.

"Little less than an hour." His voice was tight, his dark eyes pinned on hers with a ferocious intensity.

She nodded and swallowed against her painfully constricted throat. "I am not from here."

Silence.

"Where are you from?" someone asked.

"Another world."

More silence, heavier than before.

Amerie burst into laughter. Aisling lifted her head. Fear and honesty poured from her eyes. Amerie's jaw snapped shut.

"When I... faint here, it's my other body waking up in my other life. My first life. I can only be here when I'm asleep in that world. And the other way around." She forced her lungs to inhale. "I was on the island for months. I thought it was just a dream. But I fell in love with it. I craved being there every day. I preferred sleeping to being awake. Then Morana came and everything changed."

She kept her gaze down, letting the words she'd kept to herself for too long fall from her mouth like vomit, acidic and raw on her tongue. "I thought my mind made this whole thing up as a reprieve from the shit life I lived. I thought..." she shook her head. "I thought you guys were figments of my imagination. But I became addicted to you. I started losing my mind a little bit in the other world. All I could think about was this one."

She forced her voice to strengthen. Forced herself to tell them everything. They heard about her mother and her neglect. Her father and his refusal to accept her. The brutal beatings her stepmom gave her. She told them about living on the streets for years and barely making it out alive. They learned about her life as a barista and her new baking skills.

She told them how devastated she became each morning when she awoke and of the void she'd been fighting as she traveled between planes.

"The stronger I become here, the weaker I am there, and the harder it is for me to make it through the void." She lifted her chin. "I'm still coming to terms with the fact that this isn't a dream. Some days it seems like it still is, like it's too good to be true. But you have to know that I never intended to hurt any of you or put you in danger. I have fallen in love with this life, this world. And with all of you." Tears threatened her eyes. She clenched her jaw. "I have to choose. My soul... it won't make it another switch."

Troy wouldn't even notice her absence. No one else would, either.

"I choose this life. I choose this world as my soul's home. The next time the pull takes me will be the last time I go there. The next time I enter this body, I'll be staying in it."

She was met with a deafening silence.

The fire cracked and popped. A door shut somewhere.

She prepared herself for their rage. Prepared to be torn to shreds for her lies and deception. It would be what she deserved, but it wouldn't keep her from staying in this world. She would go to her island, live off the land, and learn how to fish properly. She would rather spend the rest of her days there in peace than in her other life. Morana was more than welcome to join her.

The bond thrummed with a steady warmth – Morana's answer wrapped in unwavering loyalty.

Kaida broke the silence, her voice both matronly and commanding. "This changes nothing. We accepted Aisling the second she stepped into the Pit. She is Morana's bond. She is a rider of the Ferox."

No one spoke. Aisling forced her breaths to even and slow.

"So..." Amerie started carefully, "you know a lot about coffee?"

Aisling stared blankly. Nodded.

"You can't drink caffeine, you bimbo," Cielle muttered. "You'll be awake all night and annoying the next day."

"She's always annoying," Elaila said dryly.

Aisling watched the interaction with wide eyes. They didn't hate her? They didn't seem to care much at all.

"You could feel the bond even in the other life, correct?" Oryn asked. Aisling nodded. "Interesting." He shared a look with Kaida. "Could you feel it before the actual bonding?"

"I felt something." She placed her hand on her chest. "It was a pull. Like something inside of me knew I wasn't supposed to be there. I was supposed to be here."

Aedan leaned forward, his eyes bright as he assessed her. His voice was an awestruck whisper. "A plane stepper."

Aisling nodded once.

He pursed his lips. "Interesting. I've only read about your kind, and what I've read is minimal. There is almost no information about it." She didn't know how to respond. He shrugged and laughed. "While this shocks me, it does not change the way I feel about you, Aisling. I must admit I am more intrigued about this other world than anything. Do you know about the governing styles? The issues plaguing it?" She nodded, still unable to comprehend their reactions. Excitement twinkled in his eyes. "Are you available tomorrow? There is so much you could teach me."

"Take her in the morning," Oryn replied. "Her flying is good enough that she can skip a lesson."

Aedan glanced over his shoulder, murmuring to himself as he found a napkin and furiously scribbled on it. Kaida watched him for a moment before turning her gaze to Aisling, nodding once in approval.

"You knew," Koen whispered, his eyes darting between Kaida and Aisling. "You knew this whole time."

The room quieted. Aedan stopped writing, his shoulders tensing at Koen's accusation.

Kaida didn't flinch. "Yes."

Aedan whipped his head to Kaida in shock.

Devastation and betrayal made their way onto Koen's face, quickly masked with resentment. "This whole time..." His voice shook. "You knew how terrified I was. And you said nothing."

Kaida stared at him, her silver eyes glowing with the challenge. "It wasn't my call to make, Koen. It was always hers. And I respected her decision to wait."

"What if she never chose?" he cried as he stood and paced beside the fire. "What if she fainted and never came back? How were you going to explain that? Would you have buried her? Burned her?" His concern tainted the already thick air. "What if she died here, Kaida? What would have happened to her soul on the other side? What would have happened to Morana if her bond died?"

A flip switched at the mention of her dragon. Aisling stood, her veins bubbling with a plethora of emotions threatening to drown her. "Don't yell at her."

His eyes burned as he whirled on her. "She –"

"Did the right thing." Aisling let him see the fire in her own eyes, let him see the ugly truth she'd worked to keep hidden for so long. "Don't be mad at her. Be mad at me. I was weak. I didn't want to tell you because I didn't know which life I wanted. Not at first. I didn't know if I would be accepted or if you'd treat me the same way you did when I first got here. I didn't want to deal with that forever. So I waited. I learned. I watched the way you guys interacted with each other."

She looked into every pair of eyes in the room. "I waited until now because I was terrified," she choked on a sob, "terrified, that the truth would change the way you looked at me. I have spent my entire life invisible. I have been useless. Weak. I am worth nothing there. But here, I'm someone. I have something tangible to fight against. I have people to fight for. So I kept it to myself because I thought it would be easier than letting you know the truth of who I am. The truth of who you've allowed in your ranks."

A tear sliced down her cheek. She didn't stop it. "I don't know why it happened or how. I don't understand much about being a plane stepper at all, but I know that because of all of you, because of Morana, I want to live again. I don't question why I'm alive anymore or wish that I wasn't. For the first time in my entire life, I am looking forward to having a future."

Her whole truth laid bare. Her fractured soul finally had nothing else to hide.

Aisling turned on her heel and left the room without waiting for a response. She tugged on the bond as a steady stream of tears fell down her face. Morana met her in the Pit a heartbeat later. "I need..." Aisling rasped, unable to speak. Morana extended her leg in a silent answer.

They were in the sky in the next breath. The chill sunk into her bones. She ignored it, focusing only on the wind and infinite heavens around her. The sea churned far below with hissing white caps against the deep blue of the water.

Morana knew what she needed. A constant warmth flooded the bond, anchoring Aisling against the whirlwind of her thoughts. Her mind quieted. The deep ache in her chest lessened. Her body sagged as the weight of her secret disappeared. The truth was freed, and she'd never been more exhausted in either one of her lives.

Whatever happened now, whatever they decided to do with her, she could handle. She had lived two lives simultaneously with a fractured heart. She had ridden a dragon and fought against creatures set on killing her. She had traveled worlds.

She knew who she was.

She was a fighter. She didn't just survive. She followed her dream and changed her fate.

It would be enough for her.

Morana descended as the chill settled in Aisling's bones with a shiver. The warm light of the Pit guided them back like a beacon. Neera waited in the sand with Koen beside her. Aisling's coat and gloves were in his hands. The rest of the Ferox and the King stood in the large doorway.

Aisling didn't speak as she dismounted and donned them, her body sighing in relief at the warmth against her skin. She didn't make eye contact with anyone as she clipped back into the saddle and Morana launched back into the sky to begin their patrol.

FORTY-SIX

The continent blurred under Morana's wings. Even in the darkness, it was beautiful.

The small town of Anguid shimmered below. Tiny buildings and taverns scattered across the grass and rocks. Warmth seeped from the chimneys of stone houses. A twinkling of music rang out as they ascended over the town square.

They traveled north where nothing but rocks and sharp cliffs stood against the sea. The land curved to the west, shifting from rock to dirt in a blink. Flickers of small fires lit the ground under them as they passed over livestock fields and small towns. Dirt turned to lush green grasses. Forests popped up. Mountain peaks licked the clouds.

Aisling felt Koen's stare on her skin but refused to acknowledge it. Neera flew beside Morana in silence. Their wings made no sound in the crisp night air. The moon peeked between clouds, dousing Morana in a silky sheen of light. She blew a steady stream of shadow, blanketing herself from the light as they traveled south.

The scent of warm salty air hit Aisling's nose, and she worked to keep from crying as the memories of the island came flooding back.

If she could go back in time, would she change it? Would she have run from Morana instead of helping her?

No. She had needed Morana more than she could ever understand. Even now on her back and cutting through the sky, she didn't fully understand how desperately she needed her dragon.

The bond between them flared with light, pure and unyielding. Aisling rested her hands on each side of the pommel, stroking Morana's scales in answer as if she could make the beast feel her devotion.

The sea was calmer down south as they flew over small cities and villages. There was a calmness, a peace, which transcended the constant state of fear the people had gotten used to. She smiled as they danced in the streets and swam in the sea under the moonlight. Music drifted into the clouds.

They passed over the field where Morana ate all that time ago. Aisling was thrilled to see hundreds of livestock in the fences. Morana turned her head, her eyes flashing, and Aisling let out a laugh. "No food right now. When we get back I'll let Declan know you're owed."

They turned north, following the coastline toward the Latebros mountains they had slept under. The sea raged. House-sized waves crashed against the dark stone cliffs with relentless power. Morana banked to the sea, bypassing the mountains with a low rumble in her chest as Neera sailed high overhead.

Her head snapped to the cliffs on the left. Aisling saw it a second later – a small flicker of flame halfway up the cliff face. Aisling threw her intent down the bond and Morana followed without hesitation, chirping once to inform Neera.

Morana flew at sea level past three rock archways. Her wings brushed against the surface of the cold water as they neared the rock face. At the last second, she banked upward. Aisling fought against gravity, her knuckles white around the pommel. The saddle clips strained as gravity threatened to pull her under.

Morana's massive claws found purchase just under the ledge of the opening. She angled forward enough to take the pressure off Aisling's clips. A second later, her shadows blanketed them from view. Aisling held her breath at the sound of voices inside.

A man's pinched voice snorted. "They have seven. We have almost two hundred. They don't stand a chance."

"Their beasts are bigger," another male voice responded, his tenor deep and brawny.

The first man chuckled. "Size doesn't matter when you're that out-numbered."

Their fire crackled. Aisling held her breath.

"If we take out the big fucker and the white one next week, they don't stand a chance."

"Too bad the beasts don't follow a single command," the first man snorted. "I think this is the stupidest batch that bitch has produced."

The bond stilled.

Favilla.

"Maybe she's tired," the other said.

"It's what she's made for, innit? What they're all made for. Might as well put her to use."

"She's tiring out. They're making too many. It's getting impossible to transport them all. If she goes, we won't have nothing."

The first man laughed, shrill and raw against the roaring of the sea. "You can't push a female too far, idiot. It's what they're made for – pushing and poking and prodding. The only way you push them too far is if they die." The fire cracked again, sending a tendril just above Morana's shadows. "We push until we get what we want. Beast and human alike."

"And if we go too far?"

"Then she dies, and we still have an army perfectly hidden in plain sight. The King is stupider than people realize."

One of them coughed. A shrill screech echoed from deep within the rock. "Stupid fucking things," he murmured. "The Ferox almost does us a blessing some days."

The second man hesitated. "The beast they caught to mate with her, what is it?"

"You don't know?"

"I'm asking, aren't I?"

"No one knows what it's called. They've never seen another. But it was big enough to fuck her, so that's all that mattered."

Morana let out a splitting rumble, shaking the rock enough to send shards crumbling into the sea.

Silence followed.

Feet shuffled across stone.

Morana was covered in shadow and in the air before they peered over. Her wings pushed against gravity in silence. They broke through a thick cloud above a mountain peak. The shadows dissipated. Aisling gulped a breath. Neera's bright eyes were the first thing Aisling saw.

"Favilla," she breathed, the first words she had spoken to Koen in hours, "They're talking about Favilla."

Koen's eyes widened in shock. Morana and Neera chirped. "You're sure?"

"Yes." Her hands shook as she brushed loose hair from her face. "The beasts are in there, too. We heard them." Morana rumbled in agreement.

Koen's face tightened. He glanced down as if he could see through the clouds. "What else?"

"They're attacking next week. They want to take out Soren and Morana." She glanced northward. "I know Kaida said she only wanted to be woken if there was blood but –"

He shook his head. "This is better than blood. It's a promise of it."

They flew north a second later, the dragons pushing their wings to the limits as they speared for Anguid.

Soren took up half the sky above them.

Neera and Morana had talked to him through their bond as they flew toward Anguid. He woke Kaida. The pair was already in the sky by the time Aisling and Koen arrived. Kaida stopped their crusade just before the mountain range.

"It'll be a three-part attack," Kaida called over the wind. "Morana first. Then Soren. Neera's net will catch any stragglers. We will not speak the entire time. Use your bonds and the dragons will use theirs."

They dipped low with the moon as their only companion. Neera and Morana flew under Soren's wings, hidden from the light as they crept closer to the flickering flame, the beacon of hatred in the darkness. The bond twinged with anticipation. Morana strained to keep the shadows contained, leaving a trail of darkness on the surface of the sea as they passed over the rolling waves.

Soren slowed. Morana moved forward from under his wing and climbed to the ledge where the men were still talking and screeches echoed from the cavernous space behind them.

Morana didn't stop under the ledge like before. She hovered in front of it. Her shimmering scales glowed luminescent in the moonlight.

The reflection of their fire danced over her, painting her in rich shades of orange and red. A lurch of satisfaction rolled through Aisling at the horror on the men's faces, both of them ashen with mouths parted in shock.

Let this be the last thing they saw: the dragon of shadow and death and the woman who shared its soul.

She winked. Morana exhaled, dousing their light and bathing them in thick darkness.

They screamed.

Morana lifted. Soren took her place seamlessly, shoving his massive maw into the mouth of the cave and igniting the darkness in flames of bright blue.

The screams multiplied. Not just human screams, Aisling realized with blood-curdling pleasure. Soren pushed and pushed his flame into the darkness until the screaming stopped. When he was satisfied, he came to Morana's side. Neera's net went up last, a brilliant red-orange shield against the dark of night.

Two beasts fell through, their skin sizzling as they hit the water below.

Another one fell.

Three more.

They counted fifteen in total, all burnt and impaled by the unforgiving shards of rock below. They waited for more, but none came. An eerie silence hung where death had been.

The first glow of sunrise tinted the sky in a pale lavender. Morana glistened in it, dipping and diving with the current as they flew home.

FORTY-SEVEN

Neera and Morana chirped like school girls when they entered the Lair. Aisling found Declan inside and insisted Morana get the extra meal she was promised. Koen talked with the big burly man in the front corner of the Lair just beside a narrow door. Both men's brows were knitted together. Aisling stepped to Koen's side. "Gareth, right?"

The man's face relaxed. He nodded, his warm eyes too familiar for her to place. "And you're Aisling?"

"I am," she smiled, extending her hand. "I've heard wonderful things about you. It's a pleasure to officially meet."

He took her hand with both of his. "An honor. If you or Morana need anything –"

"You'll be the first to know." She said a polite goodbye to him and Declan and walked into the hallway with exhaustion of every form threatening to break her.

"Aisling," Koen called, his deep voice bouncing off the rock walls. He fell into stride beside her.

She didn't look at him. "Where did Kaida go?"

"She's with Aedan in the common room."

"What happens now?"

"I'm not sure," he admitted. "Kaida and Aedan have to figure it out. We did enough for right now. We get to sleep for a little."

She walked down the stairs. Her door beckoned. Rest beckoned. "I haven't slept in this bed yet," she thought out loud. She'd wanted to, but her other life usually took her before she had the chance and left her crumbled unceremoniously on the stone floor.

"The beds here are as nice as they look."

"I think I'd even love my shitty apartment bed right now." She thought of the thrifted mattress on the floor and the scratchy sheets with a grimace. "No. I take that back."

Her hand clutched her doorknob. His hand landed on top of hers. She stared at it, ignoring the rush of heat to her system.

"When..." his voice came out strained, "when did you know you were going to choose us?"

She looked up at him. "Does it matter?"

His pained expression thawed. "Why didn't you tell us earlier? We wouldn't have -"

"Look in the mirror, Koen, and tell me why I didn't tell you the truth earlier." She shook her head and turned her attention back to the door. "Think back on all our time together from the very beginning and let me know what you come up with."

Her hand turned. His fell from her skin. She stepped into her room and slammed the door.

Aisling shrugged out of her clothes, not bothering to change or bathe. The fluffy white robe cinched at her waist, and she tumbled into the gigantic bed without shutting the decadent velvet curtains as the morning light streamed in.

She lied to Koen. He had nothing to do with her decision. If anything, he made it clearer. The tiniest twinge of guilt attempted to weasel its way into her head, but she doused it with shadow as sleep took her under.

She was again in the abyss. Again forcing herself to hold onto the warm glow of her bond and the boundaries of the brilliant white light at the end of the tunnel.

The oily sheen in the distance rippled in the windless void. She clenched her jaw against the weak pull. She would only go back to her old life one more time, and she wasn't ready yet.

Aisling plunged back into the light.

She woke in a sweaty panic and threw herself into the bath. The water and warm shades of late afternoon calmed her nerves enough to stop the trembling in her hands.

Kaida said she would just have to choose which world she belonged in to make the switch. But Kaida hadn't seen the void. Hadn't felt the bleak emptiness of it or the raw fear that slithered into every cell as it caressed her soul.

Aisling knew it was time to choose. Her weary body on the other side wouldn't be able to handle another switch. She needed to fuel this body as best she could before the sun fully set.

She threw on a basic set of leathers and ambled to the common room for energy to make it back to this plane. The girls were inside, and she inwardly cringed at memories of her honesty the night before. She filled a plate with everything and anything that was in front of her and took a seat at the table. Amerie rested back in her chair. Elaila sat silently, her gaze planted on something out of the window. Cielle leaned forward. "Favilla is still alive?"

"Barely it sounds like," Amerie responded.

"Kaida's been with Aedan all day. I don't think she's slept yet."

They continued talking while Aisling finished two plates full of food. Despite sleeping, she was exhausted. Would it be better when she made the switch? She imagined it had to be. Her soul would be one again, forged anew.

"Tell us about your other life," Cielle turned and prodded, her face open and warm.

Aisling paused. "You don't - you're not mad?"

"Why would we be mad? This is so wild," Amerie laughed.

Cielle brushed a short hair from her face and tucked it behind her ear. "You could have told us as soon as you landed here."

"I didn't even know. Kaida ended up telling me the next morning. I didn't know if she was lying."

"What made you realize she wasn't?"

"The bond," Aisling answered. "I felt it in my other life. It's like Morana could still hear me. She could still feel my emotions. I knew a dream wouldn't do that."

"Amazing," one of them whispered.

"We aren't mad at you," Elaila said, turning her face toward them at last. "If anything, we're upset with ourselves that you felt you couldn't tell us sooner."

Aisling swallowed another bite and put her fork down. "You guys did nothing wrong. You've treated me like one of you from the beginning. None of the guilt is on anyone but me."

"Guilt has no place here," Cielle murmured. "We all have issues. We will never look at you differently because of your past. We care about the now and the future."

"And we care about you," Amerie said, reaching across the table and holding Aisling's hand. "Since you showed up like the badass you are that day. I fell in love with you instantly." She squeezed her hand. "It's platonic though, babe. You are gorgeous, but…"

Aisling smiled while a burning pressure built behind her eyes.

"You're our family now," Elaila insisted, her dark hair hanging like a curtain around her face. "Don't ever think of yourself as no one again. You're a member of the Ferox. You ride Morana. You are worth more than you know. And we plan on making sure you feel it every day."

Aisling didn't try to stop the tears that raced down her cheeks. She needed to feel them, needed to feel the warmth and the emotion of each drop. Relief coursed through her. "What would you like to know?" she asked weakly.

There was a moment of silence. Then they all spoke at once.

She lifted her hands and burst into laughter. "Okay. Write it all down. And when I come back, I'll tell you everything."

"Where are you going?" Koen asked. His silhouette lurked in the doorway.

"You have *got* to stop creeping around like that," Cielle hissed.

Aisling glanced out the windows. The sun was close to setting. Time wasn't on her side. "To my other life."

The room fell into tense silence.

Elaila spoke first. "Are you coming back to us?"

Aisling rolled her eyes. "Of course."

Cielle went to stand. "Do you want us to be with you?"

She shook her head. "I don't think Morana would appreciate it. It was just her and I at the beginning. It should just be us now. Besides, you need sleep. I'll be back in the morning like always."

Elaila stood anyway and pulled Aisling into a tight hug. Amerie and Cielle joined. The four women stood together, limb entangled in limb for a long minute. "Come back to us," one of them whispered through a thick throat. Aisling swallowed her emotions, refusing to believe this was the last time she would see them, and nodded as she stepped out of their love. She smiled weakly at her friends before walking to the door, sidestepping Koen.

His hand gripped her elbow. She glanced up at him over her shoulder.

He said nothing as he held her gaze. It was neutral. Neutral, but thick with something she didn't want to understand just yet. She forced her breathing to remain even despite the warmth flowing through her blood.

"You going to say something, Koen? Or can you let her go so she can return to us already?" Amerie said, her voice silky and taunting.

His grip disappeared. Aisling felt his stare on her as she walked down the hall. Felt the searing heat of it against her back as she entered the Lair.

Her blood pulsed with every step. She was going to make it back here. She had to. Fear wouldn't get her anywhere. She was going to come back and get to live the life she was born to.

Morana's head peered out from her door. The violet eyes were gentle as Aisling placed her hands on either side of her snout. "I don't know how to do this," Aisling whispered. She closed her eyes and rested her forehead on Morana's glimmering scales. The void haunted her every thought, every breath. She could feel the sticky tendrils of nothing clinging to her skin, pulling at her soul to keep as a treasure. "What if I never come back?"

"Oh, but what if you do?" Oryn responded. Aisling jumped back, shocked to see him leaving Nyssa's door. "*What if* is no way to live your life, Aisling. You will come back because this is your home." He rested his hand on her shoulder with a comforting squeeze. "All you have to do is fall asleep. The bond will anchor you here. Follow it home." He placed a kiss on top of her head before disappearing through the Lair door.

She glanced at Morana. "Do you think it's that easy?"

Morana blinked once. *Yes.*

Aisling grimaced. "There's only one way to find out, I guess." She waited for her dragon to get comfortable in the sea of blankets before crawling into the crook under her wing. "Do you think I'm making the right choice?"

Yes.

"Are you sure you made the right choice?"

A huff. *Yes.*

She rested her head against Morana's stomach and sighed.

Aisling knew she was making the right decision. This life would give her everything her other couldn't. There was a future here for her. A family. A dragon. A life so violently full of love and hope. There was something to fight for that was more than just her own survival.

This place was her home. Kairossen. Anguid. The Pit. Morana's room. All hers.

Her vision darkened. A tug pulled at her stomach.

"Bring me back, Morana," she whispered as the darkness took her under. "Bring me back home."

FORTY-EIGHT

Aisling swam against the darkness, away from the golden cord anchoring her to Anguid, to Morana. Her arms burned as she hauled herself forward through the inky shadows toward the world she no longer wished to be part of. She cried out as her soul shuddered against the pull and the innate longing to be where she belonged.

She had to see Troy one more time. He was the only reason she had stayed divided for so long. The only anchor she had to her old life. She needed to sever their cord as cleanly as possible.

As she pulled and dragged herself forward toward the inky oil curtain one final time, the bond shuddered in pain, and Aisling nearly lost herself to her agony. The void laughed at her, tickling her with its darkness and sinking its terrifying cold nothingness into her soul in a taunt.

Aisling bared her teeth and clawed her way back into her old life for the last time.

FORTY-NINE

She was awake two hours before her alarm.

The time wasn't wasted with a shower. She cleaned her apartment and threw out anything that wasn't important, which ended up being almost everything.

Aisling forced herself to stare at the horrific reflection in the mirror.

Her skin had become nearly translucent. The light in her eyes, weak to begin with, had gone out. They were brown pits of nothing now.

Her cheeks were hollow. Every bone pulled against her sallow skin. Valleys dipped between her ribs. Her hip bones jutted out like shards of rock from the cliffs.

Dead. She looked dead.

She smiled, pulling the skin taut against her face.

Good. This part of her was dead. She would kill it.

She went to work an hour early and lost herself in baking. The hum of the mixer settled her weak, restless heart. Her hands sank into the dough at a slow tempo while excitement coursed through her sluggish veins for her future.

Eva showed up after some time and fell in line perfectly with Aisling's rhythm. Vivienne came in next. Then the other two. Troy said hello to everyone but her. She tried to reach him, but he didn't allow her to get a glimpse of his hazel eyes all morning.

His voice was a sledgehammer to her heart. A heart that once belonged to him. He was the only reason she had even come back. She didn't know what she wanted to say to him, but she couldn't leave him like this.

It felt selfish to choose her own happiness. After everything they had been through, did she owe him to stay? Would it be right to remain miserable so long as they were miserable together? It would only be a matter of time before he found something better. She would never have that luxury. She had to seize her happiness.

She came up beside him, blatantly ignoring the line of customers. "Troy –"

He walked away. Bitterness coated his steps. Aisling's already damaged soul hollowed with every inch he distanced from her.

"Excuse me?" a familiar voice called from the counter. Aisling gritted her teeth and turned. "I asked for non-fat milk."

Red Lips. Her dark hair was still perfectly styled in a sharp bob, not a single stand out of place. She pushed the cup toward Aisling with an impatient click of her nails.

Aisling felt herself snap. Felt the last piece of her old life crumble in her heart.

She took the cup, opened the lid, and stared into the frothy milk she knew was non-fat.

She lifted her eyes, meeting Red Lips's, and spit into the coffee.

She shut the lid, placed the cup on the counter, and pushed it toward her with a rictus grin.

Red Lips cocked her head, her eyes searching Aisling's face for a long moment. "I was wondering when you'd grow a fucking backbone," she murmured, dark and husky, before winking and tossing a wad of cash in the tip jar. She left without her coffee, ignoring the gasps of the other customers as her heels clicked along the floor.

Ryan bolted through the kitchen door; his eyes lit with silent fury. Aisling didn't give him time to speak.

"I quit," she laughed, and threw her apron to the floor. She walked out the front doors of the café a moment later, a grin on her face as she passed the line of shocked customers. The weak morning sun hit her face, and she turned up to bask in it, wondering if it was the same sun in her other life.

"What the *fuck* is your problem?" Troy yelled just feet from her. She whirled on her heel. His apron fluttered in the morning breeze. They stared at each other in the middle of the sidewalk. People bypassed them with a wide berth.

"Oh, so you can talk to me."

"You're ruining yourself, Ash!"

"No, I'm not." She smiled. "I was already ruined, Troy. I'm fixing myself."

"What are you going to do now?"

"Live."

"Where?"

She angled her head. "You know where."

He scoffed. "What – so you think you can live in a dream? You think you can sleep all day and night and not have to deal with the consequences?"

"Something like that."

He stared at her, disgust and worry bright in his eyes. She memorized them – the deep green outer ring and spots of brown, the tiny dots of gold that showed in the sunlight. It would be the last time she'd see them. The first person, the only person, in this life who had seen her soul for what it was would be nothing more than a painful memory.

"You're insane," he whispered.

Her grin felt gruesome. "Maybe. But I don't want to get to the end of my life and be haunted by what could have been. I told you I'm tired of surviving. I have a chance now to live. I'm going to take it."

"In a *dream*, Aisling? It's not real!" His finger pressed into his chest, his voice breaking. "I'm real! I'm real and I'm standing in front of you *begging* you to look at me. I'm begging you to see me again, Aisling. To remember who you are and what you mean to me." A tear fell down his cheek. "But you've lost yourself. And I've lost my soulmate to a fucking dream."

"What if it is real?" she snapped. "Have you ever thought about that? That there could be more than one world, one life?" She looked at the sky. "It's infinite, Troy. We aren't the only ones looking at it." She moved, stopping just inches from his bewildered face. "I ride the sky. I dance in the wind and part the clouds. I douse the heavens in shadow. I will choose that over this any day."

The air between them thinned. She held his gaze, watching as his shock morphed from pity to sorrow. He took a tentative step back and shook his head. His voice came out weak, nearly inaudible against the din of the city. "I love you, Aisling. Really and truly, I do. You mean *everything* to me. But I can't handle you destroying your life like this. I can't... I can't watch you die like this," he choked on a sob. "I hope you find what you're looking for."

He walked back into the café, narrow shoulders slumped as he silently wept.

Aisling stood in the middle of the sidewalk and stared at nothing as her heart, as her soul, finally shattered.

FIFTY

Troy,

I want you to know that I love you. I will always love you until my dying breath.

I am so sorry I wasn't there for you when you needed me. I will live every day with that guilt and self-loathing. You deserve so much more than me. I think you can see that now.

I understand what you said and why you said it. I've been too much lately. Too much of nothing, if we're being honest. I know I promised to be here with you, but it became impossible.

I've been living two lives. My soul has been stuck in two worlds, and I haven't been able to function in this one for a long time.

I didn't know it was possible. There's a term for what I've been doing. It's called 'plane stepping' – when a person can have a foot in both worlds, and their soul is divided in sleep. Every time I woke up here, I was asleep there, and the other way around. I have no idea why I can do it and neither does anyone else.

At first, I thought it was just an ornate dream. You know, we discussed it. But I couldn't shake the feeling of it being right. I felt so at peace there, like it was somewhere my heart could finally relax and just be. I've never once felt that way here.

When Morana fell out of the sky and into my life, I thought I had created a friend to heal my loneliness. But I felt her even here. I felt her in my chest, a pulling tug that took my breath away.

Morana took me to her home when she healed. I met the rest of the Ferox. The leader, Kaida, heard about my 'fainting' spell and knew exactly what I was. So I've known for a while, I guess, what I am.

But how could I explain it to you? How could I tell you that I would eventually have to choose which life to dedicate my soul to before it shattered, and that one of them would mean losing you?

I only told the Ferox the truth yesterday. Or last night. Honestly, I don't remember. Time is confusing now. But I just told them. And they accepted me without hesitation, knowing I hadn't been fully there the whole time, and I wondered why you couldn't have given me the same courtesy. I wondered why someone I loved couldn't give me the same understanding that I desperately needed. I don't blame you though, I want you to know that. None of this is your fault. I handled it so poorly that it's actually embarrassing.

The other life is better than this one.

The Ferox consists of seven dragons and seven riders. We are the main force against the Cruento. They're this group hell-bent on making women secondary beings. They stole our eighth dragon a few years ago and have been forcing her to mate. They have their own creatures because of it. They're dumb, but they're vicious. They're what attacked Morana and why she landed on the island with me.

The Cruento attack innocent people all over the continent of Kairossen. The beasts attack from the sky and the Cruento members, hidden in plain sight, capture women of all ages and force them into a trafficking web. You can only imagine how terrible it is. And we can't tell who the men are because they have no discerning signs. It could be anyone.

We fight against them. For women. And for everyone. Because in the end, the Cruento don't just attack women. They attack mothers and daughters, wives and sisters. They ruin homes and decimate entire villages.

The Ferox is wonderful. Kaida is the leader. She's wonderful and terrifying. She's very tiny with silver eyes. Her dragon is Soren. It's ironic because he's the biggest one, and she's the smallest human.

Oryn is her twin. He's tall and lean and handsome and so, so kind. I have a feeling you would fall in love with him instantly if you ever met. His dragon is Nyssa. Her wings are dipped in gold.

Amerie is a firecracker. She's bubbly and bright but a menace in a fight. She took me as a friend without a moment of hesitation. Her dragon is Calen.

Cielle is steady and reliable. She's someone you want as a friend. Her dragon is Aylim. She looks like the moon. I know it sounds weird, but if you could see her you'd understand.

Elaila is strong and painfully kind. Her story is devastating. It's amazing to see her now after knowing all the horrible things that happened to her before her dragon found her. His name is Osiris.

Koen is... I'm not sure. I don't know how to explain him anymore. I thought he hated me. But now? And god, he's so hot. You'd never be able to speak to him.

Anyway, his dragon is Neera. She's Morana's best friend.

And Morana... she's wonderful. She breathes shadow instead of fire, which is funny because her scales are so stunningly bright. She chose me, which led to us bonding.

The bond is hard to describe. It's like there's a cord around my heart that's a direct connection to hers. We can speak through it with emotions. I can feel her here now. I cannot tell you how beautiful it is to have a soul connection like this. How understood I feel now. How SEEN I feel.

And I want to be part of it. I want to be able to fight for those who need it. I have a chance to be the person I needed in this life.

I wasn't lying when I told you I wanted to live. I just don't want to live here anymore. I can't do it, not with the cards I've been dealt. This other life will give me what I need. My soul knew it long before I did.

I know now that I deserved so much more from this life than what I was given. I know that I'm strong and fierce and capable. I deserve this happiness.

You do, too. You deserve to wring out every drop of happiness from this life, Troy. Go to school, move somewhere else, do something to find your joy. You're smart and capable and funny, and so wonderfully, painfully loyal. The world could be yours if you took it.

There are no words to describe how much you mean to me. You were the one thing that kept me tethered to this life. No one in either world meant more to me than you. I hope you know how loved you are. That even in my other world, my soul will still hold nothing but love and adoration for you.

And I hope you dream. They aren't just something your mind makes up in your sleep. They can be an answer your soul has been searching for. If you find one that brings you peace, brings you joy, I want you to go after it with everything you have. Don't run away from something that seems too good to be true.

One day, I hope you can forgive me for this decision. Whenever we reconnect, in whatever world or afterlife, I hope we can share a cheap ice cream cone and talk about everything and nothing.

Until then, you can either toss everything I have piled up or keep it. If you donate the one pile, please donate to the shelter I scribbled on the sticky note. It's the only one I ever felt safe in.

I want you to know that it doesn't hurt. I was never in pain. I simply fell asleep and let myself dream.

You are my soulmate. The love of my life. And I will love you in every life, every world, every breath.

-Ash

PS- now can you see why I never invited you over?

Aisling wiped the tears from her cheeks and placed the note on the counter beside the meager pile of clothes he could donate. She didn't spare a final glance at her apartment before she crawled onto her mattress.

What a story her life would make in the end. Homeless. Barista. Baker. Plane stepper. Dragon rider. Shadow bringer. Dream conqueror.

The bond shimmered.

Aisling smiled as she fell asleep in her old reality for the last time, letting her breathing slow until her heart stopped beating, her last thought only of the bond in her chest, her guiding light home.

FIFTY-ONE

She was nothing, but she was shining.

The bond glimmered in the eternal darkness, her anchor against the unending void.

She'd been here for hours. Maybe days. Time stopped being real.

There was no point in fighting the darkness. It became her, and she it. It didn't reach for her anymore. It eased her forward through the bleak expanse of nothing toward the light she knew was home.

Her shattered soul was healing. The cracks filled as her new life replaced the old one. The bond glowed white hot. It extended into her bloodstream with an effervescent sheen of power, of joy. She laughed in the darkness as the weight of her old life fell away. Possibility replaced it. Hope and fight took its place.

She was Aisling, Shadow Bringer and Harbinger of Death. She bowed to no one. Dragons bowed to her. She was the light in the darkness, the dream turned reality.

The darkness softened as she eased down toward the light. She twirled her shadowed fingers in the brightness, in the glow of her new life, and smiled. The bond fluttered as she descended, as her mended soul entered her new body for the first and last time.

Aisling's heart pounded in a steady rhythm. She opened her eyes.

FIFTY-TWO

Bright amethyst eyes stared at her from above.

Aisling gasped at the strength of the bond. She could feel *everything* – Morana's excitement and nervousness, her apprehension and tension.

"I'm back," she whispered, her voice low and strong despite the shock still coursing through her. Morana's relief was palpable. Aisling gazed in wonder at the pearlescent scales glistening in the low, warm light of the torches. She stroked the bony plates with a smile. "All yours."

Morana huffed before blinking once. *Yes.*

She was Aisling's, and Aisling was hers.

Aisling shut her eyes, soaking in every sensation she could. The smell of smoke and brine filled her nostrils. A dragon snored down the hallway. Morana's scales lay beneath her fingers.

Her skin begged to touch the sky. She needed the wind and infinite openness against her.

"I need to fly," she whispered, the urge stronger than anything she'd ever felt before. Her dragon blinked once before extending her leg. Aisling climbed up and sat bareback as Morana stalked into the Pit and lurched into the air.

She'd never felt anything so exquisite. Whatever she felt before was nothing compared to this. The wind was in her blood, a song of freedom and power. She didn't feel the chill as Morana climbed through the clouds. The morning sun rested on the horizon, sending rays of pink and purple and yellow in a welcome that brought tears to her eyes.

Her soul was finally healed. The weight of her first existence, the suffering and constant fear for her future was gone. There were no cracks, no jagged edges or empty holes. She was whole and full and herself.

She allowed a single tear to fall for her old life. A tear for the abusive, neglectful mother she hadn't seen or heard from in over a decade. The father who never wanted her. For the hurt and pain she had endured by the people who were supposed to unconditionally love her.

And she allowed a tear for Troy. For the love she would always hold for him, the love she knew he still held for her, and the hurt he would feel because of her selfishness.

The bond shimmered with Morana's happiness. Aisling let her tears fall into the ether and sent a wave of her own through the bond, laughing as Morana roared her claim and joy through the sky. They flew until the sun ascended and the pink and purple morphed into a brilliant blue. They landed in the Pit and Aisling jumped down.

"Do I look different?" she asked.

Morana blinked twice. *No.*

"Hmm. I feel..." she muttered, looking over her body like she'd never seen it before. Her hair was still long, her body strong and lean. There was something different, but she couldn't place it. Morana stood before her, blinking slowly in boredom. Aisling rolled her eyes. "Fine. Go eat." Morana turned to the Lair doorway. "Wait!" Aisling took her dragon's face in her hands and stared into her beautiful eyes. "I'm forever grateful you chose me, Morana. I hope I can make you proud with this life we're going to live." She placed a quick kiss on her nose.

Morana paused before resuming her walk into the Lair. A minute later, a flood of warmth drowned the bond and Aisling clutched at her chest, the sensation of love overwhelming enough to leave her breathless. She walked slowly to the common room despite the excitement buzzing in her veins. Her stride felt surer, more confident, than ever before.

Elaila's soft laugh twinkled through the open door of the common room. Oryn's lyrical voice and Amerie's squeal of delight came next.

Her steps faltered.

Real. This was real.

She had chosen to live. Chosen a family.

Tears threatened to fall at the overpowering rush of peace that sank into her bones. She took a few steadying breaths and leaned against the stone wall to calm her heart until it wasn't a thundering beast in her chest.

Koen's deep laugh came from inside. It was rich and velvety against her skin. Electricity tingled down her spine in a way she'd never felt before. She stifled her gasp of surprise, willing the feeling to go away. A minute passed. She regained control of her body, pointedly ignoring whatever just happened, and sucked in a heaving inhale.

Aisling stepped into the doorway of the common room.

A deafening, roaring silence greeted her.

Six pairs of eyes landed on her.

A blush crept up her cheeks as the silence dragged on.

Finally, Kaida leaned back in her chair with a sly smile on her face and lifted her glass. "Welcome home, Aisling."

They were the most beautiful words she had ever heard.

Amerie glanced around the table. "Is no one going to talk about how good she looks?" She jumped up and threw her arms around Aisling, swallowing her in a bone-crushing hug. She pulled back, her warm hazel eyes dancing over Aisling's face and body. "Seriously," she whispered, "when this war is over, you and I are going out to have some fun." She wiggled her brows and Aisling let out a rough breath of a laugh.

"Give her a chance to breathe, you animal," Cielle said. She wrapped Aisling in a hug.

Elaila came up next and held her with fierce gentleness. "Are you okay?" she whispered.

"Perfect," Aisling replied.

Oryn took her hands in his. "Welcome home, Aisling. We are honored you chose us." He kissed the top of her head and whispered, "Amerie is right. You look wonderful."

Her brows pinched. "Morana said I looked the same."

"Morana is a dragon. She thinks all humans look the same."

"Do you feel different?" one of the girls asked.

"Yeah," she admitted with a weak smile and gestured to herself. "I don't know how though, if that makes sense."

"Your soul is fully here now," Kaida answered, still seated. "You're going to be stronger and faster. Your fighting skills will progress quickly." Aisling shot Koen a glance. He sat at the table beside Kaida, his dark gaze intense enough to send her pulse racing. Kaida smirked. "You'll have him on his ass in no time."

"I've had him on his ass multiple times."

Koen's brows lifted over tired eyes. He leaned back and rested his thick arm against the back of the chair beside him. "I look forward to it."

"So!" Amerie clapped, wiggling her brows and breaking Aisling from Koen's stare. "We have to celebrate. How about coffee?"

"Absolutely not," Cielle muttered. "I am not dealing with a caffeinated you all day. Besides, Aisling shouldn't make her own celebration drinks. It's tacky."

"I don't mind," Aisling said.

"We still have a job to do," Kaida drawled. The energy in the room shifted as they took their seats around the table. "There was no movement on last night's patrols. They're probably still reeling from the night before. Aedan's troops are inside the known Latebros passes. Whatever is left of that cave will be cleaned out by the end of the night."

"There can't be much left," Koen's brow pinched. "We annihilated it."

"Still. We need to make sure it's clean. If it's a nest, we can eradicate the problem in a single swipe."

Oryn rested his arm on the back of Elaila's chair. "And Favilla?"

His twin stared at him for a moment. "They know what to do if they find her."

Aisling's stomach churned. The joy of earlier came crashing down at the thought of murdering a dragon. The rest of the Ferox seemed to be on the same wavelength.

"If they are using the mountain passes, we need to prepare to fight there," Kaida continued.

"I thought they had already been searched?" Aisling asked.

"They have been, numerous times. That's why this is so infuriating." Kaida rolled her shoulders against the obvious tension in them. "We're training in the ravine this week. Individual drills and assault drills. Our sparring will be inside the ravine, as well. We need to prepare to fight without our dragons in case. The ravine is the closest thing we have to a cave or mountain pass." She looked at Aisling. "You'll be training twice a day. The mornings will be spent in the ravine. Afterward, you and Koen will work in the Pit."

"We'll need the lattes then," Amerie said with a feverish grin. "Right?"

Cielle dropped her head on the table with a groan.

"Fine," Kaida relented. "Lattes all around. Then we fly."

Aisling taught Amerie the steps and poured each drink into a mug. Kaida leaned against the stone wall, her silver eyes missing nothing as she watched the girls work. "After you get settled, Aisling, I want to hear about this other world."

"Oh yes, please! I've been dying to hear about it." Amerie smiled and walked a handful of mugs to the table.

Kaida took a mug from Aisling. "I always wanted to ask the other girl, but with everything going on, I didn't have the chance before she disappeared."

Aisling cupped her mug between her hands. "How long was she here?"

"Only a few weeks, but Neera held off on bonding with her. I think she knew it wouldn't last."

Aisling wondered if Morana –

"She never thought that," Kaida answered as if she could read Aisling's mind. "You were a done deal. We just had to wait for you to realize it."

"Did the girl ever say anything about her other life?"

"Nothing. She was quiet and reserved. It was almost impossible to talk to her, actually." She shrugged and sipped her drink. "Then she told us she was pregnant. I knew then that she wouldn't stay."

To do all of this pregnant... Aisling couldn't imagine. It would be an impossible choice. Would she risk her child's life to make herself happy? Or would she rather suffer to keep the baby safe? She cringed. Kaida nodded. "I know. No one wins in her situation."

Aisling felt a crushing sense of sorrow for this mystery woman saddled with an impossible choice. "Do you remember her name?"

Kaida frowned. "It was almost three decades ago now. Give me a minute." She shut her eyes with a frown. "Delilah. Her name was Delilah. I remember because it sounded like a flower."

Aisling's heart faltered. Her fingertips prickled before going numb. The mug fell from her hand and shattered on the floor, spraying hot coffee in every direction. A shrill ring filled her ears, her mind.

Delilah.

Her mother's name.

Warm hands gripped her elbows to keep her upright. She was somehow walking. Somehow seated on a couch. She saw nothing, heard nothing except the ringing in her ears.

It all clicked at once. The hatred her mother had for her, the constant blame she felt as a child, all because her mother had given this life up.

"My mother," she croaked. The hand on hers stilled before continuing to stroke the top of her knuckles. The warmth soaked into her, thawing the freeze in her lungs. She inhaled sharply. "It was my mother."

Kaida and Oryn exchanged a look. "How old are you?" Oryn asked.

"Twenty-six."

Kaida's face paled. Oryn bit his bottom lip – the first time Aisling had ever seen him look remotely flustered. "Can you tell us about her?"

"Is that the best idea right now?" Koen murmured from her side, his thumb pausing on her skin. Aisling swallowed thickly and squeezed his hand in answer. The deep crease between his brows relaxed as he met her gaze. She inhaled sharply and pinched her eyes shut at the memories.

"My mother had a problem with drugs since I was a baby. It's why my father never wanted more from her and ended up leaving. He made it clear that she never did drugs before I came along."

Every gear finally clicked. There was no more jam, no more blockage or confusion as to why she'd been treated so horribly.

"She would always talk about going to another world. I just assumed it was where she went when she was high. But she had this grand sense of self. She would constantly tell me about all the potential she had before I came along. As I grew up, I thought she had a mental illness, but she refused rehab or help. She insisted she wasn't insane." Aisling cleared her throat. "It got worse the older I got. She was erratic. It wasn't safe for me to be with her."

"How old were you?" Oryn whispered.

"At this point? When I knew I had to leave? Sixteen or seventeen, I think. She didn't even remember my birthday, so I just added a year every New Year's Day."

The common room was silent. Aisling dove into the memory she kept locked away in the pits of her soul, letting every bit of pain latch onto her heart.

"She attempted to use me as a bartering chip for drugs one night. We were in this shack full of men. There was smoke everywhere. Guns were spread on the table. And I was so upset because I needed to be asleep. I had a history test the next day that I wanted to do well on." Her throat tightened at the memory, the sheer terror that coursed through her when she realized what her mother was doing. "She told the men I was worth two worlds combined." Aisling lifted her face to the sky, refusing to let a tear fall over her mother. "I didn't know what that meant then, but now it makes sense."

It wasn't the drugs that ruined her mother's life. It was Aisling. She had ruined her mother's chance at happiness, at living wild and powerful and strong like Aisling was doing now. Her mother never forgave her for it. She had ruined –

"Stop it," Kaida commanded, her voice a tug in Aisling's chest. "You are not to blame for your mother's decision. She had every opportunity to stay here. We were going to tell her that, but she disappeared. We would have raised you as our own. The two of you would have wanted for nothing."

How wonderful would her life had been if she had grown up here? Her heart ached with the thought.

But it wouldn't be *her.* She wouldn't have known the struggles and hardships. She would have been weak in a different way, weak mentally.

"Guilt has no business in your heart, Aisling. Anger, yes. But guilt?" Kaida's jaw feathered. "You will never feel guilty for being born. You are a survivor. You should be proud of yourself for what you've accomplished. You're everything that she was not."

"If you saw her today, right now," Oryn asked, "would you be able to forgive her for everything because you know the cause of her cruelty?"

Aisling wanted to say yes. She wanted to be a good person, be the bigger person. She wanted to say she forgave her, but it would be a lie.

She shouldn't have been left alone as a child for days at a time, forced to eat crumbs and dead bugs from the floor. She shouldn't have learned how to use the bathroom by herself because she kept getting horrific diaper rashes. Her throat should never have been raw from crying desperately for someone to love her, hold her. Her mother should have been there.

Aisling was not a currency to hand out. She wasn't something to barter or exchange. She was a human being who was worth something despite everything she had endured.

"No," Aisling answered. "I wouldn't."

Kaida's answering smile was dazzling. "Good. You came here to live. Do not lose yourself now to something you cannot change. You killed that life for a reason. Remember that."

"Your life starts now," Oryn said.

The bond warmed in her chest.

FIFTY-THREE

The ravine was just as dark and cold as she remembered.

Morana didn't seem to mind as she cut through the jagged rocks time and time again, pushing them out to sea like a rocket of blinding white.

It was an exercise in trust when they started the assault training. The dragons came at each other from every direction in the dark. Riders shouted at each other in warning. Roars and voices clattered against the sharp rocks at a deafening volume.

"No talking!" Kaida shouted at her breathless riders after their fourth run. The dragons hovered over the sea, each of their eyes bright. "We won't have the advantage of seeing what's happening if we fight in darkness. This needs to be as realistic as possible, so everyone shut up and run it again."

They did. Again and again, they attacked each other in silence. Aisling gritted her teeth as the other dragons barely avoided Morana's claws and teeth. She contained her own screams as tails and jaws whipped just inches from her face.

Aylim thrived. Her silver scales glimmered as she threw her tiny body into the deepest, tightest crevasses of the ravine, dodging and taunting the other dragons until they were whipped into a frenzy. Soren and Neera roared in frustration as their gigantic bodies were forced to yield time and time again while the rest of the dragons fought in the depths.

Aylim came at Morana from below, snapping her jaws inches from Morana's stomach. Aisling felt her beast rumble, the familiar vibration and pressure of her shadows building. She yanked on the bond, forcing Morana up through the darkness and into the blue sky above.

"Control her, Aisling!" Kaida yelled. "Her advantage would be wasted here. She needs to learn."

"Did you hear that?" she said, patting Morana's scales. "You're going to get us in trouble. And on my first real day, too." A single thread of shadows leaked between Morana's teeth. Aisling kept her in the sky until it dissolved and the tension disappeared from Morana's muscles.

The rest of the dragons popped up through the opening minutes later, painting the sky with their beautiful scales. Soren let out a rumble and the rest of the Ferox followed him to the sea. They landed on the rocky beach below the Keep.

"I'm going to beat your ass," Amerie growled as she jumped off Calen and stalked toward Cielle.

"What's wrong?" Cielle asked with a wicked grin, her short hair wild from the wind. "Hate not being the fastest? Can't handle someone's dragon outmaneuvering yours?"

Amerie's fist hit Cielle square in the jaw. Cielle's head whipped to the side. She snarled before turning on Amerie. The two of them became a flash of fists and feet. Their dragons watched in amusement, not a single drop of animosity between them.

"Good," Kaida cooed. "This is what we want. Real fighting." The girls stopped at the sound of her voice. Cielle's lip bled over her chin. Amerie's eye looked suspiciously swollen. "These men will not hold back because we're women. If anything, we'll infuriate them more. Angry men become reckless men. Reckless men make mistakes." She patted Soren's leg. "So let's make them livid. Cielle and Amerie, keep at it. Elaila and Aisling, you're paired up. Koen, watch them and critique." Elaila glanced at Aisling and grimaced.

Oryn cocked his head. "I'm honored, sweet sister."

"Don't be," Kaida grunted and stalked into the open mouth of the ravine, her bright hair a beacon in the darkness. Oryn followed with a fearsome grin Aisling had never seen before.

"Don't worry," Elaila whispered as they followed the twins into the ravine. Jagged rock stretched skyward around them. "They can't actually hurt each other. It's this weird twin thing."

"They can still beat the shit out of each other," Koen laughed from behind them.

Elaila shrugged. "Yeah. And it's fun to watch."

There was no preamble with the twins. Kaida turned, and Oryn moved in tandem like they shared the same brain. Pale hair danced in the darkness as they came at each other with deadly brutality, barely missing fatal hits with ease. Aisling's jaw fell open.

"They were mercenaries for Aedan's father as teenagers," Elaila murmured. "They're the best fighters in the kingdom."

"Get to it!" Kaida shouted as her fist connected with Oryn's stomach. The rest of them moved to find open spots amidst the rocks and sand.

"Don't worry about hurting me," Aisling said to Elaila as they paired up. "He's never once worried about that."

Koen crossed his arms over his chest and lowered his chin. Elaila rolled her eyes. "I still have bruises from him, I think."

"You poor thing!"

Elaila's eyes twinkled with delight. She pouted. "I know. So brave."

"You going to talk the Cruento to death or what?" Koen asked.

"Do you think we could?" Aisling lifted her brows.

Elaila opened her mouth, but Koen spoke first. "Whoever throws the first strike gets one free punch at me. I won't block or fight it."

The girls instantly moved on each other.

Aisling marveled at her new body. Kaida was right. It was stronger. She moved quicker than she ever had before. A new grace laced her steps as she deftly maneuvered over the rocky ground. Her punches carried more weight. Eventually, Elaila swiped a long leg at Aisling's ankle, sending her sprawling on the ground.

She was breathless and sweaty and aching, but so violently alive. She got back up and dusted the sand off her leathers, winking at Elaila in invitation.

Koen shouted pointers but never stepped in as Aisling was handed her ass repeatedly. After what felt like hours, Aisling crashed to the sandy ground after a well-placed swipe to her knees. She grabbed Elaila's dangling hand and pulled her to the ground beside her. In a single swift arc, she landed on top of Elaila's chest and used her knees to pin Elaila's arms to her side. Elaila gaped at her from below in shock. "Yield," she said breathlessly, a grin lighting her sweaty face.

"That's her favorite move," Koen muttered.

Aisling rolled off Elaila and onto her back in the sand. "You don't know any of my moves."

"I know all of them."

"Who gets to punch you?" Elaila asked.

"Neither."

Both girls shot up. "That's not -"

"You hit each other at the same time. It doesn't count."

"I think we both get to punch you, then," Aisling challenged.

Elaila rested her forearm on Aisling's shoulder. "Unless you're that scared of us?"

A squeal echoed against the stone behind them. Cielle and Amerie rolled on the ground, both laughing hysterically as the other became covered in sand.

Kaida sat piggyback on Oryn, her small legs dangling high above the ground as they joined the rest of the group. Neither of the twins had a spot of blood on them despite their brutal fight. She looked at Amerie and Cielle. "You two better?"

"No," Cielle said as Amerie helped her stand. "I still want to beat her to a pulp."

"So back to normal then," Koen responded dryly.

"Let's get back. Wash up before you eat. You all look terrible." Kaida lifted a brow at Elaila. "How did it go?"

Elaila beamed. "She pinned me!"

"And we both get a free punch at Koen," Aisling answered, looking sidelong at him with a cheeky grin.

"What!" Amerie shouted. "How do I get one of them?"

Kaida and Oryn's eyes flashed with delight as Koen shook his head. "A win for everyone then," Oryn sighed and carried his twin out of the ravine to the beach. The dragons rested in the sand, each with their wings spread wide to absorb the sun's rays. Morana opened one eye at their approach and yawned dramatically.

"Why don't they sleep outside?" Aisling asked no one in particular.

"It's safer in the Lair," Cielle answered. "Warmer, too."

"Especially if you're a diva like Morana," Amerie said, blowing a kiss to Aisling's dragon. "Poor Maura worked nonstop to make those blankets."

Aisling balked. "I thought they all had blankets."

"No way. Only her."

They rode back to the Pit and walked the dragons into the Lair. She headed toward her room, but Koen called from the hall. "No point in cleaning up. We're training after this." She groaned and turned on her heel, walking past him defeatedly into the common room where trays of food waited. They ate in companionable silence and finished just as the rest of the Ferox strolled in. Aisling and Koen walked into the Pit where the warm sun baked the sand beneath their feet. Aisling sighed as she crumbled to the ground and let the heat seep into her aching body.

"That's the worst way to train," Koen drawled from above.

She pinched her face and looked up at him. "Yeah, but it feels great. Try it."

"No."

"Your loss." She shut her eyes. A moment later the sand shifted. She bit back a smile as his warm scent hung in the air beside her. Her chin fell to the side. "Weak."

He breathed a laugh, his eyes closed. "Yeah. I know."

She couldn't take her eyes off him. He was relaxed and calm, a state she had rarely seen before. The sun hit the angles of his sharp jaw and cast shadows on the muscled planes of his chest.

He turned toward her and she flinched out of her trance. "What do you want out of this life?"

"Happiness," she answered automatically. "I want to live, not just survive."

"And you think you can find it here?"

She had found it the second Morana crashed from the sky. Meeting them, meeting him, had just been a bonus. She traced the strong line of his nose and the full curve of his lips with her eyes. "I already have."

Koen returned her gaze until a door shut from somewhere inside. He blinked and turned his face to the sky. "We could start training like this."

"How do you mean?"

"Since you're always knocked on your ass, you should know how to fight from the ground."

"You're so charming."

He rolled to his side and rested his head on his hand. "I'm serious. All the training we've done means nothing if you're on the ground. It puts you at a major disadvantage. You only got Elaila at the end because she was tired, too."

"Wow. Way to build me up." He did have a point, as annoying as it was. She sprawled her limbs at her sides. "Fine. Teach me."

"There's two ways," he cleared his throat, refusing to look at her. "The first is getting your feet on my chest and throwing me over your head."

"That's obviously not going to happen."

"You'd be surprised."

"What's the other way?"

She could have sworn a blush crawled up his cheeks. "You wrap your legs around my waist, then swing me off balance and onto my back. It puts me on the ground and you on the offensive."

"Are you trying to make me look stupid?"

"I never have to try to do that."

She scowled. "Fine."

He was on top of her a breath later. Aisling's eyes widened as his weight settled against her. He pinned her arms to the ground. His face hovered just inches above hers.

Every inch of her was going to burst into flame, and she didn't want Morana to douse her in shadow.

"Now bend your knees," he murmured, "And put your feet on my chest."

She followed his command breathlessly, contorting herself until her knees were pressed against her chin and her feet were on his chest.

"Push me off."

She hesitated.

"Push me, Aisling."

Her legs exploded upward, taking him with them. She gasped at her new strength as his fingers uncurled from her wrists. He flew to the side, landing diagonally behind her with a grunt. She twisted onto her stomach in shock. "Are you okay?"

He sat up, his face and hair covered in sand. A grin lit his face. "Again."

He flew every time. She insisted he go dead weight at one point, fearing he was letting her push him off, but she threw him easily. "You're stronger," he said at one point as he dusted sand off his shirt. "Since you…"

"Yeah, I can feel it. It's weird."

"Why?"

"Because I was never strong before."

"That's not true."

She shrugged. "It's not a lie either."

"You were strong in every way that counted." He stared down at her. "Ready to try the other option?"

She nodded and watched in wonder as Koen lowered and settled on top of her with practiced grace. She forced herself to breathe, to ignore the jolt of heat that ran through her every time his breath pressed against her neck.

"Now wrap your legs around me," he murmured. Her legs lifted slowly, wrapping around his lean waist and locking at the ankles. His jaw feathered. "Flip me onto my back."

"I don't know how," she whispered.

"Use that awful core of yours."

Her blood flared at his insult. She exhaled sharply and tightened her knees against his sides, pulling him flush against her before twisting her body to the right as hard as she could. Koen fell with her. He grumbled as his back hit the sand and her weight landed on his chest.

She wrapped her fingers around his thick wrists, slammed them into the ground, and stared down at him with tumbling exhilaration.

"Strong," Koen whispered, his chest heaving underneath her, eyes bright.

FIFTY-FOUR

Aisling was up before sunrise.

Morana stretched in the Pit, blinking slowly against her sleepy eyelids. The bond flickered with annoyance.

"Morning, sunshine," Aisling cooed. "Time to fly." Morana extended her leg. Aisling shook her head. "No. We've been through this. It's been three days now. You fly. I run." The dragon blinked twice before plucking the bond painfully. Aisling gritted her teeth against it. "Fine. Go ahead and sleep. I'm going on a run. If something happens to me and you aren't there, you'll be pissed."

Morana's annoyance ran rampant down the bond. Aisling walked from the Pit and shook out her limbs, willing them to warm before she began. The chill in the air didn't help. She threw her hair back into a simple ponytail and took off through the long grasses, keeping an eye out for any jagged rocks along the way. She pushed herself at a brutal pace, refusing to let this new body, new life, go to waste. She was going to wring out every drop of it she could.

The sun peeked from the horizon as she darted around the ravine. Morana appeared above, her scales catching the first rays of pink and purple light. Aisling ended her run at the northern cliffs with her hands on her knees, every breath a pant. Morana landed beside her. They watched the sunrise and brought in the new day, the new possibilities, together.

She hadn't dreamed since she'd permanently made the switch. Her sleep was nothing but black nothingness, but she didn't mind. If the cost of switching worlds was the inability to dream, she would take it. This life was her dream.

She didn't allow herself to think of her mother after the revelation. Kaida and Oryn were right. It didn't matter anymore. This new life was not going to be spent wasting time on old grudges or hurt.

But thoughts of Troy were harder to control. She forced herself to remember their good times and ignore the horror that had been their relationship before she left.

The sun made its full appearance, and Aisling rid her mind of any hurt to focus only on the bright possibilities of her new day. She ran back in a full-out sprint. Morana sailed above like a moving finish line, disappearing into the Pit when Aisling reached the doors.

Aisling stretched outside before making her way to the common room for breakfast. Cielle sat across from the fire with a book in hand. "Morning," Aisling called out.

Cielle put her book down, brows pinched. "Morning yourself. Why are you so sweaty?"

"Went on a run."

She whistled. "Making us all look like shit now, I see."

"Hardly," she said over her shoulder as she piled toast and eggs on her plate. "How was patrol?"

"Nothing to report. Oryn already told Kaida and went to bed."

Aisling wrinkled her nose. The Cruento men from the cave had said it would be a week. They were nearing the deadline.

"I know. But no news is good news. So we'll take it." Cielle took a sip of her tea. "Aedan is here."

"Oh, where?"

"Kaida's. He came last night."

She hadn't heard anything last night. After dinner, Cielle and Oryn went on patrol and she learned how to play cards with Amerie and Koen until far too late. The two of them took her for everything she had, which was nothing, but Amerie gloated anyway.

"Are they serious?"

Cielle laughed. "He is. He's made it glaringly obvious that the castle is hers. He designed his room for her and an entire wing strictly for the dragons."

Aisling gawked. "She's not?"

"She isn't sure, I don't think. I don't know why. He's the King. And even if he wasn't, he's kind and gentle and strong. And so good looking."

Aisling agreed with a lift of her brows and a nod. "Oryn doesn't care?"

"Nope. He just doesn't want to hear about any of it."

"Must be a brother thing."

"Do you have any siblings?"

Aisling choked on her tea. "No. Could you imagine my mother with another child? It's just me. Do you?"

"Nope. Just me and my dad. Mom passed away a few years ago."

Aisling flinched. "I'm so sorry. I didn't mean to pry."

"That's not prying. It's general knowledge. Dad and I are close though. He lives here, you know." Aisling tilted her head in question. Cielle smiled. "Gareth. That's my dad."

Aisling's jaw dropped. "That's why he looked so familiar..." She let out a laugh. "So you lived here your whole life? Or?"

"Yeah. Well, Mom and Dad used to live in Impellor when Dad was in the King's Guard. But then we moved to the Keep. When I was six,

I was sick one day and home from school. Dad let me come to the Lair to hang out with him even though Mom fought against it. Aylim took one look at me and pounced. Dad freaked out but Aylim wrapped her tail around him and threw him across the room. Then she closed her eyes and rested her head against my little chest, and that was that."

"Six is so young!"

"I know. Kaida and Oryn refused to let me bond with her until I grew up. We've been bonded seven years now. I came just after Amerie did."

"So your mom died after you bonded?"

"Yep. It was too hard for Dad to stay in the Keep with the memories and all, so Kaida and Oryn built him an apartment in the Lair. You've seen it, the little door at the entrance." Aisling nodded. It was inconspicuous and perfectly hidden. She thought it was a closet.

Amerie walked in and nodded a silent hello before grabbing a piece of toast. "What are we talking about?"

"How did you get here?" Aisling asked.

"I... walked?"

Cielle laughed. "To the Ferox."

"Oh!" Amerie snorted. "Calen found me after I ran away. I thought I was going to be a snack, but here we are."

Aisling took a bite of breakfast. "Why did you run away?"

She sighed. "My dad is like, really old-fashioned. As in, very pro-Cruento. They were making me marry this decrepit old man. And obviously, you don't waste this," she gestured to herself, "on someone like that. So I ran. Calen found me in the middle of the night and guided me here."

"That sounds awful," Aisling cringed.

"You should have seen the man. Moles everywhere. White hair. Crusty lips." Amerie shivered. "Sometimes I see him in my nightmares."

Cielle marked the page on her book and put it to the side. "Tell us more about you. What do you like to do in your free time?"

"I have no idea. I never really…" Aisling swallowed.

"I like to read," Cielle volunteered. "The Keep's library is mostly old tomes, but they have some good stuff there."

Aisling leaned forward. "There's a *library* here?"

Cielle smiled, warm and gentle. "I'll take you."

"Morning," Elaila chirped. She sat beside Aisling. "I like to write."

"Do you like to eat?" Amerie asked, pointedly glaring at the empty spot in front of Elaila on the table.

Elaila rolled her eyes. "Excuse me for wanting to say hello before gorging myself."

"Excused." Amerie grinned. "My hobby is boys." All four girls laughed. Amerie shrugged. "It's hard here for obvious reasons. But if we ever end this stupid war, I'm going to gorge myself."

Aisling didn't know why the question fell off her tongue. "The guys here, you haven't…"

"Ugh, no," she scowled. "Oryn only enjoys the company of other equally beautiful men. And the only time Koen looks at me is when he glares."

"He doesn't *always* glare at you," Cielle argued. "Just, over half of the time."

"Well, now he seems to be markedly happier, so maybe I'll only get a glare every once in a while." She trained her bright eyes on Aisling. "Keep it up."

Aisling blushed, her heart twisting in her chest. "I don't –"

Cielle pushed Amerie off her chair. "Are you incapable of having a single conversation like a normal person?"

Amerie's head popped up from the floor. "I'm going to beat your ass again today, Cielle. Mark my words."

"Consider them marked." Cielle rolled her eyes and mouthed a sorry to Aisling.

Elaila sighed heavily as she grabbed a plate. "You'll find a hobby, Aisling. It'll take time."

"I liked baking," she offered.

"If you can bake and make coffee, I think I'll marry you," Amerie joined Elaila at the buffet.

"Who's getting married?" Kaida asked as she walked in with Aedan.

"I'm marrying Aisling," Amerie said nonchalantly.

Aedan glanced between the two of them in confusion. Kaida nudged him with her elbow. "They're joking."

"It wouldn't be the worst thing to see," he said quietly. Kaida's jaw dropped.

Amerie kissed his cheek. "You'd get a front-row seat, Your Highness."

Aisling couldn't stop the laughter from bubbling up her throat at the absurdity of it all. Koen walked in with his dark hair ruffled like he had just gotten out of bed. A few glimmers of blonde twinkled in the morning sun. The corners of his mouth hinted at a smile at the sound of the laughter-filled room. He filled a plate and sat down with Kaida and Aedan.

"We're going to pause the ravine training today. The dragons need a break." Kaida took a bite of eggs.

"So do we," Amerie groaned. Kaida's brow lifted.

"Aisling," Aedan said from across the table, his bright eyes pinning her to her seat, "would you be willing to discuss your other world with me today? I know it's all a bit raw, but any information would be -"

"Absolutely. I don't know much, I'll be honest. But I know enough."

He smiled. "Enough is all I need."

"Before or after training?" Koen asked.

"Are those bruises not enough for you?" Kaida pointed to a few small blotches of blue on his arms. Aisling grimaced. She hadn't learned the extent of her new strength yet and it showed. Yesterday she made him grimace after a punch and apologized profusely enough that he threw her on her back to shut her up.

"I didn't mean -"

Kaida leveled her with a glare. "He needed them, trust me."

Koen glanced around Kaida to look at Aedan. "We'll do afternoon training."

"Hello!" Aisling chimed in. Koen and Aedan paused. She lifted her brow. "I'm sitting right here."

"Would you prefer to train in the morning or afternoon?" Koen asked, a smile in his eyes.

"Afternoon."

"This new life suits you, Aisling," Aedan remarked. "There's something radiant about you now."

"So I was dull before?"

He stuttered. "No, no. That's not what I was saying at all."

"Hmm."

The King sat stunned; his mouth parted in silent mortification. Kaida burst into laughter. The rest of the riders echoed it.

"So you call it a...democracy?" Aedan repeated slowly, his pen scribbling furiously on his notebook.

Aisling nodded. "Yes. The people vote on their leader." She glanced again at the beautiful room he had brought her to in the Keep. A few loveseats were scattered haphazardly across from a roaring fire and giant windows that faced the sea. She sat in one opposite of the King.

"And if the people don't agree with who won?"

"They deal with it. That's the beauty of it, I think. You had your say, but it doesn't mean your say is the only right opinion."

"Outstanding," he muttered to himself. "And tell me, what of monarchies? That's what this – I – am considered, correct?"

"Correct. They were popular a long time ago. They've kind of fallen by the wayside now. It worked before we knew how big the world really was."

"How big was it?"

She drew him a crude map, cringing as she finished. "This is a poor portrayal, but it's the basic gist." She pointed to the larger land masses. "There are hundreds of countries in these. It's not one single kingdom." His eyes widened as he took it in. They talked at length about everything political and geographical until she admitted she knew nothing else. Aedan switched gears then, delving into human rights and the issues plaguing her first world.

Tea and small snacks came and went multiple times until Aisling was positive her bladder would explode. Aedan leaned back against his chair and stretched his arms into the air. "You have been a wealth of knowledge, Aisling. Truly. I have learned so much in such a short period."

"Happy to help."

He continued staring at her for a moment before shaking his head. "When I heard Morana had bonded, I was floored. I thought to myself – it would take a very special person to handle that magnificent beast. And when I met you, I was shocked. Not that you weren't wonderful, Aisling. But you were normal. And it was so refreshing to see that someone could have flaws and struggle and still be worthy enough to bond with one of the most dangerous souls in the kingdom.

"I knew from the beginning that you did not see yourself as someone worthy of such an honor. But I held onto hope. Because what are we without hope? We need it like we need sunshine and water and air. We need to believe that good can still happen even when the world screams at us that it's impossible. And over time, you morphed into what you are now – fearless and strong and inspiring. Your plane stepping ability was a shock, of course, and something we need to look into further, but it simply added another layer to your wonderfully intricate history."

He smiled. "Your life has been full of trials and tribulations. This life will be no different. But I have full faith that you will excel here. You are proof that a little hope and strength of will can change the course of fate."

A blush ran rampant on her cheeks. "Thank you, Your Highness. I'm honored." She inhaled deeply. "Since we're being honest, I want to tell you that you're doing the right thing. This war is just. It's necessary. No group of people can truly succeed when they oppress another. I've seen it happen before, and it never ends well. The only time there will be peace is when every group of people recognizes each other as their equals, not their enemy." She cleared her throat and stood. "I am honored to be fighting for you. And I hope with time, I can make you proud. But until then, I am begging you to let me leave so I don't wet my pants."

Aedan's laughter bounced off the stone walls. He gestured to the door. "Go, Aisling! Don't ever ask me for permission for anything ever again." She threw him a grateful smile before sprinting from the room. His voice echoed from the doorway. "And stop calling me that. My name is Aedan to you!"

Aisling finally found relief in the lower-level bathrooms. She walked through the hallway, following the smell of freshly baked bread and roasting vegetables. Leonard's voice punctuated the air, accented by the slamming of pots and pans.

She poked her head in and watched the kitchen staff scurry around the room. Memories of the café rushed her. She ignored the pain they brought.

"You cannot hide that beautiful face from me, Aisling," Leonard called out with his back to her. She started. He turned and gave her a wink. "Come sit, come sit."

She pulled out a stool and sat at one of the enormous islands in the middle of the room. Leonard dropped a small plate in front of her. "Eat this. You are too pretty to not feed."

"What is it?"

He flicked his hand in the air. "What is it, she asks! Taste it and stop asking silly questions." She smiled and dipped a spoon into the soft mound before her. Her eyes fluttered shut as the lightly whipped dessert melted on her tongue, the taste of creamy chocolate and orange zest making her taste buds scream in delight. "Good, yes?"

She nodded vehemently and took another bite. "What is it called?"

"Mousse."

"I've never made it."

"You said you like to bake, yes? Tell me, what is your specialty?"

She laughed. "Oh, there was no specialty. But I did like making bread. Twisted morning buns were my favorite."

He stared at her. "Morning buns?"

She glanced around the busy kitchen. "I could make them for you if you'd like. I know you're busy but –"

Leonard took the stool from under her and threw it to the side. He shouted, and a young girl came to his side a heartbeat later. "Get Aisling anything she needs, sweet girl. And find her space in the oven. And…" He listed a string of commands. The girl nodded, her eyes darting over Aisling in quiet question.

Leonard stalked off to yell at someone else. The girl listened as Aisling rattled off the ingredients she needed and came back with everything in a small basket. Aisling got to work, falling into the calming rhythm of kneading and mixing with natural, practiced ease. She rolled out the dough and spread the spice mix before folding, rolling, and slicing it into strips. Each strip twisted beautifully and she waited the allotted time for them to rise before placing them in the oven. The smell hit her nose minutes later, a scent she was now very familiar with. It wafted across the kitchen, and she took pleasure in the way the staff turned their heads to smell them, too.

She placed them on the island when they were done, pleased with their golden brown skin and distinct plaits. Leonard came from nowhere and plucked a bun from the counter. His eyes widened as he chewed. He handed her a piece of paper and a pen. "Honor me by giving me your recipe."

She obliged. He thanked her profusely while she packed the buns into a tiny basket. Leonard swallowed her in a hug as she left and made her promise to come back soon. Slyly, Aisling handed the young girl a bun. She made her way through the meadow to the Pit and into the common room, delighted to find everyone there.

Unceremoniously, she placed the basket in the middle of the coffee table and plopped onto a couch with her legs folded beneath her. Elaila's curious blue eyes slid to hers before she peeked into the basket and pulled out a bun. She bit into it and gasped, covering her mouth with her hand. "You made this?"

Aisling smiled. The attention of the room swiveled to the basket. She held her breath as everyone took a bite and exhaled with relief as their eyes widened in surprised delight.

"I'll propose tonight," Amerie said around the food in her mouth.

"Leonard let you cook in his kitchen?" Oryn asked. She nodded. He lifted his brows. "You continue to surprise us, my darling." Kaida and Cielle murmured their agreement.

Koen reached for a second bun. She slapped his hand away. "I haven't had one yet."

"Do you even know how to be a gentleman?" Amerie goaded. He glared at her. "See?" she said, gesturing to his face, "He always looks at me like this."

Aisling smiled as she took a bun and bit into it, savoring the familiar smell and taste like a woman starved. She had missed baking more than she realized.

And she missed her friend who ate her bakes like a man starved. He would have fit in the Ferox beautifully, she thought to herself as she swallowed the bitter taste of her secretive heartbreak.

FIFTY-FIVE

It had been over a week since she made the switch, over a week since they learned of the upcoming attack, and the Cruento hadn't made a peep.

Kaida and Oryn were on edge. Aedan refused to leave the castle, insisting he be there for his people when the time came. He increased the number of soldiers in every major city. The soldiers along the Keep's walls were on constant vigil.

The Latebros raid had yielded nothing. The cave was empty save for the crispy bones, ashes, and melted metal that remained after Soren's blue flames. The mood in the Ferox soured when Aedan's report came in. It was a secret hope for everyone that they had finally weaseled out the enemy, but again they were somehow outsmarted.

They ran drills at all hours until they were able to fly and fight in the ravine in total darkness. The dragons were frustrated and frequently allowed themselves small bursts of flame or shadow to release the tension. Aisling managed to land a single punch on Oryn and took it as a victory despite the bruises he left on her. She and Cielle teamed up against Amerie and somehow ended up in a fit of laughter on the ground with tears falling down their cheeks. Kaida made them do pushups until failure as a result. Aisling could barely do five.

Three riders at a time did night patrols. They flew the perimeter of the continent before diving through the innards, checking forests and fields for anything out of place. Aisling caught a few glimpses of Impellor from the sky and marveled at the beauty of the large stone castle and the bustling city around it.

Tension simmered in the common room. Exhaustion seeped into their bones. Kaida begrudgingly decreased training sessions and insisted everyone take two full days to rest and recuperate.

"Even patrols?" Elaila asked.

"Even patrols. We won't be at our best if we're running ourselves ragged. They'll strike when we're at our weakest."

"So we cannot allow ourselves to become weak," Oryn finished.

Kaida nodded. "Exactly. So take the next two days to relax. But do not," she glared at Amerie, "leave this place. We need everyone here."

Amerie feigned hurt. "Why are you looking at me when you say that?"

"Don't make me regret giving you a break," Kaida demanded as she left the room with Oryn on her heels.

Cielle whistled. "She is missing him something terrible."

"This might be the longest she's been without him," Elaila answered. "She's having as tough a time as we are."

"At least she has a man," Amerie pouted. "I have been stuck with myself for -"

Koen groaned. "I am begging you not to finish that sentence."

"I don't consider it begging if you aren't on your knees, Koen."

Cielle rolled her eyes and looked at Aisling. "Library?"

Amerie and Koen were still squabbling as she chased Cielle down the hallway and out the door. They walked through the simple flower field and entered the Keep. Cielle pushed open a narrow unmarked door and gestured for Aisling to follow her up the shallow twisting staircase.

The smell hit her first – sweet and musky and nostalgic. She stepped onto an ornate red rug and gasped at the sheer number of spines facing her. Dust glittered in the windows. Soft rays of sunlight licked the shelves through large windows. Cielle urged her forward. "This section," she pointed to the left, "is boring stuff like history. Aedan always has us in here doing research. The stuff you might like is over here."

They walked to the right wall where the shelves were smaller, coming only to Aisling's shoulders. "This is the good stuff," Cielle whispered despite the empty room. "I've read most of them. Aedan brings new books when he can."

Aisling's fingertips grazed the spines. Calmness seeped into her skin. "It's wonderful," she whispered.

Cielle smiled. "It is. And you are free to use it anytime." She looked past the shelves. "There are couches over there by the windows. You get a view of the sea, too. It adds to the mood, depending on what you're reading."

Aisling picked up a random book and curled onto one of the plush couches. Her gaze traveled over her left shoulder to the sea. The waves were calm as they crested and crashed on the sand with foamy lines. The sun peeked from behind a scattering of thin wispy clouds and flooded her body with its warmth. She couldn't stop the smile from lifting her lips as she cracked open the book and began reading.

"Hey," Cielle whispered, gently nudging Aisling's shoulder. She shot up. Her book crashed to the floor. The sun had begun its descent, casting a warm orange glow on its way down. "It's time to eat."

Aisling blinked rapidly. "How long was I asleep?"

"I have no idea. I fell asleep too." Cielle shrugged. "There's something relaxing about this place. Sometimes if I can't sleep I come here."

"I'll keep that in mind." She put her book back on the shelf and followed her friend down the stairs and through the field. Aylim and Calen flew above them before dipping down into the Pit.

"Aylim goes insane if she doesn't fly every day," Cielle explained. "She's like a dog without a job. She'll get destructive."

They walked into the common room. Oryn and Koen were playing some sort of board game on the couches. Elaila sat beside Koen with a notebook in her lap and her pen dancing across the pages. Kaida sat at the table with four maps in front of her. Amerie sat beside her, murmuring and pointing while Kaida nodded. Elaila looked up and smiled. "How was the library?"

"Wonderful," Aisling said. She filled a bowl with potato soup and grabbed a few pieces of crusty bread. "Reminds me of the one I used to go to all the time."

Amerie popped up at the buffet. "You never told us about your other life."

"Maybe she's not ready to," Cielle said.

Aisling shook her head. "No, I'm ready. We've just been so busy."

"We aren't doing anything now," Kaida rolled the maps and placed them to the side. "We have the whole night to listen."

The rest of her team filled their plates and sat at the table, listening intently to everything she had to say. The sun sank below the horizon. They nibbled at sweet breads. They drank tea. Then more tea. And more sweet treats. Until Aisling's mouth was exhausted and her voice cracked. Her drawings of various things were scattered across the table. The fire roared behind them, casting the room in a warm orange glow.

"I have questions," Oryn started after a momentary speaking hiatus. "Cars."

A corner of her mouth lifted in a smile. "Cars."

"How do they work?"

"I have no idea. I never got to drive one. I know they have complicated engines that use gas to function." Amerie giggled and Aisling rolled her eyes. "Not like that. It's liquid, like oil, but black."

"Fascinating," Oryn murmured as he stared into the fire.

Kaida yawned. The girls copied her without realizing it. She stood and stretched her tiny body. "I might not sleep tonight because of all that. Be prepared for a thousand questions in the morning."

Aisling smiled. "I'll have answers, I hope."

Kaida grinned and walked out. Oryn followed, squeezing Aisling's shoulder as he passed her couch. Amerie leaned forward with a devious look on her face that Aisling knew meant trouble. "What are the boys like? What's dating like?"

"I have no idea," Aisling admitted, resting her palms on her thighs. "I've never been on a date. No one ever showed any interest in me like that. But I watched people go on dates at the café, and it looked wonderful."

She and Troy would create stories for the couples on dates. First dates were always easy to spot – deliciously awkward and too smiley. Troy's favorite story was always that the couple had no idea they were related. Aisling liked to switch it up each time, but her go-to was always that the couple had a feeling they were soulmates, forced together by the strings in their hearts. Troy never bought that one. She shrugged. "I'm sure it's a lot like it is here."

"I highly doubt that," Amerie responded. She made a face. "The men here..."

"Come on," Cielle pulled at Amerie's shirt. "Before you get mopey." Amerie stuck her tongue out but followed her friend. Elaila passed by silently and smiled softly before disappearing into the hallway. Aisling glanced at Koen, his eyes locked on the fire.

"I think I'm going to go to bed, too," she said. He didn't respond as she walked to the doorway. She glanced over her shoulder to where he sat stone-faced and staring into the flames. "Night," she murmured, not waiting for a response before walking to her room and letting sleep take hold.

FIFTY-SIX

Morana joined her in the Pit, her violet eyes again sleepy and heavy. Aisling felt it, too. She had stayed up far too late last night. A very large part of her wanted to ditch the morning run, but her new mindset wouldn't allow it.

"I know," she patted Morana's long neck. "I'm tired, too. But this will wake us up. And you look *so* good in the sunlight."

Morana huffed before puffing her chest and blinking once in agreement.

Aisling walked outside and started her stretches as the deep blue sky dyed a heavy lavender. White puffy clouds hung before her mouth with every breath.

"How far are we going today?"

She whirled on her heel and jumped back at the sight of Koen dressed in his leathers behind her. His hair stood in every different direction like he had just rolled out of bed. But his face was bright, his eyes warmer and more open than she could remember. "We?"

He nodded. "How far?"

She blinked at him. "I just run to the cliffs. Then I watch the sunrise before coming back."

Neera appeared in the sky with Morana at her tail. They flew toward the ravine, riding on the current as much as they could while their bodies woke up. Aisling couldn't help her puzzled look as she stared at Koen. "This is not for training," she said slowly. "It's just for me. So you don't have to be here."

"I know."

Her eyes narrowed. He smiled from the corner of his mouth, a playful gleam in his eyes she couldn't help but match.

Aisling bolted, taking the run at a much faster clip than she usually did. Koen's footsteps sounded behind her, heavy and uneven at first. He fell into stride beside her quickly.

They raced through the grasses and over rocks, past the ravine, and to the cliffs, pushing each other faster. She stopped just before the edge and rested her hands on her knees. Koen turned from the cliff at the last second with fast, shallow breaths. She glanced up and watched him pace the edge of the rocks with his arms clasped on top of his head.

His shirt waved in the wind, but she could still see the outline of his body beneath. His cut muscle and lean frame rippled with every breath. A delicate sheen of sweat glistened on his face. She swallowed and shook her head, but not before Morana sent something light and airy down the bond like a laugh.

"Now I watch the sunrise," she breathed, ignoring her dragon and lowering herself to the ground. She wrapped her arms around her knees. He followed suit beside her. The waves were angry below, a change from the peaceful lapping while she read yesterday. Each crash was a roar against the rocks. Seafoam splattered in every direction.

The sun appeared, shifting slowly over the horizon at a snail's pace and painting the paling lavender sky with shards of pink and orange. The clouds bordered on silk, and Aisling wondered if Morana knew how stunning she looked in the sky as the sun reflected off her scales.

"Why the running?" Koen asked, finally breaking the comfortable silence they had settled into.

"Why not?"

"Do you need more in training?"

She grimaced. "No. Not at all. I just... like the way it feels. It feels good to be alive."

He pursed his lips in silence for a few heartbeats. "When Neera found me, I was trying to jump off the cliffs." Her stomach dropped. She turned to him in question. He smiled, an almost pained look. "Yeah. I was sick of it all. My father was a terrible man. My mother was unavailable, and I didn't think I had a way out. I thought I could do it best at the cliffs. But Neera got to me before I could get there."

Aisling didn't know what to say. She knew that feeling, knew how inescapable, how daunting but necessary it felt when the world felt like it was closing in and there was no way out. She reached for his hand and gave it a soft squeeze in answer. He swallowed thickly. "Kaida and Oryn know, but that's it."

"I won't tell anyone," she swore.

"You knew that feeling too?"

"Unfortunately." Memories of her old life crawled back. Crying on Troy's shoulder. Debating what the whole point of her life was. "But I'm glad I didn't – I'm glad I'm here. Grateful for every breath."

Koen nodded once and watched Neera dip toward the sea, her wings brushing the surface. His voice came out soft, contemplative. "It does feel good to be alive." He grimaced. "You were right, you know?"

"About?"

"Everything," he sighed. "I was an asshole to you."

"I know."

He laughed and tucked his chin to his chest. "When you told me to look in the mirror and find the reason you couldn't tell us your truth? I died inside a little bit."

She cringed. "That was really rude of me to say, actually. It –"

"No," Koen insisted, his eyes intense as they locked onto hers. "It was the right thing to say. You should have said it much earlier."

"Next time, then."

"There won't be a next time. I swear it." His voice came out soft, almost tortured. "I'm sorry. For everything. For what I said, and how I acted. For how I made you feel, all of it. It wasn't fair to you. And now that I know everything you were going through, I hate myself for it." His throat bobbed. "I'm going to make it up to you. I promise."

"You don't have to make it up to me," she whispered.

"Yes, I do."

"Why?"

"Because," he said, his mouth opening and shutting twice before snapping shut. "Just because."

"Descriptive."

He blew out a heavy breath and smiled softly. "I know. I'm trying."

"I know. And I appreciate it." She cocked her head as a thought tumbled from her mouth. "But this life – my new life, isn't going to be stained with grudges and old anger. What if we both agreed to start fresh? I wasn't pleasant either. We could forget everything that we said and did and start new with a clean slate. Would you be open to that?"

Koen stared at her with something she'd never had directed at her before. And Aisling knew. She knew she was on the precipice of something new. Something violently wonderful. Her heart thundered as that intangible something filled her veins, pounding through her like a freefall into fire.

He nodded once.

"Great," she said with quiet relief, extending her palm toward him. "I'm Aisling."

He smiled, bright and blinding, and took her hand in his. "Koen."

"Come here often?"

He barked a laugh, and she found herself joining him. "I haven't really explored this area if you can believe it," he admitted. His eyes found the dragons in the sky. "But it's beautiful. I can see why you like starting the day here."

She extended her legs and rested her hands on the cool ground behind her. "It's the best. Plus, now Morana's warmed up should something happen."

"That's brilliant."

"I know. Don't look so surprised."

They fell into an easy silence. The wind fluttered through her hair and tickled the grass beneath her hands. The sun's warmth trickled into her as it crested over the horizon, and she lifted her face to it, soaking in as much of it as she could as if she'd never feel it again. When the warmth soaked into her bones, she sighed and stood. Koen's hand wrapped around her wrist, a pleading look in his eyes. "Do we have to go?"

"Yes," she laughed. "Or we'll miss breakfast."

He groaned and released her wrist. "You run back, too?"

"No."

"Oh, okay. Great." He started walking toward the Pit where Morana and Neera were already flying. Aisling stepped beside him and gave him a doe-eyed smile before pushing him to the ground and breaking into a full sprint. She laughed at his growl and pushed herself faster until her hair fell from its braid and her shirt billowed behind her. Until her legs screamed and her lungs ached. Until she couldn't stop the laughter in her chest or dim the light pulsing down her bond.

"Why are you all sweaty?" Amerie bit into a slice of toast.

"Went on a run," Aisling answered beside Koen at the line of breakfast trays. He filled his plate and dropped a slice of toast on top of hers. Cielle and Elaila walked in and grabbed food before the four of them joined Amerie at the table.

"Ew, why?"

"To feel alive," Koen answered, glancing across the table at Aisling from under his lashes. Her stomach pitched forward. She grabbed her water, suddenly needing to do something with her hands.

"That sounds awful," Amerie murmured.

"Just admit you're slow and we can move on," Elaila quipped.

Amerie gasped. "I'm the fastest one here and you know it! I'll race you today and smoke every single one of you losers."

Cielle snorted and jerked her chin to Oryn's usual seat. "Where's Oryn?"

"He's getting his beauty sleep. Something Koen would know nothing about."

He glared at Amerie. "It's not fair to the others if I sleep too much, Amerie. You know that."

Aisling stood and worked automatically while they bickered, frothing the milk as best she could without her giant machine. An ache formed every time she made coffee in Troy's absence, but she breathed through it until it dulled. She searched in the cabinets for something sweet to drizzle but came up empty. Instead, she sprinkled cinnamon on top and walked over to the table with lattes in the biggest mugs she could find.

Amerie squealed and took a sip with an obnoxious groan. Cielle and Elaila both rolled their eyes but took their mugs with whispers of thanks. She sat down beside them and took a sip. They weren't the best she'd ever made, Troy's were always so much better, but they weren't the worst either.

"Cinnamon?" Koen asked. A frothy line of milk rested above his top lip. She leaned forward and brushed it off with the pad of her thumb.

"You have latte lip," she laughed. "Yeah, cinnamon. Usually, I like to use caramel, but we don't have any here. At least, not that I could find."

The table was silent. Koen's eyes were locked on hers, his jaw tight. Amerie's mouth hung open. Aisling shrank into herself with embarrassment. "Sorry," she whispered.

"What's latte lip?" Elaila asked softly. Aisling could have kissed her for the swivel of attention.

"It's when the foam sticks to the top lip. People had them all the time and had no idea. Troy and I would make bets on how long it would take before they noticed."

"What was the longest?"

She pinched her face in thought. "Almost an hour. I would have told the guy, but he was really rude, so I let him leave with it all crusted."

"I'll pay you to make me one of these every day," Amerie said with her lips on the rim of her mug.

"With what money?" Cielle shot back.

Aisling laughed. "Please don't ever pay me for coffee. I'll throw it back at you, or spit in your drink."

"You can spit in my drink all you like if you keep making them," Amerie shrugged. Cielle clicked her tongue in disgust and elbowed her. Aisling dared a glance at Koen.

"Who is Troy?" he asked, his voice low.

Her friend's name spoken aloud sliced her chest. She swallowed. "He is, well, he was –"

The walls shook as the peal of bells rang out across the Pit.

FIFTY-SEVEN

They sprinted into the Lair.

Aisling's pulse roared at the vicious fire in Morana's eyes, the promise of a fight. It traveled through the bond and ignited her with a ferocious need for vengeance and blood.

Declan tightened her saddle and gestured to where he had laid out Aisling's armor. She donned it quickly, finally clasping it at her back without help. Declan handed her the necklace of light. She threw it on, marveling at the way it made her armor glisten like Morana in the sunlight.

Kaida stormed in, somehow already dressed in her battle gear with her hair perfectly braided atop her head. "Heading toward Nitorum. Estimates of well over thirty." Aisling pictured the town on the map, just south of Impellor and west of the Latebros mountains.

Oryn directed Nyssa to the Pit. The rest of the dragons followed with frantic energy. Smoke wafted through the air as it leaked between their teeth.

Kaida shoved two extra daggers into Aisling's leathers. "We'll start with swords when we get back."

"Daggers are better," Amerie whispered as she threw her hair into a braid.

Kaida led the riders into the Lair. They stood in front of their dragons, each taking a moment with their bond before mounting.

Aisling didn't miss the quick kiss Cielle placed on Gareth's cheek or the worry in his eyes as he watched his daughter clip into Aylim's saddle.

The bond pulsed with shadow as Aisling clipped in. She felt the raw energy, the need to fight, and savored it. "Control it, Morana. We aren't there yet."

Soren let out a bellowing roar that shook the ground beneath them. His wings opened, blocking the sun, and Morana's neck twisted in anxious anticipation.

"Wait!" screamed a high feminine voice. "Wait, please!" Maura ran into the Pit, waving a folded scrap of paper above her head.

Oryn leapt off Nyssa. "Maura? What..."

The seamstress handed him the paper, her breaths heavy and mouth wide as she looked at the dragons and riders. Oryn's eyes flared as he read the note, his gaze immediately going to Kaida. "Impellor. They're attacking Impellor."

The dragons went silent. Aisling's breath left her lungs. Impellor. The capital. Aedan's home.

"How many?" Kaida asked through a thick throat.

"Over a hundred," he whispered.

Aisling's stomach hollowed. This was it, the attack the men had promised. They made an army and were coming to destroy everything they hated. Everything she loved.

"We split up," Kaida called after a blink of hesitation, her throat bobbing.

The dragons shifted and chirped loudly in distaste. Soren silenced them by snapping his maw, the sound echoing in Aisling's bones.

"Koen, Oryn, and Amerie will go to Nitorum," she ordered. "It's a smaller attack, so make quick work of it. Neera's shield must be perfect. Cielle, Elaila, Aisling, and I will go to Impellor."

No one spoke. The dragons didn't make a sound. They had never been split up before. The Cruento never attacked twice in a day. It was one of the first things she learned.

Kaida's eyes glittered as she looked at her riders. "Every single one of you better bring your sorry asses back to this Keep at the end of this. I will accept nothing else."

There was no time for formalities or well wishes. Soren took to the sky with Nyssa at his tail. The rest of the dragons joined them and flew south at a blistering pace. Aisling didn't have time to think or worry. She trusted Morana with her life. She trusted the Ferox. And she trusted fate. It had led her this far.

Oryn and Kaida sat up on the back of their beasts and rested their hands over their hearts as they stared at each other, both tight-lipped and paler than usual. They nodded at the same time. Soren and Kaida banked right. Nyssa led Oryn south.

Amerie blew kisses at the rest of them as she followed Oryn. Cielle and Elaila waved back.

Koen pulled up beside Aisling. "Do not get off Morana," he yelled. "Whatever happens, stay on her back."

Aisling could only nod, her voice lost somewhere in her throat as emotion drowned her. She had the overwhelming urge to shout at him to be careful, but she knew he would be. He was strong and capable and brave. He would be fine.

It didn't stop the flood of panic that ran through her at the thought of them splitting up.

Neera and Morana bumped noses before Morana pulled away and followed Soren. She covered the back of the group as Soren, Aylim, and Osiris pushed ahead.

Aisling smelled it before she saw it just minutes later. Smoke, raw and acidic in the air. It burned her throat the closer they got to the city.

The lush greenery beneath them changed drastically in just a few swipes of Morana's wings. Hundreds of houses and buildings stood open for the taking. Panic surged in her heart for the people below. Had they heard the warning bells? Had they escaped?

The screams suggested not.

A stone castle came into view, magnificent and bold against the landscape. Great plumes of black smoke lifted from its walls, now crumbling and folding against the fires burning inside. Long spears flew through the air from what was left standing of the castle walls into the fray of black beasts above.

Soren lifted his head to the sky and unleashed a roar of beastly rage that shook the heavens. Osiris, Aylim, and Morana echoed it, their promise of death the last thing these beasts would hear. A horn blew from the castle. The spears disappeared.

The beasts littered the sky in a tangled mass of wings and chaos. There were at least a hundred, Aisling decided with a roll of nausea. More than she had ever seen together at one time. Their flames were unrestrained and wild, dousing the sky in a flurry of heat.

People ran in every direction below. Men swung swords and axes at each other in a frenzy. Aisling clenched her jaw. There was no way to tell who was Cruento and who wasn't.

This was what they meant when they said chaos breeds chaos, she realized. This was why the Cruento was the invisible enemy.

"Get as many as you can out of the air in the next five minutes," Kaida shouted. "Then we unleash Morana." Soren dove in the next breath and took out three beasts with his jaws alone. They fell from his teeth in bloody pieces. Morana flew higher and paused at the clouds as she looked back at her rider, fury rampant in her violet eyes.

Aisling smiled. "Gut them, Morana."

FIFTY-EIGHT

Morana obliged.

She was the light of death as she plunged into the mass with her teeth and rage exposed. The beasts fell before they understood what happened. Aisling lifted her daggers, swiping wildly at the claws and teeth that threatened her dragon. Blood drenched her instantly, and she basked in the warmth, the liquid of retribution.

Their shrill screeches were music to her ears. She craved the sound as Morana destroyed every beast she came across.

She glanced down at the crumbling city beneath her.

Blood rained onto pulsing fires. Scorched earth spread in every direction. Bodies lie scattered unceremoniously, both human and beast.

Human screams became white noise. The clanging of swords below was the rhythmless beat Morana danced to.

Aisling plunged her daggers into a beast's extended neck, laughing as her small blade sliced through a main artery and splattered her face with blood. Morana dodged its body as it tumbled from the sky.

Soren flanked Morana, his low chirp a beckoning for Osiris and Aylim. They appeared a heartbeat later tight against Morana's side. Kaida gave her a simple nod, the command implied.

Aisling pulled the necklace from beneath her armor and lowered herself against Morana's back just before she dove forward, straight into a clump of black beasts.

They snapped their mouths in glee, their black eyes thrilled for the fight.

Aisling laughed when they realized what was leaking from her dragon's mouth.

Morana opened her maw. Shadow enveloped the sky.

Unfaltering, unyielding darkness.

Morana pulled upward at a sharp angle just in time for blue flames to douse where she flew. Screams rang out from the air and land. Morana kept pushing upward until the shadows banked, and Aisling flinched against the brightness.

Blue streams of fire pulsed through the darkness. Red and orange followed, catching any stragglers Soren might have missed.

Cielle and Elaila screamed their fury into the sky. Aisling's heart, now a raging beast in her chest, echoed the call. The bond glowed bright and strong as Morana dove again, attacking the beasts hovering around the shadows until her darkness gave way to light.

Black bodies littered the ground below. Red rivers flooded the streets. Orange flames danced into the hazy air.

Again and again, Morana unleashed her void. The Ferox answered with death. Morana and Aisling attacked the stragglers one by one until her shadows faded.

Hours passed with the arc of a blood orange sun.

Osiris and Aylim worked as a team to herd the remaining twenty beasts toward Soren. Morana sailed just above the castle in a constant loop looking for a clump of Cruento to blind, but they were unassuming. Unremarkable. Pathetically average. The soldiers were better fighters, but there were more Cruento than Aisling had ever imagined. There was no way to blind them without blinding the Kairossen soldiers, too.

Hundreds of Cruento had descended on the capital city like rats in an open dumpster. They scurried through streets with their swords swinging at anything that moved, rabid anger etched on their faces.

In the madness, Aisling wondered how someone could believe in a cause so painful for another human being. How someone could fight to the death over the enslavement of an entire group of people based on nothing of importance.

A flash of golden hair from just outside the ruined castle grabbed her attention.

He ran into the fray, long swords in each hand. His hair was tied behind his head in a low bun. The energetic, intelligent eyes she knew were replaced by a fury unmatched by anyone but the dragons. Dried blood spotted his glistening armor.

Aedan leapt into the fight, a King fighting for his people and wearing no crown. Aisling held her breath as he demolished all in his path. His sword was an extension of him; he was a dancer, twisting and slicing through the men as if they were butter. Anwir stood at his back with matching daggers, swinging and dodging wildly, his tight face stoic as always.

Morana looked to the sky. Aisling did, too. The dragons had made quick work of the rest of the beasts. Only a handful scattered through the clouds, and Aylim and Osiris were hot on their trails. Soren slapped one with his tail and it fell like a ragdoll, crashing on top of a building in a plume of dust. Aisling glanced back at the fight.

Aedan was covered in frank red blood.

She cried out as a sword pierced his side.

He didn't break, didn't falter. His blade swung, knocking the man out a second later. He removed the sword from his side with a grimace before returning to the fight.

But he was slowing. His steps became jagged. His face paled.

Another blade plunged into his back.

Aisling shrieked. She couldn't let it happen. Couldn't let this man of hope and kindness fall to the enemy. "Morana!" she begged. "Please!"

Her dragon didn't hesitate. They landed on top of a small crowd of Cruento with a sickening crunch. Kairossen soldiers cheered and swiped their blades in a frenzy at the startled rebels. Morana feasted, killing whoever was unarmored beneath her claws. "Keep your wings up!" Aisling shouted as she unclipped and slid down Morana's leg to the ground.

She unsheathed her daggers and sprinted through the mess toward Aedan, now sprawled on the stones. His skin was gray, the light in his eyes dimming by the second. She felt for a pulse. It was there – faint, but there. His blood poured onto the ground.

"Aedan! Listen to me," she panted. "You are not going to die. I will not allow it. Your people will not allow it." She stood behind him and hooked her elbows under his armpits. With a grunt, she dragged him to Morana, leaving a trail of bright red blood in her wake. "Kaida will be furious with you if you leave her, and I will be, too, because you are a good man and a good King. You are kind. You're everything a leader should be."

She unhooked one arm and shoved her dagger into the side of a man getting too close. He collapsed with blood spurting through his weak armor and shock on his face. She picked the King back up. "I did not travel worlds for you to leave like this, okay? So fight it. Fight the darkness and stay here with us because we can't do it without you." Her voice remained calm and even despite the ice-cold fear in her veins. "I'm bringing you to Morana. Then we'll get you help."

The King fell from her arms as the bond snapped in pain. Her hand covered her chest. Every breath was agony. She turned.

Two Cruento beasts snarled, their teeth deep in her dragon's beautiful hide. Blood raced down Morana's glimmering scales.

Aisling could only think of the beach. Could only picture the wound and the blood and the unnatural terror that came with it.

Morana's scream shattered the sky. Osiris and Aylim dove toward her, but not fast enough.

"Fly, Morana!" Aisling yelled, guttural and agonizing, through the din of war. "Fly!" She tugged on the bond with everything she had. "Go! I'll find you!"

Morana spared her a single pained glance before launching into the air. The two beasts remained latched to her scales as she climbed further and further into the clouds. Osiris and Aylim were there a second later. Blood poured from the sky.

The bond shrieked in agony. Aisling couldn't breathe. Could barely stand.

But the bond was still there. Morana was still there.

So she turned to the nearly lifeless King on the ground. The castle had all but crumbled. Flames licked the clouds around her. She had nowhere to take him now.

But she could fight.

Every sparring practice had been an exercise in absorption. She watched Koen wield his blade with dominating precision. Watched Elaila dance with hers and Amerie twist her body for maximum effect. She devoured Oryn's calm and Kaida's swiftness. She watched Cielle's unyielding brutality with open eyes and soaked in every talent of her family.

Aisling didn't know what her strength was, but she knew she was strong, and that would be enough.

She stood over Aedan's body and swung her daggers with the erratic but all-consuming pulse of adrenaline screaming in her blood. Men came from everywhere, anger and hate twisting their faces in grotesque masks as they lifted blades toward her King.

She remembered Koen's teaching. Remembered her power and her fury. Remembered the girl she was before, and watched in awe as her new soul demolished the memory while knocking men down in her wake. Her blades sank into flesh, every tear and rip and scream a song in her heart.

Blood flew. Spit and slurs coated the air.

Her blade found flesh and painted it red.

Her muscles screamed in agony. Every breath was heavy and hard.

She kept fighting.

Until a sharp pain ran down her spine, and darkness took her under.

FIFTY-NINE

KOEN

Three hours of blood and carnage passed.

Between the three of them, the Cruento beasts didn't stand a chance. Amerie and Calen were menaces. Oryn and Nyssa showered the sky with metallic flames. Neera's shield protected the town while he did what he always did: find safety for the innocent and kill the guilty.

By the time the last beast hit the ground, Koen had the blood of three more men on his swords. It never bothered him. Their blood was a purge of evil for Kairossen. It was therapeutic and necessary. He pictured wiping his father's blood off his sword and smirked at the image.

Amerie patrolled the sky while he and Oryn did a final check of Nitorum. There was nothing amiss. The people were shell-shocked and terrified. It didn't matter how many years had passed – the worst part of the job was seeing the destruction and terror in the eyes of everyone who witnessed the attack. His nightmares consisted mostly of their faces, blurred and amorphous, but always radiating nothing but fear. He would remember the burnt bodies scattered around, the newly orphaned children screaming for their parents, and wake up covered in sweat, unable to function until Neera had taken him in the sky to let the wind calm him.

Oryn would stay to comfort the people until the soldiers arrived. His presence evoked a calm that Koen would never be able to replicate. "If Neera is able," Oryn said after they swept the town, "go to Impellor. Help them."

Koen didn't hesitate.

He yanked on the bond and Neera answered, her wings splayed and ready as he charged into the saddle. She was in the air before he clipped in, racing north through the smoke-filled clouds toward Impellor.

Toward Aisling.

He prayed she had listened to him and stayed on Morana's back. Morana would keep her safe. She would ruin the world for her.

He knew the feeling. Knew it well, and had decided that morning to stop fighting it.

The bond flickered as they closed in on Impellor with something acidic and bitter on his tongue. The castle he had grown to know and love was long gone, its massive stone columns replaced by pillars of black smoke reaching for the clouds.

A single silver dragon patrolled the hazy sky.

His chest pounded. Neera rumbled low and shook her head, pushing them faster toward the decimated capital city as the tanginess of her worry covered the bond.

Cielle nodded once at him as he passed by, her lips in a tight white line while she scanned the sky. Soot and blood covered her. Her armor was shredded at her arms, but she didn't seem to notice or care. Aylim chirped at Neera. A flurry of emotions ran down the bond too fast for him to interpret.

They landed beside a pile of bloodied bodies. Red stained the stone below in a deep crimson. Osiris stood at what had been the entrance to the castle, his bright blue scales covered in a thick layer of dirt, grime, and blood. His unnerving white eyes latched onto Neera. Remnants of clothing hung from his mouth. Soldiers helped the wounded and hunted for stray Cruento through the empty burning streets, immune to the shock of dragons surrounding them.

Elaila appeared with a wildness in her eyes that only came out when her bloodlust had been quenched. "Koen," she breathed, almost collapsing before him. "There's so many of them. Cielle helped me tie them up, but Osiris had to -"

"Where is she?" he ground out.

"In there," Elaila answered with a bob of her throat, pointing to another open room in the ruined castle with trembling fingers.

A dragon screamed.

The bond stilled before a wave of agonizing pain ran through him. He rested his hand on the wall and panted against it. He followed the scream, his heart nearly exploding with every step as Neera's bond convulsed in panic.

Soren's red eye came out of nowhere, stopping him in his tracks. The narrow slit of a pupil pulsed as they stared at each other, neither willing to give in.

A dragon screamed again, and Koen knew. He knew which one it was. Knew something had gone horribly, horribly wrong.

"Soren!" Kaida cried from inside, her voice uncharacteristically pitchy. The beast moved, allowing Koen into the crumbled room.

Morana lay sprawled on the stone floor. Blood pooled beneath her. Two massive chunks of her hide had been torn to shreds. The brightness of her scales was dimmed to a dull matte white.

Men rushed in with buckets of water, dodging debris and cleansing her wounds as a doctor shouted orders. Morana groaned in agony as poultices from the castle's underground storage found her wounds. Soren stood beside her, lowering his head and chirping softly as her purple eyes found Koen's. There was nothing inside but utter devastation. Agony and fury and despair.

"Where is she?" he whispered, unable to keep the tinge of fear from his voice.

Kaida choked on a sob and covered her mouth with her hands as she stared at Morana. Her tiny shoulders shook. The bright hair that she always had braided and pinned was down and frizzy. Blood clung to every strand. A tear ran down her cheek.

"Where is she?" Koen asked again, his voice cracking with desperation.

"Aedan is hurt," she whispered. "The medical team has him in makeshift surgery now. They're trying to stabilize him so Soren can bring him back to the Pit."

"I don't give a fuck about –"

"She saved him," Kaida blurted, turning to face Koen. "She got off Morana and fought for him when he couldn't fight anymore. That's when Morana was attacked. Aisling told her to fly and get help. But by the time we got there..."

Morana let out another gut-wrenching cry.

"They took her," Kaida murmured. "She's gone."

Koen stopped feeling his body. Stopped hearing anything but the pounding of blood in his skull.

Kaida pulled out a cord with a vial on the end. Inside the vial was a thick red liquid. "They left this."

Aisling's necklace. Their only ability to know where she was in the shadows.

They took her light and bled her.

A brutal, diabolical taunt.

He took the necklace from her and put it around his neck, shocked to see his hands steady despite the fury thundering through his veins. "Where are they?"

Kaida blinked. "Elaila –"

He left the room. Left Morana in her agony. Left Kaida in her guilt and sorrow.

His footsteps echoed into the open sky as he passed a tearful Elaila and entered the small makeshift room behind her. Two dozen men stared back at him, their hands and legs bound painfully tight. Burns marred their skin. Anger boiled in their eyes.

"Where is she?" he asked, his voice flat and low.

No one answered. Someone whimpered. Another spit at his feet.

He didn't feel his blade leave its sheath. Didn't feel it in his hand or feel the delectable crunch of it against bone. Didn't feel anything but roaring hatred as the head went rolling across the floor.

Someone threw up.

He kept the blade at his side and asked again.

Another head rolled across the stone, its eyes forever wide in shock.

He didn't care. He stopped feeling human, stopped feeling anything but the raging bloodlust that drowned every inch of him.

Aisling had chosen this life. Chosen them.

She wanted to fight.

Just hours ago, she wanted nothing more than to feel alive. He knew she craved the wind in her hair and the sky at her fingertips, just like he did.

He refused to believe that by choosing to live, Aisling had also chosen her death.

Her blood could not stain the fresh slate she had graciously given him that morning. The clean slate that he had done nothing to deserve. A hundred years would pass, and he still would never earn the kindness she gave him.

Aisling came into his life in a flash of brilliant white scales and ruined him without uttering a word. He refused to believe that the little time they had spent together would be it. Refused to believe he wouldn't have what he had imagined for so many weeks, what he had attempted to quell before giving up and drowning in the thoughts, the hope.

There was so much more he wanted to know about her. So much more he wanted to experience with her. He wanted to watch her bake and let her wipe the latte from his lip and fly side by side together with nothing but their dragons and the sky as their companions.

He wanted to show her everything. Wanted her to feel alive at his side.

He needed her to know that the last words he had said before parting weren't what he wanted to say. He'd been too much of a coward to say what he really wanted to. What he'd felt since the day she appeared on Morana's back.

What he did say, she ignored.

He laughed at that. It was bitter and acidic in his chest. He hated it.

The men on the ground started at his laugh. He watched in glee as their faces morphed from defiance to raw terror.

Good. Let them fear him. Let them see the rumors of his wrath weren't exaggerated. He was the Blade of the Ferox – the judge, jury, and executioner. Let them realize they would never see the light of day again.

He stepped forward. They flinched. "Where is she?"

No one answered.

He set himself loose, Aisling's face the only thing he could see as blood painted the air.

SIXTY

AISLING

Her head ached.

Something rough and smelling of sweat covered her eyes and mouth.

Strong calloused hands clasped her biceps. Thick fingers dug into her skin, but she didn't cry out at the pain. Her feet scraped along the hard floor. Her head lolled between her shoulders. She flexed her fingers and toes, relieved they still worked. Every muscle ached with the simple movement.

The further they walked, the stronger the smell of damp earth got. It was sickly sweet, almost nauseating. She gagged silently against the thing covering her mouth, retching at the additional sourness of sweat on it.

Her skin pebbled against the cold. Every step they took dropped the temperature until she nearly shivered in their arms.

A door creaked open.

"All quiet?" a gruff voice asked. A grunted response was his answer. They walked forward, less confident than before, and threw her to the ground. She groaned as stone slammed into her already aching body.

"Dumb bitch," one voice muttered.

"Welcome home, princess," the first man cooed. "We'll let you get comfortable."

The door slammed shut. She removed her binds with shaky hands and blinked rapidly.

It didn't help.

She was surrounded by darkness.

No windows. No sunlight. No wind or breeze.

She reached forward. A door the size of the Lair's stood before her made of metal and reinforced with multiple beams. Slowly, she crawled along the wall and used the pads of her fingers to visualize the layout.

Jagged rock was the only thing that met her skin.

The room was gigantic. She couldn't see, but she guessed it was at least double the size of Morana's room in the Lair. She ran into something metal and hissed against the pain. Her fingers explored that, too, finding a steel bath full of painfully cold water.

She grimaced. She would not be washing in there no matter how bad things got.

The ground beneath her was rock as well. There was some dirt, but not enough to cover the stones.

Underground. Wherever she was, it was nowhere near the surface.

A shrill terror lit through her. She swallowed thickly, closed her eyes, and took deep breaths. She could do this. She had survived tough situations before.

Memories of the battle flooded her mind. Aedan lifeless on the ground. Smoke and blood tainting the air. Morana's flesh torn apart.

Aisling yanked on the bond. It was still there, barely glowing, but it had to mean Morana was still alive. There was no immediate answer.

Acidic panic crawled up her throat. She bit down on it. A steady stream of rage boiled in its wake.

She had made it too easy for the Cruento. If she had just listened to Koen and stayed on Morana's back...

No. She would never let Aedan die like that.

Koen would be livid with her. She could see the darkness in his warm eyes and the set line of his jaw as he clenched his teeth in annoyance. She could picture the muscles in his biceps flexing before he threw her to the sand in punishment.

The thought gave her comfort. She would hold onto it as she fought to get back to the light, get back to her family and her dragon.

She did not choose this life to die. No matter how brutal it would be, she would force herself to live.

The shadows stirred before her.

Her breath caught in her throat.

Leather stretched.

Something clicked against the floor.

Hot air puffed in her face.

A pair of sapphire blue eyes glared from just above her.

"Favilla," Aisling breathed.

TYSM

Can you believe I'm writing one of these? Me either. Be patient. I've had a glass of Oyster Bay and feel emotional.

A – none of this would be possible without you, babes. Thank you isn't enough for what you've done for me, but it's all I have to offer. Thank you for your unwavering patience, support, and encouragement. You're my safe place and my soul's home. Thank you for loving me as much as you do. And for constantly refilling my water bottle. You a real one and I love yas.

K – I could write an entire novel based strictly on how much I adore you, love. Know that everything I do, I do for you. (PS please give your dad and I a break and sleep in past 7am one day xoxo)

Mom and Dad– you have no idea I'm even writing a book right now. I can't wait to see the looks on your faces. Thank you for keeping the book I wrote about Snookums (RIP). It kept the little nagging voice in my head to write alive. I like to think that cute little guinea pig is looking down on me and smiling at his legacy.

Brody – your snores kept me company every day, sweet boy. Thank you for being patient and loving and the most low-maintenance dog I have ever known.

Sleep Token – I stumbled on you about 3 chapters into this book and never looked back. The soundtrack for this series will always belong to you, specifically: The Love You Want, Mine, The Apparition, and Jaws. Please make more music soon or I might die. xo

Thallia, Caitlyn, and Shreya – thank you for not laughing at my first drafts. You're the first people to have ever seen my work, and you made the process painless and a lot less terrifying than I imagined. Your feedback was exactly what I needed, and I consider myself lucky to have worked with you.

Chelsea, Gina, and Kaylee – thank you for unknowingly lending me pieces of your personalities and hyping me up when I was confident in my failures. Also for being my friends. I adore each of you with the force of a thousand suns.

And if you've made it this far, I'd like to thank you, Reader. Time is a valuable commodity, one many take for granted. I am overwhelmed with gratitude that you decided to spend your precious time with something I created. You mean so much to me, and I'm forever thankful to have come into your life, even if for such a short time. xoxoxo

About the Author

Bridgette is a simple woman. She likes Diet Coke, warm bread, and watching TV with the subtitles on.

Her past contains ten long years as a RN, a stint as a certified Personal Trainer and group fitness instructor, and an attempt at being a runner that ended with hip surgery.

When she isn't writing, you can find her cursing at Peloton instructors with sweat/tears in her eyes, baking, or trying to convince her toddler to be still for five minutes (has never happened, fyi).

You can also find Her at bridgettehooper.com, @BHooperAuthor on Instagram, or @bridgettehooperauthor on TikTok. Word on the street is She's very friendly/amazing/etc. and would love to hear from you. xo

www.ingramcontent.com/pod-product-compliance
Lightning Source LLC
Chambersburg PA
CBHW020549120726
47903CB00001B/193